R.M.- good
Elm Good ✓ **P9-DBT-022**

**Praise for *New York Times* and *USA TODAY*
bestselling author Susan Mallery**

"Mallery's prose is luscious and provocative."
—*Publishers Weekly*

"Mallery is at her addictive best. The bestselling
author crafts vivid characters and a winning story
about the risk and joy of second love,
studded with warm, alluring sex scenes."
—*Publishers Weekly* on *Irresistible*

"Susan Mallery's gift for writing humor and
tenderness makes all her books true gems."
—*RT Book Reviews*

**Praise for bestselling author
Tanya Michaels**

"Readers should rush to read [*A Mother's Homecoming*],
as [it] will touch their hearts and move them deeply."
—*RT Book Reviews*

"Tanya Michaels has done it again. She delivers
another seamless romance of two people
just doing their best."
—*RT Book Reviews* on *A Dad for Her Twins*

SUSAN MALLERY

New York Times bestselling author Susan Mallery has entertained millions of readers with her witty and emotional stories about women and the relationships that move them. *Publishers Weekly* calls Susan's prose "luscious and provocative," and *Booklist* says, "Novels don't get much better than Mallery's expert blend of emotional nuance, humor and superb storytelling."

While Susan appreciates the critical praise, she is most honored by the enthusiastic readers who write to tell her that her books made them laugh, made them cry and made the world a happier place to live.

Susan lives in Seattle with her husband and her tiny but intrepid toy poodle. She's there for the coffee, not the weather. Visit Susan online at her website, www.SusanMallery.com.

TANYA MICHAELS

Three-time RITA® Award nominee Tanya Michaels writes about what she knows—community, family and lasting love!

Her books, praised for their poignancy and humor, have received honors such as the Booksellers' Best Bet Award, the Maggie Award of Excellence and multiple readers' choice awards. She was also a 2010 *RT Book Reviews* nominee for Career Achievement in Category Romance. Tanya is an active member of Romance Writers of America and a frequent public speaker, presenting workshops to educate and encourage aspiring writers. She lives outside Atlanta with her very supportive husband, two highly imaginative children and a household of quirky pets, including a cat who thinks she's a dog and a bichon frise who thinks she's the center of the universe. You can visit Tanya online at her website, www.TanyaMichaels.net.

BESTSELLING AUTHOR COLLECTION

New York Times and *USA TODAY* Bestselling Author

SUSAN MALLERY

One in a Million

TORONTO NEW YORK LONDON
AMSTERDAM PARIS SYDNEY HAMBURG
STOCKHOLM ATHENS TOKYO MILAN MADRID
PRAGUE WARSAW BUDAPEST AUCKLAND

Recycling programs
for this product may
not exist in your area.

ISBN-13: 978-0-373-18055-4

ONE IN A MILLION
Copyright © 2003 by Susan Macias Redmond

A DAD FOR HER TWINS
Copyright © 2008 by Tanya Michna

CONTENTS

Dear Reader,

Have you ever had one of *those* days? When everything goes wrong? Your car won't start. You spill on the one shirt that is not only your favorite color but makes your tummy disappear. Your throat gets scratchy right before the biggest presentation of your life. You know what that's like. Sometimes it feels like instead of a bad day, we have a bad week or even a bad month!

When I sit down to write a book, that's the woman I'm thinking about. The reader having a really bad time who needs an escape. A delicious romantic adventure with a sexy guy who will not only make her toes tingle, but also may fold the laundry and fix breakfast. Is that too much to ask? And if he's funny, smart and caring along the way, well, why not? Isn't that what romance novels are for?

Stephanie Wynne, my heroine in *One in a Million,* is kind of having a bad patch of life right now. She has three kids, a business that needs her attention and a broken washing machine. The last thing she needs is a guy good-looking enough to star in her personal fantasies. Except there he is. And he's just so... kissable. Is it really wrong to give in? Wouldn't you?

One in a Million has been out of print for several years, so I'm delighted my publisher is reissuing it. I hope you love the story as much as I do. For more information about other books or to find out about my next release, *Barefoot Season,* please visit my website, www.SusanMallery.com. I'm also on Facebook at www.Facebook.com/SusanMallery.

ONE IN A MILLION

Susan Mallery

Chapter 1

Good-looking men should not be allowed to show up on one's doorstep without at least twenty-four hours' notice, Stephanie Wynne thought wearily as she leaned against her front door and tried not to think about the fact that she hadn't slept in nearly forty-eight hours, couldn't remember her last shower and knew that her short, blond hair looked as if it had been cut with a rice thresher.

Three kids down with stomach flu had a way of taking the sparkle and glamour out of a woman's day. Not that the man in front of her was going to care about her personal problems.

Despite the fact that it was nearly two in the morning, the handsome, well-dressed stranger standing on her porch looked rested, tidy and really tall. She glanced from his elegant suit to the stained and torn football jersey she'd pulled out of the ragbag when she'd run out of clean clothes about two days ago because...

Her tired brain struggled for the reason.

Oh, yeah. The washer was broken.

Again, not something he was going to sweat about. Paying guests only wanted excellent service, quiet rooms and calorie-laden breakfasts.

She did her best to forget her pathetic appearance and forced her mouth into what she hoped was a friendly smile.

"You must be Nash Harmon. Thanks for calling earlier and letting me know you'd be arriving late."

"My flight out of Chicago was delayed." He drew his dark eyebrows together as he looked her up and down. "I hope I didn't wake you, Mrs...."

"Wynne. Stephanie Wynne." She stepped back into the foyer of the old Victorian house. "Welcome to Serenity House."

The awful name for the bed-and-breakfast had been her late husband's idea. After three years she could speak it without wincing, but only just. If not for the very expensive, custom-made, stained-glass sign that had replaced a front window and the fact that her kids would object, Stephanie would have changed the name of the B and B in a heartbeat.

Her guest carried a leather duffel and a garment bag into the house. Her gaze moved between his expensive leather boots and her own mouse slippers with their tattered ears. When she finally headed upstairs to her own bed, she must remember *not* to look at herself in the mirror. Confirming her worst fears would cause her to shriek and wake the boys.

The man signed the registration card she'd left on the front desk and she processed his credit card. Once she'd received approval, she handed him an old-fashioned brass key.

"Your room is this way," she said, heading up the stairs.

She'd put him in the front bedroom. Not only was it large and comfortable, with a view of Glenwood, but it was one of only two guest rooms that weren't under her third-floor apartment. When she wasn't completely booked, she found it much easier to have guests stay there than to constantly keep at her kids to stay quiet. Being loud and being a boy seemed to go hand in hand.

Five minutes later she'd explained the amenities of the room, said she would be serving breakfast from seven-thirty to nine and asked him if he would like her to leave a newspaper outside his door in the morning.

He refused the paper.

She nodded and headed for the hallway.

"Mrs. Wynne?"

She turned back to look at him. "Stephanie, please."

He nodded. "Do you have a map of the area? I'm here to visit some people and I don't know my way around."

"Sure. Downstairs. I'll put one out for you at breakfast."

"Thank you."

He offered her a slight smile, one that didn't touch his eyes. It was late and she was so tired that her eyelashes hurt. But instead of leaving that second, she hesitated. Oh, not more than a heartbeat, but just long enough to notice that the overhead light brought out brownish highlights in his close-cropped black hair and that the hint of dark stubble on his square jaw made him look just a little bit dangerous.

Yeah, right, Stephanie thought as she turned away. Apparently she'd moved into the hallucination stage of sleep deprivation. Dangerous men didn't come to places like Glenwood. No doubt Nash Harmon was something completely harmless like a shoe salesman or a professor. Besides, what he did for a living was none of her business. As long as his credit-card company put the right amount of money into her bank account, she didn't care if her guest was a computer programmer or a pirate.

As for him being somewhat good-looking and possibly single—there hadn't been a wedding ring on his left hand—she couldn't care less. While her friends occasionally got on her case for not being willing to jump back into the man-infested dating pool, Stephanie ignored their well-meant intentions. She'd already been married once, thank you very much. Nine years as Marty's wife had taught her that while Marty looked like a grown-up on the outside, he'd been as irresponsible and self-absorbed as any ten-year-old on the inside. She would have gotten more cooperation and teamwork from a dog.

Marty had cured her of ever wanting another man around. While on occasion she would admit to getting lonely, and yes, the sex was tough to live without, it beat the alternative. She already had three kids to worry about. Getting involved with a man would be like adding a fourth child to the mix. She didn't think her nerves could stand it.

Despite his late night, Nash woke shortly after six the following morning. He glanced at the clock and compared it to his watch, which was still on Central Time. Then he rolled onto his back and stared at the ivory ceiling.

What the hell was he doing here?

Dumb question, he told himself. He already knew the answer. He was in a town he'd never heard of until a couple of weeks ago, to meet family he hadn't known he had. No. That wasn't completely true. He was in town because he'd been forced to take some vacation and he hadn't had anywhere else to go. If he'd tried lying low in Chicago, Kevin, his twin who was already camped out at Glenwood, would have been on the next plane east.

Nash sat up and pushed back the covers. Without the routine of work, his day stretched endlessly in front of him. Had he really gotten so lost in the job that he didn't have anything else in his life?

Dumb question number two.

He knew he was going to have to get in touch with Kevin sometime that morning and set up a meeting. After thirty-one years of knowing nothing about their biological father save the fact that he'd gotten a seventeen-year-old virgin pregnant with twins and then abandoned her, he and Kevin were about to meet up with half siblings they'd never known they had.

Kevin thought finding out about more family was a good thing. Nash still needed convincing.

By 6:40 a.m. he'd showered, shaved and dressed in jeans, a long-sleeved shirt and boots. While it was mid-June, a cool fog hung over the part of the town he could see from his second-story window. Nash paced restlessly in his comfortable room. Maybe he would tell his hostess to forget about breakfast. He could go for a drive and eat at a diner somewhere. Or maybe he'd just keep going until he figured out why, in the past few months, he'd stopped sleeping, stopped eating, stopped giving a damn about anything but his job.

He grabbed the keys for his rental car, then headed downstairs. At the front desk, he tore off a sheet of notepaper and a pen, then paused when he heard noises from the rear of the house. If the owner was up, he could simply tell her he was skipping breakfast in person.

He followed the noise down a long hallway and through a set of closed swinging doors. When he stepped into the brightly lit kitchen, he was instantly assaulted by the scents of something baking and fresh coffee. His mouth watered and his stomach growled.

He glanced around, but the big, white-on-white kitchen was empty. A tray sat on a center island. A coffee carafe stood by an empty cup and saucer. Plastic wrap covered a plate of fresh fruit. By the stove, an open box of eggs waited beside a frying pan. Through a door on his left, he heard mumbled conversation.

He started toward the female voice and crossed the threshold. A woman stood on tiptoe in front of shelves. As he watched, she reached up for something on the top shelf, but her fingers only grazed the edge of the shelf.

Nash stepped forward to offer help, but at that moment the woman reached a little higher. Her cropped sweater rose above the waistband of her black slacks, exposing a sliver of bare skin.

Nash felt as if he'd been hit upside the head with a two-by-four. His vision narrowed, sound faded and by gosh, he found himself experiencing the first flicker of life below his waist that he'd felt in damn near two years.

Over an inch of belly? He was in a whole lot more trouble than he'd realized. Apparently his boss had been right about him burning out.

A loud shriek brought him back to the here and now. Nash moved his gaze from the woman's midsection to her face and saw his hostess staring at him with wide eyes. She pressed a hand to her chest and sucked in a breath.

"You nearly scared the life out of me, Mr. Harmon. I didn't realize you were up already."

"Call me Nash," he said as he stepped forward and reached up for the top shelf. "What do you need?"

"That blue bag. There's a silver bread basket inside. I'm making scones and I usually put them in the larger basket but as you're my only guest at present, I thought something smaller would work."

He grasped the blue bag and felt something hard

inside. After lowering it, he handed it to her. She took it with a shake of her head.

"I always meant to be tall," she told him. "Somehow I never got around to it."

"I wasn't aware it wasn't something you could get around to. I thought it just happened."

"Or not." She unzipped the bag and pulled out a silver wire basket. "Thanks for the help. Would you like some coffee?"

"Sure."

He led the way back into the kitchen. While he leaned against the counter, she ran hot water into the carafe, then drained it and wiped it dry. After filling it with coffee, she turned back to him.

"Cream and sugar?"

"Just black."

"The scones should be ready in about five minutes. I had planned to make you an omelet this morning. Ham? Cheese? Mushrooms?"

Last night he'd barely noticed her. What he remembered had been someone female, tired and strangely dressed. He had a vague recollection of spiky blond hair. Now he saw that Stephanie Wynne was a petite blonde with wide blue eyes and a full mouth that turned up at the corners. She wore her short hair in a sleek style that left her ears and neck bare. Tailored black slacks and a slightly snug sweater showed him that despite the small package, everything was where it needed to be. She was pretty.

And he'd noticed.

Nash tried to figure out the last time he'd noticed a

woman—any woman—enough to classify her as pretty, ugly or something in between. Not for two years, he decided, knowing that figuring out the date hadn't been much of a stretch.

"Don't bother with eggs," he said. "Coffee and the scones are fine." He glanced at the tray. "And the fruit."

Stephanie frowned. "The room comes with a full breakfast. Aren't you hungry?"

More than he'd been in a while, but less than he should have been. "Maybe tomorrow," he said instead.

A timer on the stove beeped softly. Stephanie picked up two mitts and pulled open the oven door. The scent of baked goods got stronger. Nash inhaled the fragrance of orange and lemon.

When she'd set two cookie sheets of scones onto cooling racks, she dug through a drawer and pulled out a linen napkin, then draped it in the silver basket.

"This morning we have orange, lemon and white chocolate scones," she said as she pulled a small crystal dish of butter from the refrigerator. "They're all delicious, which is probably tacky of me to say seeing as I made them, but it's true. Being a man, you won't care about the calories, so that's a plus."

She offered him a smile that made the corners of her eyes crinkle, then nodded toward the door next to him.

"The dining room is through there."

He took the hint and moved through to the next room. He found a large table set for one. The local paper lay on top of a copy of *USA TODAY*.

Stephanie followed him into the room, but waited until he was seated before serving him his breakfast.

She poured coffee, removed the plastic wrap from his plate of fruit and made sure the butter was within easy reach. Then she wished him *"bon appétit"* before disappearing back into the kitchen.

Nash picked up one of the still-steaming scones. The scent of orange drifted to him. His stomach still growling, he took a bite.

Delicate flavors melted on his tongue. Hunger roared through him, as unfamiliar as it was welcome. He sipped the coffee next, then tried a strawberry. Everything tasted delicious. He couldn't remember the last meal he'd enjoyed, nor did he care. Instead he plowed through four scones, all the fruit and the entire carafe of coffee. When he was finally full, he pulled the copy of *USA TODAY* toward him and started to read.

A burst of laughter interrupted his perusal of the business section. He frowned as he realized he'd been hearing more than just Stephanie in the kitchen for some time. The other voices were low and difficult to make out. A husband? Probably.

The thought of a Mr. Wynne caused Nash a twinge of guilt. He didn't usually go around looking at other men's wives and admiring their bare skin.

He turned the page on the paper and started to read again, only to be interrupted by the sound of footsteps racing down the hall. He looked up in time to see three boys running toward the front door.

"Walk! We have a guest."

The command came from the kitchen. Instantly three pairs of feet slowed and three heads turned in his direction. Nash had a brief impression of towheaded boys ranging in age from ten or twelve to about eight. The two youngest were twins.

Stephanie stepped into view and gave him an apologetic smile. "Sorry. It's the last week of school and they're pretty wound up."

"No problem."

The boys continued to study him curiously until their mother shooed them out the door. The twins ducked back in for a quick kiss, then waved in his direction and disappeared. Stephanie stood in the foyer with the door open until a bus pulled up in front of the house. Through the window in the dining room Nash could see the boys climb onto the bus. When it pulled away, Stephanie closed the front door and walked into the dining room.

"Did you get enough to eat?" she asked as she began to clear his dishes. "There are more scones."

"I'm fine," he told her. "Everything was great."

"Thank you. The original scone recipe dates back several generations. My late husband and I rented a guest house from an English couple many years ago. Mrs. Frobisher was a great one for baking. She taught me how to make the scones. I also make shortbread cookies that melt in your mouth. I would be happy to leave a few in your room if you'd like."

Nash told himself that her mention of a "late husband" didn't mean much more than that he didn't have to feel guilty for noticing Stephanie's bare stomach. The entire point of their encounter earlier that morning was that he wasn't as dead inside as he'd thought. Good news that was not particularly meaningful.

He glanced at her face and saw the expectant expression in her blue eyes. His brain offered a replay of her conversation and he cleared his throat.

"If it's not too much trouble," he said.

"None at all. The boys prefer chocolate chip cookies. I guess shortbread is an acquired taste that comes with age."

She offered a polite smile and carried his dishes out of the dining room.

Nash flipped through the sports section, then closed the paper. The news no longer interested him. Maybe he would go for that drive now and explore the area.

He rose, then paused, not sure if he should tell his hostess he was leaving. When he traveled it was usually on business and he always stayed in anonymous hotels and motels. He'd never been in a bed-and-breakfast before. While this was a place of business, apparently it was also Stephanie's home.

He looked from the kitchen to the foyer, then decided she wouldn't care what he had planned for his day. After fishing his car keys out of his pocket, he walked across the gleaming hardwood floor and out to the curb where he'd left his rental car.

Two minutes later he was back in the Victorian house. He walked into the kitchen, but it was empty. He crossed to the stairs and glanced up. Was she cleaning his room, or had she gone up to her private quarters?

A loud bang made him turn toward the back of the house. He followed the rhythmic noise past the kitchen and pantry into a large utility room. Stephanie sat on the floor in front of a washer. An open manual lay on her lap and there were tools and assorted parts all around her.

In the ten or fifteen minutes since she'd cleared his table, she'd changed her clothes. The tailored slacks and attractive sweater had been replaced by worn jeans and a sweatshirt featuring a familiar cartoon mouse. As he watched, she jabbed the side of the washer with a large wrench.

"Rat-fink cheap piece of metal trash," she muttered. "I hate you. I will always hate you. For the rest of your life, you're going to have to live with that."

He cleared his throat.

Stephanie gasped and shifted on the floor so that she faced him. Her eyes widened and her mouth twisted into a half smile that was as much sheepish as amused.

"If you keep sneaking up on me like this, I'm going to be forced to put a bell around your neck."

Nash leaned against the door frame and nodded at the washer. "Is there a problem?"

"It's not working. I'm trying to use guilt, but I don't think it's helping." She glanced from him to her jeans and back. "I thought you were heading out."

"The battery in my rental car is dead."

"Did you try guilting it into behaving?"

"I thought a jump would be more effective."

"Sure."

She tossed down the wrench and rose. Wearing athletic shoes, she barely came to his shoulder. She gave the washer one more kick, then walked toward him.

"Lead the way."

Nash straightened. "I could take a look at that if you would like."

Stephanie appeared doubtful. "You don't strike me as the washer repairman type."

"I'm not, but I'm pretty mechanical."

"Thanks, but I'm going to get a professional in. I'll go get my car keys. Why don't you meet me in front?"

Stephanie waited until Nash had started down the hallway before running upstairs to get the keys out of her purse. When she reached the top floor, she told herself that her rapidly beating heart had everything to do with the effort required to climb two flights of stairs and nothing to do with her guest's appearance. She figured she was being about sixty percent honest.

The truth was Mr. Elegant-in-a-Suit looked just as good in jeans as he had all dressed up. Daylight suited him, as well. Despite the fact that he couldn't have gotten more than four hours of sleep, he looked tanned, handsome and rested. She, of course, had dark circles that had defied her heavy-duty concealer and a bone-deep weariness compounded by a broken washer and an as-ever challenged bank account.

She took the back stairs down to the rear entrance and climbed into her minivan. After backing out of the driveway, she positioned her car so her bumper nearly touched his.

Jumper cables proved to be something of a challenge, but after rooting around in the garage for a few minutes, she found a set behind a box of old spare parts for some mystery machine. She picked them up and turned, only to run smack into Nash.

"You all right?" he asked as he grabbed her upper arms to steady her.

All right? With her nose practically touching his chest and her hands thrust into his rock-hard stomach?

He smelled good, she thought wistfully as she inhaled the scent of soap and man. Something deep inside her, that feminine part of her dormant for the past three years, gave a slight hiccup of resurrection and slowly stirred to life. Awareness rippled through her. Awareness and sexual interest.

Telling herself that the good news was that this would be a great story to tell her friends the next time they managed to sneak away for a girls'-only dinner, she stepped back and cleared her throat.

"Okay. While I'm out today I'm definitely getting you that bell." She handed him the jumper cables. "Hooking them up is going to be your problem. I know what a car battery looks like, but if I used those things, I would probably electrocute myself and set both our vehicles on fire."

"No problem. I appreciate the help. Are you sure I can't repay you by looking at the washer?"

"Thanks, but no. Think of this as part of our service here at Serenity House."

Nash studied her for a few seconds before turning and walking toward the parked cars. Stephanie sighed in relief. While the offer to pay her back was really nice, she had less than no interest in an amateur messing around with her washing machine. Whenever Marty had decided to "help," he ended up completely breaking whatever had only been partially broken before. Now she hired experts at the first sign of trouble. Easier and certainly cheaper in the long run.

She followed Nash to the curb and watched as he popped the hoods on both vehicles. He stretched out the cables and clamped one end to her battery.

"What brings you to Glenwood?" she asked as he walked to his car and she did the same.

"I'm visiting family."

Huh. She wouldn't have picked him for the small-town type. "I don't know anyone named Harmon in the area."

He opened his car door. "Actually their last name is Haynes."

"The Haynes men?"

He frowned slightly. "You know them?"

"Sure. Travis Haynes is our sheriff. Kyle, his brother, is one of the deputies, as is his sister, Hannah." Stephanie tilted her head. "Let me see. I think Hannah is only a half sister. I never heard the whole story. There are a couple more brothers. One's a firefighter and one lives in Fern Hill."

"You know a lot."

"Glenwood isn't the big city. It's the sort of place where we all keep track of each other."

Which was one of the things she liked about the area. While owning a bed-and-breakfast had never been one of her dreams, if she had to run that kind of business, far better here than somewhere cold and impersonal.

Nash moved into his car and turned the key. The engine caught.

When he stepped back out, Stephanie studied his

dark hair and strong jaw. "I can see the family resemblance," she said. "Are you a cousin?"

"Not exactly." He released the jumper-cable connection. "I don't know much about them. Maybe you could fill me in later."

A shiver shimmied through her. Anticipation, she realized. Great. In the time it took to serve breakfast and dig out jumper cables, she'd developed a crush. She was thirty-three. Shouldn't she be immune to that kind of foolishness?

He coiled the cables, then handed them to her. "If it's not too much trouble."

"Not one bit. Hunt me down when you're ready. I'm usually in the kitchen after the boys get home from school."

"Thanks."

He smiled. Unlike last night's, this one reached his eyes. They brightened for a moment, which made the cold foggy morning suddenly less dreary.

Oh, she had it bad. And as soon as her long-legged, hunky guest drove off in his rental car, she was going to give herself a stern talking-to. Falling for one pretty face once had turned her life into a disaster. Did she really want to risk that a second time?

She was a sensible woman with children and bills. The odds of her finding love with a decent responsible guy had to be substantially less than one in a million. She would do well to remember that.

Chapter 2

Nash circled around Glenwood and started out on the interstate. He checked his watch and when he'd traveled twenty minutes, he drove off at the next exit, turned around and headed back to town.

With his car battery charged, he meandered through the picturesque residential neighborhoods. Ancient trees lined many blocks, the heavy branches touching over the streets and providing tunnels of shade. Big lawns stretched out in front of well-kept houses. Bikes and sports equipment littered the edges of driveways while bright blooming flowers provided color.

The quiet small-town neighborhood wasn't anything like the lakefront in Chicago where he currently lived. No big city lurked in the background. Despite the geographical differences, he was reminded of life back where he'd grown up. Possum Landing, Texas, might not have been as upscale as Glenwood, but it had the same friendly feel.

He made a couple of turns without any thought of direction. He just wanted to keep moving. Eventually he would have to get in touch with his brother and deal with the pending family reunion, but not just yet.

After his next right turn, he drove onto a wider street lined with huge Victorian houses. They were similar to Stephanie's. All restored, all elegant and framed by massive trees. A discreet sign in front of one indicated it was also a bed-and-breakfast, with a restaurant. He briefly wondered why Stephanie hadn't opened her business here rather than on the other side of town before dismissing the query and returning his attention to getting lost.

He continued to drive through the neighborhood, turning left, then right. After ten minutes he found himself facing a large shopping mall, which he had driven past the previous evening on his way in from the airport. He was about to turn around when his cell phone rang.

Nash checked the caller ID, then pulled over and hit the talk button.

"What's up?" he asked, even though he had a good idea of the answer.

"I'm checking on you," Kevin, his twin brother, said. "Did you flake out on me at the last minute or are you really here?"

"I'm in town."

"You're kidding."

Kevin sounded surprised. Nash shared the feeling.

The last place he'd expected to be was here. Given the choice he would be at work—getting lost in an assignment, or training or even paperwork.

"What changed your mind?" his brother asked.

"I wasn't given a choice. You told me to get my butt here or you'd drag me yourself."

"Right. Like me telling you what to do has made you do anything." Kevin laughed. "I'm glad you made it, though. I've met with a couple of the guys. Travis and Kyle Haynes."

Their half brothers. Family they'd never known about. Nash still couldn't get his mind around the concept. "And?"

"It went great. There's a physical resemblance I didn't expect. Our mutual father has some pretty powerful genes. We're about the same height and build. Dark hair, dark eyes."

Someone said something in the background Nash didn't catch.

Kevin chuckled. "Haley says to tell you they're all good-looking. I wouldn't know about that. It's a chick thing."

Haley? Before Nash could ask, Kevin continued.

"We've set up a dinner for tomorrow night. All the brothers will be there along with their wives and kids. Gage is here."

Gage and Quinn Reynolds had been Nash and Kevin's best friends for as long as they could remember. They'd grown up together. Three weeks ago Nash had found out Gage and Quinn shared their biological father with Nash and Kevin.

"I haven't seen Gage in a couple of years," Nash said. "How's he doing?"

"He's engaged."

"No way."

"Remember Kari Asbury?"

Nash frowned. "The name's familiar."

"He dated her when he left the service and came back to Possum Landing. She took off to New York to be a model or something."

"Oh, yeah. Tall. Pretty. They're getting married?" It had to have been years since they'd seen each other.

"Yup. She moved back and the rest is history. Apparently it all happened pretty fast."

"Even though Gage kept saying he wanted a family, I figured he was going to stay single forever. I hope it works out."

Nash meant it. He wanted his friend to have a happy marriage. To be sure about the woman he married. Not to always wonder what wasn't exactly right between them.

"Gage will be at the dinner tomorrow night," Kevin said. "You're coming, too, right?"

"That's why I'm here." To meet his new family. To try to get involved in something other than work. Maybe to find a way to feel something again.

Was that possible or was he like a kid wishing for the moon?

He didn't want to think about it so he changed the subject. "How's the leg?"

"Good. Healing."

His brother had been shot in the line of duty. Kevin

was a U.S. Marshal who had been in the wrong place at the wrong time during a prison riot.

"Do you have a limp?" Nash asked.

"Some, but it's supposed to go away."

"You'll have the scar. Women love scars from bullet wounds. Knowing you, you'll use it to your advantage."

"Funny you should say that." Kevin cleared his throat. "I would have told you before, but you were away on assignment. The thing is, I've met somebody."

Nash thought of the woman's voice he'd heard earlier. "Haley?"

"Yeah. She's…amazing. We're getting married."

Gage's engagement had been a surprise. Kevin's left Nash speechless. He stared out at the tree-lined streets and couldn't think of a single thing to say.

"You want to meet her?" Kevin asked.

"Sure."

Why not? His brother had been born wild. Nash figured any woman strong enough to tie Kevin down had to be an amazing combination of sin and steel.

"We're staying at a bed-and-breakfast in town."

Kevin named the street and Nash realized it was the one he'd been on a few minutes ago.

"I'm about two miles away," he said. "I'll be right over."

"A minister's daughter?" Nash said as he stared at Kevin.

His fraternal twin grinned. "Not what you expected?"

"Not even close. What happened to all bad girls all the time?"

His brother shrugged. "I met Haley."

"That had to have been some meeting."

Kevin grinned. "It was."

He motioned to the parlor just to the left of the foyer, then led the way into the formally furnished room. Nash glanced around, noting that this B and B seemed larger and more elegant than Stephanie's. There were crystal chandeliers and some kind of tapestries on the wall. Her place was more homey.

Kevin limped to a long, high-backed sofa in a rich floral print. As he settled onto the cushions, he rubbed his thigh.

Nash took a chair on the opposite side of the coffee table. "You've seen a doctor for that, right?"

"When it happened and again back home. I'm healing. In another few weeks I'll be back to normal, but until then it aches from time to time. I know I'm lucky. The bullet missed the bone."

What he didn't say was if it had hit eighteen inches higher and a little to the left, he wouldn't have made it at all. Nash didn't like to think of anything bad happening to his brother.

"I thought you promised we weren't going to have to worry about you anymore," he said.

Kevin shrugged. "If I hadn't drawn the short straw, I would have been in Florida on a drug bust instead of delivering a prisoner. It wasn't my fault." He grinned. "Not that I'm complaining. If I hadn't been in Kansas, I wouldn't have met Haley."

"A minister's daughter," Nash repeated. "I still can't believe it. So where did you two hook up? Church?"

"A bar."

The answer came from the doorway. Nash turned and saw a young woman walking into the parlor. As he stood he saw she was of medium height, with short fluffy blond hair and hazel eyes. She was pretty enough, curvy, dressed in a snug T-shirt and shorts. His gaze automatically went to her bare legs and he waited for the kind of reaction he'd experienced when he'd seen that sliver of Stephanie's stomach that morning.

Nothing.

Which didn't make sense. If he hadn't had sex in forever and he was finally starting to feel something, why didn't Haley ring any bells?

"You must be Nash," Haley said as she approached. She tilted her head. "Wow—you're tall, like Kevin, and really nice-looking. The same dark hair and dark eyes, but you don't look very much alike." She wrinkled her nose. "What is it with this gene pool? Aren't any of you going to be fat or balding or at least kind of unattractive?"

Kevin beamed at his fiancée. He wrapped an arm around her and brushed a kiss against her temple. "Haley speaks her mind. You'll get used to it."

"If not, I'm sure you're polite enough not to say anything to my face," Haley said cheerfully.

She sank onto the sofa, pulling Kevin next to her. Nash sat down, as well. After linking hands with Kevin, Haley leaned forward and studied Nash.

"I'm really excited about the whole brother-in-law

thing," she told him. "I'm an only child. I had way too many mothers, but no siblings. I always wanted other kids around. Some of it was to take the heat off me. I mean I couldn't even think bad thoughts. It's like everyone could read my mind. How awful is that? Okay, sometimes it was really great to have so many people worrying about me, but it could be stifling, too."

Kevin bumped her shoulder with his. "Slow down. You're going to scare Nash off. He's not the sociable twin."

Her gaze became as penetrating as a laser. "Really."

Nash shifted uncomfortably. "Congratulations on your engagement," he said in an effort to distract her. "If Kevin wasn't completely honest about his past, I'd be happy to fill in the details."

Haley giggled with delight. "Ooh, stories about when Kevin was bad. He's told me a few things, but not about the women. There had to be dozens, right? Hundreds, even?"

Now Kevin was the one squirming in his seat. "Haley, you know everything important. I love you. I want to spend the rest of my life with you."

She sighed and rested her head on his shoulder. "Isn't he the best? I can't wait to get married. Speaking of which, are you dating, Nash?"

Kevin stood and pulled Haley to her feet. "I think you've terrorized my brother long enough."

"What?" she asked as she put her hands on her hips. "What did I say?"

He gave her a little push. "I won't be long."

"Did I upset you?" she asked Nash.

He stood. "Not at all. From what I can tell, you're exactly what my brother needs in his life."

"Ha." She tossed her head and walked out of the room. "I'll be upstairs," she called back. "Planning the wedding. A really big wedding."

"Have fun," Kevin said, then flopped back on the sofa. "She's a handful."

Nash sat down. "Interesting young woman."

"I think so. She's smart, funny, fearless. She gives with her whole heart. I'm still learning how to do that, but she makes it so damn easy to love her."

Had that been the problem? Nash wondered. Had Tina not been easy to love? Had the work got in the way?

"Enough about me," his brother said. "How are you doing?"

"Fine," Nash said. "Great."

Kevin didn't look convinced. "I didn't think it was possible to pry you away from work."

Nash shrugged, rather than admit the vacation hadn't been his idea. "I'm here, ready to meet the family."

"Yeah, right." Kevin's expression turned serious. "You've always been quiet, but since Tina died, it's been worse than usual. Are you coming out of that?"

As Nash had never been willing to acknowledge what he felt about his wife's death, he didn't know if he'd recovered or not. Still it was easier to say "Sure. I'm doing great."

His brother shook his head. "You still blame yourself. It was never your fault."

"Whose fault was it?"

"Maybe no one's. Maybe it just happened."

"Not on my watch."

"You can't control everything."

Nash knew. The realization was one of the reasons he'd stopped sleeping, stopped eating, stopped living. But knowing that didn't seem to change anything.

"Tell me about the Haynes family," he said to change the subject.

Kevin continued to watch him for a couple of seconds, then nodded, as if agreeing to the tactic. "The couple I've met have been good men. They're as surprised by all this as we are, but friendly enough." He smiled. "They're all cops."

Nash knew there were four brothers and a sister. "You're kidding."

"No. They're all—" He broke off and laughed. "Wait. I forgot. One of them is a rebel. He's a firefighter."

Which wasn't the same as being a cop, but it was close. Kevin was a U.S. Marshal, Gage a sheriff. Nash worked for the FBI and Quinn, well, Quinn walked his own road.

"It's in the blood," he said.

Kevin nodded. "That's what they're telling me. Earl Haynes was sheriff of this town for years. He has a bunch of brothers and they're all in law enforcement. Maybe we're following our destiny."

Destiny? Nash didn't believe in that kind of crap. He'd gone to work for the FBI because he'd been recruited out of college. Of all the offers he'd received, it was the one that had appealed the most.

"I've seen Gage," Kevin said. "We've known him and Quinn all our lives, played together, fought, made up. I'm having trouble getting that we were always brothers."

"We acted like brothers," Nash said. "Still, I'm with you. I figured we were good friends, nothing more."

Did the new knowledge change anything? He wasn't sure.

"The dinner tomorrow night is going to be a zoo," Kevin said. "The guys, their wives and kids. If I can pull together lunch with just a few of the brothers are you interested?"

"Sure." Nash didn't like crowds.

Kevin jerked his head toward the ceiling. "There are a few empty rooms. Want to come stay here?"

"I'm okay where I am."

"You sure?"

He knew Kevin thought he was avoiding contact with the world, but that wasn't it at all. If his brother pressed him he would say that packing and unpacking was a pain, which was a lie, but would get him off the hook. The truth was something else. For the first time in two years, he'd actually felt a glimmer of interest in something other than work. He knew his sexual stirrings and physical hunger didn't mean anything, but he was intrigued enough to want to stick around and see what happened next.

Nash hung out with Kevin and Haley until early afternoon, then headed back to Serenity House. When he entered the high-ceilinged foyer, he hesitated, not sure what to do with the rest of his day. As much as he wanted to check in with the office, he knew it was too soon. Calling now would simply prove his boss's point.

He walked through the dining room and into the kitchen. The tidy room was empty. He strolled into the hallway and listened. There was only silence. A quick check of the garage told him what he'd suspected. He was alone.

The knowledge should have relieved him. He didn't like a lot of company, preferring solitude to vapid chatter. He liked the quiet. Only not today. Right now he felt restless and out of place. It was as if his skin had suddenly gotten too small.

He turned toward the stairs and took three steps, then stopped. He didn't want to read or watch TV. He considered another long drive, but that didn't appeal to him. Finally, in desperation for a distraction, he moved into the back of the house.

In the utility room he found the washer still in pieces. He opened the lid and stared at the tub full of clothes and water, then studied the dial. After skimming the manual, he figured out the washer had stopped right before the spin cycle. He pushed aside the parts and tools, then settled on the floor. There was a schematic of the interior of the machine, along with a parts list. Nash laid the diagram flat on the floor and began sorting through tools and parts.

Over an hour later, Nash had found the problem and, he hoped, fixed it. He'd just started on reassembling the machine when he heard a door slam in the house. The wrench he'd been holding dropped to the floor.

He swore good-naturedly as he picked it up. If he was dropping tools in anticipation of seeing Stephanie, he was in even more trouble than he'd first thought. Finding her sexy was one thing, but actual nerves weren't allowed.

He turned as the footsteps approached, but instead of the petite blonde he'd been expecting, a boy stepped into the room.

Nash remembered the other two kids had been younger and identical twins. So this one would be Stephanie's oldest. He offered a smile.

"Hi, there."

The boy didn't smile back. He folded his arms over his chest and narrowed his eyes as he studied Nash. "You're not the repair guy."

"You're right. I'm Nash Harmon. I'm a guest here."

Nash wiped his hand on a paper towel and held it out. The boy hesitated, then slowly offered his own hand.

"Brett Wynne."

They shook slowly. Nash had the feeling he was being given the once-over and judging from Brett's expression, he wasn't measuring up.

"Why are you messing with our washer?" Brett asked. "Guests aren't supposed to do that sort of thing. If you break it worse, Mom's gonna be real mad. Plus it'll cost more to fix."

The boy looked to be about eleven or twelve. Tall and skinny, with light blond hair and blue eyes like his mother. Of course his father could have had blue eyes, too.

He looked hostile, protective and painfully young.

No kid that age should have to feel as if he was all that stood between his family and a hostile world.

Nash carefully set the wrench on the ground. Brett's fierce scowl and hostile words brought back memories from a long time ago. Back when Nash had felt *he* was the one responsible for making sure his mom and brother were safe. The accompanying feelings weren't comfortable.

"You have a point," he said quietly. "I *am* a guest here. The thing is, this morning the battery was dead on my rental car, so your mom gave me a jump. I wanted to pay her back for that. She'd been working on the washer when I found her and asked her to help me. She's a real classy lady, so I knew she wouldn't let me pay her. That's when I thought of the washer."

Brett's expression softened a little, but he didn't look a whole lot more welcoming. "What if you break it worse?"

"Then I'll pay for the repairs. The point of doing someone a favor is to make her life easier, not more difficult." He casually cleared some space on the vinyl floor covering. "I'm pretty sure I figured out what was wrong with the machine."

"Yeah?" Brett sounded skeptical. "Show me."

Nash scooted back to give the kid a clear view of the machine. "That part back there came loose, which meant this section moved forward. These two pieces got in the way, and this one ended up a little bent."

Brett crouched down and stared as Nash pointed to the problem areas. He explained what he'd done so far and how he was now putting the machine back together.

"I'll stop if you want," he said.

Brett sank onto the floor. His blue eyes widened in surprise. "You mean if I say not to do any more you won't?"

"That's right."

Brett glanced from the washer to Nash and back. "I guess it would be okay for you to finish up. Maybe you haven't made it worse."

High praise, Nash thought, holding in a grin. "Want to help me?"

"Yeah." Brett sounded eager. Then he gave a shrug. "I mean I'm not doing anything else right now."

Nash handed him the wrench and showed him where to tighten the edge of the casing. "Turn that there."

Fifteen minutes later, the washer was nearly back in one piece. Brett had given up being distant and sullen and now bombarded Nash with questions.

"How'd you figure out what had happened? You ever take a washer apart before?"

"When I was a teenager," Nash told him. "With computer chips and electronics a lot of home appliances are getting pretty complicated, but this washer's older. That made it easier to see what was wrong. Your mom had already taken it apart. I just poked around."

He didn't mention that Stephanie had been trying a combination of guilt and physical abuse on the old machine. Thinking about how she'd stopped to kick it as she'd walked out of the room that morning made him smile.

"My bike chain came off once," Brett said. "I got it

back on and tightened up some stuff, but I guess that's not the same."

"You're pretty mechanical," Nash told the kid. "You handle these tools well."

Brett pretended nonchalance. "I know."

Just then someone cleared her throat. Nash glanced over his shoulder and saw Stephanie standing in the doorway to the utility room. The twins were right behind her, peering at him from either side of her hips. She didn't look happy.

"I know you're trying to help, Mr. Harmon, but this isn't your responsibility."

Before Nash could speak, Brett scrambled to his feet. "It's okay, Mom. I think Nash really fixed it. He knows about machines and stuff. We're just putting it back together. Let's test it."

Stephanie's doubt was as clear as her frown. "Brett, the washer isn't a toy."

"Good thing," Nash said as he stood and looked down at her. "Because I wasn't playing."

Chapter 3

Had she already mentioned that the man was tall? Stephanie had to tilt her head back to meet Nash's dark gaze. Once her eyes locked on to his, she didn't think an earthquake would be enough to break the connection between them.

What exactly was the appeal? His chiseled good looks? The hint of sadness even when he smiled? A body big enough and muscled enough to make him the most popular guy in a "drawing the human form" class? Her sex-free existence? That voice?

I wasn't playing.

She knew what he'd meant when he spoke the words. He wasn't playing at being Mr. Repair. He was just trying to help. But she wanted him to mean something else. She wanted him to mean that he thought she was sexy, mysterious and, seeing as this was her personal fantasy, irresistible. She wanted him to mean he wasn't playing with her. He wanted it to be real, too.

Yeah, that and a nod from a genie would miraculously get the piles of laundry clean, too.

"Stephanie? Are you all right?"

Good question.

"Fine."

She forced herself to look away from his face and focus her attention on the nearly assembled washer. The scattered tools on the floor were enough to remind her of Marty, who had loved to play at fixing things. He knew just enough to be dangerous to both himself and her monthly budget. Like she needed that kind of trouble again.

"Tell me exactly what you did," she said. She would need the information to tell the repair guy.

Before Nash could speak, Brett launched into an explanation that involved calling tools by their actual names and pointing out various washer parts on a diagram so detailed, she got vertigo just looking at it. She did her best to pay attention. Really. It was just that the utility room was sort of on the small side and Nash was standing close enough for her to inhale the scent of his shampoo and the faint hint of male sweat. It had been a really long time since she'd seen a man perspire.

And it wasn't going to happen again any time soon, she told herself firmly. Men, good-looking or not, weren't a part of her to-do list. She was going to put any illicit or illegal thoughts of Nash Harmon right out of her mind.

The bad news was she'd assumed that her reaction to

him that morning had come from a lack of caffeine and low blood sugar. As she'd had enough coffee to float a good-size boat and she was still full from lunch, she couldn't blame her current attraction on either of those states. There had to be another explanation.

"Mom, you're not listening," Brett complained.

"I am. You got a little technical on me. I guess it's a guy thing."

She watched as her son tried to decide between being huffy at her inattention and pleasure at her calling him a guy.

"There's a simple way to ease your mind," Nash said.

Reluctantly she looked in his direction, careful not to get caught up in his lethal gaze.

"Let me guess," she said. "You're going to turn it on and prove to me that it works."

"Exactly."

He smiled, and staring at that was nearly as dangerous. When his mouth curved, her stomach swooned. The sensation was more than a little disconcerting.

"Okay, let her rip." She bent down to the twins and rested her hands on their shoulders. "You two brace yourselves. If the washer starts to hiss and shake I want you to run for cover. Okay?"

They nodded solemnly.

The three of them watched as Nash closed the lid, then pushed in the dial. There was a second of silence followed by a click. Then, amazingly, the old washer chugged to life. She heard the sound of the tub turning, followed by water gurgling down the drain.

"I don't believe it," she said. "It might actually be working."

Brett grinned. "Mo-om. It *is* working. Nash and I fixed it."

"Wow!" She brushed his cheek with her fingers. "I'm impressed."

Adam tugged on her shirt. "I'm hungry, Mom. I want my afternoon snack."

"Me, too," Jason said.

"Meet me in the kitchen." She turned her attention back to Nash. "I don't know how to thank you. Of course I'll discount your room for the work. The last time the repairman was here, he charged me a hundred dollars."

"Forget it," he said as he crouched down and began collecting tools. "You helped me out this morning. I'm returning the favor."

"Jump-starting your car hardly compares with fixing my washer. I have to pay you something."

He glanced up. "Then I'll take an afternoon snack, too."

That wasn't enough, but it would have to do for now. Brett planted his hands on his hips.

"What do I get?"

"My undying gratitude."

"How about a new skateboard?"

She winced. The one he wanted had special wheels or a secret finish or something that cranked up the price tag to the stratosphere.

"We'll talk," she told her oldest.

"You always say that, but we never have the conversation," he complained as he stalked out of the room.

She watched him go and was pleased when he turned into the kitchen rather than heading toward the stairs and up to his room. Brett was twelve—nearly a teenager. She didn't want to think about handling a teenage boy all on her own. She didn't like to think about dealing with any of it all on her own. Unfortunately, she didn't have a choice. The past few years had taught her that alone was a whole lot better than marriage to the wrong guy.

She turned back to Nash. "How about coffee and shortbread cookies?"

He finished putting the tools in the box and stood. "Sounds terrific."

"I'll bring them into the dining room in about five minutes."

She started to leave, then stopped. The washer clicked over from spin to rinse. "I still can't believe you fixed that. I have laundry piled up to the ceiling. We've been running out of clothes. I really do appreciate your help."

"I was glad to do it." He leaned against the washer. "My work keeps me pretty busy. I'm not used to having a lot of free time and this gave me something to do."

She laughed. "Uh-huh. Next you'll be telling me I was doing *you* the favor by letting you work on the washer."

"Exactly."

"Nice try, Nash, but I don't buy it."

She headed for the kitchen. Every single cell in her

body tingled from their close encounter. Did sexual attraction burn calories? Wouldn't it be nice if it did?

She started a fresh pot of coffee, then got out glasses for the boys. Brett poured the milk while she set out grapes, string cheese and a plate of cookies. By the time that was done, the coffee had finished. She poured it into a carafe, then set it on the tray, along with short-bread cookies, grapes and some crab puffs she'd been defrosting.

"Be right back," she told her children as she picked up the tray and walked toward the dining room.

Nash stood by the front window, staring out on to the street. When she entered, he turned and smiled.

"Thanks."

"You're welcome." She put down the tray. "Let me know if you need anything else."

"I will."

She would like to tell herself that he was talking about more than just the food. While she was busy imagining that, she could pretend that his gaze lingered on her face and that his relaxed stance belied pulsing erotic tension building just below the surface of his calm facade. Or she could be realistic and get her fanny back to the kitchen.

Being reasonably intelligent, she chose the latter and left Nash in peace. The poor man hadn't asked for her sudden rush of hormones. If she didn't want to embarrass them both, she was going to have to find a way to get her wayward imagination under control. If logic wasn't going to work, she was going to have to think of more drastic measures.

"Tell me about school," she said as she slid onto the chair between Adam and Jason.

Her twins were in third grade, while Brett had just finished his first year in middle school.

"Mrs. Roscoe said we're her best class ever," Adam told her. "We beat all the other classes." He gave his twin a triumphant grin.

Jason ignored him. "We got our summer reading lists today, Mom," he said. "I've picked out five books already. Can we go to the library this week?"

"Sure. You'll all want to think about summer reading. We're going to have to talk about how many books you'll be getting through. Are there book reports?"

Adam reached for the backpack he'd left on the floor and pulled out a folder. He passed a single sheet of paper to her.

Stephanie scanned the directions, then glanced at Brett. "What about you?"

He rolled his eyes. "It's up in my room. We have to do about two pages. I want to do mine on the computer. Are we getting a new one? You said we'd talk about it when school was out."

"You're right. And unless I'm reading the calendar wrong, school isn't out yet."

"We've got four days left."

"Which gives me ninety-six hours until you can start bugging me."

Brett tried to hide his smile, but she saw it. He'd been after her for a new computer for the better part of a year. While there was nothing wrong with the one they had, it didn't play the really cool games. She figured she could probably put him off until Christmas when her "twenty dollars a week" fund would have reached computer size. Then the new computer would be a family gift.

Adam bounced in his chair. "I have a new joke," he announced. "Knock knock."

"Those are baby jokes," Brett said as he took a cookie.

"They are age-appropriate," Stephanie told him. "I listened to yours when you were his age."

Brett sighed, then dutifully went through the joke with his brother who squealed with delight when he repeated the word *who* enough for Adam to ask him why he was being an owl. Jason giggled at his older brother.

As the three of them took turns talking about their day, Stephanie found her attention sliding to the man in the next room. He was sitting out there alone while she was in here with her family. She kept having to fight the impulse to invite him to join them. Which was crazy. She'd never once encouraged guests to befriend her children. Besides, if Nash was alone, it was by choice.

He was probably married, she told herself. Or he had a serious girlfriend back in Chicago. She knew he had family here—he'd mentioned the Hayneses, although not how he was related to them.

Indecision made her fidget in her seat until she couldn't stand it anymore.

"I'll be right back," she told the boys and stalked out of the room.

This was insane, she told herself. She was asking

for trouble. Worse, she was asking for humiliation. She needed therapy.

As there was no psychologist standing by to offer advice, she walked into the dining room only to find Nash where she'd last seen him. Standing in front of the window looking out on to the street.

A quick glance at the tray told her he hadn't touched the food she'd brought him. He hadn't even poured any coffee.

He turned around and raised his eyebrows in silent query.

After clearing her throat, she tried to figure out what to say. Nothing brilliant occurred to her so she was left feeling slightly awkward.

"You must miss your family," she said.

His eyebrows lowered and drew together. "I haven't met them yet."

What? Oh. "I meant your family in Chicago."

"I don't have any there. I'm not married."

Score one for the hormones, she thought, trying not to feel or look relieved. The good news was that when Nash left, she would have a great time remembering all the surging feelings she'd experienced while he was here. It would be a lot more interesting than sorting coupons or ironing.

"Okay." She sucked in a breath. "You can tell me no. It's completely crazy and not even why you're here. I don't usually even ask. Why would you want to?" She shook her head. "Forget it."

She took a step back.

He blinked at her. "Was there a question in there for me?"

"I don't think so." She waved toward the kitchen. "We're just hanging out in there. The boys tell me about their day at school and they have a snack. You seemed..." She tried a different line of thought. "You're welcome to join us if you'd like. Or you can simply run screaming from the room and I'll get the message."

He looked surprised, and not exactly comfortable with the idea. Of course. He was a sexy, successful, single guy. Men like that didn't hang out with three kids and a single mom.

Heat crawled up her cheeks and she had a bad feeling there was a blush to match. "Never mind," she said brightly. "It was a silly suggestion."

She started toward the closed door that led to the kitchen, but before she'd gone more than two steps, he called her back.

"I would like to join you," he said.

She eyed him. "Why?"

He smiled and her internal organs did a couple of synchronized swimming moves.

"Because you asked and it sounds like fun."

"I'm not sure about fun, but I can promise loud."

"Close enough."

Now that he'd accepted, she felt foolish about her invitation, but it was too late to retract it. She moved to the table and collected the tray, then tilted her head in the direction of the kitchen.

"Brace yourself," she said and pushed open the door with her shoulder.

All three of her boys were talking at once. They barely noticed her, but the second Nash walked in behind her three pairs of blue eyes widened and three mouths snapped closed.

"This is Mr. Harmon," she said as she put the tray on the counter.

"Nash," he said easily.

"Okay. Nash. These are my boys. You've already met Brett, who is rapidly becoming a macho tool guy. And these two—" she walked to the table and put her hands on their shoulders "—are my twins. Jason and Adam. Say hi to Nash."

The twins offered an enthusiastic greeting, but Brett didn't say much. His expression turned wary and Stephanie wondered if he was about to say something that would make her cringe.

"We're having chocolate chip cookies, grapes and string cheese," she said quickly in an effort to forestall Brett. "You're welcome to that or the shortbread."

"How about shortbread and grapes," he said.

"No problem."

As she bustled around the kitchen, he pulled out one of the two empty chairs. Brett sat across from the twins, which meant Nash would be across from her. It was only a snack, she told herself. She could handle it. At least she hoped she could.

As she worked, she tried not to notice the silence. Her normally ten-thousand-words-a-minute kids were all staring at Nash. But before she could think of something to ease the escalating tension, Nash broke the ice himself.

He leaned toward Jason and Adam. "I'm a twin," he said.

The boys grinned. "No way," Jason said.

"Not identical, like you two. Kevin and I don't look very much alike. But we're still twins."

"Cool." Adam offered a shy smile.

Nash turned to Brett. "I heard school is out this week. Are you excited about summer?"

Stephanie saw her oldest wrestle with his innate excitement and his need to be standoffish.

"Summer's good," Brett said at last.

"There's a community pool," Jason said. "We go swimming every week. And there's sleepover camp at the end of summer. And Adam and me are gonna play volleyball at the park."

"Sounds like fun," Nash said.

"Brett's seriously into baseball," Stephanie volunteered as she carried a plate to the table, then returned to collect the coffee. "His team made the city finals."

"What position do you play?" Nash asked.

"First base."

She could see he was itching to say more, but for some reason didn't want to. As if wanting to talk to Nash was a bad thing.

Stephanie sighed. Brett considered himself the "man of the family." He took his responsibilities seriously. While she appreciated the effort, sometimes she wished she could convince him that it was far more important to her for him just to be a kid.

Conversation flowed for about twenty minutes until she glanced at the empty plates in front of her three.

"Looks like you're done eating to me. Guess what comes next?"

Adam smiled shyly at Nash. "We do our homework now."

"It's when I used to do it, too," he admitted. "I liked every subject but English. What about you?"

"I like 'em all," Jason announced and pushed back his chair.

He carried his plate to the counter by the sink, then gave Stephanie a hug. She hugged him back. As she felt his small back and warm, tugging hands, she reminded herself that jerk or not, Marty had done one thing right. He'd given her these boys. They were worth all the heartache and suffering she'd endured along the way.

When all three of them had trooped out of the kitchen, she turned to the table. Nash would go now, she thought. Which was fine. She'd tortured him with her family long enough. Whatever feelings of loneliness he might have had would have been erased. No doubt he would be grateful for some solitude.

"Good cookies," he said as he rose.

"Thanks. I won't tell you how much butter is in each batch."

"I appreciate that."

He carried his plate and mug over to the sink, which was a bit of a surprise. Then, before she could say anything, he turned on the water and began to rinse them off.

Stephanie thought about rubbing her eyes. She had to be having some kind of hallucination. A man? Doing work? Not in her world.

"You don't have to do that," she said, trying not to sound stunned.

"I don't mind helping."

As he spoke, he collected the boys' plates and rinsed those off, too. Then he opened the dishwasher and actually put the plates inside. She couldn't believe it. She didn't think Marty had even known where the dishwasher was, let alone what it was for.

When Nash reached for the glasses, she came to her senses.

"Hey, I'm the hired help around here, not you," she said as she stepped in close and took the glass from him.

Their fingers touched. Just for a second, but it was enough. Not only did she hear the faint ringing of bells, she would swear that she saw actual sparks arc between them. Holy wow. Sparks. She didn't think that kind of stuff was possible after age thirty.

Nash looked at her. His dark eyes seemed bright with what she wanted to say was passionate fire, but was probably the light from the overhead fixtures. Awareness rippled through her, sensitizing her skin and making her want to fling herself into his arms for a kiss that went on for at least six hours, followed by mindless, intense sex. Right there, in front of the appliances.

She swallowed and took a step back. Something was really wrong with her. Seasonal allergies? Too much television? Not enough? She felt soft and wet and achy inside. She felt unsettled. All of this was so out of the ordinary, so unexpected and so extreme that it would be really hilarious…if it weren't so darned terrifying.

Nash wondered if Stephanie really was issuing an invitation with her parted lips and wide eyes or if that was just wishful thinking on his part. No doubt the latter, he told himself as he heard footsteps on the stairs.

The boys walked into the kitchen. Adam and Jason each had a backpack with them while Brett carried a math book and several sheets of paper.

Nash figured it was time for him to excuse himself. Homework seemed like family time. But before he could say anything, Jason patted the chair next to him and offered a winning smile.

"I have to finish my calendar for summer. I wrote something about each of the months. Wanna hear?"

Nash glanced from the boy to Stephanie who gave him a shrug, as if to say it was his call. When he looked back at Jason, the boy pulled the chair out a little.

What the hell, Nash thought. He crossed to the table and took the seat.

"So your calendar is only three months long," he said.

"Uh-huh. We did pictures. See— I colored fireworks in the sky for July, coz that's when it's the fourth and we always go to the park for fireworks."

Jason opened a large folder and withdrew a folded sheet of construction paper as he spoke. Nash admired the crayon depiction of fireworks, then bent close to see what Jason had written underneath.

"It's a poem," the boy said proudly. "The teacher

said we could copy it from the board if we wanted. I can read it to you."

The last sentence sounded more like a question than a statement. Nash nodded. "Sure. Go ahead."

Jason cleared his throat, then read the poem. When he was finished Adam quietly pushed a spelling list toward him.

"I got 'em all right," he said in a low voice.

Nash studied the word list, and the big A at the top of the paper.

"You did great. There are some big words here."

Adam beamed.

The twins pulled out more papers and talked about their homework. When they'd explained everything they had to do, they started the work. But it wasn't a silent process. They asked questions, shared each step, bickered over the pencil sharpener and asked for more snacks, another glass of milk or even water. Stephanie kept gently steering them back to their assignments.

"They're usually more focused than this," she said as she pulled food out of the refrigerator. "The last couple of weeks of school are always crazy."

Nash remembered what that was like—the unbearable anticipation of an endless summer with no homework. Being here with the boys reminded him of a lot of things. How he and Kevin were supposed to do their homework as soon as they got home, but with their mom out working, there was no one around to make sure it happened. Nash had always done his, but Kevin had usually ducked outside to play. Later, when their

mom got home, they fought about it. Nash had retreated
to his room to get lost in a book.

As he glanced at the three bent heads, he realized he didn't have any children in his life. No kids of
friends, no neighbors with little ones running around.
He couldn't remember the last time he'd spent any time
with a child. It wasn't that he didn't like them; they
simply weren't a part of his world.

Had someone asked him what it would be like to
spend an hour or so with three boys, he would have
assumed time would go by slowly, that he would feel
awkward and restless. But his usual underlying sense
that something was wrong seemed to have faded. The
twins were friendly enough and while Brett obviously
didn't want him around, Nash understood enough of
what he was feeling not to mind. When Nash had been
his age, he'd done exactly the same thing.

Stephanie came over and put her hand on Brett's
shoulder. "How's it going?"

"Fine."

Nash wasn't sure that was true. Brett hadn't written
anything on his paper in nearly ten minutes.

Stephanie smiled at Nash. "Brett is in an accelerated
math group. He's already starting on algebra, and it's a
little tough. Unfortunately I was never a math person.
Still, he's way better at it than me."

Brett winced. "Mo-om, I'm doing fine."

"I know, honey. You're doing great."

Nash glanced down at the open book. "I remember
algebra," he said.

She drew her eyebrows together. "Let me guess. You *were* a math person."

"Sorry, yeah."

"Figures."

"The thing I always liked about it was the rules. Once you learn them, you keep applying them. Things need to happen in a certain order, otherwise you get the wrong answer."

She shook her head. "That would be me. The queen of the wrong answer. It was all that do-this-first stuff that made me crazy. Why can't you just do an equation from left to right, like reading?"

"You can. Sort of. Like this problem here." He pointed. "You do what's in the parentheses first, then go from left to right."

"Why?"

"Because that's how the steps work. If you're building a model car and you glue down the hood before you put in the engine, it's not going to look right."

She groaned. "Is this where I tell you I can't put a model together, either?"

Brett tapped his pencil on the table. "Can I have my book back, please?"

"Sure."

Nash handed it over. At that moment Adam claimed his attention to discuss what color green would do best on his mountains for his report on Wyoming. As Nash checked out the various options, he saw Brett read the first problem again, then start writing on his paper. When he'd finished his calculations, he plugged the answer back into the original equation and quickly solved it. His wide smile told Nash that he'd gotten it right.

Nash handed Adam a colored pencil, then caught Stephanie's eyes. She mouthed "thank you." Apparently she'd picked up his attempt to help Brett without actually helping. Her gaze darkened slightly as several emotions skittered across her face.

He tried to read them, but they came and went in a heartbeat. He was left with a sense of sorrow, as if she had something she regretted.

Of course she did, he told himself. Everyone did. Regrets were a part of life. But for the first time in a long time, he wanted to ask another person what was wrong. He wanted to learn more about her, to understand what she was thinking. He wanted to connect.

His interest was more than sexual and that scared the crap out of him. Feeling—getting involved—would be a disaster.

He told himself to get out of there right now. To leave before he got trapped. Before it was too late. But even knowing it was wrong to stay, he couldn't seem to force himself to stand and walk away.

It was just a couple of hours, he told himself. What could it possibly hurt?

Chapter 4

Nash stayed through dinner. Stephanie had no idea why, nor could she decide if it was a good thing or a bad thing. The man was nice enough, the twins already adored him even though Brett remained standoffish. She appreciated the opportunity to converse with an adult for a chance. So the situation should have been a big plus.

Except she didn't know what was in it for him. Why would a good-looking, intelligent man want to hang out with her and her kids? She opened the refrigerator and put the milk and butter back in the door, then frowned. That didn't sound exactly right. Nash's appearance and mental state didn't have anything to do with her confusion. Why would *any* man not be running for the hills? Weren't guys supposed to hate other men's children in a relationship? Not that he had any designs on her. Despite the fact that he made her long for satin sheets and champagne, she doubted he saw her as much more than an efficient hostess. After all, her luck just plain wasn't good enough to hope for more.

So why had he stayed? Why hadn't he retreated to the quiet and privacy of his room or gone out somewhere for dinner?

You could ask, a small voice in her head whispered.

Stephanie nearly laughed out loud. Sure she could, but that was so not her style.

"We're done," Brett said.

She turned around and saw that the table was indeed cleared, the dishes scraped and neatly stacked by the sink and the table wiped off.

"Very nice job," she said. "Everyone finished his homework, right?"

Three heads nodded earnestly.

She smiled. "Then I guess this is a TV night."

"All right!"

Brett pumped the air with his fist. The twins tore out of the kitchen. She heard their footsteps on the hardwood floor and was able to guess their destination.

"Stop right there," she yelled after them. "We have a guest. Use the TV upstairs."

"Why?" Nash asked from where he leaned against the counter.

She turned toward him, ignoring the continual sexual impact of his presence. Not only did she not want to make a fool of herself, but there was still a minor in the room. "The downstairs TV is for our guests."

He gave her a slow, sexy smile that could have melted the polar ice cap. "I'm not much of a TV watcher. It won't bother me if it won't bother you."

Stephanie figured she wasn't going to fight the point. If the man wanted to be generous, her kids would be thrilled. She smiled at Brett. "Looks like this is your lucky day. Go tell your brothers, and keep the volume down."

Brett grinned and raced down the hall. "We can stay down here," he yelled.

"Simple pleasures," she said as she turned toward the sink. "If only life stayed that easy."

"Complicated comes with growing up," Nash said as he also approached the sink. He was closer so he got there first.

As she watched, he turned on the water and began rinsing dishes. Just like that. He even used the sponge to clean off the worst bits.

Stephanie wanted to pinch herself to see if she was dreaming. He was helping again. *Helping.* Without being asked, without complaining. Just doing it.

Some of her confusion must have shown on her face because he looked at her and asked, "What's wrong?"

She wiggled her fingers toward the dishes. "You don't have to do that."

"I don't mind."

He didn't mind. Wow. Every time she had asked Marty to help, he'd howled like a wet cat, then had a list of fifty reasons why he couldn't. However hard she pushed, he pushed back harder. He threatened, cajoled, or had a temper tantrum to rival a three-year-old's. His goal had been to make the experience so miserable that she would stop asking. Eventually it had worked.

"So who trained you?" she asked. "I happen to know that most men aren't born being so handy around the kitchen."

He finished rinsing the dishes, then opened the dishwasher and began placing them inside. "I was married for a while, but most of my 'training' as you call it, came from being raised by a single mom. She worked a lot of hours and came home beat. I pitched in to help."

Wow times two. "You give me hope," she said.

He straightened. "In what way?"

For once her reaction wasn't about sex. "You seem like a great guy. Successful, articulate, not a serial killer—at least not as far as I can tell. You didn't have a father around, either. So maybe my boys will turn out okay, too."

He gave her another slow smile. "They're going to be great. You're doing a terrific job with them."

"I try."

"It shows."

The compliment left her feeling flustered and fluttery. She had to clear her throat before she could speak again. "If you don't mind me asking, what happened in your marriage?"

He put the last three glasses into the dishwasher. "Tina passed away a couple of years ago."

"I'm sorry."

The words were automatic. She figured Nash was in his early thirties, which meant his wife would have been around the same age. What would have taken such a young woman? Cancer? A drunk driver?

"What brought you to Glenwood?" he asked. "Or are you a native?"

The not-so-subtle change in subject ended any thought she had of actually asking her questions.

"Dumb luck," she said.

Nash picked up the dishcloth and rinsed it, then started to wipe off the counters. She was nearly dumb-struck. Rather than stand around with her mouth open, she forced herself to get the detergent out from under the sink and pour some into the dishwasher.

"We always moved around a lot," she said, trying not to stare as he finished up with the counters. "Marty had wonderful ideas of fun places to live and we wanted to experience them all."

Not exactly the whole truth, she thought sadly. This was the made-for-TV version of her marriage. The one she told mostly everyone. Especially her children.

"We spent eight months living in a forest and nearly a year working on a ranch. There was a summer on a fishing boat and a winter in a lighthouse."

Nash leaned against the counter and folded his arms over his chest. "With the kids?"

"It was a great experience for them," she said, trying to sound enthusiastic when all she felt was tired. "They have great memories."

All good ones. She'd done her best to ensure that. Whatever her feelings about her late husband might be, she wanted Brett and the twins to remember their father with a lot of love and laughter.

"I experienced worlds I didn't know existed." And would have happily died in ignorance of, given the choice. She pushed the delay button on the dishwasher, setting the start time for midnight.

"I'd homeschooled Brett through third grade, which went well. He's very bright. But Marty and I were worried about socialization. We knew it was time to settle down."

It hadn't exactly gone that way, she remembered. Marty had wanted to keep moving, but she'd demanded that they settle. Despite having an eight-year-old and four-year-old twins, she'd flat-out told him she would leave him if necessary. The previous winter Adam had spiked a 105-degree fever while they'd been stuck in the godforsaken lighthouse. With a storm raging around them, there'd been no way to get to the mainland and a doctor. She'd spent thirty-six hours in hell, wondering if her son was going to die. In the dark hours before dawn, right before his fever finally broke, she'd vowed she wasn't going to live like that anymore.

"As luck would have it, the day we arrived in Glenwood we got word of an inheritance. We fell in love with the town right as we found out we had enough money to buy a place and settle down." She offered a practiced smile. "This house was on the market and we couldn't resist. It was the perfect opportunity to have both a home and a growing business."

Nash glanced around at the remodeled kitchen. "You've done a great job."

"Thanks."

What she didn't tell him was that there was a mortgage on the old Victorian house. She also didn't mention the fights she'd had with Marty. There'd been enough money to buy a regular house outright instead of this place, but that had been too boring for him. As the inheritance had come from his side of the family, she hadn't felt she was in a position to argue too much.

"It was all coming together," she said. "We closed escrow and started the remodeling. The boys started school. We were just settling into the community when Marty passed away."

His dark gaze settled on her face. "So it's been a while."

"About three years. Marty was killed in a car accident."

"Leaving you with three children. That had to be tough."

She nodded slowly because agreement was the expected response. It's not that she'd wished Marty ill, and she certainly hadn't wanted him dead, yet by the time he was killed, any love she'd ever felt had long since died. Only obligation had remained.

"Brett mourned the most of the boys," she said. "The twins were only five. They have some memories and Brett tells them stories, but it's not very much. I wish they had more."

She meant that. What did it matter if Marty had refused to grow up and be responsible? He was still the boys' father. She wanted them to remember him as fun and loving. To think the best of him.

"You're doing great," he said. "They're good kids."

"No potential serial killers?"

"Not a one."

"I hope they're okay. I worry about them growing up without a father. I was an only child, so my experience with boys was limited to those I knew in school. I'm trying to encourage the whole 'be macho' thing, while still keeping them on this side of civilized."

"You mean no spitting indoors?"

She shuddered, then grinned. "Exactly. No spitting, no writing on the walls, no dead animals' skins."

"Pretty strict rules." One corner of his mouth twitched slightly. "How about a couple of skulls?"

"Animal or human?"

"Does it matter?"

"Of course. Animal is fine, as long as they're small and we bought them from a store. I want clean skulls."

"Typical girl. Dirt is fun."

"Easy for you to say. You're not stuck doing the vacuuming."

Nash dropped his hands to his sides and took a step toward her. Just one step, but her breath caught as if she'd just climbed a mountain. He was closer. Much closer. The light mood their conversation had created suddenly thickened. Air refused to flow into her lungs. She felt hot, shivery and more than a little out of control.

When his eyes darkened, she told herself it was a trick of the light, nothing more. It had to be that, because thinking that Nash might also be feeling some flicker of sexual attraction was more than she ever hoped for. It was also outside the realm of possibility.

She wanted to throw herself into his arms and beg

him to kiss her. She wanted to rip off her shirt and bra, baring her breasts. Surely that would be enough of a hint. Not that he would be interested in her breasts. She'd had three kids and parts of her were not as perky as they once had been. Miracles could be worked with an underwire bra.

So she could just rip off her shirt and leave the bra on. Still a good hint for him.

Right, she thought with humorous resignation. He would respond by ripping off his shirt, too, right after he wrote her that check for a million dollars.

"I don't want to keep you," she said at last. It was the mature thing to say. The right thing. How disappointing when he nodded.

"I'll see you in the morning."

"I'll be the one baking," she said, keeping her voice light.

He smiled, then walked out of the room. She allowed herself a last look at his rear, then pulled out a kitchen chair and sank onto the seat.

She had to get a grip. Yes, the attraction was nice. The quivery feelings reminded her that she wasn't dead yet. All delightful and completely meaningless messages when compared with the fact that men were nothing but trouble and getting involved with one would make her an idiot times two. Oh sure, she'd heard rumors that there were male members of the species who were actually helpful, responsible and on occasion behaved like partners, but she'd never experienced it firsthand. What were the odds of her encountering one at this point in her life? Even more important, what were the odds of her encountering one in someone who made her hormones belly dance in supplication?

"Is he gone?"

She looked up and saw Brett entering the kitchen. "By 'he' I assume you mean Nash?"

Her twelve-year-old nodded.

"He went up to his room."

Brett pulled out a chair and sat next to her. "Why's this guy hanging around?"

"Maybe he's a film producer doing research on the perfect American family."

Brett rolled his eyes.

Stephanie grinned. "Do you have a better answer?"

"No, but it's totally weird."

"I think it's nice. Don't forget, he fixed our very temperamental washer. The piles of laundry stretching to the ceiling and I are grateful." She touched Brett's shoulder. "You helped him with that. I thought you liked him."

Her son shrugged.

What was going on? Did Brett feel threatened by Nash in some way? Stephanie hadn't dated since Marty's death. Maybe having another guy around made him feel as though his father was being replaced.

"Hey, don't sweat it," she said, leaning close and wrapping her arms around him. "Nash is a guest here. Which means his home is somewhere else and he's going to be leaving us in a couple of weeks. In the meantime, he's nice, he cleans up after himself and I like having another grown-up to talk to. Nothing more. Okay?"

As they were alone, Brett burrowed into her embrace. He'd reached the stage where he didn't allow hugs and kisses in front of other people, but when it was just the two of them, he was still her little boy. Sort of.

He raised his head and looked at her. "Do you still miss Dad?"

She studied his dark blue eyes and the mouth shaped just like Marty's. "Of course I do. I loved him very much."

Brett nodded, as if reassured.

Stephanie told herself that under the circumstances, the lie didn't matter. Her first responsibility was to make her children's world as safe and stable as possible. A dark stain on her conscience was a small price to pay for that.

The teenaged waitress stared at the four men at the table. "I'm new in town," she told them, "but I have to tell you there's something pretty amazing in the water. You're Haynes brothers, aren't you? I recognize you from what I've been told. Every one of you is tall, dark and delicious. You guys all married? Anyone want my number?"

Nash was less surprised by the unsubtle come-on than he would have been before meeting Travis and Kyle Haynes. Kevin had arranged for the four of them to meet up for lunch. Even if he hadn't known about the relationship between them all, he would have guessed something was up the second he saw them.

The four men were nearly identical in height and build. Their dark hair was the same shade and the shapes of their eyes and mouths were similar. Travis and Kyle were a few years older, but still obviously related.

"Thanks, but not today," Kyle said as he took the menus from the young waitress.

"Your loss," she said.

"Probably, darlin', but you should stick to guys your own age."

"What about the stuff they say about older men knowing their way around a woman?"

Kyle grinned. "All lies."

"Why don't I believe you?" She gave a sassy wink, took their drink order and headed off.

Kevin shook his head. "Friendly girl."

Travis Haynes unrolled his paper napkin and set his flatware on the table. "Our family has something of a reputation in this town. Four generations of Haynes men have had their way with a large percentage of the local female population. The four of us have tried to change things, but that sort of legend doesn't die easily."

"Apparently not," Nash said. He looked at his twin. "We don't have a reputation in Possum Landing. We must have been doing something wrong."

"Or right," Kyle said. "Being good with women isn't something to be proud of. Now being a good husband and father—that's a hell of a lot more important."

"Agreed," Travis said. He looked across the table at Nash. "Are you settled in?"

"Yeah. I'm staying at a B and B on the other side of town."

"Stephanie Wynne's place," Kyle said. "Her oldest

boy is friends with my oldest son." He smiled. "It's a small town. There aren't many strangers and even fewer secrets."

Travis passed out the menus. "Everything's good here. I'd recommend the burgers, but then I'm a man of simple tastes."

Kevin looked at Nash, then back at Travis. "We're not exactly sushi eaters ourselves."

Kyle leaned forward. He and his brother wore identical khaki uniforms. Travis's name badge proclaimed him sheriff, while Kyle's said he was a deputy.

"Are you two finding this as strange as we are?" Kyle asked.

"Discovering family after all this time?" Nash opened the menu, then closed it. "We had no idea our father had any other children."

"It was one thing to find out that our best friends were actually half brothers," Kevin said. "But when Gage told us about all of you, I was surprised."

The waitress reappeared with their drinks. All the men had ordered iced tea. She took their orders—four burgers, hold the onions, and fries, then disappeared.

"There are five of us," Travis said. His dark brows drew together in a frown. "We have a half sister— Hannah. She works at the sheriff's office, too. She's in communications. Her mother is Louise, who—" He shook his head. "This is going to be confusing as hell."

"Talk slow," Kevin said.

Kyle chuckled. "Travis is good at that—what with being mentally challenged."

Travis turned to his brother. "I can still take you."

"With what army?"

Their playful banter reminded Nash of his relationship with Kevin. Warm, affection and constant.

"There are four Haynes brothers," Travis said. "Craig's the oldest. He lives in Fern Hill with his wife, Jill, and their five children."

Nash had taken a drink of his iced tea and nearly choked. "Five?"

Travis grinned. "We have a lot of kids. I'm married to Elizabeth. We have four girls. Next is Jordan. He's married to Holly. They have three girls."

"I'm the youngest boy in the family," Kyle said. "I'm married to Sandy. We have five kids, too. Four girls, one boy. Hannah's our half sister, through our father, so she's your half sister, as well. She's married to Nick. They have two girls." He turned to Kevin. "You and Haley are staying at the B and B Nick owns with Louise, Hannah's mother."

Nash set down his glass. "I'm never going to keep this straight."

"It'll get easier with time," Travis said. "There's also Austin Lucas, who isn't officially one of the Haynes men. He's sort of an adopted member of the family. He and his wife, Rebecca, have four kids, three boys and a girl."

"Wait until we start telling you which kids are from a previous marriage," Kyle said.

Kevin held up his hands. "I don't think I want to know."

Nash tried to do the math to figure out how many

people could show up at the dinner that night, but lost count somewhere after twenty.

"That's a lot of family members," he said. "Kevin told me your father doesn't live around here." He shook his head. "I guess he's our father, too. I don't think of him that way yet."

Kyle and Travis glanced at each other. "He's in Florida with wife number six or seven," Travis said. "I've lost count. None of us stay in touch with him."

"Why?" Kevin asked.

"He's…" Travis hesitated. "He wasn't a great father to us."

Nash leaned forward. "Don't worry about offending us with anything you say about him. As far as Kevin and I are concerned, Earl Haynes is just a guy who got a seventeen-year-old virgin pregnant and then walked out on her."

"That was Dad's style," Kyle said quietly. "He was chronically unfaithful. He and his brothers believed that if they slept in their own beds at night, that was about as good as it had to get. They didn't worry about details like being true to one woman or giving a damn about their kids."

"We wanted to be different," Travis told them. "Each of my brothers and I knew how unhappy we'd been and we were determined to keep history from repeating itself. After three generations of bastards, we wanted to make something of our lives, to get involved with our wives and kids. To be good men."

Kyle chuckled. "To have daughters."

"Why would that matter?" Nash asked.

The waitress arrived with their burgers. Once they were served, Kyle reached for the mustard in the center of the table.

"Until Travis and Elizabeth got married," Kyle said, "there hadn't been a girl born to a Haynes man in four generations."

"Not counting Hannah," Travis said. "We didn't know about her." He glanced at Nash.

"Right. Okay, no girls except for Hannah."

"Travis and Elizabeth had a daughter. Then Sandy and me, then Craig and Jill," Kyle said. "Holly and Jordan were next. He's the one who came up with the theory."

"Which is?" Kevin asked.

"Haynes men can only have girls when they're in love with the woman."

"That's crazy," Nash said.

"There's a lot of female Hayneses running around," Travis pointed out. He nodded at Kevin. "Just you wait until you and Haley are having kids."

Kevin grinned. "I look forward to our children, whatever their gender."

"Good," Kyle said. "Because you're probably going to have a lot of them."

Chapter 5

Nash left the diner after lunch and headed back for the B and B. He'd enjoyed meeting his half brothers, although he found the thought of their large families overwhelming. Five kids. That seemed like a lot.

He'd never much thought about having or not having kids of his own. After marrying Tina, he'd wanted to wait for a while before they started a family. She'd pressured him, but he'd refused to agree. Not until things were more stable between them. He'd assumed there would be children in his future, but when he thought about them they were vague shadows playing on the field at some sporting event. Not real people. Not like Stephanie's kids.

Thinking about Brett, Adam and Jason reminded him of the previous evening. He'd enjoyed helping with homework and staying for dinner. The boys were a lot of fun, each with a distinct personality. Brett was still waiting to accept him, but Nash respected that. Jason was ready to charm the world while Adam was shyer. As for Stephanie...

Better not to go there, he told himself. As it was, he'd had a restless night filled with erotic dreams of his hostess. He couldn't remember the last time he'd awakened so damn hard. Not since he was a teenager and in the throes of adolescent hormones. Back then he'd had lots of desire but little knowledge about what was supposed to happen between a man and a woman. Now he knew exactly what he wanted to do to and with Stephanie, should he ever get her in his bed.

He grinned as he realized a bed wasn't required. He'd been pretty creative in his dreams. Based on what he remembered, he could happily make love with her just about anywhere. One particularly vivid nocturnal event had been of him holding her up against a wall. She'd wrapped her bare legs around him and he'd—

He groaned as heat and pressure poured into his groin. Determined not to arrive back at the B and B with a hard-on the size of Argentina, he concentrated on the road and forced himself to think about how the houses lining the streets would look if they were all painted green.

The distraction nearly worked. By the time he pulled up in front of the B and B, he was no longer hard, although a dull ache lingered. It throbbed in time with his heartbeat. Experience told him it would go away... eventually.

He climbed out of his rental car and started toward

the large house. As he walked along the path, he heard sounds coming from a small gatehouse by the driveway. The front door was open.

Nash changed directions. When he reached the gatehouse, the faint sounds became a song on the radio. He followed the music into an empty living room in the midst of being sanded and patched. Stephanie stood in a doorway about fifteen feet away. She had a piece of sandpaper in each hand.

That morning she'd been dressed in what he thought of as her "public" clothes. Tailored slacks, a dark pink sweater. While he'd been gone, she'd changed into jeans and a T-shirt. A scarf covered her head.

As he watched, she reached up and rubbed at a spot well above her head. Her T-shirt rode up, exposing a bit of stomach. Instantly his groin sprang to life. What was it about this woman and her belly? Shouldn't he be finding her breasts erotic, or even her legs?

"You need a ladder," he said conversationally.

She jumped and squeaked, then glared at him. "I have to go to the grocery store in the next couple of days. I swear I'm going to swing through the pet department and buy you a collar with a bell."

"It's not going to fit."

"I'll put it around your wrist."

"You'll have to wrestle me into submission first."

He'd meant the comment as a joke, but at his words, her eyes darkened and awareness sharpened her features. Tension crackled in the empty room.

So this attraction wasn't all one-sided, he thought with satisfaction. Not that the information meant anything. Stephanie was a single mom with three kids. Which meant she wasn't exactly the kind of woman looking for a good time with no commitment. Too bad.

He might want her, but there was no way he would take advantage of her. He'd grown up with a single mom and he knew how hard that life could be. He wasn't there to contribute to the problem.

He ignored the tension and the need snapping between them and pointed to the bare walls.

"Is this going to be the presidential suite for Serenity House?" he asked.

Stephanie blinked slowly, as if coming out of a trance. "What? Oh. No. It's for me and the kids."

He glanced around at the old gatehouse. It wasn't huge, although there was a second story. "Why would you want to move?"

"It's always been the plan." She rubbed a piece of sandpaper against the door frame, then shook her head and leaned against the wood. "When Marty and I bought the property, we'd intended to fix this place up and move here. That way there would be more rooms to rent out. When he died, my first priority was to get rooms ready for paying guests and this project got put on the back burner. I'm hoping to get it done by midsummer."

"Isn't there more room for you and the kids at the main house?"

"Technically, yes, but when we have a lot of guests, the boys have to be quiet. We're on the third floor with guests underneath. They really try to cooperate, but they're young. Plus I hate reminding them all the time.

I don't want their only memories of their childhood to be 'stop making noise.' We're all willing to sacrifice space for privacy."

"Makes sense. Mind if I look around?"

"Help yourself."

He walked through the living room. There was a fireplace at one end, with built-in bookcases on either side. Large windows opened up to the street. The door on the right led to a short hallway and the stairs. There were two bedrooms in back, a bathroom, a kitchen that led to a small dining room, which opened on to the living room. Stephanie stood in that doorway. At the very rear of the house was a utility room with washer and dryer hookups.

Nash climbed the stairs and found a good-size master bedroom with a private bath. The ceilings were high on both floors, and the rooms had big windows, molding and lots of painted wood trim.

He returned to the living room. "Very nice," he said. "Only three bedrooms, though. Will the twins share?"

"They already do and they love it, so that's not a problem."

Nash watched her work for about thirty seconds. When she stretched up past her reach again, the flash of belly skin hit him like a sucker punch.

"Go sand something closer to the floor," he growled and grabbed a piece of sandpaper.

She spun toward him. "What?"

"You're not tall enough. I'll do that."

Her gaze narrowed. "I'm perfectly capable of doing this myself."

"Not without a ladder." He set his hands on her upper arms and gently moved her out of the way. For a brief second he had the impression of curves, heat and feminine scent, then he deliberately turned his back on temptation and went to work on the top of the door frame.

"I can't let you do this," she said.

"Never turn down the offer of free labor. It may not happen again."

"But you're a guest."

"I'm restless and bored. I need something to do."

She laughed. "Right. How silly. Of course I'm the one doing *you* a favor by letting you help me. Why didn't I see that before?"

"Beats me."

He glanced at her over his shoulder. Her chin jutted out and she had her hands on her hips, as if prepared to do battle.

"Just say thank-you and let it go," he told her.

"But I…" She sighed. "Thank you, Nash. I appreciate the help. As long as that's what we call it. Your attempt to guilt me into this by pretending I was doing you a favor was pretty pathetic."

"I've always been told I think fast on my feet."

"I'm a mother of three boys. That makes me a professional in the guilt arena. You're not even close to my league."

He chuckled and returned his attention to the sanding. Under the layers of paint was beautiful old wood, still in great shape.

"Whoever built these houses knew what they were

doing," he said. "Good-quality material and great construction."

"Whenever I panic about the mortgage, I remind myself that the B and B will outlast the payments by at least a century. Not that I plan to be around that long."

"The boys will appreciate the inheritance."

"I hope so. If one of them wants to take over the business, that's great. If not, I won't push them. They can sell the house and split the money."

"You're doing some long-term planning."

"I'm a detail person. I try to be responsible. My husband used to tell me I was anal. I guess that comes from being an only child." She knelt on the floor and started sanding the baseboards.

"Not necessarily. I was the responsible one in our family," he said. "As my brother and I are fraternal twins, I can't claim to be the oldest. It's just the way things worked out. I did the right thing and Kevin was a professional screwup. He used to get grounded about three times a week."

Now Nash could smile at the memory, but when it was happening, he used to worry a lot about his brother and how much his mom had to deal with.

"Did he turn out all right?" Stephanie asked.

"Yeah. When we were still in high school, Kevin stole a car. He and his buddies were just joyriding, but the owner pressed charges. It was the last straw for my mom. Kevin was packed off to military school. Apparently the experience scared some sense into him. From there he went to college. After that he became a cop. He joined the U.S. Marshals a few years ago. That's where he is now."

"Talk about a turnaround," she said.

"He's done well." He was pleased by his brother's success, if a little surprised by his sudden engagement.

Nash moved to the dining-room side of the door frame and continued sanding. "Kevin and I had lunch with two of my half brothers today. Travis and Kyle Haynes."

"How did that go?"

"Okay. They filled us in on all the brothers and their families. I don't think we're going to be able to keep everyone straight. They're all married and have kids."

Stephanie rubbed the sandpaper along the baseboard, while Nash tried to keep his attention on his work and off her fanny. With her kneeling like that, her butt stuck up in the air. He was charmed.

"I can't imagine what it would be like to discover a ready-made family," she said and glanced up at him. "What? Am I doing this all wrong?"

"No. You're fine."

"You're looking at me."

He couldn't argue with that. "Want me to work with my eyes closed?"

She rubbed her cheek with her free hand. "Do I look awful?"

"That's not possible."

Her eyes widened and color crept up her face. She ducked her head and began sanding with short, intense strokes. "Great compliment," she murmured.

"I wouldn't mind that one stitched on a pillow for my really bad days."

The tension had returned, and with it a longing to do more than just make love. He wanted to touch her and hold her. He wanted to connect.

Where the hell had that thought come from? Nash frowned and returned his attention to his work. No connecting, remember? No relationships. No messy emotions. No disasters.

She cleared her throat. "About your family. There are four brothers and a half sister. At least that's what I've heard. Wait, if she's a half sister, is she still related to you?"

He appreciated the change in subject. "Apparently. She and the brothers share the same father, as do Kevin and I."

"I'd heard that Earl Haynes was something of a ladies' man. How did he meet your mother?"

Nash sanded harder. "She was seventeen and working in a concession stand at the convention center in Dallas. Earl Haynes was in town for a few days. They met, he was charming. Next thing she knew, she was pregnant and he was gone."

He glanced at Stephanie. She sat back on her heels.

"That's horrible," she said.

"Agreed. She'd been raised in a strict home. She didn't know much about men or the world. She tried to get in touch with Earl, but couldn't find him. Her parents made things pretty ugly for her. She gave birth to twins and when she turned eighteen a couple of months later, they threw her out."

Stephanie sucked in a breath. "Just like that?"

"Yeah. By then Earl was back in town for his yearly convention. She went looking for him and found him in the arms of another woman. He told my mom that he didn't care about her, and never had. As for his kids, they were her problem."

He'd been an infant at the time and remembered nothing of what had happened. Yet just thinking about what that bastard had done filled him with fury.

"She ran down to the hotel lobby, crying her heart out," Nash continued. "The woman he'd been with realized she'd made a mistake with Earl, as well. Edie Reynolds took her home to Possum Landing and gave all of us a place to stay while my mom got a job and saved money for an apartment. My brother and I grew up there. It turns out that Edie's two sons were also fathered by Earl Haynes, so Gage is in town, as well, and Quinn, his brother, should be arriving shortly."

Stephanie shook her head. "I never could follow soap-opera plot lines, and this is a whole lot more complicated. After moving to Glenwood, I heard a lot about Earl Haynes and his brothers. They were known as local lady-killers. I'd always assumed the talk was just a bunch of rumors, but I guess it was true. What's so interesting is that his sons are terrific men. I guess they used to be pretty wild, but all of them have settled down. You heard about the wives and kids. Brett is in class with one of their boys. I think the twins know a couple of their daughters. There are so many, it's hard to keep them straight. But they're all good kids."

"They have some crazy notion that Haynes men have

boys when they're not in love with the women they're getting pregnant and that they only have girls when they are."

She laughed. "Oh, please. That's *so* not possible."

"Apparently there are plenty of girls to prove the theory. Neither Kevin nor I have kids to put it to the test."

"I've never heard of such a thing. Of course if it's true, you're going to have to be prepared not to have any boys." Her expression turned wistful. "I really love my sons, but I wouldn't have minded a little girl. Sometimes I miss things like hair ribbons and dresses."

"It could still happen."

She grinned. "Do you see a star parked over my house? There's no way I would ever get married again, so the odds of another child seem slim."

He felt her words down to his gut. Right up until that moment, he'd been enjoying their conversation, but now he only wanted to walk away. He started sanding again. Slow down, he told himself. Stephanie's reluctance to marry again didn't matter to him. Not one bit.

"You must have loved him very much," he said into the silence.

"What? Who?"

"Your husband. You don't want to marry again because you loved him so much."

She blinked several times, then attacked the baseboards. She used the sandpaper like a scrub brush, then abruptly straightened.

"Look," she said. "There are a lot of reasons I don't want to get married again, but none of them are because

I loved Marty too much. I know that sounds horrible, but it's the truth."

Nash didn't know what to do with the information, nor did he want to understand why the knot in his gut suddenly went away.

There was a moment of awkward silence, then they both spoke at once.

"Go ahead," he told her.

Stephanie started sanding again, this time with a little less energy. "Fertility-gender legend or not, you're going to be an uncle several times over. Brace yourself for the onslaught."

He hadn't thought of that. "No wonder the dinner tonight is at a pizza place," he said.

She laughed. "You sound as excited as if you were facing a root canal without anesthetic. Are all the family members expected to be there?"

"Pretty much. Earl is hanging out in Florida with wife number six or seven. He wasn't invited. But all the brothers, kids, half sister and spouses will be there."

"Sounds like fun."

Maybe to her. Kevin was engaged, as was Gage. Quinn, the only other single guy in the extended family, had yet to show up. Which meant Nash would be the odd man out.

He'd spent his life like that, he reminded himself. It was how he preferred things. But that didn't mean it was going to be comfortable.

"Want to come with me?" he asked. The invitation was impulsive, but he didn't withdraw it. "You said the boys know a lot of the Haynes kids. They'd have a good time. You could check out the girls and see if the legend is true."

Stephanie dropped her piece of sandpaper and wiped her hands on her jeans, all the while considering the invitation. She didn't object to spending some quality time with the featured player in her erotic fantasies, even if she wasn't sure why Nash would want her and the boys along.

"Won't it just be family?" she asked.

"Too much family. You could protect me."

He spoke lightly, but she thought she saw something dark and lonely in his eyes.

Get a grip, she told herself. She had to stop reading things into Nash's expression that just weren't there. The man wasn't lonely. He was fine. Most people were fine. The thought of her protecting him was laughable.

"I'll let you have the biggest piece of pizza," he promised.

She had to admit that she was curious about the Haynes family. And a pizza dinner out would thrill the boys. Then there was the issue of being in the same room as Nash—a way she was starting to enjoy spending her time.

She looked at his dark eyes and the way his mouth curved in a half smile. Maybe if she said yes he would accidentally brush his hand against hers. Maybe they would sit close enough together that she could imagine what it would be like to be in bed and all tangled up with him. Not that she needed much help in that department. He was already the star of her intricately detailed daydreams.

What did she have to lose?

"We'd love to join you," she said. "What time do you want us to be ready?"

This was *not* a date, Stephanie told herself that evening as she pulled off her red sweater and grabbed one in teal. It was an evening out at a pizza parlor, so there was no reason for her to sweat what she was wearing. Really.

She pulled on the teal sweater and studied her reflection. The color made her eyes look bluer, but the thicker knit made her look as though she didn't have breasts. Complicating the decision of what to wear was the thundering herd of elephants in her stomach and the faint tremor in her fingers. The latter had caused her to nearly put her eye out while applying mascara.

A knock on the door was followed by Brett calling, "Mom?"

She gave her reflection one last glance and figured this was as good as it was going to get. She fingered her short hair, briefly wished (for the thousandth time in her life) to be tall, then told her oldest to come in.

He pushed open the door and stepped into her room.

"What's up?" she asked as she crossed to the dresser and studied her small earring collection. There were simple gold hoops, a pair of dangling enameled flowers in light pinks and reds and several inexpensive pairs she'd bought on sale. She picked up the gold hoops.

"Why are we going out?" Brett asked.

She glanced up into the mirror and studied her son's reflection. He stood beside her four-poster bed, both arms wrapped around a post, as he swung back and forth. His shoulders were slumped and his expression was solemn.

"Whoa—you're upset because we're going out for *pizza?*" she said as she fastened the first earring. "Are you feeling okay?"

He gave her a halfhearted smile. "The pizza part is fine."

"What about hanging out with your friends and playing video games? Is that what has you bummed?"

The smile broadened. "No."

"Hmm, I don't think it's because we're letting your brothers come along. I know we talked about locking them in the closet when you and I want to leave, but I think it would hurt their feelings. The minivan doesn't have a trunk, so we can't leave them there."

"Mo-om, I don't want to lock Jason or Adam in a closet."

"Good to know." She finished with the second earring and turned to face him. "That only leaves Nash as the problem."

Brett dropped his gaze and stared at her bedspread. While she would admit that the floral print was very pretty, she didn't think it deserved to be studied with that much intensity.

She walked over to Brett and put her hand on his back. "He's a nice guy. What can I say? He invited us to join him tonight. He's just found out he's related to the Haynes brothers. You know how many of them there are. Plus their wives and their kids." She lowered her voice. "Nash didn't exactly admit this, but I think he wanted us along because he's a little nervous. I think he wants us to be a noisy distraction. That's it."

Brett looked at her. The concern had faded from his eyes. "Yeah?"

"Yeah."

He smiled again. "We're really good at being noisy."

She brushed the hair from his forehead. "I would say you and your brothers are experts."

Nash held open the door to the large pizza restaurant. When Stephanie and the kids had entered, he walked in and saw the small desk up front. The hostess there gave him a big smile. "How many?" she asked.

"We're part of the Haynes party," he said.

"Okay. Through to the back. There are two double doors. You can't miss it. Just follow the noise."

The twins raced ahead with Brett trailing behind them. Nash put his hand on the small of Stephanie's back and urged her forward. As they got closer to the room, the sound of conversation spilled into the main restaurant.

Stephanie leaned close. "Sounds like little more than controlled chaos," she said.

He looked at the dozens of people milling around in the huge room. "I think controlled is stretching it."

They stepped inside where they were greeted by Travis and Kyle. He introduced Stephanie and her kids, then met several wives, two more brothers and three kids.

"This is never going to work," a pretty woman with light brown hair said. "It's only been ten minutes and your eyes are already glazed." She reached into her purse and pulled out a plastic package. "I thought this might happen so I brought name tags."

A petite redhead handed over a box of her own. "Great minds, Elizabeth," she said. "I brought them, too."

The redhead turned to Nash. "I'm Jill, Craig's wife. Craig's the oldest of the brothers." She glanced around the room, then pointed to a tall, dark-haired man with gray at his temples. "Craig's easy to keep track of. He's the best-looking of the brothers."

"He is not," Elizabeth said, then laughed. "I guess we all have our favorites."

"Fortunately that is usually the guy we're married to. Anything else would make these gatherings awkward." Jill looked at Nash, then at Stephanie. "Are we terrifying you? I guess this is really strange. We're such a close-knit family that we don't even think about it, but I remember when I had to meet everyone. It was a little intimidating." She frowned slightly. "Actually it was a lot easier for me back then. Only Travis, Kyle and Austin were married. There weren't as many kids. Did you know that Austin isn't officially a Haynes? It's more of a family member by adoption."

Nash shook his head. "You can't start adding more people," he said. "Not without written permission."

As he spoke he spotted his brother, Kevin, across the room. Haley was next to him, staring at him with a look of love and devotion that made Nash feel he'd accidentally witnessed something personal. He turned away.

"Listen up, everybody," Elizabeth said loudly.

A boy of about fourteen stuck two fingers in his mouth and gave a sharp whistle. The room went quiet.

"We have name tags," she continued, waving the box over her head.

"And pens," Jill added.

"Right. Everyone come get a name tag. If you're an adult, put your name first, then a dash and your spouse's name. If you're a child, put your name on top and your parents' names underneath. If you're too young to write, come see me or Jill. Any questions?"

"Is there going to be a quiz?" Travis asked.

"You bet. And if you fail, you are in big trouble, mister. Don't be messing with me."

Travis looked pleased at the prospect.

"After you've filled out your name tag," Elizabeth continued, "take a seat at one of the tables. We want to save the big one at the far end for the adults. You kids can sit at the other tables with your friends."

Jill handed out name tags while Elizabeth passed around several pens. Nash saw Adam and Jason race over to stand with their mother. She talked them through filling out their tags. He waited until they had finished, then wrote his own name. It was only when he glanced around the room that he realized every other tag had either a spouse's name on it or parents' names. Kevin and Haley had put each other's names with theirs on the name tags, as had Gage and Kari.

"Getting ready to bolt?" Stephanie asked when she'd peeled the back off her tag. "I'm fairly comfortable in crowds, what with running the B and B and all, but even I'm a little overwhelmed by all this."

"I'm doing okay," he said, taking the tag from her and placing it on her sweater, close to the neckline. "I won't pass the quiz, though."

She grinned. "I figured if they called on me, I'd cheat by saying everyone was a Haynes. At least then I'd be able to pass with about eight-five-percent accuracy."

"Good idea."

His gaze fell on to the tag he'd just pressed into place and he saw that she didn't have a name after hers either. They were the only two unattached adults at the gathering.

Elizabeth waved them over to take a seat at the large table. Nash found himself seated between Stephanie and Jill. Kevin was on Stephanie's other side.

When everyone was settled, Craig stood. "As the oldest of the Haynes brothers, I would like to thank all of you for coming." He smiled. "We are here tonight to welcome our new brothers." He motioned across the table. "Gage Reynolds, Kevin Harmon and Nash Harmon."

Nash found himself standing, along with Kevin and Gage. There was a round of applause. When they were seated, Craig continued.

"I know we're all anxious to get to know each other. I suggest we start by going around the table and stating our names, where we live and what we do for a living. Oh, and don't forget to introduce your children."

"Yeah, don't forget us," a little dark-haired girl said. The adults laughed.

"As I already have your attention, I'll start," he said

when there was quiet. "I'm Craig Haynes. My beautiful wife, Jill, is sitting right here." He put his hand on her shoulder. "We have five children, the oldest of which is that tall, good-looking eighteen-year-old. Ben was offered a football scholarship at UCLA."

He continued to introduce his five children, then concluded by saying Jill had the hardest job of all—she kept them in line—while he was just a cop.

Travis went next. He rose and introduced his wife, Elizabeth, and their four children. They went around the table. Every single Haynes brother was a cop, until Jordan stood and proclaimed himself as the only Haynes sensible enough to go into firefighting rather than law enforcement.

Austin Lucas was next. He had the Haynes basics—tall, dark hair and eyes—that distinguished the brothers, but his hair was much longer and he wore a small gold earring. Austin mentioned that he was a Haynes in spirit and heart, rather than by blood.

Gage was next. He talked about his life in Possum Landing, where he was the local sheriff. He introduced his fiancée, and said that his brother, Quinn, should be arriving any day now.

When a tall, dark-haired woman rose, Nash figured she was the half sister he'd heard about. Her introduction confirmed the fact. She explained that her mother, Louise, was home babysitting their latest daughter who had been born only six weeks before.

When it was Nash's turn, he stood. "I'm Nash Harmon. Kevin's twin brother. I'm the smart one."

Everyone laughed.

He grinned when Kevin reached around Stephanie and punched his arm. "I live in Chicago," Nash continued, "where I'm a negotiator for the FBI."

As he added a few more details, he glanced down and saw Stephanie looking at him with surprise. Hadn't he told her what he did for a living?

"I figured there would be more of you than Kevin and I could ever hope to take on on our own," he said lightly, "so I convinced my temporary landlady to take pity on me and help balance the numbers. This is Stephanie Wynne. Her three boys are…" He glanced around at the other tables, then spotted Jason and Adam frantically waving. "Over there."

He sat down. Craig rose again. Just then several servers entered the room. They had large trays covered with pitchers of root beer, iced tea and beer. When everyone had a drink, Craig raised his glass.

"Welcome," he said.

Chapter 6

Nash lost count of the number of pizzas consumed by the Haynes family. They simply kept on coming. Pitchers of drinks were continually refilled, as well. By the time the kids asked to be excused to go play video games and the adults had started moving the chairs around to form small conversational groups, even the servers were looking exhausted.

He'd spent most of dinner talking with Stephanie and Jill, but after the meal, he found himself in the company of his brothers.

Brothers. The word still surprised him. How could he and Kevin have been a part of this family for so many years and not have known? How could a man like Earl Haynes get an innocent seventeen-year-old pregnant, abandon her to return to his real family, then produce such honest, sincere, caring offspring?

He crossed to the pitchers of drinks left on the table and poured himself another glass of iced tea. After two beers, he'd switched to the nonalcoholic drink. He wasn't worried about driving, they'd brought Stephanie's minivan and she'd taken the wheel on the way over. Instead he considered the fact that too much beer would make his hostess even more of a temptation than she already was. When sober he found her delightfully intriguing. While drunk he might find her irresistible. Not a good thing for either of them.

He took a drink and surveyed the crowd. He could put a name to the men, but he was still having trouble connecting which spouse belonged with which partner. Hannah was easy. As the only female Haynes, she had many of the physical characteristics of her brothers—she was tall, dark-haired and attractive. Her husband was the only blond male in the room. But after that, things got fuzzy. Was Kyle's wife the average-height brunette with brown eyes or the average-height woman with light brown hair and green eyes?

"Is it making you crazy?"

He turned toward the speaker and found a slender woman standing next to him. Her name tag read "Rebecca—Austin." Underneath were the words "Honorary Haynes through love."

"The guy with the earring," he said.

She smiled. "That would be my husband, yes. He's something of a bad boy."

She spoke the words with a smile and Nash saw the affection twinkling in her eyes.

He glanced over to the man in question and saw him

with a young child on his hip. As he spoke with Travis, Austin absently brought the child's hand to his mouth and blew on the palm. The little boy laughed loudly.

"You seem to have changed his ways," he said.

Rebecca shook her head. "Actually he changed them all on his own. He was always the quiet rebel, but he's mellowed."

Austin looked content, Nash thought. He was a man comfortable and at peace with his world. Two things Nash rarely experienced.

He turned his attention back to the woman in front of him. She was lovely, with classically beautiful features that spoke of a gentler time. Unlike the other wives who were dressed in jeans and casual shirts, Rebecca wore a long dress edged in lace. Her dark, curly hair came to the middle of her back. She reminded him of a character in one of those British period movies—the kind that made him head directly for ESPN if he ever turned the television to one by accident.

"Are you overwhelmed?" she asked. "It's a huge family."

"I'm getting the adults," he said. "The kids are going to take longer."

"We all have trouble with that. At one time or another, each of us has had to stop one of the children and ask who they belong to."

She took a step closer and lowered her voice. "When Travis told us that there were long-lost Hayneses around, everyone was thrilled. When I heard you were all single, I was doubly delighted."

He raised his eyebrows. There was no way she was asking for herself.

She laughed. "I have a friend. D.J. doesn't know it yet, but she's ready to settle down. I was planning on fixing her up with one of you. The thing is, you're not all single, are you?"

"Gage and Kevin have had a change in circumstance in the past few months."

"So I heard." She grinned. "I had high hopes for you, Nash, but they've recently been dashed."

She turned and nodded across the room. He followed her gaze and saw Stephanie talking with Jill.

As Stephanie spoke, she moved her hands. A smile tugged at the corners of her mouth. Jill responded and they both laughed. He was standing too far away to hear the sound, but he imagined it and smiled in return.

"Oh, my," Rebecca said. "It's worse than I thought."

"It's not anything."

"Really?"

"Yes." He wasn't about to tell her about his no-relationships rule. "I'm only in town for a couple of weeks."

"Sometimes plans change."

"Not mine."

"Too bad." She shrugged. "But if you're leaving that quickly, you wouldn't be right for D.J. even if you were available. Which leaves the mysterious Quinn Reynolds. Maybe I can fix them up."

Nash considered the idea. On the surface Quinn was a charmer, with plenty of stories and a woman on each arm. But underneath...he wasn't like the rest of them.

Quinn lived in a world that would break most men. He did things, saw things, no human should endure.

"Quinn's a great guy," he said. "But more than a little dangerous."

Rebecca looked intrigued. "D.J. enjoys a challenge."

"Quinn would be that. But he's a loner. Women tend to have one purpose in his life, and it's not cooking."

He'd expected Rebecca to be shocked, but instead she grinned. "How fun. That would make D.J. completely crazy."

Nash wouldn't have used that word to describe Quinn's relationships with his women, but then he didn't know this D.J. person, either.

"You want to torture your friend?" he asked.

"No, but I can't figure out another way to get her happily married."

"Okay, then." Nash took a step back. Sometimes women completely confused him.

Rebecca excused herself. As she walked away, Stephanie joined Nash. She glanced at her watch.

"Would you mind if we collected the boys and left? It's a school night and they're already wired enough from school getting out in a couple of days. If I have any prayer of a decent bedtime for them, I need to get moving now."

"Sure. Want me to help?"

"Please. Why don't you look for the twins? They'll be together and more cooperative. I'll pull the car up front and get Brett."

They said goodbye to the Haynes family, then walked into the main restaurant. The video-game room was by the door. Nash spotted Jason and Adam on a bench by the wall. Adam stood as he approached, but Jason only blinked sleepily.

"Time to head home," Nash said.

"I'm ready," Adam said.

Jason rose, then held out his arms. "I'm tired."

Nash stared at him. A small child holding up his arms was a pretty universal symbol. Even living a child-free existence, Nash got it right away. Jason wanted to be carried.

Nash hesitated. It wasn't because he thought Jason would be too heavy or that Stephanie would mind. Instead he paused because something inside of him warned him that this was potentially problematic. He didn't do relationships—not with women, not with friends, not with kids. Relationships required a level of letting go he didn't permit himself. Control was all that stood between him and chaos.

Jason's implied trust made him uneasy. He'd only known the kids a couple of days. So why was Jason so comfortable around Nash?

"He wants to be carried," Adam said, as if he thought Nash didn't get it.

"I know."

There didn't seem to be a graceful way out of the situation and Nash didn't want to make a scene over nothing. So he bent forward and pulled the boy up toward his chest. Jason instantly closed his arms around Nash's neck and rested his head on his shoulder. His small legs wrapped around Nash's waist.

Nash put one arm around the boy to hold him in

place, then motioned for Adam to lead the way. Instead the eight-year-old tucked his fingers into Nash's free hand and leaned close.

"Is Mommy bringing the car around?" he asked sleepily.

"Yes. Come on."

He led the way to the front of the restaurant, then out into the night. Brett was already waiting on the sidewalk. He took one look at the three of them, then turned away. But not before Nash saw the hostility flare in his eyes.

The brief glimpse of the twelve-year-old's raw hurt and anger stirred something familiar in Nash.

Stephanie drove up and broke his concentration. Then he got caught up in settling the twins. As he was about to climb into the passenger seat, Kevin stepped out of the restaurant.

"What did you think?" his brother asked.

Nash looked back at the pizza place. "Good people."

"I agree." Kevin grinned and slapped him on the back. "See you soon." He ducked his head into the minivan. "Nice to meet you, Stephanie. If this guy gives you any trouble, you let me know."

She smiled. "So far he's been terrific, but if that changes, I'll call."

"You do that. Night."

Kevin stepped back into the restaurant. Stephanie watched him go.

"You have a great family," she said. "You're lucky."

Nash had never thought of himself that way, but in this case, maybe she was right.

* * *

Stephanie sucked in a breath and did her best to hold on to her temper. "Brett, it's late, it's a school night and you're behaving like a brat. If you're trying to convince me that you're not mature enough to handle evenings out on a weeknight, you're doing a great job."

Her oldest flopped back on the bed and stared at the ceiling. Since arriving back from their dinner out with Nash and his family, Brett had been sullen, uncommunicative and mouthy. She couldn't figure out what the problem was. Sure he was inching closer to being a teenager, but hormones couldn't kick in over the course of a couple of hours, could they?

She sank onto the bed and put her hand on his stomach. "I know you had a good time. I saw you laughing."

"It was okay."

"Just okay? I thought you were having more fun than that."

He shrugged.

She began to rub his stomach, something she'd done when he was little and not feeling well. "I'm not leaving until you tell me what has your panties in a bunch. I'm just going to sit right here. After a while, I might start singing."

He continued to stare at the ceiling, but she saw his mouth twitch. All the boys thought she had a horrible voice and begged her not to sing. Plus, he would really hate the panty remark. She wondered which one would get to him first.

"I don't wear panties."

"I do the laundry. I already know that." She leaned over him. "How about I just stare at you?"

She made her eyes as wide as possible and forced herself not to blink. Brett pressed his lips together, but it was too late. First he smiled, then he grinned, then he giggled and turned away.

"Stop staring at me!"

She relaxed her face and sat back. "I will if you'll talk."

He turned on his side so he was facing her, but instead of looking at her face, he studied the blanket. "Do you still love Dad?"

She was unprepared for the question. Brett didn't want to have this talk very often, but whenever he did, she felt uncomfortable. She always went for the easy answer, rather than the truth, because that's what Brett wanted to hear. Because she wanted her son to remember his father as a good person and his parents as happy together.

"Of course I still love him," she said gently. "Why do you ask?"

He shrugged.

"Is this about Nash? Are you worried that something's going on between us?"

Another shrug.

"He's being nice," she said. "I like him, but that doesn't mean anything. He's on vacation. When his vacation is over, he's going back to Chicago."

Where the handsome widower probably had dozens of elegant, sophisticated women vying for his attention.

Where he wouldn't even remember a single mom with three kids who had an embarrassing crush on him.

"Do you want to, like, you know, go out with him?"

Honestly she would much prefer to stay in with Nash, but that wasn't what Brett wanted to know. Two weeks ago she would have told her son that she never planned on dating or getting involved with a man ever. But Nash's arrival had shown her that there were some empty places in her life. While she would never be stupid enough to risk marriage, she wouldn't mind a little male companionship now and then.

"I can't imagine Nash and me on date," she said truthfully. "But your dad has been gone three years. While my feelings for him haven't changed, there will come a time when I want to start dating again."

Brett's blue eyes filled with tears. "Why? Why can't you just love Dad?"

"Because he's gone." She pulled him into a sitting position, then drew him into her arms. "When you get a little older, you're going to think girls are a whole lot better than icky. I promise. So you're going to go out. You may even have a girlfriend."

He writhed in her arms. "Mo-om."

"Just listen. So you have this girl you really care about. Will you still love your brothers?"

He looked at her. "What does that have to do with anything?"

"Just answer the question. Will you still love them?"

"I guess. If they're not being dopey."

"Will you still love me?"

"Sure."

"That's my point. The human heart has the capacity to love as many people as we want to let into our lives. If I start dating or not, nothing about my feelings for you, the twins or even Dad are going to change. There's more than enough room for everyone."

"But I like thinking about you with Dad."

"You can keep thinking about that. I didn't leave him, honey. He died. We mourned him and we still love him. That's the right thing to do. But it's also right to live our lives and be happy. Don't you think your dad would have wanted that for all of us?"

Stephanie knew that Marty would have loved the idea of being mourned endlessly by his wife and children, but she wasn't about to lay that guilt on her twelve-year-old.

Brett nodded slowly. "But you're not going out with Nash."

"I'm not."

"Promise?"

"Nash and I will not go out of this house on a date." She made an X over her heart. "But that's as much of my life as you get to dictate, young man. And should I decide to go out with someone, you're going to have to accept the idea. Agreed?"

"Yeah. No problem."

"Good."

She kissed his forehead, then released him. After he scrambled under the covers, she tucked them in around him, said good-night and walked out into the hallway. After closing the door, she moved down the stairs.

She wondered when Brett had started to consider

Nash a threat. Was there something in his behavior, or was her son able to subconsciously pick up on her strong attraction? Not that it mattered. She'd been very comfortable agreeing to no dates with Nash. Somehow she couldn't see him offering to take her to dinner and a movie. He wasn't a "dinner and a movie" kind of guy. Nash was more late-night walks along the river and hot, passionate kisses up against the crumbling stone wall of the ancient castle.

Stephanie smiled. At least he was in *her* imagination. As there was neither a river nor a castle nearby, she was probably safe. Not that she wanted to be.

She reached the main floor and turned toward the kitchen, then stopped when a slight movement caught her attention. As she spun around, she saw Nash pacing restlessly across the living-room rug. He glanced up and saw her, came to a stop and shrugged.

"I'm a little wound up from the dinner," he said. "I'm not ready to go up to bed. Am I bothering you?"

Not in the way he meant. "Of course not. I have to make cookies for the twins to take to school tomorrow. There are few things less interesting than watching someone bake. You want to come into the kitchen and be bored for a while? It will probably help you sleep."

"Sure."

As soon as he agreed, she wanted to stop and bang her head against a nearby wall. Watching her might be boring for him, but having him near was wildly exciting for her. She really didn't need to spend more time with him. Hanging around with Nash only seemed to encourage her overactive imagination. Before their dinner tonight she'd thought he was sexy and roguishly charming. After their dinner, she was starting to like him.

She'd enjoyed watching him interact with his family. He'd been caring and understanding with the dozens of kids running around, attentive and interested in his brothers. She'd been stunned to find out what he did for a living. So much for her theory that he was a professor or sold shoes. Instead he inhabited a dark and dangerous world, which only made him more physically appealing.

Stephanie told herself that she had to stop imagining Nash as the bare-chested caveman whisking her off into the wilderness. The poor guy had signed on to be her guest, not the star of her erotic fantasies. If he knew what she was thinking, he would be forced to run screaming into the night.

She collected ingredients for chocolate chip cookies and set them on the counter. Nash took a seat at the kitchen table, then half rose.

"Can I help?"

She shook her head. "I've done this so many times, I don't have to look at a recipe. But if you behave, I'll let you have a sample fresh from the oven."

"Deal."

She grabbed a couple of eggs and put them next to the canister of flour. "So what did you think of tonight?" she asked.

"It went well. I'm not sure I can keep everyone straight."

"I wouldn't want to try," she admitted. "The name

tags were a great idea." She measured brown sugar. "Where in Chicago do you live?"

"I have a condo by the lake. I can walk to a lot of great restaurants. There's a good jogging trail nearby."

"I've never been, but I can't imagine you do much jogging in the winter."

"True. Then I hit the gym."

And he had the body to prove it. Although she doubted Nash worked out to be buff. No doubt it was required for his job. She tried not to sigh at the image of him in a ratty T-shirt and shorts, lifting heavy weights. Instead she channeled her energy into vigorously whipping her eggs.

"I grew up with one brother and my mom," he said quietly. "I've never had any experience with a large family."

"The Hayneses will take some getting used to," she said. "But they'll be worth the effort."

He nodded. "What about you? Are you one of seven?"

"Not exactly." She opened the bottle of vanilla and picked up her measuring spoons. "I was an only child. My parents were artists. Very focused on their work and each other." She gave him a slight smile. "They didn't believe in paying attention to the outside world. Things like electric bills and empty kitchen cupboards didn't faze them. I grew up pretty quickly. Someone had to be the responsible one and it turned out to be me."

His dark gaze settled on her face. "Was that tough?"

"Sometimes." When she wanted to be a kid, like her

friends. "But I learned a lot, too. I was really prepared for the real world when I left for college."

"Did you want a big family?"

"Sure. While I was growing up, I thought it would be terrific. I had it all planned, from my husband to our five kids to our assortment of dogs, cats and small rodents."

She'd thought the same when she'd married Marty. But by the time she'd figured out she'd made a horrible mistake and discovered she was pregnant in the same week, her plans had changed. She'd resigned herself to having one child. The twins had been an accident. A blessing, but an unplanned one.

If only, she thought. If only Marty had been more willing to be a grown-up instead of an overgrown child. If only she'd seen the truth earlier. Except then she wouldn't have her boys, and she loved them more than anything.

"Stephanie?"

"Huh?" She glanced up and saw him watching her.

"Are you all right? You got pretty quiet."

"Sorry. Just thinking."

He rose and crossed to the island. "About your late husband?"

"Yes, but not in the way you think." She didn't want Nash to worry that he'd made her miss Marty.

"Was it being out with me? The whole 'meet the family' circus?"

"No. That was great. I really enjoyed tonight." She tried to smile, but he was standing only a couple of feet of counter space away and his intense, dark stare took her breath away. She cleared her throat. "I don't get out that much."

"With three boys and your own business, you probably don't have time to date much."

"Date?" She laughed. "Like that ever happens."

"Why doesn't it?"

"Good question."

She dumped the dry ingredients into the batter and began to stir. As the mixture thickened, she had to really push to get the wooden spoon through.

"I'll do that," he said, stepping around the island and moving next to her.

Before she realized what was happening, he'd taken the spoon from her and was making quick work of the mixing. She blinked in surprise.

"Why do you do that?" she asked. "Why are you always so happy to help?"

"Why not?"

She didn't have an answer she was willing to share. Telling him she'd long ago learned not to depend on anyone made her sound pathetic.

"Do these go in next?" he asked, nodding toward the open bag of chocolate chips.

"Yes." She dumped the chips into the batter.

"So why don't you date?"

She stared at the swirling mixture, rather than risk looking at him. Dangerous, dangerous question. "I just…there aren't many men interested and I don't seem to meet any."

"Interested men?"

"Any men."

"So it's not that *you're* not interested."

"I—" The questions were going from bad to worse. Interested? Was she? Not in love. She'd learned that lesson in spades. But in a good man? Someone who would be fun and funny and caring? Someone who would hold her and ease the trembling ache deep inside?

"I could be interested," she admitted softly.

"Good."

He dropped the wooden spoon into the bowl and turned toward her. Before she realized what was happening, before she could catch her breath or even consider if this was as crazy as it seemed, he'd pulled her into his arms. Just like that. She was pressed up against his hard, masculine body and then his face was getting closer and she knew he was going to kiss her.

Stephanie's last rational thought was that it had been twelve years since a man other than Marty had kissed her and that there was a more than even chance she'd completely forgotten what to do.

Then Nash claimed her mouth in a warm, tender, erotic kiss that made her heart freeze in midbeat and her brain completely shut down. There wasn't any thinking, there was only feeling. Feeling and doing.

He pressed his lips against hers with just enough pressure to make her want more. Strong, large hands settled on her back. She felt his fingers, the heat of his palms, the brush of his thighs against her own. His scent surrounded her, enticed her, made her legs weak and her muscles slack. She had to wrap her arms around his neck to stay standing.

Then his mouth moved against her. Slowly, discovering, teasing. He brushed his tongue against her lower lip. She had no will and parted instantly. Excitement raced through her. The sound of her breathing filled her head. She wanted with a desperation that should have terrified her, but instead only made her reckless. She wanted deep, hot kisses and wild abandon. She wanted his hands everywhere. She wanted to touch and be touched, to be wet, to be filled. She wanted to lose herself in an orgasm that would shake the very fabric of the space-time continuum.

So when he again swept his tongue against the inside of her lower lip, she moaned low in her throat. When he moved inside and brushed against her, letting her taste him, feel him, dance with him, she responded with an intensity that was as foreign to her as the fiery need spiraling through her.

She kissed him deeply, matching each thrusting stroke with one of her own. When he moved his hands from her back to her rear, she arched against him, flattening her belly against an impressive hardness.

They both strained to get closer and closer still. Heads tilting, tongues mating, hands roving, they gasped and kissed and nipped and surged.

She traced the length of his spine, then felt his high, tight rear end. As her fingers dug into his flesh, his arousal flexed against her stomach. He slipped his hands to her hips, then to her waist. At the same time, he pulled away from her mouth and instead began to kiss her jaw, her neck, then that sweet spot right below her ear. He licked the sensitive skin and while she was still caught up in the pleasure, he sucked on her earlobe. At the same moment, his hands closed over her sensitized breasts.

She had to bite her lip to keep from screaming. Long fingers cupped her curves, while his thumbs and forefingers caressed her hard, aching nipples. Need raced through her. Need and desire and longing for more. She wanted to tear off her clothes, and his. She wanted him to take her right there, on the counter. She wanted it hard and fast, her legs spread, him buried deep, thrusting and thrusting until they both lost control in a shuddering release.

"Nash," she breathed and reached for the buttons on his shirt.

He grabbed the hem of her sweater and started to tug. Right then, there was a loud creak from overhead.

Stephanie knew it was just the old house settling as the night temperature dropped, but it was enough to remind her of the fact that they really *were* in her kitchen and that she had three children sleeping upstairs. She stiffened slightly. Nash read the signal for what it was and immediately stepped back.

His face was flushed, his eyes dilated, his mouth damp from their kisses. He looked like a man more than ready for a walk on the wild side. She had a feeling she looked just as…aroused.

Just don't think about how long it's been since you had sex, she told herself. The reality would be too depressing for words.

In the silence of the kitchen, their breathing sounded loud and unnaturally fast. Nash recovered enough to speak first. Or maybe he wasn't as nervous as she was.

"I haven't kissed anyone in a while," he said, his voice thick with passion and slightly wry. "I don't remember it being like that."

She had to clear her throat before speaking. "Me, neither."

"You okay?"

She nodded.

"Want me to apologize?" he asked.

"No. Not unless you're sorry." Oh, please, not that. She couldn't stand that.

His dark eyes crinkled at the corners as he smiled. "Not even close."

He raised his hand toward her, then dropped it back to his side. "I'd better head upstairs before... Well, before we start at it again."

She didn't want him to go, but she knew it was for the best. Ah, maturity. Why was it never as much fun as acting like an irresponsible kid?

"Sleep well," he said as he turned to leave.

"Unlikely," she said before she could stop herself.

He glanced at her and grinned. "Tell me about it."

Chapter 7

Stephanie thought about looking at the clock, but the first time she'd checked it had been about ten to four in the morning. She doubted it was much past four now. Although she'd managed to doze on and off for a few hours, she'd spent most of the night alternating between reliving the incredible kiss she and Nash had shared and pulling the pillow over her face to muffle her shrieks of embarrassment.

What had she been thinking? *Had* she been thinking?

No, she told herself. She hadn't been thinking at all. She'd been reacting. She'd been feeling and touching and wanting. Not thinking.

If she'd taken the time to consider her actions, she never would have allowed herself to respond with such wanton abandon. She'd been crazed with passion—a new experience for her. Her feelings of need had spiraled out of control in less than ten seconds of first contact. What did that say about her?

Stephanie didn't have an answer. In all the years she and Marty had been married she'd never felt so needy. So alive. So desperate.

"Desperate?" she murmured into the night.

She didn't like the sound of that. It made her think of pitiful people doing inappropriate things without considering the consequences.

Oh, like wanting to do it right there on the counter, next to the batch of cookie batter?

She pulled the pillow over her face and groaned.

She wasn't desperate, she told herself forcefully. If she was desperate, she would be out eyeing all the single fathers in town. She'd met a few at school events. A couple had even asked her out. While she'd appreciated the invitations, nothing about them had sent her into sexual spasms the way Nash did. She'd thought they were nice, pleasant men who didn't tempt her in the least. She'd found it tragically simple to remember that she absolutely didn't want to get involved again because a relationship with a man meant taking on more responsibility. Thanks but no thanks.

With Nash it was different. She found it far too easy to forget her rules and instead focus on how the man looked as he walked through a room. She could spend an embarrassing amount of time thinking about his mouth, his voice, his hands. And all that was *before* he'd kissed her. Now that she had actual evidence of the potential, she could easily spend the better part of her day considering the sexual possibilities. They could—

Stephanie sat up in bed and clicked on the lamp on her nightstand.

"Snap out of it," she whispered aloud. "You're a mature, responsible woman with a successful business and three kids. You have more guests arriving in a few days, summer vacation starting at the end of the week and laundry multiplying like rabbits. You simply cannot waste your days thinking about making love with Nash Harmon. It's not right. It's not healthy. It's not likely to happen."

The last was the most tragic, she thought as she flung herself back on the bed. If only he would creep into her room in the dead of night and take advantage of her. If only he would—

She sat up again, but this time it wasn't to give herself a stern but useless talking-to. Instead her mouth dropped open as a horrifying thought occurred to her.

She and Nash had kissed. Right there in her kitchen. It had been painfully real and erotic and incredible and wow. But she didn't know why he'd done it or if he was going to regret it come morning. Regardless, she was going to have to face him and act as if nothing had happened. She was going to have to pretend not to be affected by his presence or his voice, and she was going to have to act that way in front of her children.

She moaned, then rolled onto her side and hugged the pillow close. Why hadn't she thought that part through before she'd allowed herself to come unglued in his arms? What if *he* was having seconds thoughts?

What if he thought she was some sex-starved freak and all he wanted was to pack his bags and move out? What if he was laughing at her?

Each thought was more awful than the one before. Stephanie endured the potentials for humiliation for as long as she could, then gave up and threw back the covers. She wasn't going to lie here for another couple of hours, looking for trouble. With her luck, it would come looking for her, regardless of her opinion on the matter. Better to face the day with a smile and a happy heart.

She crossed to her bathroom and clicked on the light. It was worse than she thought. In addition to spiky hair and pale skin, she had bags the size of carry-on luggage under her eyes. Scratch that starting-the-day-with-a-smile stuff. She was going to have spend the next hour with a cold compress under her eyes.

Nash heard footsteps on the stairs shortly after five that morning. He figured it was probably Stephanie getting an early start to her day. While he wanted to get up and join her in whatever she might have planned, he didn't think she would appreciate the interruption.

Instead he continued to sit in the tufted chair in front of the window and stare out at the faint hint of light on the eastern horizon.

He felt good. Hell of a thing to admit, but it was true. Life coursed through his body. Desire rumbled just below the surface and threatened to surge back into existence at any moment. Interest prickled at the edges of his mind. He no longer wanted to get lost in his job—instead he was making plans, anticipating.

When had that happened? It wasn't all about the kiss and his reawakened sexual need. Oh, sure, he wanted Stephanie. All she had to do was name the time and place and he would be there. But this feeling inside was about something more.

Was it finding out about his family? Was it a combination of things? Was it that he'd finally been forced to look up from his work long enough to remember there was a world out here? Did it matter?

As he stared out the window, he had a sudden flashback to what she'd felt like in his arms. How her body had yielded to his. Curves to hard planes. She'd smelled so damn good. His fingers flexed as he recalled the feel of her breasts and how she'd moaned when he'd brushed against her tight nipples.

His body reacted quickly and predictably. Nash chuckled as blood sprinted to his groin. The ache there thickened until it bordered on uncomfortable, but that was okay with him. Feeling all of this beat feeling nothing, and he'd been feeling nothing for a long time.

Since well before Tina's death.

He closed his eyes against the growing light. He didn't want to think about her. Not today. He didn't want to live in the past or wonder what he could have done differently. He just wanted to be.

Life beckoned. He heard the call, felt the stirring inside himself. Was he going to answer? Was it safe?

He opened his eyes and considered the question. There were no guarantees. He'd always known, but

Tina's death had reminded him in an ugly way. Joining the rest of the world would mean taking risks. He could never forget that he had to stay in control. He couldn't risk letting that go, not even for a second.

His cell phone rang. Nash grabbed it from the desk by the window and glanced at the display screen. He recognized the number and punched the talk button.

"Harmon."

"Tell me you're on a beach somewhere enjoying the sun."

Nash grinned. "Jack, it's a little after five in the morning on the west coast. There isn't any sun."

His boss swore. "Sorry. I always forget about the time difference. Did I wake you?"

"No. I was up."

"Want to tell me why?"

Nash thought about Stephanie and what they'd done the previous evening. "Not a chance."

"Huh. I can't decide if your being cryptic is good or bad."

"I can't help you there."

"You mean you won't. Never mind. I'm not calling to mess with you too much. I thought I'd bring you up-to-date on what's going on around the office."

"Right." Nash grinned. "You're calling to check up on me. Why don't you admit it?"

"Because I don't have to. Marie's pregnant."

Nash's grin broadened. "Don't sound so broken up about it."

"She already has eight or nine kids. Why does she want another one? What if she doesn't come back? She keeps my life running smoothly. I don't want to have to train some other assistant."

"Hold on. I want to pause a moment and feel the compassion."

Jack swore again. "I know, I know. I should be happy for her."

"You would be if it weren't so inconvenient for you."

"Right."

Nash shook his head. "For one thing, Marie only has two children, not eight or nine. For another, she loves her job more than most of us do. She's not going to quit."

"That's what she says, but I don't believe her."

"That's your problem."

Jack called him a name, then brought him up-to-date on several projects. "So how are you feeling?" he asked when he was done.

"I felt fine before I left and I still feel fine," Nash said.

"You know what I mean. I worry about you. Too many hours, no time off. Hell, Nash, you don't even call in sick."

"That's because I don't get sick."

"You work late, you work holidays. It's not natural. I don't want you burning out. I need you at the top of your game."

"So your concern is all about you."

"Damn straight." Jack was quiet for a second. "You need to talk to somebody."

Nash's chest tightened. "I did."

"You had the required sessions with an in-house psychologist because I threatened to fire you if you didn't. I'm talking about someone outside the bureau. Tina's death was a shock to all of us. Violence leaves a scar."

The conversation was a variation of one they'd had a dozen times before. "I've dealt with it in my own way."

"That's what scares me. Do you still blame yourself?"

Nash knew the right answer. He was supposed to say that he didn't. That it was just one of those things. Instead he told the truth.

"I should have known. I should have done something."

"You're good, but you're not that good. No one is."

But Nash knew he was supposed to be. He was supposed to be one of the best.

"So you're having fun?" Jack asked in a change of subject.

Nash thought about what he'd been doing for the past few days. "Yeah. I am."

"Good to hear. Take it easy. Relax. Become one of the living again."

"I'm working on it."

"I wish I could believe that. You need to get laid."

Nash chuckled. "Funny you should mention that. I was just thinking the same thing myself."

"For real?"

"Yup."

"That's the best news I heard all day. Good for you."

"Don't be so enthusiastic," Nash said. "You're starting to worry me."

Jack laughed. "Fair enough. Okay, you go find a

good-looking broad and I'll hold things together here. See you in a couple of weeks."

"Sure thing. Bye."

Nash pushed the end button on his cell, then tossed the phone back onto the desk. Jack was old school, and the least politically correct guy Nash knew. But he was a good man who genuinely cared. He wanted Nash to let the past go—not just for the sake of his team, but for Nash himself.

Nash wasn't ready to let anything go, not yet, but he was willing to take his friend's advice about finding a "good-looking broad." He already had one in mind.

Nash showered and dressed, but waited until close to seven before going downstairs. After what had happened the previous night, he wasn't sure what to expect. At the bottom of the stairs he saw that the kitchen door was closed and the dining room door was open. Taking that as a hint, he crossed to the dining room and found his usual place for one already set. The local paper, along with *USA TODAY,* sat to the left of his napkin and flatware. A basket of still-warm scones sat next to an empty coffee cup. Before he could check the carafe, the door to the kitchen pushed open and Stephanie entered.

She had returned to her B-and-B-owner uniform of tailored slacks, low-heeled pumps and a sweater that clung to her upper body in such a way as to interfere with his brain waves. Makeup accentuated her blue eyes…eyes that were not looking directly at him.

"Good morning," she said politely as she carried a

full coffeepot over to the table. She unscrewed the lid of the carafe, then filled it with the steaming liquid.

"What would you like in your omelet?" she asked. "I have several cheeses, an assortment of vegetables, bacon, ham and sausage. Or you could have the meat on the side."

She offered him a friendly smile that didn't chase away the air of nervousness.

So she'd decided to go the "all business" route to deal with whatever morning-after jitters she might be having. Nash could have wished for something else, but he understood her decision. She didn't know him from a rock. She was a woman with responsibilities and they didn't include playing footsie with the paying guests.

"An omelet would be great," he said. "Cheddar cheese and whatever vegetables you have around. I would appreciate a side of bacon, as well."

"No problem. It will be about fifteen or twenty minutes. The boys are due down any second and I want to get them fed. Is that all right?"

"Of course."

She nodded and left, all without ever looking directly at him. Nash took his seat and opened the paper, but he didn't actually see the print.

Was she having second thoughts about last night? Did she regret the kiss? When they'd parted, he would have bet she'd been as pleasantly surprised and turned on as he had been. But after several hours to reflect, she could have decided it had all been a mistake.

He didn't want her to think that. He wanted her to want him as much as he wanted her.

Nash shook his head. Okay—he had it bad. He was on the verge of behaving like an idiot over a woman and he couldn't remember the last time that had happened.

The sound of feet clattering on the stairs caught his attention. The boys were arguing over whose turn it was to pick up in the family room upstairs. Apparently they all tried to get in the kitchen door at once because there were shouts of "Stop pushing me," and "Get out of my way!"

Nash smiled as he imagined the three of them shoving and laughing and then bursting into the kitchen. He heard Stephanie's warm greeting, then the sound of chairs being pulled out.

For the first time in years, he found himself not wanting to be by himself. As he sat alone in the dining room, he listened to murmurs of conversation and explosions of laughter, all the while wishing he could be a part of it. Then, without considering the consequences of his actions, he picked up his carafe of coffee, his cup and the basket of scones, then walked into the kitchen.

Once again, conversation ceased. He could feel the boys looking at him, but his attention centered on Stephanie. She had just set a carton of eggs onto the center island. Her head snapped up and her mouth parted slightly. Color crept up her cheeks.

"The dining room was a little empty this morning," he said by way of explanation. "Would you mind if I joined you in here?"

Emotions raced across her face, but they went too quickly for him to read them. If she hesitated for too long, or looked too uncomfortable, he was going to head back to the dining room and keep out of her way for the rest of his stay.

The corners of her mouth turned up slightly and her blush deepened. When she finally met his gaze, he saw a heat flaring in her eyes that matched the one raging inside him.

"That would be nice," she said.

The twins shifted their chairs to make room for him between them. He set his coffee and scones down on the table and collected an empty chair. When he was seated he saw that Brett didn't look as happy to see him as everyone else did.

Before he could think of something to say to the pre-teen, Jason flipped back the napkin on the basket and peered inside.

"Whatcha got?" he asked, then wrinkled his nose.

"Don't you like scones?"

Jason shook his head. "They taste funny."

Nash offered one to Adam, who shrunk back in his chair as if he'd been offered bug guts. Nash glanced at Brett and raised his eyebrows.

Brett reached across the table and took one. "They're still kids," he said as he set the scone next to his toast. "They don't like these yet."

"Makes sense," Nash said, trying not to smile. The way Brett talked, he was pushing forty instead of barely turned twelve.

Nash poured himself a cup of coffee. Behind him, Stephanie cracked eggs into a frying pan.

"There's a talent show today," Jason announced. "At school. A girl in my class is going to dance ballet." He wrinkled his nose. "She's got this funny-looking skirt thing. A tutu. It sticks out and is all stiff. But if you throw it across the room it goes really far."

"A boy in my class plays the drums," Adam said from Nash's other side. "And three girls are going to sing a song from the radio."

"Sounds like fun."

Adam nodded.

The twins chatted all through breakfast. Brett didn't say much, but he kept his eye on Nash. Stephanie slid their scrambled eggs onto their plates, then whipped up Nash's omelet. While he finished eating, the boys stood and began collecting their backpacks. There was a flurry of activity as each child received a hug, a kiss and lunch money.

"Have a good day," Stephanie said as she tucked change into Adam's backpack and closed the small zippered compartment. "I love you."

She gave them each another quick hug, although Brett ducked out of her embrace. Then the boys thundered to the front of the house and outside. The door slammed behind them.

Nash finished his breakfast and poured himself another cup of coffee. Stephanie pushed open the door to the dining room and watched out the front window until they were all on the bus.

As she stood there, he remembered his own mornings as a child. His mother had always made sure she was there to fix them breakfast and pack their lunches. Then she'd walked them out of the house. The last thing she'd said every school morning through to his high-school graduation had been that she loved them each more than she could say and that they were the best part of her world.

For a while, he had stopped believing her on both counts. Now, looking back with the hindsight of an adult, he knew that nothing had changed on her part.

Stephanie returned to the kitchen where she fussed with dishes, munched on an extra piece of bacon and fluttered nervously until Nash used his foot to push out the chair across from his.

"Have a seat," he said.

She glanced from him to the chair, then sighed. "Okay. I guess we need to talk about it."

She poured herself a cup of coffee and joined him at the table.

She looked at him, then away. Color climbed high on her cheeks, retreated, then returned. Nash figured it was all up to him.

He decided to start with something easy. "Was my joining you and the boys for breakfast a problem?"

"What?" She'd been tracing a pattern on the table. Now she raised her head and stared at him. "No. Of course not." She smiled. "I thought it was nice. If you want to plan on joining us for the rest of your stay, I'll just set an extra place in here, rather than the dining room. It's not a problem at all."

He'd half expected her to ask him why. Why did he want to join them? Not that he had an answer. On some level he knew that being around her and her kids allowed him to forget. Without work to distract him, there was too much time to think. But that was only one of the reasons. The others all had something to do with him enjoying her and the boys' company.

"I'd like that," he said. "So if that's not the issue, what is? Last night?"

She swallowed, then nodded slowly. "*Issue* isn't exactly the word I'd use. I thought..." She looked away. "You're so calm."

"And you're not?"

"Isn't it obvious?" She clutched her coffee cup in both hands. "I just... I guess what I really want to know is why it happened."

Funny, that wasn't his most pressing question.

He knew that she had to be around thirty, maybe a couple of years older. She was smart, successful, pretty and sexy as hell. But right now she looked ready to jump out of her skin with nerves and embarrassment. Because of him? He would like to think he got to her that much, but he had a feeling that might be wishful thinking on his part.

"You're attractive," he said, wondering if she really didn't know why he'd wanted to kiss her. "Very attractive and I enjoy your company. I had a pretty universal male reaction to both of those facts."

She pressed her lips together and nodded. "Okay," she said, her voice almost a squeak. She cleared her throat again. "So you're talking about, um, you know, interest."

Sex. He was talking about sex. "Interest works, but only if it's returned."

This time there was no question that she was blushing. Her cheeks flushed to a bright red and she nearly dropped her coffee cup.

"I'm not really used to talking to adults," she said in a low voice. "Men, I mean. I don't think I was very good at it before and the lack of practice has only made me worse."

"Then we'll take it slow. The conversation, I mean."

Her eyes widened slightly. "Okay. Well, then I should probably start at the beginning."

He had no idea what she meant. "The beginning?"

"Yeah. I met Marty my last year of college. I was so thrilled to be out on my own and not responsible for anyone but myself. I'd dated some, but hadn't fallen for anyone before. Not like I did with Marty. Everything was so exciting. Marty…" She sighed. "He was a few years older. Charming, funny. He'd switched majors so many times that he was still a junior after five years of school. I remember thinking that he was so full of life and so interested in me."

She looked at him. "I told you my parents are artists, but what I didn't tell you was that their art is the most important thing in their lives. I remember growing up knowing that no skinned knee, no problem with a friend could ever compete with the perfect light on the right view. While they painted, I didn't exist."

"Marty was different?"

"I thought so. He focused so intently on me that I didn't realize I was just the latest in a long line of fleeting passions. He swept me off my feet and I married him less than two months later. Within six weeks, I realized I'd married someone just like my parents."

Nash leaned toward her. "In what way?"

"He wasn't responsible. He wasn't willing to think about anyone but himself. He didn't care if the bills got paid on time or if they turned off our electricity. He didn't worry about showing up to work on time. There were so many other fun things to be doing. I'm sure a mental health professional wouldn't be surprised that I'd replaced my parents with someone exactly like them, but it was a shock to me. I was devastated."

He wanted to reach across the table and take her hands in his, but he didn't. Instead he sipped his coffee, then asked, "Why didn't you leave?"

"I wanted to," she admitted. "I considered my options, thought about what I wanted and decided that I wasn't going through that again. But right before I packed up to go, I found out I was pregnant with Brett."

She moved her cup around on the table. "Marty was thrilled. He swore everything was going to be different, and I wanted to believe him. I thought it would be wrong to take his child away from him, so I stayed. He went from job to job, city to city, state to state, and we went with him. Every time I managed to save a few dollars, he spent them on something crazy like an old beat-up motorcycle or a weekend of river rafting. I waited for him to grow up, to realize he had responsibilities. I found creative ways to make money at home. After a few years, I told him we couldn't continue that way. I would homeschool Brett through kindergarten, but if we weren't settled by the time he was in first grade, I was leaving."

She leaned back in her chair and shrugged. "Brett

was three. That gave Marty another three years to get his act together. In the meantime, I started taking night courses whenever I could. Business, mostly. If I had to leave, I wanted to be prepared. Once Brett was of school age, I knew I would be able to take care of us both."

"Then the twins came along," he said.

"Another unplanned pregnancy," she agreed. "Suddenly I had a four-year-old and infant twins. There wasn't any money. I had to pay the doctor off in weekly installments. The week I brought the twins home, the city turned off our electricity. It was hell. Through it all Marty said we'd be just fine. He kept not showing up for work or quitting. About a year later, I snapped. I packed up the kids and I left him. I knew that it would be hard on my own, but caring for three children was a whole lot easier than caring for four."

If Marty hadn't been dead, Nash would have found him and beaten his sorry butt into the ground.

"He followed me and begged me to come back." She looked at Nash, then away. "Brett adored him. I gave in. I didn't love him anymore, but I felt guilty for leaving. Isn't that crazy? So I stayed. Then one day he got a letter from a lawyer. One that said he'd inherited a bunch of money. I told Marty I wanted to put it on a house. I thought if we could have that much security, I could stand the rest. We were passing through Glenwood at the time, so we decided to buy here. But Marty couldn't just buy a regular house and own it outright. This monstrosity fit right into his dreamworld. I thought it was better than just blowing the money on a sailboat so we could go around the world and I agreed. Then he died."

Nash didn't know what to say. "You've done a hell of a job."

"I've done my best to think about my boys. I want them to be happy and secure. I want them to know they're important to me. None of which is my point."

She squared her shoulders. "I'm thirty-three. I've been responsible for someone else since I was old enough to order groceries on the telephone. By the time I was ten, I was paying all the bills and managing the household money. My parents took off for France when I was twelve. They were gone for five months. I was scared to be by myself for that long, but I got through it. I was the grown-up with Marty and I'm the grown-up now. My point is, I'm not looking for another responsibility. I've heard that men can be partners in some relationships, but I've never seen it."

Nash heard the words, but he wasn't sure why she was telling him. He added her parents to the list of people he would like to have words with, but that didn't help.

"I'm impressed by how well you've held it all together," he said.

She nodded. "But you don't know why I'm telling you all this."

"Right."

She sucked in a breath and stared at the table. "That kiss last night was pretty incredible. The fact that you didn't go running screaming from the room when you saw me this morning tells me that you maybe didn't mind it too much."

He knew this was difficult for her, but he couldn't help laughing. "You're understating my position," he said. "I wanted you. I still want you."

Her mouth formed an "oh" but no sound emerged. She glanced at him, her eyes wide and stunned.

"That's clear," she whispered. "I, ah, appreciate your honesty. The thing is, I haven't allowed myself to have a sexual thought since Marty's death. I don't meet many men, but the ones I do meet either take off at the thought of a woman with three kids, or they're too much like Marty and I'm the one running. I don't want a relationship. I don't want to get involved. But…"

Her voice trailed off.

Nash leaned toward her. He wasn't sure what direction she was heading, but if it was the one he thought… where could he sign up?

"I thought that part of me was dead," she said. "It's not."

"Good to know."

She smiled slightly. "I thought so. And that made me wonder, what with you leaving town at the end of next week and all…"

He put the pieces together, rearranged them and did it again. He came up with the same answer. Which meant he was doing it wrong. No way his luck was that good.

She stared at him. "You really need to talk now."

"You want me to say it?"

She nodded.

If he got it wrong, she would throw her coffee in his face and he'd be forced to look for new quarters. He could live with that. If this was going to be his fantasy, too, he might as well just go for it and prepare himself to be shot down.

"You're not interested in a relationship," he said.

"Right."

"You liked the kiss."

"Uh-huh."

"A lot."

She grinned. "A lot works."

"What you're looking for is something more along those lines. An affair while I'm in town and when I leave, it's over. No strings, no regrets, no broken hearts. Until then, we keep each other company at night. Am I close?"

Chapter 8

He was close, Stephanie thought as embarrassment and horror swirled in her throat. So close that he'd grasped the concept in one seemingly easy try.

It was one thing to *think* about hot monkey sex with a virtual stranger who happened to be handsome, hunky and heart-poundingly erotic, it was another to have the object of her desire figure it all out and say it back to her. Out loud.

In the light of day, the idea sounded sleazy and off-putting and completely improbable.

Without thinking, she pushed herself to her feet and bolted from the room. She had no particular destination in mind—just a need to be away from Nash.

As she raced along the hall, she tried to tell herself that she hadn't done anything wrong. She was an adult, Nash was an adult. He'd kissed her and they'd both liked it. So what was the big deal about suggesting taking things to the next level? Didn't people do that all the time?

Maybe, she thought frantically. But not her. She'd been with exactly one man in her life—her husband. The rules and social mores of the modern dating world were completely beyond her. She had never asked a man to hold her hand before, much less ask him to have an affair.

She reached the bottom stair, but before she could put her foot on it, someone grabbed her arm.

She stopped and sucked in a breath. Okay—not someone. Nash. She ducked her head because she could feel heat on her cheeks. Not only from what he'd figured out about what she wanted, but because running hadn't exactly been mature.

Silence stretched between them, lengthening like taffy. Finally it snapped with an almost-audible crack and he spoke.

"I apologize," he said quietly. "Apparently I misread the situation and insulted you."

His words were so at odds with what she'd been thinking, she couldn't help turning around and staring at him. His dark gaze settled on her face as he shrugged.

"Wishful thinking on my part," he said. "I projected what I wanted on to you."

He was taking the fall for this? She couldn't believe it. "I… You…" She blinked. "Projecting?"

"The kiss was hot. It made me want more."

She processed the statement. The ripples of horror

changed to tingles of excitement as she considered the possibilities. "You don't mind that I'm interested in a no-strings affair? You don't think that's tacky and cheap and sleazy of me?"

His mouth curved into a slow smile as fire flared in his irises. "Do I look like I mind?" He released her arm and reached up to stroke her cheek. "You're attractive, sexy and you kiss like a wet-dream fantasy come to life."

Oh, my. Speaking of wet, his words made her go all squishy inside. An ache began between her thighs and spread out in every direction. She felt both weak and incredibly powerful. Desire swept through her—the kind of desire she'd hadn't felt in what seemed like a lifetime.

"Why don't you ask your question again," she said. "I'll try not to run this time."

His expression tightened and grew more intense. Around them, the air thickened as tension crackled. She could feel the hairs on her arms and the back of her neck standing up. Her gaze locked with his.

"Are you interested in an affair?" he asked, his voice low and heavy with what she was pretty sure was sexual need. "Sex, fun and when my time in town is up, we both walk away. No regrets. No expectations."

It sounded wicked. It sounded perfect.

"Yes," she whispered. "That's exactly what I want."

She couldn't believe she'd spoken the words aloud, but before she could give in to self-doubt, he pulled her close.

"It's what I want, too," he murmured. "I've been

hearing rumors for years, and I finally get to find out if they're true."

Rumors? "About me?"

He pressed his mouth against her neck. Delicious tingles tiptoed down her spine, making it nearly impossible to think.

"Not you specifically," he told her. "Older women."

Stephanie had already placed her hands on his shoulders and if his thick muscles didn't feel so good as she pressed her fingers against him, she would have snatched them back. Instead she shifted a little, without actually breaking contact with his hard body.

"Older women?"

He raised his head and grinned. "You said you're thirty-three. I'm thirty-one. Ever since I first figured out the possibilities between a man and a woman, I've been hearing stories about how great it is to be with an older woman. All that experience. All that latent desire as they reach their sexual peak. I've always wondered if everything they say is true."

She supposed there were two ways to respond to his challenge. Duck and run, or challenge him back. While her first inclination was to do the former, something told her there was more fun to be had in the latter.

"Of course it's true," she said as she leaned close. "I hope you can keep up."

He gave a low, throaty laugh right before he claimed her mouth.

The hot, hungry kiss took her breath away. His lips pressed against hers with enough pressure to make her a hundred percent sure he wanted her as much as she wanted him. She parted instantly and he swept inside.

He tasted of coffee and sin. She shivered in delight at the first brush of intimate contact. Heat poured through her, making her legs weak and her breathing catch. Need exploded, surrounding her, crashing over her, making her want with a desperation that left her ravenous and achingly alive.

As she tilted her head to deepen the kiss, he pulled her closer still. They touched everywhere. Her breasts flattened against his chest, his arousal throbbed along her belly. His hands roamed her back, moving up and down in a rhythm that matched the pounding of her heart.

While she traced the breadth of his shoulders, he explored her waist, then her hips. One hand slipped to her rear and squeezed. His fingertips just grazed the very top of the back of her thigh. The light contact shouldn't have been anything special, yet it burned through her clothes and singed her skin.

Unexpectedly Nash bit down on her lower lip. She gasped. When he drew the sensitized skin into his mouth and gently sucked, the gasp turned into a moan.

They had to get closer, she thought, need turning frantic. Closer and naked and touching. Now. This instant.

The message traveled from her brain to her hands. Even as he shifted so that his fingers grazed her nipples and jolts of wanting arrowed down to the thick swollen dampness between her legs, she tugged at his shirt. The fabric pulled free of his waistband. She fumbled with buttons, unfastening the first two. He slipped his hands under her sweater. She caught her breath in anticipation. His large, warm hands cupped her breasts.

Her thin bra felt like a steel barrier keeping him from touching bare skin. Torn between wanting to get his shirt off him and wanting to feel his skin on hers, she tried to shimmy out of her sweater while still unbuttoning his shirt. At the same time, she turned and bumped the bottom stair with her foot.

Nash caught her as she started to fall. His strong arms held her upright.

"We need to take this upstairs," he murmured as he kissed along her jaw to her left ear.

"Okay."

Her head fell back in supplication. She silently begged him never to stop. His hands returned to her breasts and she couldn't think…couldn't do anything but feel. It was all too good, too amazing, too incredible. The wet heat of his mouth, the way he flicked his tongue against the sensitive skin below her ear. Then there were his fingers and the way they teased and played and pressed against her nipples. Not hard, not soft. Just right. Very right.

"Stephanie?"

"Uh-huh?"

"Hang on."

He swept her up in his arms, just like Rhett Butler carrying Scarlett. After an initial moment of being disconcerted, she felt light and feminine and too sexy for words.

"I wish I was naked right now," she said.

His dark eyes brightened with need. "Me, too. My room's closer. Is that all right?"

She couldn't answer because he was kissing her, but she tried to tell him "yes" with her lips and her tongue. Apparently he got the message because the next thing she knew, they were on the second floor and heading down the hall.

He pushed open his door and stepped inside. The blinds were open and sunlight filtered through the lacy curtains. The door bumped closed behind them, then they were next to the bed and she was sliding to her feet.

The second she felt firm footing beneath her, she wrapped her arms around his neck and leaned against him. He hauled her close and deepened the kiss.

Every part of her body screamed for his touch, for nakedness, for release. She tried to kick off her shoes, but her brain wouldn't focus on anything but the feel of his mouth against hers and refused to send messages to muscles. Nash fumbled with his shirt, then chuckled.

"We're not making progress," he said as he broke the kiss and took a half step back.

He finished unfastening buttons and shrugged out of his shirt. She managed to slip off her shoes and reach for the hem of her sweater. But before she could pull it off, he bent low and kissed the bare skin below her bra band. Soft, damp kisses tickled along her ribs. Savoring the delicate caress, she froze with her hands clutching her sweater, her arms half-above her head. He cupped her breasts, then reached for her sweater and finished the job.

He returned his mouth to hers and kissed her. As he teased her tongue, he unfastened her bra and pulled the straps down her arms.

Her already taut nipples brushed against the hair on his chest. The contact both tickled and aroused. Every part of her was so hypersensitized that she desperately wanted more of everything. She clung to his shoulders and turned her torso back and forth so her nipples slid against his bare skin. At the same time she sucked hard on his tongue and pressed her belly to his arousal.

Nash groaned low in his throat, brought his hands up to cup her breasts and rubbed her nipples with his thumbs. Pleasure spiraled through her chest, then dove deep and landed between her thighs. Heat increased, as did the swelling. She was so ready, she thought desperately. They were both still half-dressed and she was shaking with need.

She dropped her hands to her waistband and unfastened her slacks. He followed her actions, which moved them closer to naked, but left her breasts wanting more.

In a matter of seconds, she'd pulled off the rest of her clothes. Nash pushed down his jeans and briefs, tugged off his socks, then gave her a brief kiss, followed by the command "Don't move."

He disappeared into the bathroom. She heard fumbling, three swear words, then something hard fell on the floor. He reappeared holding a box of condoms.

The sight of birth control should have been sobering, but Stephanie was too far gone for rational thought. She didn't want to know how or why he'd been prepared, but she was grateful.

When he rejoined her, he tossed the condoms onto the nightstand, then urged her to sit on the bed. From there he eased her onto her back and knelt next to her. One leg slipped between hers. As he bent low and took her right nipple in his mouth, he pushed his rock-hard thigh up against her waiting dampness.

The combination of the pulling, sucking kiss and the pressure against her pulsing need nearly sent her over the edge. She gasped wordlessly and dug her fingers into his hair.

"Don't stop," she breathed, not wanting either point of contact to end. She pulsed her hips shamelessly, rubbing herself against him, squirming to get closer, to get the pressure higher, faster, harder.

He switched his attention to her other breast and shifted so he knelt between her legs. He moved his leg, then replaced it with his hand.

Strong, sure fingers slipped between her curls into slick flesh. He explored all of her, brushing against that single point of pleasure in a way that made her suck in her breath in anticipation. Then he shifted slightly and slid two fingers inside her.

She felt words leave her lips, but couldn't say what they were. She couldn't do anything but feel the way he moved in and out of her. Hot need pooled, then grew, then spilled over into every cell of her body. She barely noticed when he stopped kissing her breasts and instead pressed his mouth against her belly. He moved lower and lower, shifting back with each kiss, yet continuing to move his fingers inside her.

With his free hand, he parted her curls, then placed

his mouth directly over that one most-sensitive spot and gently licked her.

Air spilled from her lungs. Before she could catch her breath, he closed his lips around her and gently sucked. At the same time he flicked his tongue back and forth, and moved his fingers and then she was flying.

Her orgasm was as powerful as it was unexpected. She shook and gasped and moaned and dug her heels into the mattress. Spasms rippled through her as pleasure eased the tension that had been plaguing her for what felt like a century. He continued to touch her, softening his kiss, moving his fingers more slowly, but still filling her, taking her on and on until it seemed that she'd been climaxing for hours.

At last her body relaxed and he stilled. Stephanie felt as if her bones had melted. She might never be able to walk again, but did it matter? Did anything matter but the delightful lethargy stealing over her?

Nash pressed a kiss to her inner thigh, then shifted so he was lying next to her. He was smiling.

"I don't have to ask if that worked for you," he teased.

"Probably not. If there's a story on the news about an earthquake in the area, I guess I'm going to have to take responsibility. Or maybe it's your fault."

"I like it being my fault."

She touched his face, then brushed her thumb across his mouth. "That was amazing."

"I'm glad."

She turned toward him and put her hand on his hip,

then slid it down to his large erection. "Ready for act two?"

Instead of answering, he reached for the box of condoms. While he opened the package, she leaned over him and kissed him. At the first brush of his tongue on hers, tension returned to her body. She deepened the kiss, then pulled back to lightly bite her way along his jaw.

"You're distracting me," he grumbled.

"Really?" She glanced down to watch as he fumbled with the protection. "Want help?"

"Sure. I was never good with these."

She took the condom from him and gently slid it down his arousal. "Does the unopened package mean you haven't been practicing much?" she asked.

His dark gaze settled on her face. "I haven't been with anyone since my wife passed away. I met someone a few months ago and thought maybe…" His voice trailed off. "I bought the condoms because of that, but things ended long before we got to the naked stage."

She supposed that her friends would tell her it was dangerous to be a man's first time after the death of his wife. Of course, Nash was her first time, too. Besides, they'd agreed on a no-commitment sexual attachment. She liked him, she wanted him, and glory be if he didn't feel exactly the same. It was the perfect relationship.

"Ready to take that latex for a test-drive?" she asked.

"Sure."

She started to slip onto her back, but he put his hands on her hips and urged her to get on top. After swinging her leg over his hips, she settled above him. He brought both his hands up to her breasts and cupped her curves. The second his thumbs brushed against her nipples, she felt her insides clench. Apparently he wasn't the only one ready for round two.

She reached between her legs and grasped his hardness, then pressed the tip of him against her wetness. As she pulled her hand away, she eased down onto him.

Her body had to stretch slightly to accommodate his thickness. Nerve endings quivered as he filled every bit of her. She braced herself and began to move.

The feeling was too good, she thought as her muscles clenched hard around him. Each time she slid down over him, she felt herself tensing more and more. His hands on her breasts only pushed her closer to the edge.

"You're holding back," he said, his voice sounding strained.

She opened her eyes and saw the tension on his face. He was watching her.

"Just give in," he told her.

"I want to." She sucked in a breath as a ripple of pleasure cascaded through her. "It's just…"

"You think I'm going to complain if you come again?"

She smiled. "Good point."

He stared at her. "Come on. I want to feel you. Just let go."

With each thrust of him filling her, she found herself getting closer and closer. Soon there wasn't going to be anything to talk about.

"Do it."

He accompanied his command with a rapid pulse of

his hips. The hands on her breasts moved more quickly. He filled her again and again until the need grew to an unbearable pitch. She sat up and put her hands on her thighs, then raised and lowered herself faster and faster.

Nash figured this was one of life's most perfect moments. He was seconds from his own release, but he was damn sure going to hold back until Stephanie climaxed. Unfortunately his good intentions were severely tested by the sight of her riding him up and down like some X-rated cowgirl. With each shift of her body, her breasts bounced up and down, drawing his gaze and making his mouth water with desire. She had her head back, her eyes closed and she was lost in the pleasure of the moment. It was about the most erotic situation he'd ever experienced.

He could feel pressure building deep and low, which only meant trouble. He tried to think of something else, but how could he with her naked and bouncing, with her mouth parting slightly and her tongue sweeping across her lower lip as she—

He groaned as his release exploded from him. White-hot pleasure swept through him in a fury of rushing pleasure. He remained conscious enough to notice that she'd cried out at the exact moment he'd lost it. Even through the waves of his orgasm, he felt her body contracting around him, pulling every drop from him, making him come longer than he'd thought possible.

When they'd recovered enough for her to crawl off him and him to clean up, they slipped under the covers and lay on their sides looking at each other.

Stephanie smiled at him. Nash liked how contentment showed itself in the lines of her face and the way her knee nestled casually between his. He liked the scent of her body mingling with the fragrance of their lovemaking, and he liked how, even though they'd just finished, he wanted to make love with her again.

It had been a long time, he thought. Too long. After Tina had died, he hadn't set out to avoid women and sex. Somehow it had just happened. He'd buried himself in work and had never found his way out.

"What are you thinking?" she asked.

"That I never meant to live as a monk after my wife died."

"I'm surprised the single women in the office didn't make a play for you."

"How do you know they didn't?"

Her smile widened. "Do you have to beat them off with a stick?"

"Only a couple of times a year."

She looked away and the smile faded. "You must still love her very much."

The transition confused him for about a minute, then he figured out what she wanted to know.

"Hey." He touched her chin, forcing her gaze back to his face. "You and I were the only ones in this bed. At least on my side."

The smile returned. "On my side, too. I haven't been with anyone since Marty, but that's not about being brokenhearted. As I was trying to explain before, things were complicated."

He slid his hand under the sheet and cupped the curve of her bare hip. Her skin was like warm silk.

"Is this easy?" he asked.

"Very. The best kind of easy."

He agreed. In the past, he'd found the first sexual encounter in any relationship about as dangerous as a minefield. There were too many ways to misstep. But with Stephanie, everything had fallen into place. He'd never had a sex-only, no-strings affair before, but so far it was better than he could have hoped.

"How about a few ground rules to keep things that way," he said.

She nodded and sat up. "Good idea."

As she'd moved, the sheet had fallen away from her breasts. He found his attention sliding from her words to her body. He leaned toward her and touched his finger to the outer curve of her breast, then traced a line to the place where that pale skin darkened to a deep rose. Her nipple instantly tightened. After licking the tip of his finger, he brushed his damp skin against her nipple and waited for her breath to catch.

Damn if it didn't. As expected, his body responded with a rush of blood heading south.

"Rule number one," she said. "Lots of sex."

He raised his head slightly to look at her face. "That's a good rule. So good we should probably make it one and two."

"Fair enough. Sex and lots of it. You're only in town for a short period of time. I want to take advantage of that."

"My kind of woman."

He wanted nothing more than to lean in close enough to kiss her breasts, but figured they had better get things settled before the next round. He forced himself to drop his hand to his side and focus on the conversation.

"I'm going to assume you don't want the boys to know about us," he said.

She nodded slowly. "It would only confuse them. Brett still worries about me replacing his father and the twins would only want to bond with you."

"So I'll leave my door unlocked. You can head downstairs when you're ready to have your way with me."

"That works. We'll also have during the day until school's out at the end of the week. If you're not too busy with your family."

"I'm not." He reached for her hand and laced their fingers together. "Speaking of my family, would you mind joining me for a few of the bigger get-togethers? You and the boys?"

He wasn't sure why he made the request and he hoped she wouldn't ask him to explain.

Luck was on his side. She nodded right away. "That would be great. I had a good time and I know my kids did, too. All that family can be a little intimidating."

"I'm not intimidated."

"Because you're a big tough guy."

"You know it."

She laughed, then slipped down on the mattress. "Okay, then I'll think of it as helping out. Sort of 'you scratch my itch and I'll scratch yours.'"

"I like the sound of that." He moved closer and drew back the sheet, baring her to the waist. "So where does it itch?"

She wrapped her arms around his neck and kissed him. "Everywhere."

Chapter 9

Stephanie had never considered painting a room any-thing but a chore, yet this afternoon she found her-self humming while she worked. Suddenly the squishy swish of the roller on the walls sounded cheerful and lively. The smell didn't bother her, not with the gate-house windows wide open and the afternoon sun spill-ing into the room. Even the low-grade complaining of long-unused muscles didn't do anything to dampen her happy mood. She doubted anything short of a serious disaster could wipe the smile off her face.

Life was good, she thought as she smoothed the pale paint over the prepared wall. Life was damn good.

She giggled softly and stretched up her arm. The movement pulled at her hips, which ached from being extended when she'd parted her legs as wide as possible so she could wrap them around Nash. The discomfort only added to her exuberance. Being sore after something boring like an exercise class wasn't very inspiring, but being sore because of mind-clearing sex with an incredible lover was worth every twinge. Her insides still tingled with lingering aftershocks and she couldn't stop sighing with contentment. While she'd never considered herself an affair kind of girl, obviously this was something she should have done years ago.

"It never crossed my mind," she murmured aloud.

With three kids and a pretty hefty mortgage, she'd been more concerned about staying afloat financially after Marty's death than getting any sexual needs met. After a while it had been easy to forget she even had needs. Making love with her husband had been very nice, but over time, the memory faded. She didn't want another relationship with a man, so she'd figured intimacy was no longer available to her.

Until Nash had shown her all the possibilities. And what possibilities there were. They'd made love twice, then agreed to try and get some work done. It had been all of three hours since they'd left his bed and she couldn't wait to get back into it.

Mentally calculating the time until the boys would be turning in for the night, she wondered how she would survive that long without Nash touching her. Now that she knew he was even better than her fantasies, she wanted to take advantage of every second they had together.

"You're not working," Nash said as he walked in from the kitchen. "You're standing on the ladder, grinning."

She laughed. "If I tell you that I'm thinking about us being together will that make it okay?"

"Absolutely."

He leaned against the door frame, a tall, good-looking man holding spackle and a putty knife. He'd pulled on a dark blue T-shirt over worn jeans. She liked how he was competent in whatever he did, whether it was patching a wall or making her scream with pleasure. She liked how he was comfortable asking her what she liked when they were in bed, and offering to help out around the house when they weren't. She liked that he was a bit nervous about being around his new family and that he wanted her there to act as a buffer. Not that he'd ever said the latter, but she'd read between the lines.

What she liked most was that they were equals. He had needs, she had needs. No one was more in charge. No one was subservient. They were taking care of each other, while getting what they wanted.

She dipped the roller into the paint on the tray. "How's the patching coming?" she asked.

"All done in the kitchen." He turned his attention to the walls. "Are you sure you don't want me to do the painting in here? You're kind of short to reach the top of the walls."

"That's why they invented ladders," she said. "I like doing this. If you want to help, you're welcome to paint the windows. I already taped the glass, but I haven't started on the frames yet."

"Sure. Let me put this away."

He covered the can of spackle, then set it on the

makeshift workbench she'd created by placing a flat door over two wooden crates. After he left, she heard running water. The man cleaned up after himself, she thought happily. Did it get any better than that?

Nash returned and took a nearly empty gallon can of paint and a brush, then walked over to the large window. She watched him expertly brush the wood trim.

"So how did an FBI negotiator learn how to paint?" she asked.

"I helped paint our house a few times when I was growing up. Since then I've been dragged into a couple of projects with guys from work."

"Do you like your job?"

He glanced at her then returned his attention to the window. "Most of the time. Not when it goes bad."

She didn't know all that much about what he did, but knew it had a lot to do with negotiating with criminals holding hostages. A bad day for him would mean someone died.

"How did you get in that line of work?"

He shrugged. "I was recruited by the FBI out of college. I worked in Dallas for a while, got my master's in psychology. I went into profiling, then I attended a lecture by a negotiator. I trained, worked with him for a while and figured out it was something I had the temperament for."

"Meaning you can handle high-stress situations?"

"That and disconnect from the emotions inherent in the incident."

Low-key and distant, she thought. He'd been that

way with his family at the pizza-night dinner. Friendly, but not completely involved. She envied him his emotional detachment. If she'd been able to muster a little for herself, she might have been able to leave Marty.

"So you were probably really annoying when your wife wanted to pick a fight," she said. "There she'd be, all crabby and on edge, and you'd be rational and logical."

She'd been teasing, but instead of smiling at her words Nash looked thoughtful.

"We were different," he admitted as he continued to paint the window frame. "Tina lived on the emotional edge most of the time. Drama fueled her. I never figured she would make it as an agent."

Stephanie nearly dropped her roller. She grabbed the handle with both hands and tried not to look shocked. "She was an FBI agent?"

Nash nodded.

Who would have known? Stephanie hadn't much thought about his late wife, but if she had, she would have assumed the woman was a... She frowned, not sure what she would have assumed. Certainly not a federal agent.

"We met during training. I was one of her instructors. I thought she was too impulsive and wanted to flunk her out. I was outvoted."

She turned back to the wall and resumed painting. Better to leave a few streaks on the walls than to stand on the ladder with her mouth open. "Not a very romantic beginning," she said.

"It wasn't. I thought she was a flake, and she thought

I was a hard-nosed rule follower. She moved on and I forgot about her. We hooked up about a year later, on assignment."

Doing something dangerous, she thought wistfully. Capturing bad guys or saving innocent lives. There was tension, adrenaline followed by passion.

Stephanie didn't like the knot that formed in her stomach or the feeling of being a fairly typical, fairly boring thirtysomething single mom.

"If you two were married, you must have changed your initial opinions of each other," she said.

Nash shrugged. "We were always opposites."

"Sometimes that works."

"It didn't for you and Marty."

That was true. "I'm not sure we were opposites so much as we wanted different things," she said, thinking it was safer to think about her late husband than Nash's late wife. "Or maybe it was just that I wasn't willing to pay the price for always doing what I wanted. I didn't like always having to be the grown-up, but Marty didn't seem to give me a choice. Someone had to make sure the bills got paid on time and that there was food in the house. But there were times when I envied his ability not to worry about things like money and consequences. I could never let go that much."

"You took on a lot at an early age. I think kids who have to grow up fast never forget what it was like to be young and in charge. I had the same thing at home. My mom worked a lot of hours and my brother was a complete screwup. He was born to break rules. Even though we were twins, I always felt like the oldest."

"But he grew out of it," she said. "Kevin's a U.S. Marshal now." Kevin had changed. Grown up. Most people did. Just not Marty.

Nash turned around and looked at her. "How did this conversation get so serious? People having an affair aren't supposed to talk about anything significant."

She smiled. "I didn't know. This is my first affair, so you'll have to fill me in on all the rules."

He set the brush on the edge of the paint can and walked toward her. "The rules are whatever we want them to be."

"Really?"

There was a light in his dark eyes that made her insides quiver. As he approached, she put the roller onto the tray and leaned down. The kiss was hard, hot and left her breathless. Wanting exploded within her. She wrapped her arms around his neck and let him lower her to the ground.

"It's been less than three hours and I want you again," he murmured against her mouth. "At this rate we're not going to get a lot of work done."

"I don't mind."

"Good, because I—"

A noise caught their attention. Both she and Nash turned. Stephanie cringed when she saw Brett standing in the open doorway of the gatehouse. The look on his face told her that he'd seen her in Nash's arms and that he felt betrayed. Before she could say anything, he took off for the house.

Desire drained out of her, leaving behind guilt and confusion. On the one hand, she was glad that Brett remembered his father and still thought about him. On the other hand, while she wasn't looking for love or anything close to it, she knew it wasn't right for her to close off that part of her life simply because her twelve-year-old son might not approve. Brett had to learn that it was okay to move on with life. But was this the time to have that conversation? And if so, what was she going to say? Complicating the situation was the fact that she and Nash didn't have a relationship she could explain to her children.

There was no one to ask, she thought sadly. No one to share her worries with. Like most tough times in her life, she was going to have to wing it and hope she didn't mess up too badly.

She took a step toward the house, then stopped when Nash touched her arm.

"Brett's upset," he said.

"I know."

"Maybe this would be better discussed with a guy."

Stephanie stared at him. "You want to talk to Brett about what he saw?"

"*Want* is a little strong, but I have an idea about what he's feeling. I'm not going to tell him what's going on between us, but I can reassure him."

She considered the offer. The mature side of her argued that Brett was *her* child and *her* responsibility. While Nash was probably a nice guy and definitely great in bed, he didn't have children of his own and he had only known hers for a few days. Therefore she should be the one to make things right with her son. The rest of her wanted to toss the problem in his lap and let him solve it. Just once it would be nice not to have to sweat the right thing to say.

"I really should talk to him," she said.

Nash lightly kissed her. "Go paint," he told her. "Give me ten minutes. If I'm not back by then, come find us."

Letting go was unfamiliar. Releasing responsibility was unheard of. Stephanie battled what was right with what was easy. Before she'd made a decision, Nash left the gatehouse.

Ten minutes, she told herself as she checked her watch. He couldn't mess up too badly in that amount of time, could he?

Nash walked into the house and paused to listen. When he heard something thump against the floor, he headed for the kitchen rather than the stairs.

When he pushed open the door, he found Brett banging his way through emptying the dishwasher. The kid's shoulders were slumped and stark pain darkened his blue eyes.

"Hey," he said. "How's it going?"

The twelve-year-old spun to glare at him. "You don't belong here," Brett yelled. "You're a guest. Guests stay in the public rooms. Not the kitchen. The kitchen is for family. Get out."

Nash closed the door behind him and approached the boy. Brett clutched a pot in his hands as if he would use it as a weapon if he had to.

"Did you hear me?" the kid demanded.

"I heard all of it. Even what you didn't say."

Nash recognized the boy's helplessness, the frustration that fueled anger. He knew Brett wanted to be big enough and strong enough to force Nash out of the room, the house and his mother's life. Brett wanted Nash never to have come here, never to have existed. Now that he was here, Brett wanted him gone.

The old feelings were still there, Nash thought with some surprise as he took a seat at the table. Buried, nearly forgotten, but still real. How many times had he wanted to take on Howard? Bad enough when Howard and his mother had just been dating, it had gotten worse when the two had announced their engagement and said Howard would be adopting the boys. Like they were babies. Like they needed him.

"Your mom's a real nice lady," Nash said slowly, searching for the right words, trying to remember what would have made him feel better. "Pretty, a lot of fun."

He glanced at Brett and gave a slight smile. "She probably seems old to you, but not to me. I like her a lot."

Fear flashed in Brett's eyes. Nash leaned forward and rested his elbows on his knees.

"The thing is, I'm just passing through," he said. "I'm not sticking around. In a couple of weeks I'll go back to Chicago. That's where I live and work. That's where my life is."

His life? For the first time since Tina's death Nash realized he was lying about having anything close to a life. He had a job and that was about it. Few friends outside of work. None that he socialized with. He lived alone and he was damned tired of it.

He shook off that train of thought. Later, he told himself. Right now Brett was more important.

"I understand what you're going through," Nash said.

Brett turned away. "Yeah, right."

"Okay. Grown-ups say that all the time. It's boring and annoying, huh? But in this case, it's true. Your dad died. My dad never bothered to stick around after he got my mom pregnant. There was just her, Kevin and me. She was really young and didn't have any money, so it was hard for her. She worked a lot. She worried a lot. I hated to see that, so I filled in when I could. Sort of like you with the twins."

Brett traced a pattern on the countertop. Nash wasn't sure, but he thought the kid might be listening.

"They're still pretty young," he continued, "but *you* understand that it's hard for her. You worry. And the last thing you need is some guy coming in to mess up your family."

Brett looked at him in surprise.

Nash nodded. "It happened to us. My mom started dating this guy—Howard. He was okay, I guess. But I never really trusted him. Why was he butting in? He didn't belong."

"What happened?" Brett asked.

"They got married. I didn't want them to, but they did anyway."

There was more to the story, but Nash didn't bother going into it. He'd made his point.

"I'm not like that," he told Brett. "I like your mom and I'd like to see her while I'm in town. But I *am* leaving, so all this is temporary. I'm not looking to get married or to replace your dad. I wanted you to know that, man-to-man."

He waited while Brett considered the information. Then the kid sucked in a breath.

"Okay. I get it." He still looked troubled, but not so afraid. "I guess my mom needs someone to talk to and stuff." He gaze narrowed. "But you shouldn't kiss her where just anyone can see. My brothers wouldn't understand. They don't remember Dad much and they might think you're sticking around."

"Good point. I'll remember it." Nash stood. "Something else, Brett. You may not believe me, but it's true. Even if your mom were to find someone she fell in love with and wanted to marry, that doesn't mean the guy would be taking your dad's place. No one can do that. You might even like the guy, which would be okay, too. But your dad will always be your dad."

Brett looked doubtful, but didn't disagree. Nash figured he'd done as much as he could. He held out his hand.

"Friends?" he asked.

Brett stared at his hand, then him. Finally he moved close and they shook.

"I guess we can be friends," the boy said.

"I'd like that." He jerked his head toward the front of the house. "I'm going back to the gatehouse now, if that's all right with you."

Brett nodded. "Tell my mom I'm going to get changed, then I'll come help, too."

"I know she'll appreciate that."

Brett headed for the door, then paused. Staring at the ground he said, "Thanks for explaining things, Nash."

"You're welcome."

Nash returned to the gatehouse and found Stephanie waiting impatiently by the door.

"You nearly hit your limit," she said, glancing from him to her watch. "I was giving you ten minutes, then I was going to barge in and take over."

She tried to smile as she spoke, but he could see the worry in her eyes.

"We worked it out," he said, then explained what he and Brett had discussed.

When he was done, she sank onto the floor and pulled her knees up to her chest. "Thanks for clearing things up with him. He and I used to be able to talk about anything, but lately I've noticed things are changing. I guess it's because he's getting older. I'm not looking forward to him being a teenager. That's for sure."

"He'll get through it, as will you," he said, crouching next to her. "He's a good kid."

"Too good. Oh, sure, he can be a pain, but for the most part, he really tries to step in and help. Sometimes it's easy to let him. When that happens I do my best to remember he *is* still a kid and not my personal assistant. He's getting to that age when he needs a man around. Sometimes I think I should get over my fear of getting involved with another irresponsible guy and get married simply to take the heat off Brett. It would sure give him a break."

She continued talking, but Nash no longer heard

what she was saying. Instead he was remembering a conversation he'd had with his mother shortly after she'd told him she was marrying Howard. He'd protested the engagement, saying they didn't need Howard around. His mother had tried to explain that Howard was a good man whom she loved very much.

"But there's more to it than that," she'd said. "My marrying Howard means you don't have to be the man in the family anymore. You won't have as much responsibility. I want that for you."

At the time he'd felt as if he were being eased out of his own family. Now, looking back, he wondered if his mother had worried about him the same way Stephanie worried about Brett.

Footsteps on the walkway interrupted his musings. Both he and Stephanie stood.

"Anybody home?" a man called.

"Hey, Nash, did your landlady kick you out already?"

He didn't recognize the first voice, but he knew the second.

"Kevin," he said and headed toward the front porch. Nash assumed the other man was one of the Haynes brothers.

When he stepped outside he saw he'd been right. Kevin and Travis stood by the sidewalk. They waved at him and walked closer.

Kevin smiled at Stephanie. "I knew you'd get tired of his ugly face. Threw him out, huh?"

She laughed. "Actually he's helping me patch and paint my gatehouse. He does quality work and if he's at it much longer, I'm going to have to give him a discount on his room."

Kevin shook his head. "Nash getting his hands dirty? I can't believe it."

Nash stepped next to his brother and threw a mock punch. Kevin ducked, shot out a jab, then slapped him on the back. "Wait until you hear what Travis has to say."

Travis Haynes wore a khaki-colored uniform and a beige Stetson. He pulled off the hat and smoothed back his hair.

"Kevin and I were talking," he said. "I happened to mention that once a year the Glenwood sheriff's department along with local firefighters and paramedics get together with the army base about fifty miles from here. We break up into teams and spend a couple of days playing war games. The more experienced men are paired up with new recruits, giving them a chance to learn. What with your background and all, I thought you might be interested."

Nash could see Stephanie out of the corner of his eyes. She stood on Travis's right. At the mention of war games, she rolled her eyes.

"Gage already said yes," Kevin said. "I did, too. If Quinn shows up in time, I know he'll be in."

"I'm in," Nash said.

Kevin nudged Travis. "Told you he'd say yes."

Nash turned to Stephanie. "What about you?"

She shook her head. "I have an actual life that requires me not to play games. Why is it men refuse to stop acting like little boys?" She looked stern, but her tone was teasing.

"Everybody has to play sometime," Nash said.

Her gaze locked with his. He felt the sexual tension return and wished they were alone.

"I like a different kind of game," she informed him, then turned her attention to Kevin and Travis. "Gentlemen, I need to get back to my painting. I hope your war games are everything you want them to be."

Travis grinned. "You sound just like my wife. She makes fun of me every year."

Stephanie waved and headed back into the gatehouse. Nash watched her go, his gaze drifting from her trim waist to the sway of her hips. Heat flared inside him. He knew he had it bad and he didn't give a damn. Wanting Stephanie was the most fun he'd had in years.

"The war games start in a couple of weeks," Kevin said. "You're going to have to extend your vacation."

Nash thought of all the time off he'd accumulated in the past couple of years. "Not a problem."

"Good."

"We need to—" Travis's cell phone rang, cutting him off. "Just a sec," he said as he pulled out the phone and pushed the talk button. "Haynes." He walked a couple of steps away as he listened.

Kevin stepped closer and lowered his voice. "So what's with you and Stephanie?"

Nash wasn't surprised his brother had noticed his interest. He and Kevin might not be identical twins, but they were still closer than most brothers and didn't have a lot of trouble knowing what the other was thinking.

Nash looked at the gatehouse. "Nothing significant."

"That's not how it looked from here."

"She's great, but I'm not into permanent relationships. As it turns out, neither is she."

"You can't be alone forever," Kevin said.

"Why not?"

"It's better to be with the right person."

Nash shook his head. "You say that now that you've found Haley, but six months ago you thought alone was a fine way to be."

"You loved Tina enough to want to marry her. What happened that was so bad you wouldn't want to risk trying again?"

"Nothing was bad." Nothing specific. He couldn't point to any one event and say "this is the reason I don't want to get involved." Probably because his problem wasn't about his marriage. It was about him.

"You're stubborn," Kevin said.

"We have that in common."

"I know. Mom used to complain about it all the time." He took a deep breath. "Speaking of which, I want to invite her and Howard out here for a few days. To meet everyone. I know you're not going to like it, but you're going to have to deal with it. You can't—"

Nash cut him off with a simple "Fine with me."

Kevin stared at him. "You're serious?"

"Sure. Give them the name of Stephanie's B and B. They can stay here."

Nash thought of his recent revelations about the past. Maybe things hadn't been exactly as he'd remembered them. Maybe being twelve had colored his view of the truth. Maybe it was time to change things.

"Great. I'll call tonight." Kevin grinned. "They're going to like Stephanie."

"Don't go there," Nash growled. "You start making trouble for me and I'll tell Haley about the time Mom walked in on you with those two cheerleaders. If I remember correctly the three of you were naked."

Kevin winced. "I was only sixteen," he protested. "I didn't know what I was doing."

"You seemed to know exactly what you were doing. As for being sixteen, that doesn't help your cause. The cheerleaders were both in college."

Kevin grumbled under his breath, then nodded his agreement. "I won't make trouble with Stephanie," he promised.

Nash believed him. Kevin had never wasted his time with lies.

He knew Kevin thought he was doing Nash a favor by wanting things to work out with Stephanie. What Kevin didn't know was Nash wrestled with more than a bad marriage. His brother knew how Tina had died, but not the details. She'd been killed in the line of duty. What Kevin didn't know was that she'd been assigned as backup on one of Nash's negotiations.

His superiors had never blamed him, but Nash knew what had really happened that day. He'd been responsible for the death of his wife as surely as if he'd detonated the bomb himself.

Chapter 10

Nash put his arm around Stephanie and drew her close. She leaned her head against his shoulder and sighed. The soft puff of air teased his neck and made him think of other ways they could be touching. The blood heating in his body told him to get her upstairs right that second, but he resisted the desire growing inside him. They had the whole night to make love. Right now he was enjoying being next to her.

The night was clear and cool. Overhead, stars glittered in the sky. He could hear the faint sound of a stereo next door. The boys were in bed, but probably not asleep yet, which was another reason to wait before heading inside.

"What are you thinking?" Stephanie asked from her seat next to him on the top step of the porch. "That you're so incredibly hot for my body that you're tempted to rip off my clothes right here? And if that's not what you're thinking, you need to lie."

Nash smiled. "I was also thinking about your kids, that it would be better to wait until the little guys are asleep, then head inside."

"Good point. As long as you were thinking about it."

He turned his head and brushed his lips against her forehead. "I'm having trouble thinking about anything else."

"An excellent quality in a man." She wrapped her arms around his waist. "Dinner was fun. Thanks for joining us."

"I had a good time, too. The twins look so much alike, yet their personalities are different enough that I don't have any trouble telling them apart."

"I know. I don't understand how they can be so physically identical and so unalike on the inside. I've always wondered if some personality gene didn't split exactly in half or something."

He grinned. "That would be your technical, biochemical explanation?"

"Do you have a better one?"

"No. Yours is perfect."

She laughed. "I'm a fairly intellectual person, which explains why I beat your fanny when we were playing Go Fish."

"You are a card shark."

She winced. "Bad pun, but I forgive you. The whole evening was fun. Sometimes I get so caught up with the boys' homework schedules and their activities that I forget to take time for us to just hang out and enjoy each other's company. Life becomes a treadmill and the routine becomes all-important. Occasionally I need a reminder that it's okay to have a good time. Thanks for doing that tonight."

"My pleasure." He dropped his hand to her hip and rubbed the curve there. "You said something earlier that I can't stop thinking about."

"What?" She raised her head and looked at him.

"You wanted to know why men refused to stop acting like little boys. The implication being we don't grow up. I know you were teasing when you said it, but I wonder if that's what you really believe."

She pulled back slightly, shifting so she faced him. One of her hands rested on his knee, the other toyed with the sleeve hem of his shirt. In the porch light, he could see her large eyes and the way the corners of her mouth twisted slightly.

"You're the first man I've ever spent any time with who seems to be a grown-up," she said. "My father was completely irresponsible and I've told you about the horror of being married to Marty. I've been burned twice and that makes me less than trusting."

"Is that the real reason you haven't been dating?"

"Yikes! Talk about going for the throat."

"Is it?"

"Maybe. Probably. I don't know."

"Come on." He put his hand over hers and squeezed. "You do know."

Her gaze narrowed. "You have that master's in psychology, don't you? Now you want to try out some of your theories on me."

"You're avoiding the question."

"And doing a fine job if it, too. Okay." She nodded. "I'll be serious. Yes, avoiding boys disguised as men is one of the reasons I haven't been very excited about dating. I have three kids and no time to raise a fourth. You seem decent and normal, but this is a part-time fling, not something serious. With my past, I think I have the right to be wary."

He understood her point, but didn't like the idea of her spending the rest of her life alone. He was about to say so when he realized he didn't especially like the idea of her with someone else, either.

That made him slam on the mental brakes. No way was he thinking about anything serious with Stephanie. She was strictly temporary.

"At some point you have to be willing to take a chance," he said.

"Why? What are the odds that I'll end up with someone exactly like Marty? I seem to be destined to head in that direction. He was the first guy I really fell for. I don't want to risk it again."

"So take it slow this time. Really get to know the guy."

"The way I got to know you? Despite my claim of being responsible, I seem to be a bit impulsive in the relationship department." She laughed. "Trust me. This is much better. I'm having a great time with you and right now that's enough. I have no interest in getting married again."

They had that in common, he thought. Even though

she was saying all the right things, he couldn't help worrying about her. "What about money?"

Her eyes widened. "Gee, Nash, the sex was really great, but I never planned to pay you for it."

"That's not what I meant."

She shimmied close. "But now that we're on the subject, I think I'm good enough that you should pay me."

He laughed and hauled her onto his lap. "Do you?"

"Uh-huh."

She straddled him, her heat pressing against his suddenly hard arousal. She rocked back and forth, teasing them both.

"That feels nice," she said. "And big. Is all that for little ol' me?" Her voice was a soft purr.

"Think you can handle it?"

"There's nothing I want to do more than handle all of you. Let's go inside and get naked."

Her words set him on fire. While he wanted to take her at her word, he couldn't help holding back long enough to kiss her. Her mouth parted instantly and he plunged inside her. She stroked against him, then clamped her lips around his tongue and sucked until he thought he might lose it right there. So much for having control.

He shifted her off his lap and scrambled to his feet. When he'd pulled her into a standing position, he wrapped his arms around her and lifted until her feet were dangling. She wrapped her legs around his hips and hung on. He started toward the front door.

"I want to tell you that I can walk," she murmured between kisses, "but this is so much more exciting."

"For me, too." He cupped her rear, holding her firmly against his erection. "Besides, doesn't every woman want to be swept away?"

"Honey, you're doing that in spades."

Under any other circumstances, Stephanie would have assumed that breaking into song while dusting the main parlor was reason to think about seeing a mental health professional. It was the middle of the afternoon and she wasn't even listening to the radio. But she decided to cut herself some slack. After all, she hadn't slept the previous night. Instead of wasting seven or eight hours with her eyes closed, she'd spent them in Nash's arms where she discovered that women did indeed hit their sexual peak in their thirties. While she was more than a little tired, she figured she could catch up on her rest when Nash was gone. Far better to take advantage of his proximity, interest and skill while he was in town.

She stretched up to dust the top of a lamp and the muscles in her back pulled slightly. She smiled as she remembered the shower they'd taken that morning. How she'd gripped the shower door frame to keep from falling as he'd knelt between her legs. The hot water had poured over both of them as he'd used his tongue to make her scream and shudder and go all weak at the knees...literally.

Still humming a somewhat embarrassing medley of tunes from cartoons, she finished in the parlor and walked toward the kitchen. She had to figure out what they were having for dinner. Then maybe they'd rent a couple of movies. School was out tomorrow and none of the boys had any homework. They could—

The sound of voices interrupted her thoughts. She paused to figure out where they were coming from. She recognized Nash's low rumble and the twins, but where on earth could they be? She tilted her head. The utility room?

Following the sound, she walked through to the rear of the house. Sure enough, Nash crouched in front of Adam and Jason in the laundry. Between them sat an overflowing laundry basket.

Stephanie knew exactly what was going on. She'd told the twins to take the laundry upstairs and fold it. For the most part they were willing to do their chores, but laundry was the one thing all three of the boys hated more than just about anything.

No one noticed her standing in the doorway. As she watched, Nash touched each boy on the shoulder.

"You have a responsibility to your family," he said. "Your mom works hard to provide for you. In return, you go to school and help out when asked. Do you understand?"

Both boys nodded.

Nash smiled. "Good. If you work together as a team, the job will go that much quicker. Agreed?"

Two more nods, followed by Jason saying, "But Adam's gotta fold the laundry. I did it last time."

Adam turned on his twin. "You did not. I did it. It's your turn. You're always trying to get me to do your chores and I'm not gonna do this one."

"So this is an ongoing dispute," Nash said calmly. "How do you keep track of whose turn it is?"

Jason drew his eyebrows together. "It's his turn."

"Is not."

"So there's nothing in writing," Nash said.

Both boys shook their head. Their mouths were set in straight, stubborn lines and they had their arms folded over their chests.

"Why don't we talk about negotiating a system that would be fair to both of you," Nash said reasonably.

Stephanie held in a laugh. It all sounded really good, but these were eight-year-olds. If Nash didn't come to his senses, he was going to be talking for the next three days and would probably end up folding the laundry himself out of self-defense.

She stepped into the room and pointed at the laundry basket.

"Take that upstairs," she said firmly. "Now. You each fold half the clothes in that basket. If there is an uneven number of clothes, leave the last one on your bed. If you don't start upstairs right this instant, there will be no dessert for either of you."

Jason opened his mouth to protest. She stopped him with a shake of her head.

"Not one word," she said. "One word means you're in bed ten minutes early. Two words means twenty minutes early. If you understand and agree, then nod slowly."

Both boys looked at her, then at each other. They sighed heavily and nodded.

"Good." She stepped back to give them room to

carry out the basket. "Come let me know when you're done."

They each grabbed a handle and carried the basket into the hallway. Nash watched them go.

"I'm a professional," he said.

"You work with criminals. These are young boys. I'm going to guess that criminals are a lot more rational."

"You think?"

She smiled. "I would put money on it. But thanks for helping. I really liked what you said about them having responsibilities. I'm not sure it sunk in, but maybe next time."

He wrapped an arm around her shoulders. "You're saying I stink at parenting."

"I'm saying you're a sweetie to try."

He tugged on a strand of her hair, then released her. "Give me your car keys."

"They're upstairs on the table by the door to our apartment. Why? Is your rental acting up?"

"No. I want to put gas in your car. Mind if I go get the keys?"

She nodded because it was suddenly too difficult to speak. Okay, in the scheme of things, Nash putting gas in her car was no big deal. But the unexpected thoughtfulness made her throat get all tight and her eyes burn. As he walked to the stairs, she found herself wishing— just for a second—that he wasn't leaving in a week or so. That his stay in Glenwood might be a little more permanent.

"Crazy dreams," she whispered. "You know better."

The phone rang, offering a welcome interruption. She headed for the kitchen and grabbed the receiver.

"Serenity House. This is Stephanie."

"Hi, Stephanie. It's Rebecca Lucas. We met at that pizza dinner a couple of nights ago. I don't know if you remember me. There were so many people there."

Stephanie pictured a tall, slender woman with long, dark curly hair. "Yes, of course I remember. How are you?"

"Good. The reason I'm calling is Jill just called me. Craig—he's the oldest Haynes brother—got the evening off. His kids are out of school today. They're in a different school district. Anyway, we're celebrating with an impromptu barbecue here tonight. I think all of Nash's brothers will be coming and I wanted to invite him." She laughed. "Actually I want to invite you and your boys, as well, if that's all right."

Stephanie knew Nash didn't have any plans and she was pretty sure he wouldn't mind the invitation. She hesitated before accepting for all of them. Was that too presumptuous? Then she remembered his request that she help him out with his family.

"I'm sure it is, but let me double-check with him. Hold on just a sec."

She put the phone on the counter and moved toward the stairs. She met Nash as he was coming down and explained about Rebecca's phone call.

"You want to go?" he asked.

"Yes, but they're your family. Do *you* want to go?"

"As long as you're coming, sure."

"Good. I know the boys will enjoy the evening."

She took a step back, but couldn't seem to look away from Nash's dark gaze. Just being close to him was enough to get her heart all fluttery and her toes curling. Attraction crackled between them and she swayed slightly.

"Yeah," he said. "Me, too. Now go back to your phone call. Going out will make the evening go faster. When we get home, it will be time for the boys to go to bed."

Her stomach clenched. "Then us, too," she whispered.

"My thoughts exactly."

Stephanie carried a plastic freezer bag full of chocolate chip cookies up to the back door of the huge house. She hesitated slightly before entering. While she remembered meeting Rebecca Lucas at the pizza dinner, she and the woman weren't friends. Just walking into the house seemed rude, but knocking when there were kids running in and out seemed weird.

Before she could decide what to do, Rebecca pushed open the door and smiled.

"I saw you walking up from your minivan," she said easily. "You lost the kids in the first five feet and Kyle came to claim Nash. Let me help you with those." She took the bag of cookies from Stephanie. "We'll appreciate these."

"You said I didn't need to bring anything, but I wasn't comfortable coming empty-handed. They're still frozen if you want to pop them in the freezer. They'll keep well for another few weeks."

"Not a chance." Rebecca led the way to an oversize blue-and-white kitchen with gleaming stainless-steel appliances. "Between our kids and the Haynes kids and friends popping in, the cookies won't last two days."

She set the bag on the counter and turned to Stephanie. "The men are out getting the coals ready and all the salads are in the refrigerator. So there's not much for us to do right now but relax. May I get you something to drink?"

"Sure. Iced tea if you have it."

"Have a seat."

Rebecca waved toward several bar stools at the end of the counter. Stephanie took a seat as her hostess poured her a glass of iced tea.

"Jill's upstairs with the little ones. I think she's reading a story. Elizabeth, Holly and Sandy are outside supervising the play area. Kevin, Gage and their fiancées haven't arrived yet." Rebecca laughed. "Oh, dear. I should probably pull out the name tags. This is going to be a muddle."

Stephanie shook her head. "I'm pretty sure I have everyone figured out. What I don't know I can fake."

"Always a good plan."

Rebecca leaned against the counter. Her long curly hair tumbled down her shoulders. She wore a calf-length pale blue dress patterned with tiny white and pink flowers. There didn't seem to be any makeup on her flawless skin. She was tall, slender, lovely and looked as if she belonged in the pages of a Jane Austen novel.

"We were all very curious about you," Rebecca

admitted. "Kevin swore his brother wasn't seeing anyone."

Stephanie hadn't expected that line of questioning. She'd picked up her glass, but now she put it down and folded her hands onto her lap. "We're not exactly seeing each other."

They were, she supposed. After a fashion. Seeing each other naked. But that was different. Rebecca was talking about an actual relationship.

"I'm not sure I believe you," Rebecca said. "I saw the way he was looking at you the other night." She held up her hands. "I'm not going to say any more about it. My goal isn't to torment you. When I first heard about Nash I thought he might be someone I could introduce to my friend D.J. I don't think that's such a good idea now."

Stephanie felt as neatly trapped as a goldfish in a glass bowl. So how exactly was she supposed to respond to Rebecca's statement? There was no way she wanted Nash involved with someone else—it would cut into their affair time. There was also a hint of discomfort at the thought of him with another woman, but there was no way she was about to explore that particular emotion.

"Nash and I are friends," she said at last. "He's only in town for a couple of weeks, so *your* friend is unlikely to find him anything but temporary."

"How long does it take to fall in love?" Rebecca asked. "You might just be friends now, but that could change."

Stephanie reached for her glass. "No way. I'm smarter than that."

Rebecca raised her eyebrows. "You're not a fan of marriage?"

"It's great for a lot of people."

"Just not you."

"Something like that."

Rebecca's expression turned dreamy. "I can't imagine not being married to Austin. He and the children are my entire world. I suppose that sounds silly and old-fashioned. I have a job, although I'm only working part-time these days. I have friends. But all of that pales next to what I feel for my husband."

Stephanie was surprised by a stab of envy. "That sounds lovely," she said. "My marriage wasn't exactly like that."

"Haynes men make excellent husbands," Rebecca told her. "Austin is an honorary Haynes. Nash is one, too. He's—"

But she never got to finish saying what Nash was. Several small children burst into the kitchen, followed by a petite redhead Stephanie recognized.

"Hi, Jill," she said as the other woman approached.

"Stephanie. I heard you and Nash were joining us. That's great." She bent down when a little girl of three or four pulled on her jeans. "Sarah, I told you we're not going to have a snack. We'll be eating in about half an hour. But I will get you something to drink."

Two more children of about the same age also clamored for drinks. Rebecca agreed. After opening a cupboard, she pulled out stacks of small plastic glasses and put them on the counter.

"We have juice and milk and chocolate milk," she said.

Everyone wanted something different. Rebecca poured while Jill passed out the half-full glasses.

Stephanie found herself the odd man out and crossed to the large window overlooking the massive backyard. More children were playing on a built-in play set. Older kids sat in groups talking. She could see all the Haynes men talking together around the big barbecue pit, while their wives had pulled plastic chairs under a tree. Everyone seemed to be having a good time.

What a great family, she thought. Growing up, she would have given anything to belong to a group like this. Being the only child of parents more interested in art than real life had given her plenty of time on her own to wish for friends and cousins and family.

She returned her attention to the men. Elizabeth came up and stood next to Travis. He smiled at his wife and put his arm around her. Even from across the lawn, Stephanie could see the love in his eyes. Rebecca was right—Haynes men did seem to make good husbands. There didn't seem to be one like Marty in the bunch.

She studied each of them in turn, finally settling her gaze on Nash. He stood a little off to one side. In that instant, he appeared so alone that her heart squeezed tight. She wanted to go to him, hold him close and—

And what? He was leaving, remember?

For the first time, that information didn't make her happy.

She started to turn away from the window when she caught sight of Jason running toward Nash. Her eight-year-old flung out his arms and launched himself. Nash caught him easily. Man and boy laughed together. Stephanie felt her mouth curve up in response.

She pressed her fingers against the glass, as if she could touch them both. Longing filled her. A longing that was foolish and dangerous. Caring wasn't an option, she reminded herself. She and Nash had set down very clear rules and it was way too late to think about breaking them. It was also pointless. Even if she was crazy enough even to consider having a change of heart, Nash wasn't. Something she was going to have to remember.

Chapter 11

After dinner the men collected the trash and cleaned up the picnic area while the women and kids disappeared inside the house to take care of dessert. Nash pulled a beer out of the cooler and passed it to Craig, then took one for himself.

All the brothers were sprawled out on chairs around the cooling fire pit. Jordan leaned forward with his forearms on his knees.

"You're jealous because I wasn't afraid to be a rebel," he said.

Travis grinned. "Yeah, right, because only a really smart guy runs into a burning building. Are you crazy?"

"If he is, we probably all are," Kyle joked, then turned to Nash. "You've heard about our black-sheep brother here, right? The only non–law enforcement officer in four generations of Haynes men. Hell, even Hannah works for the sheriff's office. But did Jordan pay attention to all those years of tradition?"

"Not for a second," Jordan said cheerfully.

Nash glanced at Kevin. "Four generations of Haynes men?" he asked. He and Kevin hadn't considered other relatives beyond the half brothers and their families.

"Not all living," Craig clarified. "We have a few uncles still in the area, but we don't see them very often."

Nash watched as the four Haynes brothers exchanged a look of silent communication. Before he could ask what they were talking about, Travis nodded, then began to explain.

"Our uncles are a lot like our father. They never much believed in home and family. They think it's all a waste of time. Now that we're all happily married, they consider us sellouts."

"Why?" Nash asked. "Didn't they want you to get married?"

"No. They like women. A lot of women. Earl Haynes, our father, was the only one of his brothers to get married. I doubt he was faithful a day in his life. He used to brag that he was a good husband and father because he came home every night. In his mind sleeping in his own bed was good enough. Who he'd been with before that didn't seem to matter."

"They used to fight," Kyle said quietly. "I would hear them yelling at each other. She would beg him to stop seeing the other women and he would laugh at her. Then one day she left."

"What do you mean, left?" Kevin asked.

"She disappeared," Jordan said. "It turns out Earl asked her for a divorce. After all she'd already been through she considered that the final straw. She took off and no one has heard from her since."

Once again the brothers shared a look of silent communication, then Travis spoke.

"About three years ago our wives got together and organized a family meeting. They insisted we find out what happened to her. We hired a private investigator to track her down."

"She's fine," Travis said. "Living in Phoenix. She didn't remarry, but she's involved with someone who makes her happy."

"What did she say when you got in touch with her?" Kevin asked.

"We didn't," Craig told him. "We know she's all right. If she wanted to talk to any of us, she would know where to find us."

Kyle took a long drink of his beer. "It's not her fault," he said. "After years of dealing with Earl, she's paid her dues. She doesn't want anything to do with Haynes men and who can blame her?"

Nash understood the logic, but he wasn't sure he agreed with it. The sons were very different from the father. But if she'd left without a word…he could see why they wouldn't want to be the ones to make the first move.

"What is biology and what isn't?" Austin asked, speaking for the first time. "None of us have figured that out."

"True enough," Travis said. "How much of our father makes us who we are? Why, after three generations of womanizers, did my brothers and I finally figure out how to have successful relationships?"

"It wasn't easy," Craig said. "I made a mistake my first time out and I have the divorce to prove it."

"Me, too," Travis said. "But once I met Elizabeth, everything fell into place."

Jordan looked toward the house. "Finding the right woman makes all the difference in the world."

"I know that," Kevin said with a conviction Nash envied. After years of playing the field, of never wanting to settle down, he'd finally fallen in love.

Nash suddenly wanted to ask them how they knew for sure. How could any one woman be the right one? When he and Tina had been dating he'd never thought of her as right or wrong. She was someone he was seeing. When she'd pushed to take things to the next level, he'd agreed. When she'd demanded marriage, he'd considered his options and had finally proposed. But had she been the right one? He doubted it.

"Now we're old boring married men," Craig said. "Kids, mortgages, steady jobs and great wives."

Travis held up his beer. "Here's to not changing a thing."

The men clinked cans. Nash joined in, but he knew he didn't have anything to toast. Did he want his life to stay exactly the same? Two weeks ago he would have said yes, that he had all he wanted. Now, after spending time with Stephanie, he wasn't so sure. She'd reminded him that there was more to living than simply showing up every day. Participation was required, and he'd been going out of his way to avoid that.

The back door of the house opened and dozens of kids spilled out on to the lawn. The women followed, several holding cakes, others with plates of cookies or cartons of ice cream. Stephanie had plates, forks and spoons in her hands.

He watched her move, watched the easy way she walked and how she smiled when Adam and Jason came running up. She bent down and said something to them. They laughed, responded, then turned toward him.

Adam spotted him first. He pointed and the twins raced toward him. He had just enough time to set his can of beer on the grass, out of harm's way, before both boys plowed into him. Jason hung on to one leg while Adam wrapped his arms around his neck.

"Mom said we can have ice cream with our cake," Jason announced with glee.

Adam ducked his head. "She said I could have a corner piece. Are you having cake, Nash?"

"Absolutely."

"Then come on."

Each twin grabbed a hand and tried to pull him to his feet. He shifted his weight and stood. As he glanced over their heads he saw Kevin watching him. His brother's expression was knowing.

Nash wanted to stop and say something. That whatever Kevin was thinking, he was wrong. Nash didn't have it bad—he didn't have it at all. This time with Stephanie was a pleasant distraction, but little else. It couldn't be more…not when he considered the price he would pay for taking another chance on getting involved.

The boys didn't settle down immediately. It took three tries and several threats to finally get them into bed and the lights off. Stephanie closed Brett's door and headed for her living room where Nash was waiting for her. She sank down next to him on the sofa.

"We're going to have to give it a little time," she said. "I'm pretty sure they're down for the night, but they may take a while to fall asleep."

"So we'll talk until they do."

She angled toward him so she could stare at his handsome face. "Halfway decent in bed and he likes to talk," she teased. "How did I get so lucky?"

"It's a question you must ask yourself every morning."

She laughed. "Surprisingly I have other things on my mind when I get up."

"I am surprised. You shouldn't be thinking about anything but how good I make you feel."

Actually that was the first thing on her mind, but she wasn't about to admit that to him. Not when he was already so confident about his abilities in the bedroom. Not that he had reason to be anything but impressed with himself. Lord knows he made her entire being tingle.

"I had a good time tonight," she said. "You have a great family."

"I agree. I still have trouble believing they've been out there all this time, and I never knew about them."

"I used to dream about finding out I had a big family," she admitted. "I wanted aunts and uncles and lots and lots of cousins. Especially at the holidays. It was always really quiet at our house. My parents surfaced from their work enough to remember it was Christmas or my birthday, but they never really participated. I remember they used to give me board games as presents, but then never take the time to play with me. I used to try playing both sides myself, but it wasn't very much fun."

Nash's eyes darkened. "That's sad."

She held up a hand. "Don't look stricken. I recovered. I'm just saying more kids around would have been really nice. At least you always had Kevin."

"Not just him, but Gage and Quinn, too. We were always over at each other's houses. Gage, Kevin and I are the same age and Quinn is only a year younger, so we hung out all the time. Our moms were friends, as well." He leaned his head back on the sofa cushion. "We used to say we were like brothers. Ironically, that turned out to be true."

"Where is the mysterious Quinn?" she asked. "I keep hearing about him, but I've yet to see him."

"He works for the government. Some secret branch of the military. His work takes him around the world and he's not always accessible. Gage left a message and as soon as he gets it, he'll show up."

"He sounds a little dangerous. Why am I picturing a guy all in black and carrying really big guns?"

"I don't know, but that sounds like Quinn."

She shivered. "Not my kind of guy. Was he scary when you were growing up?"

"Not scary, but a bit of an outsider. He and his dad didn't get along." Nash frowned. "I guess Ralph isn't really his father anymore. Not biologically." He looked at her. "Ralph and Edie couldn't have kids of their own. It's a complicated story."

"I think it's great that their mom helped out your mom when she was abandoned by her own family. Even if you and your brother didn't know you were related to Gage and Quinn, you still got to grow up as close friends."

"I'm glad Edie was a caring person. My mom was in a hell of a bad situation." He shook his head. "Barely eighteen, with babies. What kind of parents would throw their daughter out of the house under those conditions? Edie was really there for her."

He reached out and covered her hand with his. "Who's there for you, Stephanie?"

The question surprised her. "I have friends. In a pinch they would come through."

"What about on a day-to-day basis?"

"Unfortunately there aren't a lot of people lining up to play second string," she admitted. "But I do okay."

"Is okay good enough?"

This line of conversation could lead to very dangerous territory, she thought. Dangerous and tempting. While she might not mind fantasizing about Nash stepping in to provide backup, reality was very different, and she had to remember to keep the two worlds separate.

"Hard question to answer, as I don't have a choice in the matter." She squeezed his fingers. "Hey, let's change the subject. Your entire responsibility for me consists of pleasing me in bed. Nothing more."

He studied her as if he wanted to say more, then nodded.

"They were talking about our father tonight," he said. "Earl Haynes was something of a bastard."

"I've heard bits of gossip over the past few years."

"He slept around and didn't seem to care about his wife or sons. All the brothers worry that they'll turn out like him."

"From what I've seen, none of them have. Are you worried, too?"

He shrugged.

She leaned close. "You can let that one go."

"Why? How do you know I'm different? I'm sleeping with you."

"Yes, but that's simply proof of your excellent taste."

The corners of his mouth curved up. "You think?"

"I know."

They were close enough that she could inhale the scent of him and feel his heat. Wanting flooded her, but she didn't act on the need. Part of it was she wanted to give the boys a few more minutes to fall asleep, and part of it was how much she liked the anticipation. After so many years of chaste living, it was fun to suddenly feel like a sex kitten.

"Having the information about your father means that you get to make informed choices," she said. "You know what to look out for."

"One of your choices was staying with Marty," he said. "Was it a good one?"

She sighed. "As far as my sons are concerned, yes. I wouldn't give them up for anything. But as far as making me personally happy in my marriage, no. Marty wasn't a good choice."

He reached out and stroked her cheek. "Are you okay? Financially?"

"Didn't we already have this conversation?" she asked.

"Yes and you didn't answer the question."

"Let me guess. You're not going to let it go until I do, right?"

He nodded.

She knew she could shut him down by pointing out that none of this was his business. But Nash wasn't asking out of anything but concern. Although she had no clue what he would do if he thought she was in need. Offer her a low-interest loan?

The thought was mildly amusing, but not much of a distraction. Was she going to tell him the truth or not?

She settled on the truth because she'd never been a very good liar.

"We're doing okay," she said slowly. "I've told you what life was like with Marty so you know that there wasn't a lot of extra cash each month. I held down the only steady job in the family, so that made things tight. When Marty got the inheritance, it seemed like a miracle."

"I was surprised when you told me he'd agreed to buy a house. It doesn't sound like his style."

"Oh, it wasn't. We had huge fights. In the end, he gave in, but with a twist. We bought this place instead of a regular single-family home."

She glanced around at the high ceilings of her third-floor living area. "At first I hated it. The last thing I wanted was a big mortgage and a lot of remodeling. When Marty died, I was furious. I'd been left with this disaster. But over time, I realized it was the best thing that could have happened. We get a lot of tourists up here, and many of them love the idea of staying at a bed-and-breakfast. I've been able to do most of the remodeling myself, which has saved a lot of money. I make my own schedule, and I'm here when the boys get home from school. A regular job would mean day care and that would be financially impossible."

"Interesting information," he said, "but you haven't answered the question."

"We do okay," she told him. "Some months are tight,

some aren't. I did manage to keep a small life insurance policy up on Marty so when he died there was some money from that. I put it away. If push comes to shove, it's my emergency fund. Fingers crossed I never have to use it." She held up one hand.

"If all goes well," she continued, "I'll use it to pay for the boys' college. So I'm fine. Really."

He smiled. "You're more than fine. You're responsible, giving and a great mom."

His compliment pleased her, which she told herself was silly. Still, she sat a little straighter and fought the urge to beam.

"I try."

"You succeed."

She shifted and, still facing him, leaned against the back of the sofa. "Okay, fair's fair. You got to ask me a very personal question and now I get to do the same."

"All right."

She thought about all the possibilities and settled on the one that troubled her the most.

"Tell me about your wife."

She watched closely, but Nash's expression didn't change.

"What do you want to know?"

"Whatever you want to tell me. Whatever…"

Her voice trailed off as a horrifying thought occurred to her. Did he not want to talk about the woman because she still mattered so much? He'd claimed not to be thinking about her when they made love, but what if he'd been lying? What if there were ghosts who—

"That's not the reason," he said.

She blinked at him. "What are you talking about?"

"I'm hedging because I don't know what to say about her, not because I'm heartbroken."

"That's a relief." She pressed her lips together. "Wait a minute. How did you know what I was thinking?"

"It was a logical assumption."

"Uh-huh."

She didn't buy that for a second. But what other explanation could there be? How strange that Nash knew her so well after just a short period of time, and despite all their years together, Marty had never known her at all. Was Marty's lack of knowledge due to some flaw within him, or had he never found her all that interesting?

"When I started working for the FBI," he said, "I quickly learned that emotional detachment was an asset. Nearly every situation is difficult on some level and leading with your heart is a good way to make the wrong decision. Staying emotionally distant was something I'd learned while I was growing up and it served me well at the bureau."

Having heard about his close family, Stephanie couldn't imagine how or why Nash would detach. Sometimes he seemed a little distant with his family, but that could have been shyness or emotional reserve. Nothing about his relationship with her and her kids indicated he was anything but emotionally available, but this wasn't the time to go into that particular subject. She filed the question away to spring on him later.

"I've told you a bit about Tina. She was my opposite. Emotional, disorganized, leading with her heart instead of her head. I wasn't even sure I liked her at first." His gaze narrowed slightly. "I'm talking about after she was an agent. I never considered her as anything but a coworker during training."

"Of course not," she murmured, believing him. Nash would never break that kind of rule.

"Dating led to more dating. After a while Tina suggested we live together. Marriage seemed like the next logical step."

How interesting, she thought. Had Tina been the one guiding the relationship? Nash almost made it sound like he was only along for the ride.

"How old were you when you got married?" she asked.

"Twenty-seven."

Okay—the right age for most guys to think about settling down. So had Tina been in the right place at the right time? Not a question she would be asking.

Stephanie resisted the urge to slap herself upside the head. She knew exactly what she was doing. If she could convince herself to believe Nash had married Tina because it was "time" and not because he was wildly in love with her, somehow that would make Stephanie feel better about their relationship. Crazy but true. She told herself to get over it.

"You didn't have a chance to have kids," she said. "I guess she passed away before you got around to that."

He shrugged. "We never talked about it. I always

wanted children. I guess Tina did, too. Then she was killed."

"How?" she asked before she could stop herself.

"In the line of duty. A bomb exploded."

She'd been expecting a lot of answers, just not that one. A bomb sounded so violent. Because it *was* violent, she thought. Violent and unexpected and shocking.

"I'm sorry," she whispered.

"Thanks."

Nash's expression hadn't changed as he talked, but there was something in his eyes that tugged at her heart.

"Want to talk about this more or change the subject?" she asked.

"Let's move on."

"Okay. So how did a guy with a twin brother and close friends learn to disconnect emotionally while he was growing up?" she asked.

He shook his head. "Easier than you might think. My mom married a guy when Kevin and I were twelve. Howard and I never got along."

That surprised her. "Still? But he and your mother are expected the day after tomorrow. Is that going to be a problem?" She frowned. "Why on earth did you want them staying here if you two aren't speaking?"

"We're speaking. And we get along."

The words sounded right, but she wasn't sure she believed them. "You're not going to be yelling at each other in the foyer, are you?"

"No. If there's any yelling, we'll do it outside where it belongs."

She smiled. "Fair enough. So is this emotional detachment you're so fond of the reason you haven't gotten involved with anyone else since your wife's death?"

"No. I've avoided relationships because I loved Tina and I can't ever love anyone else again."

Stephanie stared at him for several heartbeats, then burst out laughing. "Oh, come on. That's ridiculous. You can't love again? Did we move from real life to a TV soap? Are you saying the human heart is capable of only loving once? What about my three kids? Should I send the twins back because I already loved Brett when they arrived?"

Nash looked as shocked as if she'd pulled a gun on him. The charged silence between them made her wonder if she'd gone too far. He couldn't be serious about not loving again—people didn't work like that. But did he believe it? Had she just insulted him big-time?

She waited anxiously as he stared at her. She couldn't read his expression…not until one corner of his mouth twitched.

"You're not buying my best line?" he asked at last.

Relief swept through her. "Not for a second. Who has?"

"Everyone but you."

"I see. Are these 'everyones' women?"

"For the most part."

"Then you need to start dating women with slightly higher IQs."

He laughed and grabbed her around the waist, then hauled her onto his lap. "I prefer my women to have a little more respect than you do, missy."

She settled her hands on his shoulders and brushed his mouth with hers. "That so isn't going to happen as long as you talk like an idiot."

"Idiot, huh? I'm one idiot you can't resist."

She leaned in to kiss him again. "You're right about that," she whispered and gave herself up to him.

Chapter 12

"Batter up," Brett called, as he tossed the baseball in the air and caught it. "Adam, it's your turn."

Adam walked to the square marked on the grass in front of the house and clutched his bat. From what Nash could tell, Adam might be the quieter twin, but he was the better athlete. So far he'd been the one to hit the ball every time Brett pitched it.

Brett pitched a slow ball and Adam swung. There was a *crack* as the bat connected, then the ball flew directly back to Brett who had to jump to catch it.

"Good hit," he called to his brother.

Nash stood at the end of the porch, leaning against the house. The boys were playing in the side yard to, as Stephanie put it, "Avoid as many windows as possible."

The late morning was warm and clear—the perfect weather for the start of summer vacation.

The boys had tumbled out of bed surprisingly early, apparently too excited by the thought of no school to sleep late. Stephanie had predicted their behavior, which meant she'd left his bed around four in the morning. He'd slept until he'd heard not-so-quiet footsteps on the stairs about quarter to seven. He was tired and his eyes felt gritty, but lack of sleep was a small price to pay for spending the night with a woman who defined female beauty and sexuality.

He quickly checked his thoughts, knowing that if he dwelled on all they'd done together while in bed, he would end up in a very uncomfortable state. It didn't seem to matter how many times they made love; he always wanted her more. Last night had been no different.

He heard the front door open, then the sound of footsteps on the porch.

"They should be here any minute," Stephanie said as she stopped beside him and leaned against the railing. She glanced at him. "Are you sure you're going to be okay with your mom and stepfather staying here?"

He smiled. "I'm more than fine. I'm actually looking forward to their visit."

She didn't look convinced. "I would buy that a lot more easily if you hadn't told me you and your stepfather didn't get along."

"The problem's all on my side," Nash admitted, for the first time feeling comfortable with the truth. "Don't worry."

"I'll try not to." She turned toward the street, as if watching for cars. "If they're going to be staying here, we're going to have to be more careful about our sneaking around."

"Good point." One he hadn't considered.

She turned back to smile at him. "It will make things more exciting."

"I don't think that's possible. Not without one of us having a heart attack from the stress."

Her smile broadened. "Are you saying your affair with me is stressful?"

"I'm saying it's already more exciting than I thought possible. More excitement could be dangerous."

"But you're a big tough guy. Don't you live for danger?"

Her teasing words produced a predictable reaction. He ignored the sense of heat and heaviness flooding south. Good thing, too, because about eight seconds later a four-door sedan pulled up behind his rental car.

"They're here," he said.

Stephanie straightened. The humor faded from her eyes, replaced by worry. "Do I look okay?"

Despite the potential for an interested onlooker, he leaned forward and dropped a kiss on her mouth. "You look perfect."

Her expression cleared. "Excellent answer."

They walked to the porch steps, then onto the pathway. As they approached, the car doors opened. Nash's mother, Vivian, stepped out onto the sidewalk and smiled.

"What a lovely town. It's so charming. Nash, I swear, you're still getting taller."

He chuckled at the familiar claim, then folded her into his arms. "Hey, Mom. How was the trip?"

"Great." She kissed his cheek, then smoothed back his hair and rested her hands on his shoulders. "How are you?"

The question was about more than his state of being that day. He knew she wanted him to move on with his life, to let go of the past. To find someone else and settle down. He figured it was a "mom" thing.

"I'm good."

"Really?" Her gaze searched his face. "I hope so."

The car door slammed and she turned toward her husband. "Doesn't Nash look taller, Howard?"

"Viv, I'm going to guess our boy stopped growing a few years back," Howard said affectionately. He circled around the car and offered Nash his hand. As they shook, he patted Nash on the shoulder. "Good to see you. Life treating you well?"

"Always."

Nash stepped back and introduced Stephanie. "She owns Serenity House," he said. "You haven't lived until you've had her breakfasts."

"Nice to meet you, Mr. and Mrs. Harmon," she said. "I hope you'll enjoy your stay."

"Please call us Vivian and Howard," his mother said.

"Thank you."

There were a couple of yells from around the side of the house. Stephanie glanced in that direction. "I have three sons you'll meet later. While we live on the floor above your room, please don't worry. We're not directly overhead."

"We're going to have a lovely time," Vivian said, then tucked a strand of dark hair behind her ear. "How long have you had the bed-and-breakfast?" she asked.

"Almost four years. Would you like to see your room?"

"That would be nice."

Vivian turned to her husband. "Do you need me to carry anything in? I don't want you doing all the work."

Howard smiled at his wife. "I like taking care of you. Go on in and register. I'm sure Nash is going to insist on carrying the heaviest bag. We'll be fine."

Vivian nodded and touched Howard's arm. The contact wasn't anything special, just a brief brush of fingers, something Nash could remember having seen his mother do hundreds of times before. Yet for the first time, he saw the affection between the couple, the expression of happiness and contentment on his mother's face. She loved this man—she had for nearly twenty years.

The two women walked toward the house. Howard opened the trunk and laughed when he saw all the luggage. "Now you know why I had to rent a full-size car at the airport. Your mother isn't one to travel light. She always brings extras, just in case. I figure she packed enough for us to take a trip around the world, although she wouldn't agree. I guess if we ever did that, she'd want to bring the whole house. Just in case."

He shook his head, then started removing suitcases. Howard talked about the flight and who was looking in on their house while they were gone. As he spoke, Nash realized that there wasn't any strain between them. At least not on Howard's part.

They carried in the luggage and found Vivian and Stephanie by the registration desk.

"I was just telling your mother that the boys are pretty well behaved," Stephanie said. "There shouldn't be much noise."

Vivian shook her head. "And I was telling Stephanie that I miss the noise of having my boys in the house."

"I doubt that," Nash said. "You were always yelling at us to turn down the music or the TV or to stop revving our car engines in the driveway."

"Was I?" Vivian asked with a laugh. "I don't remember that at all."

"Would you like some lunch when you've unpacked?" Stephanie asked. "I don't have a restaurant here, but I would be delighted to make sandwiches, and I have several kinds of salad."

"That sounds lovely, dear," Vivian said. She linked arms with Stephanie. "Show me the way to the kitchen and I'll help while Howard and Nash take our things upstairs."

Stephanie looked a little startled by the suggestion. "You're a guest."

"Nonsense. I want to help. Or at least keep you company. You can tell me about your boys."

Stephanie glanced at Nash who gave her a smile. "You'll be fine," he said.

"Of course she will be," his mother said. "Now where's the kitchen?"

"Extra cheese on my sandwich," Howard called after them.

Vivian waved her fingers at him and laughed. "He always reminds me," she said as the two women turned down the hall. "As if I ever forget."

Nash picked up the key Stephanie had left on the desk and the two suitcases he'd brought in. "Ready to take these upstairs?" he asked.

"Lead the way."

They climbed to the second floor. Nash noticed right away that his room wasn't close to theirs, which meant he and Stephanie wouldn't have to tiptoe back and forth once everyone was in bed. Good planning on her part, he thought with a grin.

The room she'd chosen for them was large, with a king-size bed and a big bay window. Howard set his suitcases on the bed, took the ones Nash had carried and dropped them on the other side of the mattress.

"How are things going here?" Howard asked as he opened a garment bag and pulled out a suit, a sports coat and several dresses. "When Kevin called he said you two had already met your brothers."

"We've had a few group functions, as well as a lunch. When the whole Haynes family gets together, there are dozens of people. Everyone is married and has kids."

"Are they really all in law enforcement?"

"Except for Jordan. He's a firefighter."

Howard hung up the clothes. "Interesting. You and Kevin have followed in their footsteps. Gage and his brother, too." He returned to the bed and opened the largest suitcase. "Are they good men?"

Nash nodded. "Even the firefighter."

Howard chuckled. "Your mother worried about how things would go when you and Kevin arrived. Would the other brothers accept you two? Would you accept them? We're both glad it worked out." He scooped out toiletries and carried them into the bathroom. "We keep telling each other that you're grown up enough that we don't have to be concerned anymore, but maybe parents never let go of that."

Nash followed his stepfather into the bathroom. "You don't mean me," he said. "I wasn't the one getting into trouble."

Howard set two zippered cases on the counter. "True, but we wanted the best for you. You haven't been yourself for a while. I'm glad to see you getting back to normal."

He headed back to the bedroom and Nash followed. He knew that he'd been burying himself in his work, but he hadn't realized anyone but his boss had noticed.

"You mean because I'm finally taking a vacation?" he asked.

Howard shrugged. "That's part of it. Mostly you're smiling again. It's been a long time."

"Since Tina's death." Nash wasn't asking a question.

"No. The change happened before that." Howard picked up several shirts, then set them back in the suitcase and faced Nash. "There wasn't anything wrong with Tina. She was a perfectly nice young woman. But your mother and I never thought she was right for you.

She was flighty and impulsive. Despite the parts of your job that force you to make split-second decisions, you're a thoughtful man. You consider your options. You use reason. Tina wasn't a good match for that."

Nash didn't know what to say. Howard's comments stunned him. Apparently Howard and his mother had thought his marriage to Tina was a mistake from the beginning, but they'd never said anything.

"Now, Stephanie seems like a nice sort of woman," Howard said, resuming his unpacking. "It takes someone sensible to make a business successful. Vivian mentioned she's a widow. She was very young when her husband died."

The not-so-subtle matchmaking got Nash's attention. "Don't go there," he warned. "My stay here is temporary."

"You could move. You don't have any ties to Chicago." He smiled. "Okay, I'll be quiet. We don't care what you do, Nash, we just want you to be happy."

"Thanks. I appreciate that."

Howard mentioned something about how the Texas Rangers were doing that season. While Nash responded, he wasn't listening all that closely. Part of him was thinking about what the other man had said. About being happy. Nash couldn't remember the last time he could claim that. It had been well before Tina's death. Had it been before Tina?

Did it matter? Wasn't the more important point that he was happy now…maybe for the first time in years.

"I don't have enough plates," Stephanie said, trying not to panic. "Or glasses."

"Use plastic," Nash called as he walked through the utility room and out to the garage where there were several folding chairs.

"Use plastic," she muttered. "Easy for him to say." Although it was a pretty good idea. Did she have plastic?

She stopped in the center of the kitchen and tried to figure out if she'd stored any extra plastic glasses and plates after a birthday party for the twins. She dashed to a cupboard and pulled it open. Three unopened packages of plates sat on a top shelf she couldn't reach. At least she was making progress.

Nash returned with four chairs. "There are a couple more out there."

"We've brought down the chairs from upstairs, plus the ones in the dining room." She grimaced. "It's not nearly enough."

"Hey, stop sweating the details."

"You call having a place for people to sit a detail?"

"Sure. The kids will be happy on the ground." He put down the chairs and crossed to her. After resting his hands on her waist, he kissed her. "Thank you for offering to host the dinner."

Just being near him made her feel more calm. "I'm happy to have your family over. Really. But I need you to get those plates down for me."

When she took them from him, she happened to glance at her watch. The time made her shriek. "They're due back at any second. Get the chairs set up. I'll start stacking flatware."

Nash did as he was told and Stephanie raced to collect forks and spoons.

Kevin had called earlier to suggest another impromptu dinner for the family. Rather than cook, he'd offered to get Chinese. Stephanie had volunteered her place as the location. Vivian and Howard had taken the boys to meet Kevin and Haley at the Chinese restaurant, where they would buy enough food to feed the army that was the extended Haynes/Harmon/Reynolds family.

"Glasses," she murmured. "The sodas are already cooling in the big tub outside. I have milk and juice for the kids. I made iced tea. There's a—"

A faint double ring caught her attention. She spun in place. "Nash, your cell phone is ringing."

"Can you grab it?" he called from the utility room. "It's on the front desk with my keys."

She ran to the front of the house. The ringing got louder as she approached. When she saw the phone, she picked it up and pressed Talk.

"Hello?"

There was a moment of silence before a man asked, "I'd like to speak with Nash Harmon."

"Sure. Just a second."

She hurried into the hallway and found Nash carrying in more chairs. "It's for you," she said. "I'll take those."

"They'll wait," he told her and leaned them against the wall and reached for the phone.

She'd been about to politely retreat to the kitchen, but he put his arm around her and drew her close.

"Harmon," he said into the phone.

She couldn't hear what the man was saying, so she contented herself with relaxing against Nash's strong, broad chest. She closed her eyes and breathed deeply.

His chest rumbled as he spoke. "I thought you didn't want me taking on any more assignments," he said.

After listening for a while longer he said, "I'll think about it and get back to you." He chuckled. "None of your business. Uh-huh. Yeah, she's gorgeous. Tough luck. Get your own girl." A pause. "Okay. I'll let you know in a few days."

He hung up the phone.

"Your boss?" Stephanie asked, trying not to preen about the *Yeah, she's gorgeous* remark.

Nash nodded. "He wanted to tell me about a job opening up that I might be interested in. Different city, change of scene. He thought it would do me good."

She glanced at him. "Why do you need that?"

He tucked the phone into his shirt pocket and wrapped his other arm around her. "I didn't have a choice about my vacation. My boss insisted I take time off. He's been worried that I'm burning out."

That surprised her. "Why?"

"I haven't taken any time off since Tina died."

Stephanie's retreat was instinctive. Before she knew what she was doing, she'd pulled away far enough to lean against the opposite wall in the hall. She hated that Nash was no longer smiling.

"You're burying yourself in work?" she asked, knowing the question wasn't much of a stretch.

"Yeah, but not for the reasons you think."

She didn't know *what* she thought. She only knew she didn't want him still to be in love with his late wife.

"Then what are the reasons?" she asked, careful to keep her voice neutral.

He sucked in a breath and stared at a spot well above her head. "I told you Tina was killed in the line of duty, by a bomb blast. What I didn't tell you is that I was there. I'd been called in to negotiate a hostage situation. I convinced the guys to give up. When they came out, I knew something wasn't right, but I couldn't figure out what. Later I realized things had gone too easily. I told the team to wait, but Tina didn't listen. She was her usual impulsive self. About ten seconds after she ran into the building to free the hostages, I found out why they'd given up."

Stephanie didn't want to think about it, didn't want to imagine it, but she knew what had happened. "The bomb went off."

He nodded, his face expressionless. "Tina, another agent and all the hostages were killed."

He blamed himself. She knew that because she knew Nash, and because under the same circumstances she might have blamed herself. Foolish, but true. "No one else thinks it's your fault."

He looked at her. "You don't know that."

"Am I wrong?"

"No."

"So you blame yourself and you bury yourself in work. Now your boss is offering a different job, thinking that the change will snap you out of it."

"Something like that."

"Do you need to be snapped out of it?"

His body relaxed. "Not right now. You're good for me, Stephanie."

His words warmed her in a way that had nothing to do with heat and everything to do with her heart. He was good for her, too. He made her want to believe in love and hope and the future. He made her want…

She mentally winced. No, don't go there, she told herself. Nash was temporary, remember? There was no point in wishing for the moon. She would only end up disappointed, with a crick in her neck.

"I aim to provide a full-service establishment," she said lightly. "Don't forget to mention all this on your comment card. It will impress the management."

He moved toward her. "I'm serious. Since I've met you—"

Whatever he'd been about to say got lost in the sound of car doors slamming. She was dying to know what he'd been about to say, but they were about to be invaded by the entire Haynes family.

"Save that thought," she told him even though she knew they would never discuss this topic again. She knew because she was going to make sure it never happened. Whatever Nash might want to tell her, it wasn't the one thing she wanted to hear. Namely that he'd decided to stay.

"I could never do what you do," Howard said the next morning.

"Most of my job is paperwork," Nash reminded him as they jogged through the quiet neighborhood.

"But when it isn't, there are lives on the line. I admire your ability to deal with that."

There was pride in Howard's voice as he spoke—a father's pride in his child. Nash realized he'd heard it dozens of times before. Maybe from the first time he'd met Howard. Hell, he thought, feeling like an idiot. He'd been so busy resenting his stepfather, he'd never noticed the man cared about him. Loved him.

"You had a hard time when you started dating Mom," Nash said. "I remember Kevin and I making things tough on you."

Howard grinned. "You made me work for my place," he said, his breathing slightly labored. "But it was worth it. Besides, I was crazy about your mother. A couple of my friends were worried that she was only interested in finding a father for you and your brother, but I loved her too much to care. Of course they were wrong. I guess nearly twenty years of marriage has proved that."

They reached the corner and paused to check traffic before jogging across the street. The morning was clear and still a little cool, although it would warm up later.

"We were twelve when you two started going out," Nash said. "If she'd wanted to find someone to be a father for us, she would have started looking earlier."

Howard glanced at him, then wiped the sweat from his forehead. "You were heading toward being teenagers. That's when boys really need a man around. Your mother worried about you."

Howard had mentioned something similar the day before. "Why me? I was the good kid."

"Right. As the bad kid, Kevin got all the attention. Vivian was afraid you'd get forgotten in all the fuss. We talked about it a lot before we were married."

Nash felt as if he'd missed out on most of what was going on while he'd been growing up. "Why didn't I know about any of this?"

"You weren't supposed to. You were the child."

They reached the edge of the middle-school playground and turned around.

Howard slowed to a walk. "Whew. I'm not getting any younger."

"You're still in great shape."

Howard grinned. "You're lying, but thanks. Anyway, Kevin continued to get into trouble and you continued to be the perfect child. When Kevin stole that car, we didn't know what to do. The police were the ones who suggested the military school. We figured they would probably be able to straighten him out and with Kevin gone, you'd have a chance to shine."

Nash didn't think there were any more surprises to be had, but he'd been wrong. "I didn't think you'd sent him away because of me," he said, oddly humbled by the information.

"Not because of you. Kevin was hell on wheels. But our concern about you swayed our decision." Howard slapped him on the back. "You're both like my own sons. I would have loved Vivian as much without you two as part of the package, but just between us, knowing you boys came along with the deal made it irresistible."

Nash didn't know what to say. He felt awkward and foolish. As if he'd been playing by one set of rules all these years, when there had been a completely different game in play.

"Howard," he began slowly. "I—"

The older man smiled. "I know, Nash. I've always known. I love you, too."

In celebration of the kids all being out of school, the Haynes/Harmon/Reynolds family took over the large back room of the local pancake restaurant.

Nash sat at the big U-shaped table and listened to all the conversations flowing around him. In a crowd like this, his instinct was to withdraw—to observe rather than participate. But since his early-morning jog with his stepfather, he'd realized he'd better stop assuming anything about himself or his life. Apparently nothing was as he'd thought it had been.

All those years wasted, he thought sadly. Howard had been there for him and he'd never noticed. What else had he missed in his life?

The sound of laughter interrupted his thoughts. He looked across the table and saw Stephanie and Elizabeth laughing together. Petite, with short blond hair and a mouth designed specifically to drive him mad, Stephanie was a walking, breathing fantasy. He liked how she fit in with his family. In less than twenty-four hours she and his mother had become fast friends. She managed to keep his brothers, their spouses and kids straight.

He wanted her. That was hardly news, but the feeling this morning was different. He wanted more than sex. He wanted—

Nothing he was going to get, he reminded himself and looked away. He glanced around the table and saw Brett watching him. He smiled at the boy, who started to smile back, then instead turned away. Ironically, Nash knew exactly what the kid was thinking. He still saw Nash as a threat.

He thought about trying to reassure Brett again, but figured there wasn't any point. He, Nash, hadn't listened to Howard all those years ago. Why would Brett listen to him? Still he wished he had the right words. Life would be easier for Brett if he understood, just as life would have been a whole lot easier for Nash if he'd known that Howard wasn't a problem. All those wasted years when they could have been close.

He hated the regrets. The "could have beens." And he didn't just have them with Howard. What about his regrets with Tina? Their marriage had never been picture-perfect. Maybe if he'd worked harder to make it better. Maybe then he wouldn't feel so damn guilty all the time. Maybe—

His brain cleared. It was as if he'd been looking through a fog for the past two years, since the day of his wife's death.

Haltingly, almost afraid of what he would see, he looked at his brothers and their wives and fiancées. He looked at their faces, their eyes, and the way they were always touching. Husbands and wives in love with each other.

Love. That's what had been wrong with his marriage. He'd gone through the motions, but that's all it had been. He should never have married Tina because he'd never loved her. And it had taken him the better part of two years to figure that out.

Chapter 13

Stephanie watched the clock impatiently. It was 11:27 p.m. She and Nash had agreed she would head downstairs at 11:30 p.m. After some debate they'd decided it would be easier for her to explain her presence going up to her own floor than for him to say why he was heading down from hers.

In theory there was no reason to sneak. While it was best her children didn't know that she and Nash had become intimate, would it really matter to his parents? Not that she was going to suggest they spill the beans. In a way, having to wait heightened anticipation. She was already trembling slightly at the thought of seeing him and there was a definite heaviness low in her belly. One would think they had made love enough times for some of the thrill to be fading, but one would be wrong.

Two more minutes passed. At exactly 11:30 p.m., she picked up her shoes, a travel alarm set for four in the morning and tiptoed out of her room. She made it down the hall to the stairs without making a sound then headed to the floor below.

At the third stair from the bottom, she stepped as close to the wall as possible to avoid the creaky step, then reached the second level and headed for Nash's room.

The door was already open. She stepped inside, prepared to remind him that she had to make it back to her own bed before anyone was stirring, but she wasn't given the opportunity to speak.

He'd been standing in the center of the room, just out of the pool of light given off by the bedside lamp. As she entered, he crossed to her and pulled her close. As his arms wrapped around her body, his mouth settled on hers. The deep, sensual, demanding kiss turned her bones to liquid.

She melted against him. Wanting flooded her, barely giving her enough time to drop her shoes and set the clock on the dresser. The door closed with a soft thud, then Nash's hands were everywhere—her back, her hips, her waist, her breasts.

They'd been together enough times that he knew what she liked, what she loved and what made her scream with delight, and he used that knowledge to reduce her to a quivering shell of need. His long fingers gently massaged the curves of her breasts, moving closer to her already tight nipples without actually touching them. Anticipation built inside her.

She squirmed closer, silently begging him to touch her there, but he was slow to respond. Closer and closer still until his thumbs lightly brushed over the tips of her nipples. One brief caress, then he was gone.

She groaned her frustration. Determined to tease him as much as he teased her, she withdrew from the kiss and began to suck on his lower lip. At the same time, she cupped his rear, digging her fingers into the firm flesh and bringing his arousal more closely in contact with her stomach. They both caught their breath.

"I want you," Nash breathed. "Naked."

His words increased her need, delighting her. In a smooth dance they'd performed before, they broke apart and quickly tugged at their clothes. She finished first and slid onto the cool sheet. Nash followed.

They lay facing each other, his leg between hers, his thigh pressing against her swollen dampness. As they kissed, he cupped her left breast. Their tongues stroked and played. When he retreated, she followed. His taste, his heat, his hardness all inflamed her. She could not be naked enough with this man. She wanted to be vulnerable, hungry and bare to him. Yes, she wanted the pleasure to follow, but for now it was enough to want him.

When he urged her onto her back, she went easily. He broke the kiss and knelt between her thighs. His mouth settled on her chest. As his tongue swept over and around the tight nipple, his fingers matched the action on her other breast. Her muscles tightened as pleasure poured through her, trickling down to increase her growing ache. She felt herself swelling, readying. Already she wanted him inside her, but that was for later. First Nash would want to make her beg.

He kept his attention on her breasts until she was close to breaking. Tension filled her body, making every muscle stiffen. When she nearly vibrated with need, he moved lower, placing openmouthed kisses on her belly, then lower still.

He reached for her hands and brought them to her center, where he had her part herself for him. She drew her knees back and dug her heels into the mattress. Her eyes were closed, but she knew he was close—she could feel his warm breath fanning her dampness. She was ready, so ready. Ready and aching. Her hips pulsed in silent invitation. And still he waited.

At last he moved close and pressed his tongue against her. Fire shot through her, making her jump and gasp. The single, slow lick was followed by another and another. Gentle, easy strokes that drove her to the edge of madness. He didn't go fast enough to take her to climax, but he didn't let the tension fall off, either.

She strained to get more pressure, she rocked her hips to get him to go faster. Neither worked. She tried begging.

"Nash, please."

She felt the rumble of his laughter. In response to her plea, he inserted a finger inside her then curled it slightly, so it seemed to stroke her from the inside as his tongue did the same from the outside. He moved them in tandem. Slowly. Gently. Thoroughly. Bottom to top. Top to bottom. Over and over. Like the ticking of a clock. Ever so steady. Ever so slow.

Her entire body clenched. She couldn't breathe, couldn't think, couldn't do anything but focus on that incessant rhythm. Over and over. Tension grew and grew until she thought it would split her in two. More. She needed more. She needed—

He stopped completely. For the space of three heartbeats he hovered above her, not touching, not moving. Nothing. The wait was unbearable. Then he kissed her again, but more firmly this time, and faster.

She climaxed without warning. The release swept through her at the speed of sound, flinging her into paradise and making her cry out. Muscles contracted, her entire body spasmed in perfect pleasure. She was out of control and she never wanted that to change.

He continued to touch her, gentling the contact, until she had nothing left.

She opened her eyes and saw him smiling at her. She had to clear her throat before she could speak.

"That was more amazing than usual," she told him. "Which is saying something."

"You're easy to please."

"I'm glad you think so."

She lowered her gaze and saw that he was still hard. Her stomach clenched.

"I want you inside me," she said.

Words to live by, Nash thought as he reached for

the condom he'd left on the nightstand. As he slipped it on, he studied the flush on Stephanie's chest and cheeks. The physical proof of her orgasm pleased him. He wanted her to enjoy their time in bed.

When he'd put on the protection, he slowly pushed into her. She was hot and wet. As he filled her, her muscles contracted around his erection, testing his control. He forced himself to hold back. He wanted her to come again.

Still kneeling, he shifted his weight off his arms so he could reach out to touch her breasts. They were always exquisitely sensitive after her first release. Just lightly brushing her nipples was usually enough to get her going again. He wanted to feel her rippling contractions and watch her face as she experienced wave after wave of orgasm. Her mouth would part slightly, her eyes would widen as she tried to keep looking at him. Sometimes he would swear he could see down to her soul.

Sure enough, with the first touch of his fingers, she gasped. He felt the tight clenching of her body. He thrust into her again and contractions massaged him. Blood surged into his arousal, pressure built in his groin, and still he held back.

Their gazes locked. With each rhythmic release, she sucked in a breath and whispered his name. Over and over, as if in prayer. He was getting closer, too, but he wanted this to go on as long as they both could stand it.

In and out, in and out. He got harder and harder.

Deep inside everything collected for the surging release that was as inevitable as the tide. She continued
to climax, massaging him, drawing him in deeper. Her
breathing increased. He surged in faster and faster.
They were both gasping.

At last he had to release her breasts and grasp her
hips. He held on to her as he pumped in and out. She
half raised off the bed. Her head dropped back as one
massive contraction clenched around him…and he was
lost.

His release exploded in a vortex of heat that forced
the air out of his body. He pushed in deeper, wanting
her to take all of him. Her dampness continued to con-
vulse around him, drawing out the bliss until there was
nothing left for either of them but to fall together in a
tangle of arms and legs.

Stephanie woke with a sense of contentment. She
rolled onto her back and smiled. Last night had been
amazing. More amazing than usual, which was saying
something. But her feeling of happiness didn't just
come from a night of great lovemaking. It also came
from the recent changes in her life.

She liked Nash. Okay, she liked him a lot. She liked
being around him and talking to him. She liked his parents and his brothers and their families. She liked the
impact he'd made on her world. She liked how he was
with her sons. Man, oh, man, did she have it bad. Because liking him wasn't the problem.

She wanted more.

Stephanie sat up and tossed off the covers. "Don't be ridiculous," she said aloud. "There is no 'more' in this situation. You knew that when you started the affair."

But knowing and believing were two different things, at least in her world. She could list all the reasons it would never work—distance, her reluctance to trust a man to act like a partner and not a child, his emotional withdrawal from life since the death of his wife. Those were really big problems to get through. While they could be solved if both of them worked at it, so far she hadn't seen any indication that Nash wanted to change the status of things. Nor was she going to.

In a few days, when his vacation was over, he would leave, and she would let him. No matter what, she wouldn't make a scene. It wasn't right to change the rules at this late date.

Not that she wanted to, she reminded herself. When Nash left, she would go on with her life and she would do just fine. Sure she would miss him, but she would get over it…wouldn't she?

Stephanie didn't want to think about any of that. She stretched and swung around to put her feet on the floor. As she did so she glanced at the clock. And actually screamed.

It was eight-thirty. In the morning. Her alarm had been set for six-thirty. What had happened?

Even as she fumbled for the switch and realized she'd forgotten to turn it on, adrenaline rushed through her body, galvanizing her into action. She raced into the bathroom where she quickly washed her face and brushed her teeth. A shower was going to have to wait. She had guests to feed.

In less than six minutes she was relatively groomed, dressed and racing down the stairs. The boys were already up—their doors were standing open—and she could hear voices from downstairs. Wincing at what Nash's parents must think of her, she jogged toward the kitchen and burst inside.

"Hey, Mom," Brett said from the table.

"Mommy!" the twins said together.

They were also at the table. They were eating breakfast. Pancakes and bacon from the looks of it. She stared around the room and saw Nash standing at the stove. The man was cooking!

"Morning," he said with a smile.

While it wasn't as unbelievable as having aliens land on her roof, it was darned close. Helping out was one thing, but cooking? Marty had always acted as if she were threatening to cut off his right arm if she ever suggested he prepare a meal himself.

She felt numb with shock. "I, ah, overslept," she said. "I forgot to set my alarm."

Nash's expression didn't change, but his eyes brightened with amusement. "You probably had other things on your mind."

That was true. She'd been so concerned about setting her travel clock so that she could get back to her own bed, that she'd forgotten about her regular alarm.

"My folks are in the dining room," he continued. "They have coffee, fruit and the newspaper. Howard wanted oatmeal which I've already fixed. Mom is raving about your scones and complaining about the weight she's going to put on. I have another batch in the oven."

He nodded at the stove. "I was fixing some eggs for myself. Do you want any?"

She'd slipped into an alternative universe. "Um, thanks."

"Okay. Oh, when I took the uncooked scones out of the freezer, I didn't know which to use, so I took a bag off the top shelf. I hope that's okay."

"It's fine."

"Brett told me what oven temperature to use."

She glanced at her oldest. "Thanks, honey."

He shrugged. "Nash said you were tired and we should let you sleep."

She could feel her cheeks getting hot. Nash was the reason she needed her rest.

"Coffee?" the man in question asked.

She nodded. He poured her a cup, then added milk and sugar, just the way she liked it.

Her throat was tight and her eyes burned. She had a bad feeling she was way too close to tears for comfort. Which made no sense. So he'd been nice—was that a reason to cry?

Sense or not, Nash's actions touched her in a way nothing had for years. Maybe ever. He'd taken care of her. Just like that, with no expectation of getting something back. She hadn't known that men like him existed. He made her feel she could count on him.

"You okay?" he asked.

She nodded again, knowing it was impossible to speak.

Just then she heard the sound of several cars pulling up.

"What's that?" Jason asked and got down from his seat. He ran toward the front of the house.

"They're all here," he called.

"Who?" Adam asked as he, too, left the kitchen. Brett was on his heels.

"Right on time," Nash said, glancing at the clock.

"On time for what?" she asked, her voice only a little scratchy.

Nash grinned. "You'll see."

Howard came through the swinging door. "Seems that the gang has all arrived. Ready to assign chores?"

"Sure."

Nash slid the scrambled eggs onto a plate, along with a couple of pieces of bacon. "Eat up," he said. "You're going to need your strength. I'll be right back."

He walked out of the kitchen, heading toward the front door. Howard followed. Stephanie glanced from the plate to the door, and decided to see what was going on.

What she found stunned her nearly as much as seeing Nash cooking. Most of the Haynes clan had descended. All the brothers were there, along with Austin and several of the wives. There weren't as many children as usual. Instead of carrying food or drinks, this time everyone had gallons of paint, toolboxes, ladders and other building supplies. They gathered by the gate-house, as if waiting for instructions. Nash stood in the center of the group.

As she approached, she saw that he held a list in his hand and was assigning tasks.

"Upstairs in the master, there's some ugly wallpaper in the bathroom. Did anyone bring the steamer?"

"Sure." Kyle patted the machine he'd set on the driveway. "I'll have that off by noon. Then we can put up the new paper."

"We'll do that," Elizabeth said as she put her arm around Hannah. "It's a floral pattern and we're going to care more about getting it right."

Travis groaned. "Any of us could do just as good a job."

"Sure you *could,* but do you want to?"

He kissed her. "Not on a bet."

Several people laughed. Stephanie felt as if her feet were nailed to the grass. She couldn't move, couldn't speak, couldn't protest what was happening. She watched as everyone trooped into her gatehouse and began to work. Nash finally noticed her and walked over.

"You okay?" he asked.

"No. What are you doing?"

He stood facing her. "You'd ordered the paint and wallpaper already," he said. "I didn't pick it out."

"I know, but why are they here?"

"They're helping out because I asked. I know you've been working on the gatehouse for a long time. You want to move in there so you can get the rest of the house renovated. I want to help. I'm leaving in a few days and I would like the gatehouse done before I go. I guess I want to know that you're going to be okay."

He spoke the last bit defiantly, as if he expected her to be furious. She supposed she should be—he'd been high-handed in arranging all this. But the truth was, she was even closer to crying than before.

No one had ever wanted to take care of her before. No one had ever worried about her. They all assumed she was so damn competent that she didn't have doubts, didn't get tired, didn't sweat that it was going to come out right.

She ached down to her bones. Not just because he was being so sweet and nice and making her want to beg him to never leave, but because what he was doing was proof that he *was* leaving. If he'd considered changing his mind and staying, he wouldn't want to have the gatehouse finished.

"You mad?" he asked.

She shook her head because she couldn't speak.

"Is it okay that I'm doing this?"

She managed a slightly strangled "Yes."

"Will you be okay if I go help out?"

"Sure."

He touched her cheek, then walked toward the gatehouse.

Stephanie stood alone on her lawn and listened to the sound of people working and talking and laughing. She knew that she had to help out the others. It wasn't fair to leave everything to them. But first she had to get herself under control.

In that moment, when she'd realized what he was doing, something inside her had given way. It was as if some protective wall had crumbled to dust, leaving her exposed and vulnerable.

How could she help loving him? He wasn't even everything she'd ever wanted—he was more. A partner, a friend, a warm, caring lover who was as solid as a rock. He was her hero. A one-in-a-million kind of man.

A man who was leaving. And she didn't have a single right to ask him to stay.

By midafternoon, most of the rooms had been painted. Stephanie walked through the downstairs carrying cans of soda and bottles of water. The twins were circulating with granola bars and cookies.

The transformation of the dark old house into something bright and charming amazed her, as did everyone's friendliness. These people might be a part of Nash's family, but they made her feel welcome.

She handed Craig a bottle of water and started toward the kitchen. On the way she found Brett carefully sanding a baseboard in the hall.

"You're doing a great job," she said as she stopped and crouched next to him. "That's pretty detailed work."

Her twelve-year-old looked up at her. His blue eyes were dark and troubled. "Nash got his whole family to help."

"I know. That was really nice of him, huh?"

Brett didn't answer. Instead he folded the sandpaper in half and twisted it in his hands. "He's still leaving, right?"

As much as Stephanie wished she could say otherwise, she had to agree. "Of course he is, honey. He has a life in Chicago, remember?"

"He's not so bad, you know?" Brett's voice sounded small. "He's not Dad, but that's okay."

Her stomach dove for her toes. When had her son let go of his resentment of Nash and why hadn't she seen it happening? She hadn't wanted any of her children to connect too closely with Nash because she hadn't wanted them hurt by his leaving.

"Brett, Nash is a really great guy. He's been fun to have around, but it was always temporary. You knew that."

She winced at her own words. Of course he knew. Reminding him wasn't going to make Nash's leaving easier.

"But he likes it here," Brett said, staring at the sandpaper rather than her. "I bet he'd want to move here if you asked him to."

"I know it seems like that to you. I agree that he's had a fun vacation, which is good. But he has a regular life waiting for him. He has a job and a home and friends." But not a woman. She knew he'd been alone since his wife's death. And yes, the sex was great, but was it enough to get him to relocate? She didn't think so.

"You could ask," Brett repeated.

"I could."

But she wouldn't. Not only did she not want to put Nash in the position of having to refuse her, she wasn't sure she would survive actually having to hear him say no.

By five the gatehouse was nearly finished. Nash walked from room to room, pleased with all that had been done. All that was left was the new carpeting. As soon as Stephanie had that installed, she and the boys could move in. They'd have their own place, away from the guests. She would be safe.

He could see her here—her furniture, the boys' books and toys. They would make the small house into a home.

Could he see himself here?

The question brought him up short. Did he want to be here? Did he want to stay with Stephanie and her sons? That would mean getting involved. Emotions weren't safe, he reminded himself. Emotions were messy and couldn't be controlled. If life was out of control—

His cell phone rang. He pulled it out of his shirt pocket and pushed Talk.

"Harmon here."

"It's Jack," his boss told him. "We have a situation."

Five minutes later Nash turned off the phone and jogged toward the main house. He found Stephanie in the kitchen with Brett. She took one look at his face and blanched.

"What's wrong?" she asked.

"My boss called. There's a hostage situation in San Francisco at a bank robbery gone bad. Shots have been fired. A helicopter's on its way to pick me up." He glanced at his watch. "It's coming from the army base and should be here in about six minutes."

He'd wondered how she would react to the crisis, but except for the loss of color in her face, she was in control. "Do you need me to get you anything? Most of your family has left. Your parents took the twins to the park. I'll tell them when they get back."

"I appreciate that. I don't know how long I'll be gone. These things can take time. Then there's paperwork afterwards."

She dismissed his comments with a wave of her hand. "Don't worry about that. I'll pack your things and you can call us and let me know where you want them sent."

Her assumption that he wouldn't be coming back surprised him. Yes, he only had a few days left of his vacation but—

"I'm glad you're leaving," Brett said fiercely.

Nash turned to the boy and saw him wipe the back of his hand across his eyes. Hell.

He knelt in front of Brett. "I'm sorry I have to go, but this is important."

"I don't care."

"I care very much. About my work and about you, your brothers and your mom."

"Then don't go."

The words shouldn't have mattered to him, but God help him, he liked hearing them.

"Some bad men are holding people hostage. I have to go. If I don't some of them might die."

"Then promise to come back."

Stephanie put her hands on Brett's thin shoulders. "Honey, don't. Remember what we talked about? Nash has his own life and it's not here."

They'd talked about him? He stood and tried to read her expression. "Stephanie…" He wasn't sure what to say.

She shook her head. "We both knew this was temporary, right? So it's ending sooner than we thought. At least we're saved from having a long, painful goodbye. It's like ripping off a bandage. Faster is better."

"Faster hurts more," he said.

"But it's over quicker."

He wanted to tell her he would come back. He wanted to tell her that he didn't want to go in the first place. But to what end?

Before he could figure out what words were right, he heard a familiar sound. "The helicopter's here."

Outside several sheriff's cars had blocked off the street. Nash saw Kyle talking to one of the helicopter pilots.

Nash bent down and hugged Brett. Then he straightened and pulled Stephanie close.

"Take care of yourself," she said as she stepped back. There were tears in her eyes.

He felt as if he'd been kicked in the gut. There were a thousand things to say and no time left. His heart heavy, his chest tight, he jogged to the helicopter. Kyle slapped him on the back as he climbed in.

"Don't get dead," he called.

Nash gave him a thumbs-up, then yelled at the pilot to take off. He watched out the window until Stephanie and Brett were no more than specks. When he couldn't see them anymore, he watched anyway, knowing they were still standing there.

Chapter 14

By five in the morning the San Francisco sky had turned pale gray. Nash had lost count of the cups of coffee he'd consumed. He'd managed to talk the bank robbers into releasing the bodies of the two men they'd killed before Nash had arrived, and one pregnant woman who had gone into early labor. There were still fifteen people and three men with guns inside the ground-floor bank building.

FBI agents, local police and SWAT teams circled the high-rise. There were sharpshooters in place. The media was being kept at bay, with a live news feed being set up across the street.

Jack sat with Nash in the specially equipped vehicle in front of the bank.

"Now what?" Jack asked.

Nash didn't have an answer. Becker, the guy he'd been talking to for the past several hours, had seemed like he was ready to discuss releasing more hostages, but then had hung up unexpectedly. The bank's surveillance cameras had been disconnected by Becker and his buddies when they'd first taken hostages, so getting a look inside that way wasn't an option. A long-range camera had shown the three men having what looked like a heated argument.

"I'm guessing one of them doesn't agree with Becker's plan to give up," Nash said.

Sometimes that happened. Some criminals would rather shoot it out and face death than accept the consequences of prison. If that was the case, if a man was prepared to die, there weren't many rescue options.

"Can we take any of them out?" Jack asked.

Nash looked down at the bank floor plan he'd been given. Becker had said the hostages were being held in the vault. The door was open, but the civilians were still out of the main section of the bank. If Becker was telling the truth, then the sharpshooters could fire into the bank without hitting the hostages.

"We can't take one of them out," Nash said. "Even if we planned an armed assault for one or two seconds later, there would still be enough time for hostages to be killed. What are the odds of us getting all three of them at once? I don't want any dead civilians. Not on my watch."

Jack nodded. In this situation, Nash was in charge.

Nash rose and stepped out onto the sidewalk. The

street had been blocked off, which would be hell on the morning commute. His stomach grumbled.

Frowning, he tried to remember the last time he'd eaten. Not since arriving. The men inside hadn't, either. Or the hostages. He picked up the specially equipped cell phone that not only connected with Becker, but also activated a recording device and transmitted the call back to the FBI truck.

As he punched in the number, he shifted slightly. Then he had to move again. What the hell?

A rumbling sound grew as the ground began to roll.

Nash swore. Great. Just what his morning needed. A damn earthquake.

The rolling grew in intensity, as did the roaring sound. People began to yell. A few screamed. He looked up at the tall buildings all around him and figured he'd better head for cover. Just then the doors of the bank burst open.

A tall, dark-haired man ran onto the sidewalk.

"Don't shoot," he yelled, holding a cell phone in one hand and a gun in the other. He tossed the gun on the ground.

Nash was on him in a second. "Becker?" he yelled, even as he twisted the man's arm behind him and physically dragged him away from the bank.

"That damn building is swaying like a boat," the man cried out. "It's gonna fall and I'm not going to be crushed to death like some bug."

Behind him, still in the bank, another man was screaming for Becker to get his sorry butt back inside.

The ground continued to roll and shake, distracting everyone.

Nash grabbed his radio. "Now," he called out. "Get in there now!"

The rescue team swarmed the front of the bank. With the earthquake still rumbling Nash couldn't hear the crash of the bank's rear door being blown as the rest of the team entered that way. Three shots were fired, then there was silence. Nash clutched his radio.

"One gunman shot," a voice said. "One captured. The hostages are all safe."

"How are you going to explain the earthquake in your report?" Jack asked several hours later as he sat on a corner of Nash's temporary desk in the San Francisco office.

Nash leaned back in his chair. "Sometimes we get lucky. That's all it was."

"It was more than that," his boss said. "Before you arrived, they'd killed two people. You put a stop to that. You're good at what you do."

"Thanks."

Jack stood up. "Either I was wrong about you burning out or you got what you needed from your vacation. You're welcome to come back anytime you'd like." He grinned. "Is tomorrow too soon?"

Work. Nash's refuge. Was he ready to return so quickly?

"Let me get back to you on that," he said.

Jack raised his dark eyebrows. "You sure about that?"

Nash nodded. "I'll finish my report and see you on my way out."

"Fair enough."

He left and Nash turned his attention to the computer screen. But instead of entering his report, he found himself thinking about what had happened that morning. How a 4.2 earthquake had saved fifteen hostages. As he'd told Jack, it had been little more than dumb luck. As always, there were circumstances out of everyone's control. Even his.

He placed his fingers on the keyboard, then dropped his hands back onto the desk. Well, hell. What do you know, he thought grimly. He couldn't control the world. If he were honest with himself, he might admit he couldn't control much of anything. Life happened, and he didn't get to decide which way it was going to go. He'd never been able to decide. No matter what he wanted or expected or needed, life had its own plan and didn't consult with him.

Today he'd gotten lucky. Two years ago, he hadn't.

Nash rose and crossed to the window. He stared out at the skyline of the city, but instead of seeing the tall buildings, he saw the bomb explosion that had killed his wife.

He hadn't known. No one had known. Tina had acted impulsively. He hadn't killed her. He'd never been responsible. Maybe he'd never believed he was. Maybe wallowing in guilt over not stopping her death had been easier than facing the truth—he felt guilty because he'd never loved her.

He should never have married her. He saw that now. Maybe he'd always known that, too. But he'd been in his late twenties. It had been time for him to get married, settle down. She'd been there and she'd wanted him. He'd been flattered. When she'd suggested making things permanent, he couldn't think of a reason to say no. He cared about her, they got along. He hadn't known what love felt like. He hadn't known the possibilities.

But after a few months, he'd seen that they'd made a mistake. He'd tried to talk to Tina, but she'd refused to admit there was anything wrong. After a night of fighting, they'd gone to work and she'd been killed.

She'd deserved to be loved. Everyone did.

Including him.

Nash stiffened. Had he been the only one living out a part, or had Tina, too, been going through the motions? He would never know. He couldn't go back and make things right with her. But he could make the future better. He could let go of what had happened. He could learn from his mistakes. He could risk living again. He could risk love and belonging or he could continue to live on the outside, always looking in, never connecting.

One way was safe, one was guaranteed to be complicated and messy. What did he want? And what was he willing to risk to get it?

The twins sat on the edge of the bed and watched while she packed up Nash's clothes. According to the news, the hostage situation had ended that morning. Stephanie had been half expecting to get a phone call, but when noon came and went without a word, she accepted the fact that he was gone forever.

Reminding herself that she'd been the one to say he didn't have to come back wasn't making her feel any better. Nor were the boys' long faces.

Jason swung his feet back and forth, clunking his heels against the pedestal of the sleigh bed. "But Nash likes being here," he said mournfully.

"I know he had a good time," she said as she folded shirts and stacked them together. "You're supposed to enjoy your vacation."

Adam didn't speak. Instead he stared at her with eyes full of hurt.

Her own control was already more than a little shaky. It wouldn't take much to push her over the edge. She tried to smile.

"We'll be fine," she told the boys. "It's summer, so there's no school. Isn't that a good thing?"

They both nodded without a lot of enthusiasm. She knew how they felt. In less than a week, the B and B would be filled. She would be running around like a crazy person. But the thought of paying guests and plenty of work didn't ease the sharp pain in her chest. She felt as if her entire world had been shattered.

No more relationships, she vowed silently. She and the boys couldn't handle it. She'd gone and fallen in love with the first guy she'd slept with since Marty's death. Her sons were missing Nash, as well. If one man could mess up her life in just a couple of weeks, what would happen if she actually risked dating?

It wouldn't be the same, a small voice whispered. She sighed, knowing the words were true. She'd fallen in love with Nash. It didn't matter who she dated. He'd claimed her heart and it would be a long time before she was able to offer it to someone else again.

She dropped the shirts into the open suitcase, then faced the twins.

"I can't believe it's barely the first week of summer and you two have long faces," she said.

"Brett says he's not coming out of his room," Jason told her.

"I know. But you know what? I have a great idea that's going to make us all feel better."

Neither twin looked convinced. She didn't feel convinced, either, but she was going to pretend to be fine—for their sake. Tonight, like last night, she would lie awake, missing Nash, longing for him, wishing it could have been different. But during the day, she would keep it all together.

"We're going to the pool," she said and waited for the cheers.

"Okay," Jason muttered.

Adam simply slid off the bed and walked out of the room.

Stephanie stepped into the hall and crossed to the bottom of the stairs. "Brett, get your swimsuit," she yelled. "We're going to the pool. And yes, you have to go."

Vivian opened her door. "Is everything all right?" she asked kindly. "The boys seem very quiet today."

"They're missing Nash," Stephanie admitted. "I thought hanging out at the pool with their friends would help."

Vivian's dark eyes turned knowing. "Will it help you?"

"I'm a little old to be healed by water sports," she said, determined to keep her tone light. "But it's always fun to get out."

She waited for Vivian to ask more questions, but Nash's mother simply smiled. "Do you mind if Howard and I tag along? We're enjoying our time with the boys."

Stephanie hesitated. The last thing she needed was for her sons to bond with more people who were leaving. But it would be rude to say no. Besides, on a purely selfish level, she liked hanging around with Nash's folks. Not only did they remind her a little of him, they were good people whose company she enjoyed.

"You're more than welcome," she said. "Just be warned that it gets pretty noisy."

"No problem. Give us five minutes to get ready."

The Glenwood community pool complex was as crowded and loud as Stephanie had imagined it would be. There were actually three pools—a shallow one for children under the age of six, a six-lane lap pool and a massive round pool that dated back to the fifties when a rich newspaper baron had moved to town and donated the land and money for the structure. Over the years, the main pool had been refurbished, but the original shape had never been changed.

Stephanie led her group to a place in the shade. Most of the older kids and teenagers congregated on the cement border of the pool, while the families took up residence on the grassy slope leading to the video-game hut and snack bar. She spread out towels, double-checked that the boys had been covered in sun block, then gave them the okay to head for the water.

She promised Vivian and Howard that she would return shortly, then made her way to one of the half-dozen lifeguards on duty. There she gave the names and ages of her three boys, pointed them out and confirmed they had each attended swimming classes and were strong swimmers.

She was about to return to Nash's parents when someone tapped her on the shoulder. She turned and saw Elizabeth Haynes.

"I didn't know you were coming to the pool today," she said with a smile. "There's a group of us here." Elizabeth laughed. "I suppose we always travel in groups, don't we? Have you heard from Nash?"

As several of the Haynes brothers had still been around when Nash had left, word of his assignment had spread quickly. That morning she'd received a couple of calls asking for updates. She wasn't sure why anyone in his family thought he would stay in touch and the reminder that he hadn't didn't make her feel any better.

Still, they were nice people who weren't responsible for her broken heart and she did her best to be polite.

"I saw on the news that the hostage situation ended successfully," she said. "But other than that I don't know anything."

Elizabeth smiled. "I'm sure he'll be back shortly."

Stephanie nodded, even though she doubted she would ever see him again. Oh, they might run into each other sometime when he was out visiting family or here for the war games, but by the time that happened she intended to be well over him. Which meant she shouldn't plan on crossing paths with him for about twenty-five years.

"Are Kevin and Haley with you?" Stephanie asked. "Vivian and Howard have braved the pool."

She pointed up to where they'd placed their towels. Elizabeth glanced toward them and waved.

"Let me go tell the others," she said. "We'll join you."

Stephanie couldn't protest—not without sounding rude. And it wasn't that she didn't like the Haynes family—it was just that they reminded her too much of Nash.

It was only for one afternoon, she told herself as she returned to Vivian and Howard and prepared for the onslaught. She could survive that. Tonight, when she was alone, she would give in to the tears that hovered right beneath the surface of her self-control. Eventually the raw edge of the pain would dull into something bearable.

In a matter of minutes Elizabeth and company had

joined them. Names of children in the pool were passed around and Haley and Elizabeth took the first shift of watch. Stephanie sat next to Rebecca who made her laugh with tales of teaching her oldest son, David, the ins and outs of using the washing machine.

"He didn't believe me about sorting colors," Rebecca told her. "And there was this bright red T-shirt."

"I know exactly what happened."

Rebecca grinned. "The boy has pink underwear. He's humiliated."

Stephanie tried to concentrate on the conversation. But Kevin was with them, as was Kyle, and every time she caught sight of a tall, dark-haired man, she thought of Nash. Her heart instantly started pounding and her thighs went up in flames. Then she had to remind herself that he was gone. When that happened, a fresh wave of pain swept through her and threatened to pull her under.

She found herself wishing for the impossible and imagining what life would have been like if Nash had wanted to stay. If he'd fallen in love with her, the way she'd fallen for him.

Rebecca leaned close. "Whatever happens, I want you to know the family will always be there for you."

"I appreciate that," Stephanie told her.

She knew what Rebecca meant—that even if things didn't work out for her and Nash, the family would still look out for her. She could call on them in a time of need. Another kindness, she thought, trying to be grateful. There was no way for Rebecca to know the words sounded like the closing of a metal door, locking her in a prison of memories from which she would never escape.

The twins climbed out of the pool and ran up the slope. She picked up their towels and handed them over as the boys approached.

"How's the water?" she asked.

"Not too cold," Jason told her.

Adam frowned slightly. "Brett's talking to a girl," he said, the confusion in his voice making it clear he didn't understand why anyone sensible would want to do that.

"Really?"

At twelve? Was that the right age for that sort of thing to start? She glanced around the pool and found her son sitting on the edge on the far side. Next to him was a pretty red-haired girl with a bright smile. Brett said something, then ducked his head. The girl laughed.

Stephanie's longing for Nash increased. She wanted him to be here to share the moment. She wanted to ask him how things were going to be different as her son became a teenager. She wanted—

"Are you all right?" Rebecca asked in a low voice.

Stephanie nodded, then had to brush unexpected tears from her cheeks. She couldn't speak. Not without breaking into sobs. Control, she told herself. She had to get control.

Rebecca said something else, but Stephanie couldn't hear her. It took her a second to figure out that a loud noise had filled the sky. She looked up and saw a heli-copter approaching.

"It's Nash," Jason yelled as he scrambled to his feet.

Stephanie couldn't blame her son—that was her first thought, too. Even so, she told both him and herself it wasn't possible.

"Nash wouldn't take a helicopter back to Glenwood," she said. Assuming he was even coming back.

But Jason didn't care. He raced toward the rear fence of the complex and swung open the gate. Adam was on his heels. As she got to her feet, Brett ran past her.

"It's Nash," he called. "Hurry!"

She walked after them. Even if it *was* Nash, his return didn't mean anything had changed. She was going to have to talk with the boys tonight and remind them that Nash had been a guest and nothing more. They weren't—

She froze just inside the gate. Once again two sher-iff's cars blocked off the street as the helicopter set down. Her heart pounded painfully in her chest as a tall, dark-haired man stepped out.

Her sons flung themselves at Nash. She couldn't hear what they were saying, but Nash bent low and hugged them all. Her eyes filled with more tears. She couldn't do this, she thought. She couldn't pretend she didn't care, which meant she was about to make a fool out of herself in a very public way.

But even the threat of humiliation didn't stop her from running toward him.

Nash straightened and held out his arms. She crashed

into him and hung on, knowing she never wanted to let go. She wanted to be with this man forever. Did she have the courage to tell him the truth? Did she really think she could hide it?

"I missed you," he whispered, wrapping his arms around her so tightly she could barely breathe. "Every minute."

The intensity of his words gave her hope.

"Me, too."

He kissed her hard, then pulled back enough to look at her face. His dark eyes blazed with a fire she'd never seen before. "I want to change the rules," he said. "I don't want to be a temporary guest. I don't want to leave. I want to make things complicated and messy and permanent. I love you, Stephanie. I love you in ways I've never loved anyone before. I want to marry you and grow old with you. I want us to have one of those marriages that makes young couples sigh with envy. I want to have a baby with you. If the legend is true, you'll even get that girl you want."

She couldn't speak, couldn't think, couldn't do anything but listen to the melodic sound of his perfect words. He loved her? Really?

"You love me?"

"Yeah. Are you shocked?"

Relief and happiness and promise and hope swept through her making her feel as if she could float on air.

"I'm stunned," she said, then kissed him. "I love you, too. I know I wasn't supposed to, but I couldn't help myself."

"I'm not about to complain. Will you marry me, Stephanie? I know we have a lot of details to work out, but they're just logistics. I can relocate. Hell, I can get a different job. I just want to be with you and the boys."

Someone tugged on her T-shirt. She looked down and saw her kids standing next to them.

"Say yes, Mom," Brett told her.

Nash chuckled. "Okay, guys, we need a little privacy."

The boys grumbled, but took a few steps back. He turned back to her.

"I know the last time you ran off with someone you'd only known a few weeks, it was a disaster. So if you want to take things slow, I'll understand. I want to be a partner in this marriage. I want us to take care of each other. It's not going to be one-sided, but I'm willing to prove that to you, rather than have you take my word."

"Oh, Nash." She leaned against him and sighed. "You've already proved that a hundred times over. I love you and I want to be with you always." She looked into his eyes. "Yes, I'll marry you. There's nothing I want more."

"All right." Nash pulled her off her feet and swung her around. "She said yes," he yelled.

There was a collective cheer. For the first time she noticed the Haynes/Harmon/Reynolds clan had gathered around them.

"We have an audience," she murmured.

"I know. They're my family. Your family, now. Maybe we should give them a show."

He lowered her back to the ground and pressed his mouth to hers. It was a kiss of love, of passion and promise. Stephanie responded in kind, as words of congratulations washed over them.

My family, Nash had said with pride. He was no longer the man on the outside, looking in, she thought happily. He'd become a part of them, and of her. He'd come home.

* * * * *

Dear Reader,

Looking back on my childhood, I'm amazed at all that my mom managed to do for me and my sister! I think Mom may have been the subconscious inspiration for my heroine Kenzie Green, a single mother trying to handle everything life throws at her with optimism and a sense of humor. (It's not easy to relocate two nine-year-old twins who don't want to go!) Kenzie's fresh start in Atlanta comes with several complications, including her attractive new neighbor, widowed artist Jonathan Trelauney. Neither Kenzie nor JT are looking for love, but sometimes love finds you, anyway.

When I first wrote *A Dad For Her Twins,* my youngest child was in preschool. It's hard to believe she's now the same age as the nine-year-olds in the story! A lot changes over the years, but a mom's love for her children is constant and I still enjoy writing for Harlequin as much as ever. You can keep up with all my upcoming releases, including my Hill Country Heroes miniseries, by following me on Twitter at @TanyaMichaels or "liking" me at www.Facebook.com/AuthorTanyaMichaels.

A DAD FOR HER TWINS
Tanya Michaels

For Jarrad, Ryan, Hailey and Toni.

Our household is a never-ending source of inspiration, support and laughter.

Chapter 1

"Peachy Acres is a stupid name," Drew complained from the backseat.

Thank you, Mr. Optimism. Mackenzie Green, intrepid single mom and owner of a minivan that was older than her nine-year-old twins, sighed inwardly.

Kenzie empathized with her son's unhappiness over moving, but his negative commentary was making the four-hour trip from Raindrop, North Carolina, to Atlanta, Georgia, feel like an interminable cross-country trek. Or a voyage in space, she thought, vaguely recalling some old movie promo about no one being able to hear you scream. Too often Kenzie felt as if she were screaming on the inside.

Behind her, Leslie had adopted the prim, emphatic tone that made her sound like a cranky schoolteacher.

"I'm sure it's called Peachy Acres because *Georgia* is the *Peach* State," she informed her brother.

Drew was unimpressed. "Know-it-all. I hate when you talk like you're older than me. We're the same age!"

"A person doesn't have to be *older* to be *smarter*."

"All right!" Kenzie took a breath, reminding herself that deep feelings of maternal love prevented her from strapping the kids to the roof for the duration of the trip. Well, maternal love and state laws. "You two be nice."

She was always a touch envious when she heard about inseparable twins who dressed alike and finished each other's sentences. It would be bliss if her children could just go a day without bickering. Heck, an *hour*— she wasn't picky! Tensions were running abnormally high today; the kids had said goodbye to the only home they'd ever known.

Leslie was coping by burying her nose in a young-adult reference book about Georgia during the Civil War, despite her increased tendency to get carsick while reading. Drew, as had become his habit this past spring, was channeling his misery into anger. Would the new setting do him good, giving him the chance for a fresh start and provide distractions like the zoo and natural-science museum, or were Kenzie's difficulties with her son about to get worse?

She'd debated turning down this transfer to a Georgia branch of the bank she worked for, but the Atlanta location had far more frequent job openings than the small bank in Raindrop, including the position of loan officer, to which she was being promoted. The stress of moving and the higher cost of living seemed worth the much-improved salary and increased odds of upward mobility. Another plus was that Kenzie's sister lived in the Atlanta area. Even if the two hadn't been close as children, it would do Kenzie and her kids some good to have family nearby. Nice, *stable* family.

Besides, although Kenzie was fond of the little town they'd been living in, she was looking forward to having the kids in a different school. She'd chosen their new home based largely on the district in which it was located. At the tiny elementary school in Raindrop, there had been no gifted curriculum to challenge bookish Leslie, and many of the instructors were a stone's throw from retirement. Drew's third-grade teacher, who had only a year left to go, had lacked the energy to address Drew's growing number of outbursts in class, countermanding Kenzie's warnings that losing his temper would carry consequences. Not that Kenzie blamed Mrs. Blaugarten for Drew's behavior problems.

While Drew had always been active, last spring had been the first time he'd taken his extracurricular sports seriously. He'd been surrounded by fathers coaching teams and volunteering to work the concession stands, dads coming to watch their sons score goals in soccer or hit a baseball into the outfield. For Drew, the runs he batted in paled in comparison to the fact his father had never witnessed them, despite glib promises to be there.

"Mo-om?" Leslie's plaintive wail cut through Kenzie's thoughts. "I don't feel so—"

"Pull over!" Drew yelled in a panicked voice. "She's gonna blow!"

Kenzie signaled with her blinker as Drew urged, "Hurry!"

Spoken like someone who's never tried to drive a minivan hauling a loaded trailer. She steered gently onto the shoulder, kicking herself for not insisting that Leslie put aside her books for once and sing along to the radio or, better yet, take a catnap to make the ride pass faster.

In the grassy ditch on the side of the road, Kenzie smoothed her daughter's blond hair and handed over a bottle of water from the minicooler in the front seat. Moments later, they were back on the road. Leslie was sufficiently recovered to start bickering with her brother again.

As she stemmed off the burgeoning argument, Kenzie met her own gaze in the rearview mirror. *Are we there yet?*

"Kids? Kids, we've made it to Aunt Ann's street."

Both children had fallen asleep…during the final ten minutes of the drive. *Naturally.* Kenzie might have enjoyed the few moments of peace more if she weren't so tired herself. She'd been up at dawn to finish last-minute packing before getting the rental trailer this morning. After loading up their possessions and driving for hours, Kenzie's entire body ached.

Leslie lifted her head from its crooked angle against the seat and peered out the window. It was after seven but, due to the long summer days, still bright outside. Well-dressed children played on shiny scooters in driveways outside two-car, and even the occasional three-car, garages. The first time she'd been here, Kenzie had wrestled with twinges of resentment—who was she to question why the heck Ann and Forrest Smith needed a palatial, redbrick two-story to themselves? It wasn't *their* fault that Kenzie and the kids owned a secondhand couch with upholstery so garish it brought to mind the Las Vegas strip, or that they hadn't been able to afford replacing the dishwasher. Besides, Ann and Forrest had started a family now, so they'd probably grow into the space.

Kenzie was momentarily stymied as she approached the Smith residence. On the one hand, she didn't have enough experience maneuvering a trailer to comfortably navigate the driveway and the perfectly manicured flowering shrubs that lined it. On the other hand, she suspected the home owner's association governing the ritzy suburb had some sort of rule about staying parked in the street overnight. She pulled up to the curb for the time being and told herself she'd deal later with any uptight stipulations. The house she and the kids were buying on the opposite side of the city would be their first in an actual subdivision—with a name on the stone entrance and everything—but it didn't quite merit an HOA.

The front door to the house opened, and Kenzie's sister emerged. She'd been born Rhiannon, but these days she was Ann, wife of an economics professor at a small but credentialed local college. Kenzie, twenty-eight and technically older by a year and a half, often felt like the younger sibling. Ann was always the one giving advice, accompanied by head-shaking and sighs. She'd been that way her entire life, determined that she knew better than her crazy parents and older sister.

It had taken until the twins' toddlerhood for Kenzie to realize that, however frustrating Ann's attitude over the years, her sister had a point. Witness how differently their lives had turned out.

Well, twenty-eight is hardly old, and this move is a new beginning. Kenzie had been making slow changes to her life for the past few years. This promotion gave her a chance to create a fresh start for her and the twins. From here on out, she would be practical Kenzie Green, loan officer and suburbanite.

With help from Ann on the legwork, Kenzie had found the perfect home. It wasn't a big house, but it came with like-new appliances, and the school system was fantastic. The only drawback was that the sellers, who were moving out of the country, had put the house up early in case it took time to get an offer. They didn't want to close until mid-October; Kenzie's job started next week. Hence, the Peachy Acres apartment complex and the short-term lease Kenzie had signed. Ann had made halfhearted noises about offering her guest rooms for the interim, but even her sister's spacious home would feel unbearably cramped by the time nearly three months passed.

Besides, living out here would create complications

once school started, and involve a hellish commute. The apartment building, closer to the city, was just inside the edge of the kids' new school district. By staying at Peachy Acres until their house was ready, the twins could get settled into their classes and start making local friends. There was no way Kenzie was going to move them from Raindrop, enroll them in school near Ann's, then ask them to transfer *again,* later in the fall. She had assured her sister that letting them stay tonight was assistance enough.

"We were starting to worry!" Ann said from the driveway. "We expected you earlier."

Kenzie stretched, rubbing one palm against her lower back. "I'd planned to be here sooner, but you know how effective plans are once kids are involved."

Ann tilted her head, regarding her blankly.

What, baby Abigail never disrupted plans? Okay, that just wasn't fair.

It wasn't that Kenzie wished her sister ill, but when Kenzie had been a mother for five months, she'd been a sleep-deprived neurotic mess whose shirt was normally splattered in spit-up (Leslie's sensitive stomach had started from the cradle). Yet here was Ann, looking like an ad from a women's clothing catalog in her khaki capris, coral short-sleeved shirt and pearl earrings. Granted, she was plumper than she'd been before the baby, and Kenzie knew the pale blond bobbed hair was not her sister's natural color. Still, Ann was a vision of grace and loveliness.

Drew muscled between the two adults. "It took

for-*e*-ver because Les here had to hurl every five minutes."

"I only got sick twice! *You're* the one who ordered the big soda at lunch and—"

"Kids!" Kenzie didn't yell, but her tone spoke volumes. If Leslie ever wanted another bookstore shopping spree or Drew planned to play another video game for the remainder of his natural life, they both needed to cease and desist.

"Well." Ann's green eyes were wide. "That certainly does sound like an eventful trip. Leslie, do you feel up to eating? I have a roast beef simmering. Forrest had hoped to join us for dinner, but he's teaching a weekly night course for the summer semester. He has a meeting in the morning, Kenzie, but he can help move big stuff in the afternoon."

"Roast beef? I'm starved!" Drew ran on ahead, food being his number one priority in a three-way tie with video games and sports.

"My stomach's fine now," Leslie said, "but I'm more interested in holding Abigail than eating."

"Maybe after dinner. She's taking her evening nap. I don't want to disturb her routine."

Kenzie stumbled as she stepped up onto the front porch. Ann had managed to instill a routine in a five-month-old? Amazing. Kenzie's recollection of the twins' first year was blurred, but they'd practically *never* slept…at least, not at the same time.

Should Kenzie seek her sister's parenting advice on how to deal with Drew's recent moodiness? Ann was certainly a solution-finder by nature. But any conversation about Drew's anger would inevitably lead to a discussion of Kenzie's ex-husband, Mick Green, absentee father and Aspiring Musician. He always talked about his dream as if it deserved capital letters.

Once, Mackenzie had been his biggest fan, a dewy-eyed teenager who just knew she was marrying the next Springsteen. *Mick and Mac—gag.* Looking back with adult hindsight, she would call their marriage the biggest mistake she'd ever made, except for one thing... well, two actually. Whatever else he'd failed to provide, Mick had given her the twins.

Even when Drew was glowering and Leslie was tossing her cookies, Kenzie loved them fiercely. The thought steadied her. Her little family could handle this transitional period.

Yesterday's mistakes had yielded today's blessings... and tomorrow stretched ahead of them, full of promise.

"Need help?" The man addressing Kenzie had an intriguing voice—sort of low and growly, yet not unpleasant.

His tone, though, was laced with so much skepticism, as if she were *clearly* beyond help, that Kenzie wondered why he'd offered. Maybe it just seemed like the thing to do since she, a torn cardboard box and all of the box's former contents blocked his path. Her groan stemmed from equal parts embarrassment and sore muscles.

Glancing up from her sprawled position in the stairwell, she got her first good look at the potential knight in armor. Paint-stained denim and cotton, if you wanted to be literal, which she did. The new-and-improved practical Kenzie couldn't afford flights of fancy.

Then stop staring at this guy like he's the mystical embodiment of your fantasies.

Frankly, it had been too long since she'd had a decent fantasy, but if she had, it would look like him. Thick, dark hair, silver-gray eyes, strong jaw and broad, inviting shoulders. None of which were as relevant as her still being on her butt. She got to her feet…more or less.

As if she were having an out-of-body experience, she watched her wet sneaker slide across a piece of debris—the plaster head of a panda, she realized as she fell backward. The handsome stranger grabbed her elbow. Large hands, roughened skin. Since he was theoretically saving her from ignominious death in a dingy stairwell, she could forgive the lack of a delicate touch. The way her luck was running this morning, she would have broken her neck if he hadn't come along.

The man shook his head. "Lady." Was the undertone exasperation or amusement? Hard to tell from the single word.

"It's Kenzie," she said, grabbing the stair rail with both hands. "Kenzie Green. And thank you."

"No problem." He'd stepped back, either to keep from crushing her belongings under his work boots or simply to avoid her rain-soaked aura of doom.

She grimaced at the mess that covered half a dozen stairs. The coasters she was always admonishing the kids to use. Assorted books, her texts from some correspondence courses alongside Leslie's Mary Pope Osborne stories. Two mauve lamp shades. A statuette of a now-headless panda Kenzie had once received for donating to a wildlife fund, and various other small belongings that had been packed, taped up and neatly labeled Living Room in black marker.

"Guess they don't make cardboard boxes like they used to," she grumbled. What was wrong with the stupid box that it couldn't withstand being weakened with water and dropped down a few lousy steps?

Thank goodness Kenzie was such a levelheaded pragmatist. If she were given to the slightest bit of paranoia or superstition, she might see it as a bad sign that her first summer day in the sunny South was under deluge from a monsoon. She might be rethinking that rent check she'd written for a place where the elevator doors wouldn't even open.

"Are you the handyman?" she asked suddenly, taking in the man's clothing and an almost chemical smell she hadn't initially noticed. A cleaner of some kind, or paint? Maybe the elevator would be fixed before Ann arrived with the kids, not that Drew couldn't take three flights of stairs in a single breath. But he hardly needed new reasons to complain.

"The handyman?" Tall, Dark and Timely let out a bark of laughter that was gone as soon it came. In fact, all traces of amusement disappeared from his expression so quickly she wondered if she'd imagined them.

"I'll take that as a no," she said. "It was an educated

guess—Mr. Carlyle assured me that a handyman would be taking care of the elevators today. Which would make moving in a lot easier."

"Mr. C. *is* the handyman, in addition to being the property manager and the one who knocks on the doors whenever you're late with rent."

She stiffened. "I'm never late with rent."

He raised an eyebrow at her hostile tone. "I meant in general."

"Sorry. I take money seriously."

"You and everyone else." He grimaced absently, as if he were scowling at an unseen person. Did he owe someone money?

Oh, don't let him be one of those charming but perpetually broke deadbeats. There were too many of those in the world already. Then again, this guy wasn't technically all that charming. Hot, definitely, but not so much with the personality.

Imagining how Leslie would react to her mother calling a man *hot,* Kenzie grinned. "Well, thanks again. It was nice to almost meet you."

The corner of his lips quirked. "I'm JT. Good luck with the rest of your move." He started to pass, but stopped, watching as she wrestled with the lamp shades and books. With the box no longer intact, carting her belongings was problematic.

"I hate to impose," she began, "but were you in a hurry? It's going to take me a couple of trips to haul everything to the third floor, and if you wouldn't mind sticking around in the meantime to make sure no one…" What, stole her stuff? Who would want the book of *101 Jokes for Number-Crunchers* Drew got her last Christmas? "To make sure no one trips. I'd hate to be sued my first day in the city."

"I have a better idea." He was already sweeping up an armful of debris. After years of not having a guy in the household, it seemed bizarrely intimate to see this big man handle her possessions.

Books, Kenzie, not lingerie. Besides, people with better budgets than hers hired strangers to move their stuff all the time.

JT gestured toward the decapitated panda. "You keeping this poor fellow?"

"Sure. That's what they make glue for, right?" A couple of drops of that super all-stick compound and, as long as she managed not to chemically bond her fingers together, the panda should be as good as new.

Using the soggy cardboard in a way that reminded her of the baby sling she'd bought Ann, JT cradled the awkward bulk against his body. Between the two of them, they got it all up to her floor.

There were four units, two on each side of the hallway. Hers was the last on the left. As she unlocked her door, she heard JT's slight intake of breath, as if he were about to say something, but nothing followed. So she set down her load, turned to relieve him of his and thanked him one last time.

"I've got it from here," she said, hoping she sounded like a confident, self-sufficient woman.

"You sure?"

She thought about everything ahead—the new job, this temporary moving before the *real* move, trying to keep the kids from expiring of boredom until school started, and trying to keep them in their teachers' good graces once it did.

"Absolutely," she lied through her teeth. Next time she lectured the twins never to fib, she'd have to add the mental exception: *unless it's the only thing between you and a nervous breakdown.*

Chapter 2

"You're late." Sean Morrow glanced up from his lunch menu as JT took a seat on the other side of the table. With Sean's lean build, fair hair and expensive suit, the two men were a study in contrasts. "Dare I hope this means you were so caught up in a new painting that you lost track of time?"

"Actually, I was assisting a damsel in distress."

Sean pursed his lips, looking unsure about whether or not JT was kidding. "An attractive damsel?"

"Only if drenched waif is your type." To himself, JT admitted his words were a glib, incomplete assessment of Kenzie Green. *Good name.* Sounded like a vibrant, bright color—the kind he seldom used anymore—and it certainly rolled off the tongue more easily than *phthalo green* or *Antioch blue.*

Though Kenzie wouldn't necessarily turn men's

heads on the street, she was put together with a grace of form that belied how they'd met. She was a slight woman with layers of burnished-gold hair that were probably a lighter honey when dry. Her deep blue eyes looked like the ocean when you were so far out the shore was no longer visible, and there was something geometrically appealing about her small face—delicate blade of a nose, angular cheeks, an almost pugnaciously pointed chin that reminded him of some award-winning actress whose name eluded him. *Holly would have known.* Holly had been his link to pop culture.

She'd been his link to just about everything outside the studio, reminding him that there was a movie coming out he might like, reminding him of the names of acquaintances at openings, reminding him that he hadn't bothered to eat in nearly twelve hours. "How can I trust that you're going to help take care of this baby," she'd teased him once, "when you can't even remember to take care of yourself?"

Pregnancy had transformed her from the shyly smiling girl he'd first met to a laughing, excited woman with irrepressible humor. *I plan to decorate the nursery behind your back—I know you're the big-shot artist, but I'm scared you'll turn it into some abstract expression on spatial dynamics. I was thinking ducks and bunnies.*

"JT!" Sean's tone was pitched halfway between annoyance and concern. "Did you hear anything I said? You had that look again."

Stalling, JT sipped his water and tried to bring himself back to the present, a difficult feat given how much part of him longed to remain two years in the past. For the first few months after her death, thinking of Holly had hurt, creating electric shocks of pain that racked his whole being. Now that the sting had lessened, recalling cherished memories was comforting, beguiling. Easier than facing a future without her.

"It's hard," he said simply.

"I know." Sean lowered his gaze, a touch of sadness creeping into his own voice. "I know, man, but Holly wouldn't want you to be miserable. She would have wanted you to move on with your life. And she'd definitely want you to paint."

It wasn't as if he hadn't tried. The encaustic series he'd collaged in the weeks after the funeral—a sickening double funeral during which he'd felt he was putting his entire world into the ground—was his best work ever. But the frenzied creation of those paintings had hollowed him out somehow, leaving a void where inspiration had once been. He'd allowed Sean to hang the dark wax-and-oil images at the gallery, but couldn't bring himself to sell them.

The gallery. JT willed himself to focus. It wasn't fair that he left everything up to Sean these days; the two men were supposed to be equal business partners. JT was the one who knew art; Sean was gifted with people and finances.

Out of nowhere JT thought of the book he'd seen Kenzie holding—something about number crunching. Then there had been the reproachful set of her rosy mouth when she'd mentioned the importance of money.

I should introduce her to Sean. Though the thought was mostly facetious, it certainly wouldn't be difficult to arrange. JT lived directly across the hall from his new neighbor.

"I've lost you again," Sean muttered.

"I was thinking about setting you up on a date."

"Seriously?" Sean grinned. "Not that I've ever needed help meeting ladies, but I take it as a good sign that you're thinking about *anyone's* love life."

"I'm not a monk," JT said defensively.

JT had gone on a half-dozen dates this year, but nothing lasting had come of them. It wasn't just that he missed Holly, it was more that he was still unsure of who he was without her. They'd met in Chicago when they were both college students. He'd become an adult during the years they'd been dating; he'd become a critically acclaimed artist during their marriage. He'd been about to become a father. With all of that taken away...

Since her death, JT had slept with only one woman, an art dealer Holly had liked and respected. In a bizarre way, JT had felt his late wife would approve. Marsha had been recovering from the shock of her husband walking out on her, needing to reaffirm her own feminine attraction, and JT had craved the touch of another person to penetrate his isolation. Their affair had lasted less than a month before they parted amicably, each somewhat healthier for the encounter, but knowing they had no future together. Sean had hinted several times that JT needed more of a social life. Even Mrs. Sanchez, who lived on the second floor of Peachy Acres and had appointed herself JT's godmother, for lack of a better description, nagged that his apartment needed a woman's touch.

Thankfully, the waitress came to take their orders, which gave JT something to think about besides his inability to paint and unwillingness to date.

Would there come a day when he could once again consider painting a joy, not an obligation? Would he ever again view love as a blessing and not a dreaded danger?

Some of his best paintings had evolved from brushstrokes with no direction, just moving his arm intuitively and watching to see what evolved on the canvas. If he kept getting out of bed each morning and facing each day, one after another, would his life begin to take some kind of shape? He couldn't be certain. But in the absence of an actual plan, he supposed he'd find out.

Kenzie throbbed everywhere—muscles she hadn't realized she possessed were angrily making their presence known. She had a ton of unpacking to do, but all she really wanted was a long, hot soak in the bathtub. There wasn't time, though. Ann had called from her cell phone to say she was en route with the kids and "backup brawn." Besides, Kenzie was scared to test the bathroom's hot water. If it, like the building's elevator, the ceiling fan in her bedroom and the stove's faulty pilot light, neglected to work, she might cry.

Reminding herself that those were all minor inconveniences easily fixed, Kenzie grabbed a bottle of water from the refrigerator. Heck, she'd already relit the pilot light herself, and the worrisome smell of gas had dissipated. She sat on the brown living-room carpet, a shade probably chosen because it wouldn't show stains. That could come in handy with two kids. When the knock sounded at her door, she wasn't sure her legs would cooperate enough for her to stand, but she managed. Just barely.

Instead of the relatives she'd expected, it was Mr. Carlyle, a short man of indeterminate age. His thick hair was the color of freshly fallen snow, unmitigated by gray, and he had exchanged the navy tracksuit he'd worn this morning for an Atlanta Braves T-shirt with jeans and a tool belt.

"Afternoon, Miss Green." He peered past her at the cardboard boxes stacked beyond. Her apartment looked like an elementary student's homage to Stonehenge. "You settling in okay?"

"More or less."

"I won't bother you long, just came up to tell you the elevator's working again."

Oh, happy day! She and Forrest would need to bring the mattresses up through the stairwell, but the elevator would make everything else easier. "That's wonderful news. Thanks, Mr. Carlyle."

"Just doin' my job—and call me Mr. C. Everyone in the building does."

It's what JT had called the man this morning. For a moment, it was on the tip of her tongue to ask the property manager about the handsome mystery man. She assumed JT lived here, but didn't know that for sure. What was his last name? Did he ever smile? She ignored the random thoughts, telling herself they stemmed from exhaustion. Normally she was too worried about taking care of her own household to be nosy about others.

Kenzie had just finished giving Mr. C. a rundown of small repairs needed in the apartment when the elevator at the end of the hall dinged. The doors parted, and a teeming mass of cranky humanity spilled forth. Blond Leslie and dark-haired Drew led the way, bickering and power walking, each apparently determined to reach their mother first. Behind them, Ann's infant daughter, Abigail, was screaming bloody murder in her car seat. As Ann approached, Kenzie saw two wet circles on the front of her sister's shirt and tried not to feel relieved that Ann looked harried for a change. With them was her husband, Forrest. At first glance, he seemed to be talking to himself, but Kenzie quickly realized that he was wearing an earpiece attached to his phone and was trying to set up a tee time.

Amidst the noise—perhaps because of it?—the door directly behind Mr. C. opened, giving Kenzie a clear view of the person framed in the doorway. *JT.*

JT lived in the apartment across from her?

Her eyes locked with his, but calls of "Mom! Mom!" broke the spell. She looked toward her two kids and, in her peripheral vision, saw JT quickly shut his door. No doubt he was hiding on the other side thinking *There goes the neighborhood.*

From the two hopeless expressions aimed at Kenzie as she set paper plates on the coffee table, one would think the kids were being served their last meal.

She sat cross-legged on the floor on the opposite side—tomorrow she'd get around to assembling the white pine dinette set. "Guys, you know this is only temporary. Everything will get better soon."

"Easy for you to say," her son said morosely. "You'll meet new people at your job. How are *we* supposed to make friends this summer?"

Kenzie knew from asking Mr. Carlyle that, of the twelve units in the building, ten were currently occupied, including hers and Mr. C.'s, which was on the first floor. He'd said there were a few teenagers in the building and one toddler, but no other elementary-school-aged kids.

Drew heaved a dramatic sigh, sounding for a change just like his sister. "We'll practically be shut-ins until school starts!"

The twins had protested that they were too old for day care. Kenzie had grudgingly said they could stay here by themselves for the duration of summer break—with her coming home each day for lunch and Ann making habitual drop-ins to keep them on their toes. Yet even after they'd begged permission to stay alone, Drew managed to make it seem as if a form of torture was being inflicted on them.

"School starts in a few weeks," Kenzie told them. "It will be here before you know it!"

Leslie picked at the crust on her tuna fish sandwich. "I miss my friends."

After less than twenty-four hours? "North Carolina isn't far. We can visit sometimes. Once we move into the house, we'll invite Stacy to come stay for a weekend."

"What about Paul?" Drew demanded from around a bite of sandwich. He never let being depressed stand in the way of his appetite. In fact, if Leslie continued to ignore her own food, he'd probably ask if he could have it.

"Sure," Kenzie said. "We could invite Paul, too. *If* the two of you behave, and after we're all settled."

"You mean once we have furniture again?" Drew asked.

With a spring starting to poke through the ugly upholstery, their thrift-store couch hadn't been worth the trouble to move. At this precise moment, just about everything seemed like more trouble than it was worth. But, as she'd promised the kids, it would get better. She had a few more days before she was due at work; maybe they should check the budget and spend half a day on something fun.

"There's lots of cool stuff to do around Atlanta," she stated. "Stone Mountain, the aquarium downtown, the Coke Museum, a planetarium." When she received only halfhearted murmurs of agreement, she played her ace. "Six Flags?"

Leslie glanced up with shining blue eyes. "Really? You never let me go anywhere with roller coasters!"

"Well, it's not like we had any theme parks in Raindrop."

"You promise you'll take us?" Leslie asked skeptically.

"Yes, but I'll need to get my first paycheck before we go."

"At least that's something to look forward to," Drew allowed before his face fell again. "We may not have had roller coasters back home, but I could have spent the summer swimming at Paul's. What kind of apartment doesn't have a pool? I thought that was, like, standard."

Instead of a pool, there was a communal balcony area on the roof, complete with grill and a couple of lounge chairs, which spared her the arguments about the kids swimming unsupervised while she was at work, thank goodness. "This place isn't so bad. And it's the only three bedroom we could afford."

"Small bedrooms," Leslie muttered, joining her brother for a seat on the Whiny Train.

"You guys would rather I find a place where you can share a room?"

The twins exchanged looks of mutual horror, quickly chorused, "No, Mom," and went back to their sandwiches without further complaint.

Drew didn't speak again until he was finished. "Mom, can I ask you something?"

"Of course, sweetheart."

Leslie darted a glance at her brother, shaking her head emphatically. Uh-oh. Whatever was coming next, the twins had clearly discussed it already…and disagreed. *Big surprise.*

"What is it, you guys?"

Drew steadfastly refused to look at his sister, who was attempting to bore holes in his skull with her glare.

"Did you let Dad know we were moving? Does he have a way of, I dunno, reaching us here?"

"Oh, honey." Kenzie's heart constricted into a tight fist. "I left a message at his last known phone number, but the person who lived there said she hadn't seen your father in weeks."

"Told you." Using her thumb, Leslie crushed a corn chip on her plate. "If he cared about seeing us, or even hearing from us, he'd make it easier to find him."

"You take that back!" Drew's features contorted in fury, but beneath the youthful rage, he looked achingly vulnerable. Kenzie wanted to pull him into her lap for the hug she knew he wouldn't accept. "Dad does care."

Leslie rolled her eyes. "You really are a dummy."

"Leslie Nicole! You can apologize to your brother or go to your room."

The girl stood, her posture defiant.

"Les…" Far from sounding angry now, Drew's tone was imploring. He wanted her to share his belief that their father loved and missed them and would make more time when he finally "hit it big." Drew was the one who still allowed himself to hope, and Kenzie thought that was why he was always the angriest when Mick let them down.

Leslie tried to feign indifference. When the subject came up, she informed people that she didn't miss her father and that they were better off without him. But Kenzie had heard Leslie sniffling behind closed doors after these declarations. Kenzie watched her daughter go now, wondering what was the best way to handle the situation. Which was more detrimental—verbally bashing her ex and disillusioning her kids, or allowing them fruitless hope?

"Dad will visit us again," Drew maintained. "Eventually."

They never knew when Mick would pop back into their lives. His sporadic phone calls usually came—at an inappropriate hour—from wherever his band was playing. Most years he managed to send small, truck-stop Christmas presents that his son treasured as if they were gold. Three times since the divorce was final he'd actually sent Kenzie cash. Mick Green wasn't an evil man, but he was unreliable, inconsistent and suffered tunnel vision, keeping his eye on an unlikely prize and clinging to a fantasy of what he wanted to be when he grew up. Just as he hadn't listened when she'd said the Jagger-nots might not be such a great name for his band, he'd resisted her suggestions over the years that maybe it was time to find a different way to earn a living. Preferably something that generated income.

Would it be best if he stopped contacting the kids altogether? Given the way Drew was looking at her now, his heart visible in his sapphire eyes, she couldn't bring herself to ask Mick to do that.

"He *could* visit," she finally conceded. "I think it's unlikely we'll see him soon, but you never know."

Kenzie had never found time for another man in her life—not that there'd been a huge selection of age-appropriate bachelors in Raindrop. If she ever dated again, it would be a steady, predictable man with no creative aspirations. Someone she could depend on.

In the meantime, she'd just keep depending on herself.

Chapter 3

Though JT routinely lost track of time, his stomach always growled right on schedule at six on Friday. Enchilada night, or possibly taco casserole. His doorbell buzzed at exactly the expected hour—you could set a clock by Mrs. Sanchez—and he crumpled the drawing he'd been working on, tossing it in the general vicinity of an overflowing wastebasket. *I should empty that.* Mrs. Sanchez would bust his chops about the mess.

He opened the door of the apartment. Roberta Sanchez, who'd raised four children and was approaching double that in grandkids, lived below him with her husband, a MARTA bus driver. When she'd first heard that a widower had moved into Peachy Acres, she'd shown up with a covered pot of chicken tortilla soup. Food had followed every Friday since, with flan on his birthday.

"*Buenas noches,* Jonathan." She marched toward his kitchen with a foil-wrapped glass pan.

"Nobody calls me that," he reminded her.

Over her shoulder, she hitched a dark eyebrow. "Are you calling me a nobody?"

"Of course not."

"Then shut up. Now be a good boy and find me a clean spoon, if such a thing exists here. No wonder you are uninspired to create beauty, living in such disorganization! Have you painted at all this week?"

He rummaged through a drawer. "You sound like Sean."

"I sound nothing like that degenerate!" She sniffed. "You should have heard him flirting with my daughter Rosa in the elevator. It's inappropriate, the things he says to a married woman."

JT grinned inwardly, knowing full well that Mrs. Sanchez adored Sean, a feeling that was mutual even though Sean called her the Battle-Ax.

She paused. "You're not expecting him, are you? Maybe I should have brought more."

He eyed the pan. "That would feed an entire dinner party. Is Enrique working the night shift? You could join me."

"If you want me to join you, you should clean up this pit first." Despite her words, she pulled two plates down from the cabinet. "I'll stay. The good Lord knows my company is as close as you'll get to a dinner party. You don't want to be a hermit, Jonathan."

"I'm doing my part to uphold the reclusive artist stereotype."

"To qualify as an artist, shouldn't you produce *art* of some kind?"

Touché. "Nag, nag, nag. It's a wonder your children haven't moved farther away."

She sniffed again, not dignifying his jibe with a response.

The Sanchez family was the kind of close-knit group neither JT nor Holly had ever possessed. Holly would have loved Mrs. Sanchez; initially, that had been why he'd put up with the older woman's intrusions. But she'd won him over with her drill-sergeant tone and twinkling dark eyes. She seemed to understand his loss without ever expressing the cloying pity that made him want to withdraw more. Plus her cooking was a little piece of pepper-laced heaven.

JT didn't have a kitchen table, merely three padded, high-backed stools pushed up to the counter. He cleared away a pile of junk mail and an empty pizza box to make room for them to eat. Mrs. Sanchez pulled a carton of milk out of the refrigerator, opened it and immediately grimaced.

"Jonathan, this milk is older than some of my grandchildren."

"An unfair comparison. You have grandkids born every ten minutes!" He said it lightly, but it was the Sanchez babies that had made him leave the rooftop Fourth of July picnic last month.

Roberta had browbeaten him into attending, but he hadn't been able to bear it for long. Just as he hadn't been able to bear the empty nursery in the house he'd shared with Holly. After all the work she'd put into it, wanting it to be perfect for their child, he couldn't bring himself to paint over a single duck or bunny. The crib he'd assembled sat obscenely empty, and a month after he'd lost his cherished wife and the daughter he'd never had a chance to know, he'd bent over the railing and finally cried, ugly hoarse sobs that felt as if they were splitting him in half. From the moment the doctors had given him the news at the hospital, throughout the memorial service, he'd been too shocked and disbelieving to truly cry. Once he had, instead of feeling better for having poured out some of the pain, he'd been pissed off at the senseless loss.

He'd locked himself in his studio, barely eating or sleeping, trying to purge his enraged grief with painting. When he'd finished the series, he'd been like a man coming out of a coma, disoriented and unsure of how much time had passed. He'd wandered through his own house like a ghost, stopping in the nursery—that bright, cheerful room where he'd wept until he wished he'd died with them. Then he'd walked straight to the phone and arranged to put the house on the market, not caring where he lived as long as it was elsewhere.

"Jonathan." Suddenly Mrs. Sanchez was there, touching his shoulder. "Sit down. Eat. You need sustenance." She blessed the food, with a little pause before saying amen and making the sign of the cross. Had she added an extra silent prayer on his behalf?

It was odd. The only child of a wealthy couple, JT hadn't felt guilty that he was "disappointing" his parents by not going to law school and following in his father's footsteps. The elder Trelauney stubbornly spoke of a father-son practice even though JT had no interest in becoming an attorney. Instead of wasting his time arguing, JT had simply continued painting, ignoring his father's scorn over the "pointless scribblings." *You're on the cusp of manhood, son. Act like it! You're not some finger-painting toddler.* Yet JT had refused to feel ashamed. Now, by not painting, he felt he was disappointing Sean and Mrs. Sanchez—people who were better to him than he deserved—and that bothered him far more than his family's disapproval ever had.

Though he wasn't particularly hungry, he forced himself to take a bite of the enchiladas and was immediately rewarded with a spicy blend of rich flavors. "This is really good."

"I believe you meant great."

"I believe I did."

She reached for her glass of water. "You are a good boy, Jonathan. Even if you are a slob."

He surprised them both with a genuine chuckle.

Mrs. Sanchez looked pleased by this progress. "Mr. C. tells me that someone has moved in across from you. I'm glad. It's too quiet up here with 3A unoccupied and that flight attendant in 3B gone half the time."

JT thought of that moment yesterday when he'd heard a baby shrieking and had flung open his door. He still didn't know exactly why he'd reacted that way or what he'd expected to find. Though there had been only a handful of people on a floor that was often deserted except for him, it had sounded as if a deafening mob had descended. He'd heard plaintive shouts of "Mom" clearly directed at Kenzie. Was the baby hers, too? He didn't think so, but he hadn't stuck around long enough to inquire.

He winced at the memory and turned to his dinner guest. "It looks like my quiet days are over. The new neighbor lady has kids. Two, maybe three."

"Two," Mrs. Sanchez confirmed. "I asked Mr. C. He also mentioned she has no husband."

Was Kenzie divorced? Widowed, like himself? Technically, the presence of kids didn't require a husband in the first place. Maybe she'd never been married. There could still be a serious boyfriend in the mix. JT experienced a funny twinge in his chest he didn't want to examine too closely.

Feeling that he was being watched, he jerked his head up and found Mrs. Sanchez studying him. He didn't like the speculative gleam in her eyes.

"No," he said automatically.

She blinked. "I don't know what you mean."

Deciding this was as good a time as any to take her advice about tidying up, he rose and went to the dishwasher.

"You told me she had kids," Mrs. Sanchez said. "So you've met them?"

"Just her. Briefly." Despite his attempt to sound dismissive, the memory was vivid.

Kenzie Green had looked like the wreck he felt like on most days, yet there'd been determination glinting in her eyes and an unmistakable lifting of her chin when she'd stood to regather her belongings. He'd had the impression that life had knocked her down before and she was resolved to get back on her feet as many times as necessary.

"Well," Mrs. Sanchez prompted. "What is she like?"

"I don't know. About your height, blondish. I didn't exchange life stories with her."

"No," Mrs. Sanchez said, her voice disconcertingly gentle. "You wouldn't have, would you?"

He stiffened. "If you're so curious about Kenzie, you could have taken *her* the enchiladas instead of knocking on my door." The churlishness in his tone reminded him of his self-important father, and JT flinched.

But Mrs. Sanchez held herself above his rudeness with reproachful aplomb. "I fully intend to take her a dish this weekend and welcome her. I thought it better not to show up on her doorstep her first day, when she might be feeling tired and overwhelmed. I hate to intrude," she added with a faintly challenging air.

JT walked her to the door. "We're lucky to have you in the building, Mrs. Sanchez."

"You certainly are."

He hesitated before saying goodbye, unsure how to ask what was on his mind without putting ideas in her head. Mrs. Sanchez herself had said that, if any of her grown daughters had been single when JT moved in, she would have sent her up to deliver the homemade soup. So far, for all her fussing that he needed a woman's touch in his life, she'd lacked a spare female to nudge his way, deeming the flight attendant down the hall too frequently absent. Now there was a seemingly available woman living less than two yards from his front door. Surely Mrs. Sanchez knew better than to...

"You weren't planning to mention me to her, were you?" he demanded, unable to help himself.

"Hasn't she already met you for herself? What possible reason could I have for bringing you into the conversation? Is she some sort of art critic?"

He rocked back on his heels. "You've been known to spout the opinion that I would benefit from female companionship."

"I've also said you should eat more regularly, clean up this disorderly pigsty and go back to painting. Why would I inflict *you* on some girl who is already burdened with raising two children alone? Jonathan, *mijo,* you're probably the last thing she needs."

He stole a glance over her shoulder at Kenzie's door and tried to take stock of what he could possibly offer any woman at this point in his life. "You're undoubtedly right."

On Saturday afternoon, Kenzie excused herself to go downstairs and check the mail. She wasn't expecting anything other than standard Dear Occupant fare, but she'd been going a little stir-crazy in the apartment. The kids seemed louder than normal today, and she couldn't chuck them out into a backyard to play. Showing the resilience of youth, they were back in better spirits. During a televised Braves game the night before, Drew had allowed that maybe living in Atlanta could be kind of cool.

Punching the elevator button, Kenzie considered the evening ahead. Would their finances, currently stretched by moving expenses and utility deposits, allow dinner out and a movie? Maybe if they went to the movie first, taking advantage of matinee prices, and eschewed concessions, then drank tap water at dinner rather than paying for sodas… She reached the bottom floor and dug in her pocket for the small, silver key Mr. C. had given her. This was the first time she'd checked to make sure it worked.

She gathered the handful of mail, sorting through it in the elevator on her way back up. Coupons, catalogs, the bill that her cell phone company had thoughtfully forwarded so that she wouldn't miss this month's opportunity to pay them. One yellow envelope was addressed to Jonathan Trelauney. Previous occupant? When she noticed the "3C," she realized the mailman must have just dropped it in her slot by mistake.

Jonathan Trelauney must be JT. His full name sounded familiar, but after dealing with so many people through the bank, eventually all names caused her moments of déjà vu. She'd encountered nearly half a dozen account holders with her sister's name.

When she stepped off the elevator, Kenzie glanced at JT's envelope. She'd been unpacking all day and was dusty. Her hair was tidy, pulled back in the habitual French twist she favored for work, but she didn't have any makeup—

Oh, for pity's sake! Handing the man his misdirected mail does not require mascara and perfume. Did she even own perfume? She couldn't remember the last time she'd treated herself to anything more luxurious than scented body wash.

Annoyed with herself, she rapped on his door a bit

more curtly than she'd intended. At first she wasn't sure anyone would answer, but then she heard footsteps on the other side. JT appeared in the doorway, unshaven and *shirtless!*

Kenzie had taken a breath as the door opened; now she choked on her own oxygen. It took all her discipline not to let her gaze dwell on his leanly muscled torso or the dusting of dark hair across his broad chest. "I…is this a bad time?"

He rubbed a hand across his face. "I was sleeping on the couch."

"Oh." It seemed like a practically sinful indulgence, snoozing smack-dab in the middle of the afternoon, but then he didn't have two kids bouncing around and a zillion boxes to unpack. "I didn't mean to disturb you."

He regarded her with heavy-lidded eyes. "Did you need something?"

"Just bringing you this. It was in my mailbox." Their fingers brushed when he took the envelope, and she told herself that such a platonic touch would ordinarily not make her light-headed. It was the proximity of all that naked skin making her heart flutter. He must have a naturally golden complexion. He wasn't pale, but his color didn't seem to come from a tan, either. And, good grief, was she staring again?

Because she *was* actually staring, she noticed a splotch of dark violet paint near his rib cage. Suddenly the name clicked. "Jonathan Trelauney! I know you. Of you, rather. You're an artist."

JT was startled by two things—three, truthfully, but he was trying to ignore the unexpected sensation that had washed through him when their hands met. He didn't think the reaction came from the fleeting contact so much as her expression. Something akin to desire had flared in her eyes, and it had rocked him. No woman had looked at him like that in a long time. Hormones aside, he'd been surprised that Kenzie had heard of him. While his work had been renowned in certain circles, he was hardly a household name. Second, the *way* she'd said "You're an artist" had been filled with horrified discovery. She might as well have pronounced "You're a leper."

He frowned. "Do you follow art?" It seemed the only logical conclusion for recognizing his name, yet didn't explain her negative reaction.

"No. My hippie parents follow art. I've absorbed a few details here and there during the rare visit with them." Though she kept her voice matter-of-fact, disdain leaked into her expression. The warmth in her earlier gaze had cooled completely.

Hippie parents? "Ah. I see."

Her hands went to her hips. "Just what do you 'see'?"

"Your parents were artistic, touchy-feely types, and you—" he hazarded a guess "—rebelled by growing up to be ultraconservative."

Her burst of laughter caught him off guard. "Whatever you do, don't give up art for psychiatry, because you couldn't be more wrong. My younger sister, Ann, was the conservative in the family. *I* married a musician at eighteen."

He glanced at her baggy shirt, sensible sneakers and pulled back hair. "You married a musician?"

"Yeah. And by nineteen, I had two babies to feed and clothe, so I reevaluated certain lifestyle choices."

JT wished she looked cynical instead of vulnerable. He felt…well, he wasn't sure, but she was a virtual stranger. He shouldn't be required to *feel* anything on her behalf. If he'd been more awake when he answered the door, his normal barriers in place, he would have said thanks for the mail and dismissed her without further conversation.

He could always try that now. "Well, thanks for the—"

Behind her, the door to 3D opened, and two kids stuck their heads out, seeming surprised to see their mother talking to some shirtless dude across the hall.

"Mom!" This from the girl who looked scandalized. The boy glared silently in JT's direction.

Kenzie didn't help matters, blushing as if she'd been caught in the midst of something illicit. "What are you guys doing out here?"

"We were worried about you." The daughter fisted her hands on her hips. Mini-Kenzie. "You said you were going to run get the mail, then you didn't come back. For all we knew, the elevator was stuck between floors!"

The boy looked faintly disappointed. "I had this plan for prying the doors open. Who's he?"

"Kids, this is our across-the-hall neighbor, Jonathan Trelauney."

"JT," he told the children. "Nice to meet you."

"These are my twins," Kenzie said. "Drew and Leslie."

"Not the identical kind of twins," Drew interjected.

JT bit back a smile. "I noticed."

"Why aren't you wearing a shirt?" The boy's tone was thick with suspicion. "Doesn't your air conditioner work? If you're hot, it would be smart to wear shorts instead of jeans."

Kenzie's head whipped around as she shot her son a warning glance. "Use your manners, Drew."

"But, Mom, I was just—"

"Let's get back in our own apartment and leave Mr. Trelauney alone."

Yes, JT thought with relief. Alone would be good. He attempted his goodbye again. "Well, thanks—"

The elevator ding sounded, reminding him that Mrs. Sanchez had said she would bring Kenzie food and an official welcome today.

"—forthemail," he blurted. Then he shoved his door closed.

He caught a glimpse of Kenzie's mouth falling open. She was probably taken aback by his rudeness. If she'd known he was saving her from possible matchmaking attempts, she might have appreciated his efforts. A moment later, there was another knock. JT, trying to learn from his mistakes, was slow to answer.

"It's Sean," his friend called from the hall. "I know you're home. I just saw you shut the door in some poor woman's face."

JT ushered him in. "Don't judge me. It's complicated. You want a beer? I could use a beer."

Sean, dapper in a button-down shirt and slacks, and making JT feel like the Wild Man of Borneo in comparison, frowned. "Do you even have beer in the apartment?"

"Um…no." On his wedding anniversary, back in February, JT had gotten stinking blind drunk. After that, the thought of booze had made him sick for months and he'd avoided keeping any around. "Can I get you some lemonade?"

"All right, but only one, I have to drive," Sean deadpanned. "Tell me about the hottie in the hall."

"You can't call Kenzie a hottie," JT objected as he pulled a pitcher out of the refrigerator. "She has two kids."

"The boy and girl? She doesn't look old enough to have kids that age."

JT recalled what she'd said about marrying as a teenager, but didn't share the information with his friend; it seemed like a violation of privacy. "Why exactly are you here? Please don't tell me it's to ask if I'm painting anything. I was up until dawn, sketching and mixing colors on a canvas until my vision blurred."

"About that." Sean squirmed, looking uncomfortable, which was worrisome. Sean rarely let anything discomfit him. "Now, don't be mad."

Lemonade missed its destination, splashing on the counter rather than into a glass. JT narrowed his eyes. "What did you do?"

"I was thinking entirely of you," Sean said. "Well, mostly of you. Partially. We are business partners. Financially linked?"

"I'm aware. Cut to the chase."

Sean swallowed. "I accepted a commission for you."

"You *what?*"

"This older couple, the Owenbys, came into the gallery last night. You'd like them. Real marine-life enthusiasts, big contributors to the aquarium—"

"Sean!"

"They saw the abstract seascape mural of yours in Tennessee and want to hire you to do a much smaller version for their home."

"No."

"I told them they could leave a down payment with me and that I'd work out the details with you. Think of me as your agent."

"Which you aren't!"

"Don't you even want to know how much they're paying?"

"You had no business accepting that check!" JT thundered. He'd contact them and tell them no. Sean would refund their money. That would be that.

"I'm trying to help." Sean had raised his voice, too. It was unlike him to show such blatant emotion, which made his angry insistence doubly effective. "In case you haven't noticed, you've bottomed out."

"Gee, that escaped my attention."

"JT, I'm the best friend you've got, so get your head out of your ass and think it over. This doesn't even require the creativity of having a new idea. All you have to do is duplicate what already exists."

Pathetic. People were really willing to pay him money for that?

He wondered absently what his checking account looked like these days. He'd been coasting on some previous investments, what he'd made on the house sale and his part of the gallery proceeds. Gallery earnings, according to what Sean told him at lunch the other day, had steadily dipped for the past quarter. God, he *was* pathetic. Sean essentially did all the work in what was supposed to be a joint venture, picking up JT's slack for two years. Shame burned in his gut.

Maybe this was a way for JT to step up to the plate. Skulking around his apartment and waiting for his next great idea hadn't netted results.

"I thought it would help get you back in the habit," Sean pressed. "Kick-start your artistic drive."

"Oh, well then, I'll just slap some blue squiggly lines on a canvas and we'll all be happy, won't we?" But JT's sarcasm had lost its venomous edge. If he revisited a former painting, might it help him recapture what painting had been like back when he actually had inspiration?

He would do the painting, but he was still infuriated by Sean's high-handed techniques. Infuriated that he'd been reduced to this. He took a swig of his lemonade and walked past Sean, carrying both glasses.

"Where are you going with those?"

JT didn't bother glancing back. "To my studio to see if I can find something toxic to mix into yours."

"So is that a yes?"

"You should leave before I change my mind."

The front door opened before JT even finished his sentence, followed by a muffled whoop of triumph from the hall. JT was alone with two glasses of lemonade and the sudden fear that the only thing more pathetic than repainting something he'd already done would be painting a version that sucked.

Then again, at this point, what did he have left to lose?

Chapter 4

"I don't know, Mom," Leslie said from the beanbag chair where she was rereading *The Trumpet of the Swan.* "It still looks crooked."

Kenzie paused at the top of her stepladder to shoot her daughter a mock glare. "She who decides she'd rather read than help does not get to offer criticism."

"Would you actually let us help?" Drew asked excitedly, temporarily forgetting his handheld video game. "I didn't think I was allowed to climb up there or use a hammer."

"Well," Kenzie said, backpedaling, "there are lots of other things you could be doing if you wanted to lend a hand. Like wiping the remaining cabinets and drawers with a wet paper towel so I can finish putting away kitchen stuff."

Drew scrunched up his nose. "Lame."

Lame, huh? Then she hated to think what it said about her that she'd experienced a thrill of heady satisfaction after applying shelf liner to the pantry and closets last night.

Her moment of triumph, though, hadn't held quite the *zing* as the visceral thrill that had shot through her body when she'd seen JT's naked chest. That had been a much different sensation. Even now she tingled at the memory, glancing down guiltily to make sure the kids didn't realize their mom was having premature hot flashes over the new neighbor. She fanned herself with the framed picture she held.

"Mom?"

She almost jumped—not the best reaction at the top of a ladder. "Yes, Drew?"

"Why are you even hanging all this stuff?" he asked. "You're just gonna have to take it down in a couple of months when we move again."

For a change, he didn't sound bitter about relocating, merely curious.

"It's true that we won't be here long, but I want us to be comfortable and happy in the meantime." She indicated the pictures she'd already nailed into place. "This stuff makes me happy."

It was amazing how far some family pictures on the wall and colorful hand towels in the kitchen could go toward making a place cheerful and inviting. Mr. Carlyle had told them that residents in this particular building were allowed to make more changes than most, in terms of knobs, light fixtures and even painting the walls. Tenants were simply required either to return their surroundings to their original condition when they left or to pay for management to do so. Her short time here wasn't worth such effort, but she found herself imagining the difference she could make in the small apartment. It was cozier than it had first seemed when the atmosphere had been permeated with crankiness and the odor of damp cardboard.

There was a single bathroom, unfortunately, and it only held the toilet and bathtub. They each had a mirrored vanity and small private sink in the corner of their rooms. Like a hotel, Drew had said. Leslie had been ecstatic to have counter space for her hair stuff and lip gloss, and that she didn't have to share with her brother.

Because she was hammering a nail into the wall, Kenzie didn't realize there was someone at the door until Drew pointed it out to her. Leslie looked up with mild surprise, having been too engrossed in her novel to notice the knocking, either.

"Coming!" Kenzie called, descending from the ladder.

"Do you think it's that tall man?" Leslie asked. "The one who lives across the hall?"

"JT? I doubt it. I expect it's Mr. C. He said he'd be over sometime this weekend to fix my ceiling fan," Kenzie said. "What made you think of JT?"

Leslie shrugged. "He seems weird. Opening and shutting his door yesterday without saying anything. Standing there with no shirt and messy hair today. Like this creepy professor I read about in a mystery once where—"

"Les, later, okay?" Kenzie didn't want to open the

door while her daughter was cataloging what she perceived as JT's eccentricities after only two brief encounters. *My kid is either too quick to judge, or she's bizarrely perceptive.* After all, weren't a lot of artists known for being eccentric?

Like musicians.

She told herself that her potent physical reaction to JT earlier was just the unexpected shock of being that close to undressed male flesh, quite a rarity for her. If Kenzie ever dated again, it wouldn't be with a sleep-tousled artist sporting careless dabs of paint across his flat abdomen. No, she would take the smart route… someone like the attractive man in the shirt and slacks who'd appeared in the hallway just as JT fled into the recesses of his apartment with hardly a goodbye. *Les is right. He's a little weird.*

Luckily, not everyone in the building was mysterious, antisocial and averse to smiling. Kenzie opened the door to find a short, dark-haired woman beaming at her over the top of a foil-wrapped casserole dish.

"I'm Roberta Sanchez," the lady said in a faintly accented voice. "Welcome to Peachy Acres!"

"Thank you," Kenzie said, touched. The friendly gesture of hospitality reminded her of Raindrop; she hadn't necessarily expected to find it so close to the heart of a city. "Please come in. I'm Kenzie Green, and these are my kids, Drew and Leslie."

Drew sniffed the air like a hound. "What kind of food did you bring?" he demanded.

"Drew, don't be rude." The way her son acted, people probably thought Kenzie habitually starved him.

"How was I rude?" He rolled his eyes. "Don't you think she wants us to be interested in whatever she made?"

Mrs. Sanchez gave him a look that convinced Kenzie the older woman had children of her own. "Regardless, you should not talk back to your mother." Then she smiled, lowering her voice to a conspiratorial whisper. "And it's tamale pie."

It smelled incredible, and Kenzie's stomach gurgled with appreciation. She'd been so caught up in the visual progress she was making in the apartment that she hadn't realized how close it was getting to dinnertime. And heaven knew that when Leslie was lost in a book, she didn't stop to eat or sleep unless prompted. *Oops.* In light of her sarcastic thoughts about Drew's appetite, she experienced a little pinch of guilt.

"So it's a dessert?" Drew asked.

"Different kind of pie." Kenzie took the warm pan from Mrs. Sanchez. Breathing in the scent of spiced meat and melted cheeses, she feared she might start drooling. "Leslie, say hello to our visitor." *Which doesn't mean a halfhearted wave without glancing up from the page,* she added with telepathic sternness.

Thankfully, the girl put the book down—after carefully saving her place with a bookmark bearing the wand-wielding image of Daniel Radcliffe. "Hi, I'm Leslie Green. You live in the building?"

Mrs. Sanchez nodded. "You'll love it here."

"We're not staying long," Drew said, his eyes locked on the dish in Kenzie's hand as he practically vibrated with the unspoken question, *When can we eat?*

"No?" Mrs. Sanchez looked crestfallen. "Oh, that's too bad. I already told some of my grandchildren that they might have kids to play with when they visited. And Jonathan—JT—could use some company. This floor is practically deserted."

"Are you sure he *wants* company?" Leslie asked. "He reminds me a little of this guy in a story who kept to himself and had crazy eyes. No one could prove anything, but the characters suspected—"

"Leslie! Why don't you find some plates? We should eat this wonderful-smelling tamale pie before it gets cold," Kenzie said. Drew bounded toward the kitchen, eager to assist if it meant eating soon.

Leslie was slower, heaving a sigh as she trudged after him. "No one *ever* wants to hear about my books. I thought parents were supposed to be *happy* when their children liked to read."

"Less attitude, more cooperation," Kenzie admonished. Then she turned back to Mrs. Sanchez, who was trying not to smile. "Sorry. They're not always like this." *Sometimes they're worse.*

"I understand. I raised four." The woman's gaze held both amusement and empathy. "You seem like you have your hands full. It's just you and the children?"

Kenzie nodded. "They don't see my ex on what you'd call a 'regular' basis."

Mrs. Sanchez clucked her tongue. Something about her made Kenzie want to brew a pot of tea, sit down with the other woman and confide all her problems and doubts. Kenzie blinked, surprised by the impulse. She was accustomed to being self-sufficient. Her mother and father, bless their well-intentioned hearts, hadn't been big believers in hands-on parenting, afraid that too many guidelines and rules would "stifle" her individuality. So she'd made a lot of decisions from a young age…including the one to marry Mick.

Getting pregnant hadn't been a deliberate decision so much as a spontaneous celebration of a gig that was going to "put his band on the map." She'd never regretted having the twins, but once they were born, she had not only herself to look after but two small, dependent babies. Mick's failed attempts to be there for them had reinforced her determination to be independent. She must really be tired from the move if she was tempted to lean on a total stranger.

Straightening, Kenzie regained her composure. "Will you stay and eat with us, or do you have family waiting for you to join them for dinner?"

"Enrique and I ate early—he says waiting too late gives him heartburn at night—but I would love to stay for a few minutes and get to know you better."

Kenzie dished up three servings of the tamale pie and poured glasses of sweet tea. At her first bite of the dinner, she nearly moaned. "Oh, this is so good!" she told a delighted Mrs. Sanchez.

Drew grunted acknowledgment, but refused to slow his eating long enough to vocalize praise. Leslie looked disgusted by his behavior.

"Boys," she muttered imperiously. "Mrs. Sanchez, would you give my mom and me the recipe for this? We probably couldn't make it this good, but it might be fun to try."

"I'm pleased you like it!" Mrs. Sanchez said. "I'll bring the recipe up sometime this week."

"No practicing cooking while I'm at work, though," Kenzie told her daughter. "Sandwiches and microwaved snacks only." The kids were maturing, but not enough that she wanted them messing with a gas stove unsupervised.

When conversation revealed that Mrs. Sanchez was home most days, Kenzie thought about getting the woman's phone number so that the kids had an emergency contact right here in the building. Mrs. Sanchez seemed to know every one of their neighbors. Along with Mr. C., the first-floor tenants were a young married couple with a two-year-old who begged them to take her for rides on the elevator, a Georgia Tech grad student and the crusty Wilders.

"They've been married nearly forty years and have raised bickering to an art form," Mrs. Sanchez told Kenzie after the kids had cleared the table and returned to their abandoned book and video game. "They tell anyone who will listen that they're determined to outlive the other. If you ask me, though, they're crazy about each other and smart enough to know nobody else would put up with either of them."

The second floor, where Mrs. Sanchez and her husband lived, included a woman with six cats—Kenzie hated to think about her pet-deposit bill—and a family with two teenage daughters. Mrs. Sanchez said that should Kenzie ever need a sitter, she could give fifteen-year-old Alicia a call.

"Not her older sister, though. Boy crazy, that one.

If she was thinking about a boy or on the phone with a boy—which she always is—she wouldn't notice a child spurting arterial blood in front of her. Then there's the third floor," Mrs. Sanchez continued. "You, a flight attendant named Meegan and, of course, Jonathan. You've met him?"

Kenzie nodded. Questions bubbled up inside her, trying to pop free, but she bit her tongue. Voicing any curiosity conflicted with her resolve as a practical single mother to have no interest in him.

Mrs. Sanchez paused, her prolonged silence and dark eyes making Kenzie feel as if she had to say *something*.

"He, uh, seems nice. We didn't talk much, but he helped me carry some stuff to the apartment when I dropped a box on the stairs."

"He's a good man," Mrs. Sanchez said, her tone wistful. "Sometimes, I wish I could have known him before…"

"Before what?" The question spilled out of its own volition. *Ann would be so disappointed.* Hadn't Kenzie, approaching thirty, learned to temper her impulses with more discipline?

To Kenzie's surprise, Mrs. Sanchez wasn't quick to fill in the blanks of JT's history as she had been with the other occupants.

"Before he moved here," was all she said. "He had a different life and must have been a very different man. Maybe you can get to know him better at the Labor Day rooftop picnic. Everyone in the building comes! Well, not Meegan, if she's traveling. You'll still be here Labor Day, won't you? That's right around the corner."

Kenzie nodded. "We don't move until mid-October. We just needed somewhere to stay in the interim."

"You picked the right place! Peachy Acres is a nice group of people, but a little nosy," Mrs. Sanchez said with a grin. "Once residents know I've met you, they'll want to hear all about the new lady in 3D."

"Not much to hear," Kenzie said. "Mother of two with a desk job at a bank. Very staid."

Mrs. Sanchez raised an eyebrow. "I suspect there is more to your story than that."

Not if I'm lucky. After her unorthodox childhood and tumultuous marriage, Kenzie aspired to an uneventful life with as few surprises as possible. Although, she conceded as she walked Mrs. Sanchez to the door and thanked her again for the unexpected visit and wonderful food, not all surprises were bad. As she had the thought, she couldn't help glancing past Mrs. Sanchez at the closed door of apartment 3C. Mrs. Sanchez's earlier words ran through her head. *He had a different life and must have been a very different man.*

What kind of surprises had life dealt Jonathan Trelauney?

In art school, entire semesters could be spent in the study of perspective. There was no question JT needed to change *his* perspective. With a growl of frustration, he stood up from his desk. Maybe a change of scenery would help this afternoon. Sure as hell couldn't hurt.

In times past, he'd enjoyed the familiar scents of his workroom—the faint bite of oil, the sweet beeswax he sometimes worked with—but now he seemed to be suffocating on the stench of failure. Fresh air and a fresh outlook were definitely in order. *The roof.* He grabbed a sketch pad and a couple of charcoal pencils. Without allowing his gaze to linger on the door of Kenzie's apartment, he crossed the hall to the roof-access door, then took the stairs two at a time until he emerged into the brightness.

There was a lot to be said for natural light, but the sun overhead was nearly punishing in force. He was grateful for the rooftop breeze, even if it ruffled his pages and his hair. Impatiently pushing aside the dark strands that blew into his eyes, he tried to remember the last time he'd had a haircut. Sean had remarked that JT looked less civilized with each passing week.

JT had always been absentminded when it came to trivialities like regular haircuts—he'd been preoccupied creating his art. Now he was preoccupied with *not* creating it.

He settled himself in one of the chairs and scowled at the pencil in his hand, willing it to do something. Anything. After Sean's visit yesterday, JT had tried to work on the commissioned painting. How could he be stuck on something that was already finished? In theory, all he had to do was duplicate it—any halfway decent forger or first-year art student could do that.

The work needed something new, though, some flourish or detail or spin, otherwise the buyers weren't getting their money's worth, merely an adult version of paint-by-numbers. He'd tried throwing some paint on a canvas, playing, to see where it led…which was nowhere. Rather than continue to waste supplies, he thought he could sketch some ideas first. Finally his hand began moving, the pencil making a familiar soft scratching against the paper.

When it stopped, he stared at the thickly lettered sentence he'd written: *I am going to kill Sean.* Friend or not, the man had no business accepting a job on JT's behalf.

The sound of the metal door scraping across the concrete drew his attention. Kenzie's daughter stepped outside, blinking. When she saw him, she froze.

"You're that guy!"

He quirked an eyebrow. "And you're that kid who lives across from me."

"Leslie." She held a book in front of her, almost as though it were a tiny shield. "Mom said I could come up here to read."

There was little danger of anyone falling off the roof, with or without adult supervision, since the patio was surrounded by a tall mesh fence that slanted inward at the top. It was safe enough as long as the kid was wearing sunscreen, and all tenants had an equal right to be here. He gave her a gruff nod and hoped that she'd immerse herself in the book and leave him alone.

It took about two seconds for him to realize that wasn't going to happen.

"What are you doing up here?" she asked curiously.

"Working."

She didn't take the hint. "What kind of job do you have?"

"I paint."

"But you aren't painting now." She'd dropped her

book on a chair and studied him, her expression imperious despite her diminutive status. Something in that moment reminded him of Holly, making him want to smile. "You don't even have paints with you."

JT ground his teeth. "I sketch ideas first, then paint later."

"Oh. Can I see what you're working on?" She was walking toward him as she voiced the rhetorical question.

"No, I—" He flipped the pad closed, but apparently not before she glimpsed some of the words.

"Kill Sean?" Her blue eyes were wide.

No doubt she'd tell Kenzie they were living across the hall from a homicidal maniac. "Don't ask. It's a long story." And none of her business, although that wasn't proving much of a deterrent.

She stiffened. "You think I wouldn't understand because I'm some dumb kid?"

"I—"

"Mrs. Griffin, our librarian, said she thought I was one of the smartest students in the whole elementary school!" Leslie's bottom lip trembled. Her indignation was morphing into something far more uncomfortable. "Now I won't get to see her *or* the teachers *or* the other kids in my class because we had to *move*. I wanted to stay in Raindrop!"

It wasn't his place to warn her that life often took unexpected directions. And it wasn't as if he could counsel her on weathering the bumps, since he hadn't recovered from his own. At a loss, he pointed toward her book, his tone abrupt in his own ears. "I thought you came up here to read. I'm trying to work here."

She burst into tears.

Oh, hell. He'd wanted to dissuade further conversation, but he hadn't meant to hurt her feelings. "Wait, I… No, don't do that. Please stop."

He stood, even though he had no idea what he planned to do. Go toward her? He couldn't reassure a little girl. What would he say—that everything would be all right? Yeah, that would be really convincing, coming from him. He could tell her that recent sleep deprivation made him a jackass, but that seemed inappropriate. Certainly his entreaty for her to stop hadn't accomplished anything.

Panic rose within him. What if she got more hysterical? Should he go get Kenzie? He winced, imagining what she'd do to him for reducing her kid to sobs.

"You're still crying," he said helplessly.

Oddly enough, that penetrated the girl's sniffles and fluttery gestures. She sent him a damp glare. "Thank you, Captain Obvious."

Her reaction surprised a chuckle out of him. "Aren't you too young for sarcasm?"

"No."

Well, all right then. What did he know about kids? He recalled his wife's excitement as she talked about their becoming parents. Would he have been a good father?

Leslie rubbed one eye, scowling at him with the other. "I wasn't crying because of you, just so you know."

"Oh. Good."

"It's just…I'm a pest. I should learn, being one of the smartest kids in Raindrop. I bothered my dad once when he was working on a song. He yelled at me."

What a jerk. Not that JT had done well himself, but shouldn't her actual father do a better job of relating?

"Sometimes I wonder if Drew and I weren't such pains, whether Dad would've stuck around. Then maybe we could have stayed in Raindrop. As a family."

Despite knowing that no one else was on the roof, JT reflexively looked around for help. The situation called for someone like Mrs. Sanchez or Sean, who always knew what to say to people. JT wished he were anywhere but here. This kid's home life was none of his business, and anything he said could potentially make her feel worse.

"I, ah…there are a lot of good things about Atlanta," he said awkwardly.

"Like what?"

"We have libraries here, just like they did in Raincloud."

"Raindrop." She sighed miserably. "But the libraries here won't have Mrs. Griffin, will they?"

"Eventually you'll miss it less," he mumbled.

"That doesn't help *now*."

Her matter-of-fact statement was so true, he sent her an admiring glance. "You really are a smart kid."

"I know." Juxtaposed against the seeming arrogance in her words was the painful fragility in her expression. Her features were so much like her mother's that it was easy to picture the same vulnerability in Kenzie's eyes, although the mental image added to his discomfort. Did Kenzie know she was better off without her jerky ex, or did she—like her daughter—second-guess what went wrong and wonder if they'd made a mistake in coming to Atlanta?

"There's a great aquarium here," he said. "And some really good restaurants. Zoo Atlanta. Museums. I did a mural for a children's fine arts museum."

She looked skeptical a moment before allowing, "I guess you really are a painter."

"I really am." Or had been, once. "I even have VIP passes to the museum. I can bring guests in free of admission and stay for a little while after closing hours." Part of him recoiled in anticipation of the coming invitation. What was he doing, getting more involved with the Greens? Hadn't these few minutes on the roof been painful enough?

But he hated the expression in Leslie's eyes and his part in putting it there.

He never used his passes, and this kid was going through a rough time. Was he really such a heartless recluse that he couldn't spare a couple of hours to give her family a guided tour through a museum? Maybe he'd rediscover some inspiration while he was there.

"If your family's not already busy next weekend and your mom approves the idea, perhaps I could take the three of you to the museum for a little while, show you that Atlanta's not all bad?"

"For real?" Leslie's face brightened so suddenly she rivaled the sun. "That would be cool. Let's go ask Mom!"

"What, now?"

Nodding, she scooped up her book, then dashed toward the door. She shot a look over her shoulder, as if double-checking to make sure that he was coming. As if she was worried that, given the chance, he'd change his mind.

Yep, he thought with wry admiration. She was *definitely* a smart kid.

Chapter 5

Kenzie slid deeper into the vanilla-scented froth of bubbles, a sigh escaping her as heat seeped through her aching body. Oh, she needed this! Drew had just popped a movie into the DVD player, and Leslie was upstairs with a book. Was it possible Kenzie was about to enjoy an almost unheard of half hour of peace?

"Mom, Mom!"

You had to ask. She squeezed her eyes shut in denial, but called through the door, "What is it, Les?"

"I have to ask you something!"

"Can it wait, honey?"

Was it Kenzie's imagination, or did she hear the rumble of a lower voice out in the hallway? Her eyes opened. "Leslie, is Mr. Carlyle with you?"

"No. Mr. Trelauney."

Kenzie couldn't have grabbed for a towel any faster if her daughter had informed her that JT had X-ray vision. "Offer him a soda. I'll be out in a minute."

Sparing only a cursory wistful glance at the bathtub behind her, Kenzie hurriedly put on undergarments, followed by a faded polo shirt and a pair of denim shorts that got stuck on her damp thighs before obediently sliding into place. She looked disheveled, her hair curling in moist, frizzy ringlets about her shoulders, but at least she was dressed.

What was JT doing here? She doubted it was to bring them a neighborly casserole. Joining her daughter and neighbor in the kitchen, Kenzie was struck by how much smaller the room seemed when filled with JT's presence.

She swallowed. "Mr. Trelauney. To what do we owe the pleasure?"

Leslie bounced on the balls of her feet. "JT's gonna take us to a museum! Where he's a celebrity!"

"Let's not get ahead of ourselves, kid." The large artist looked comically uneasy next to her daughter— like a German shepherd afraid of a Chihuahua. He turned to Kenzie. "*Celebrity* is putting it too strongly, but I did some work for a museum that lets me bring guests. I told Leslie that we could *ask* about going some weekend…if you didn't mind."

"Please, Mom!" Leslie begged, looking more animated than she had since they'd first arrived in Atlanta. "I've read books about cool museums like the Louvre but I've never been to one. You said the good part about living here was all the stuff Raindrop didn't have. What do you think, Drew?"

He'd trailed his sister and their unexpected guest to the edge of the kitchen and stood against the wall, straightening just long enough to shrug his shoulders. "I'd rather go to a baseball game, but I guess a museum's okay."

"So can we, Mom?"

"Go watch the movie with Drew and let me discuss it with Mr. Trelauney."

"Okay. But he *wants* to take us. He invited us. You don't want to be rude to our new neighbor!"

Kenzie narrowed her eyes. "Out."

No sooner had Leslie gone than Kenzie wished she hadn't been so hasty. Now she was alone with JT, who looked just as good in a worn cotton T-shirt that lovingly molded his torso as he had without a shirt. *Really, Kenzie. You're a practical adult, not a hormone-stricken teen.*

"Can I get you that soft drink?" she offered.

"No, thanks. I don't want to impose."

"It seems my daughter was imposing on you. She didn't knock on your door, did she?" Maybe Kenzie should have paid more attention to whatever Les had been saying about the book with the reclusive man. If her daughter was bugging real people because of a fictional mystery, Kenzie needed to have a *long* talk with her.

"I was sketching up on the roof." He nodded toward

a pad sitting on her kitchen counter. "She came up to read and started a conversation."

Figured. When Kenzie needed Leslie to do something, she couldn't draw the kid's attention out of a story. But when JT needed peace and quiet to do his work, her erstwhile bookworm turned into Chatty Cathy. "I'm sorry if she was bothering you."

He shuffled slightly, shifting his weight. "Our conversation didn't go very well."

"Define not very well."

"Adolescent-weeping unwell."

She frowned. "You made Leslie cry?"

"I was trying to work and suggested she read her book instead of bugging me. I didn't put it that bluntly," he added quickly, "but she started crying. Said something about bothering her dad when *he* was working."

"I see." She truly did. JT wasn't the one who'd hurt Leslie. That had been Mick.

Kenzie could hear her ex-husband in her head, snapping that if the kids weren't so distracting, he would have written a hit song by now. Of course, he'd apologized later. Mick always said he was sorry; that was his standard MO. What had changed was Kenzie's ability to accept the apologies.

"I'll talk to her," she said tiredly. "You don't have to take us on a field trip because you feel guilty."

"You'll probably be doing *me* the favor," he said, surprising her by not seizing the easy out. "Sean, my business partner, says I need to get out more. Maybe someone else's enthusiasm for art will help me reclaim my own."

"Artist's block?" she asked.

"Something like that."

Beneath his dry tone, there was a...vulnerability. She felt oddly drawn to him, this big man who seemed to shoulder even bigger problems. For a second she thought she might reach out, try to smooth his troubles away with a soft caress. *Stupid.* Jonathan Trelauney was not a little boy who needed nurturing. He was like Mick, a man at the whim of his "muse" or whatever. While other people toiled nine to five, JT moved restlessly through his days—or napped through them—seeking inspiration. If he'd snapped at Leslie upstairs, had it been out of frustration with Kenzie's daughter or simply frustration with himself and his artistic gift?

Déjà vu all over again.

"Mr. Trelauney, thank you for the invitation, but I really think it would be better if the kids and I don't join you." It was the same pleasant but inarguable tone she might have used when telling a bank customer that their loan had been declined. A touch apologetic but firm. JT would have to be obtuse not to get the message.

He moved toward her almost imperceptibly, not actually taking a step but leaning as if to study her better. "You don't like me, do you?"

"I don't know you."

"And you don't want to." Strangely, he sounded almost amused.

Kenzie sighed. "Look, my kids and I are only going

to be in the building for a brief time. We're waiting for our new house to be ready. So I probably won't get the chance to know anyone all that well. Don't take it personally."

"Go to the museum with me."

His persistence startled her. "Why are you pressing this? Given the way you practically slammed your door in my face when I brought your mail, I assumed you weren't interested in getting to know us, either."

Absently, he rubbed his knuckles over his stubbled jaw. "You're refreshing to be around. And a hell of a lot better than my own company."

What was she supposed to say to that? *Refreshing?* He made her sound like fruit juice.

"As you said," he continued, "you won't be here long. Why not take this short-lived opportunity to let an artist give Leslie a behind-the-scenes tour of a museum? It'll make her happy. She misses home, you know."

"Of course I know that!" In light of his valid point and obvious willingness to accompany them, it seemed churlish to continue refusing. "Fine."

His eyes widened in mild surprise. "So it's a date?"

"If by 'date' you mean a mutually agreed upon and strictly platonic social outing intended to cheer up my daughter, then yes." Her tone was so proper that Ann would have applauded. Deep down, Kenzie knew she sounded uptight, but this man did not bring out the best in her.

He didn't seem offended, though. In fact, his lips actually twitched, as if he might...

Yowza. In their few exchanges, she'd never seen him truly smile. Now a grin transformed his whole face, making his memorable gray eyes bright with humor. But the expression was fleeting, leaving the kitchen somehow a touch darker and dingier than it had been a moment ago. She had to fight the compulsion to cajole another smile from him.

"It's a date," he repeated, giving her one last unreadable look before walking past to tell the kids that he'd see them next weekend.

Kenzie, her legs feeling unsteady, listened to Leslie's exultant whoop of delight and to the door closing as JT left. Mrs. Sanchez had said she wished she'd known JT "before." Had Kenzie just received a glimpse at the man he'd once been? Because, despite what she'd said about not forming attachments at Peachy Acres, she suspected she could very much enjoy getting to know *that* man.

JT straightened, rolling his shoulders and blinking like a man waking from a dream—that's how painting had often felt to him, a kind of altered state of reality. Though he wasn't painting, at least he'd finally put something besides death threats against Sean on the pages of the damn sketch pad. Fidgeting with his pencil, he studied the image.

Not bad. He'd almost captured the play of emotions on the woman's face. Artistically speaking, this was better than anything he'd managed in weeks. On a personal level, however, he was a little disturbed to find himself sketching Kenzie Green at two in the morning.

He doubted she would appreciate being his subject.

Amazing how someone could be so prickly and so soft at the same time. A study in contrasts. This afternoon, she'd tried to politely dissuade him from the museum visit. Despite a civil tone, there had been a chill in her gaze. Because he'd upset her daughter? Instead of being dissuaded, he'd stood there like a fool noticing that she smelled like vanilla, bringing to mind fresh-baked cookies warm from the oven.

Even hours later, he was still surprised that he'd pushed the museum invitation. After all, he'd only mentioned it to Leslie in the first place because he'd panicked at the sight of her tears…and had regretted the gesture nearly as quickly as he'd made it. He was not what Sean would call "a people person." What if they went to the museum on Saturday and it was an awkward disaster for all of them? What if he said something stupid and somehow made Leslie cry again?

Then Kenzie will knock your block off. Perversely, he found himself grinning at the prospect. He could tell she was a protective mama bear trying to do what was best for her cubs. And she was protective of herself. She handled it differently than he did, but it was there, a certain distance, an unspoken warning of "Don't get too close. I've been hurt."

He could empathize—sometimes he wasn't entirely comfortable being close to even Sean or Mrs. Sanchez. Unlike those two, Kenzie didn't know enough about him to pity him. There was no softened edge of sympathy in her dealings with him, and he appreciated that.

He hadn't realized how much he *needed* that. Kenzie Green was too caught up in her small family and over-coming their obstacles to be worried about "poor JT."

With a sigh, he glanced back at the sketch.

He missed being an artist, missed the certainty of knowing who he was. And he was damn tired of being poor JT.

Barely pausing in her phone conversation, Kenzie smiled and held up her index finger to signal that she'd be done in a moment. Ann nodded, choosing to stand while she waited. She fell into that unconscious sway that was habitual to many new mothers, keeping Abigail soothed inside her navy-and-white-checked baby sling. It was the first time she'd come inside Kenzie's new place of business, and Kenzie could see the approval on her sister's face. The marbleized floor spread from one end of the main lobby, where the tellers worked, to a row of judiciously spaced mahogany desks—one of which Kenzie now occupied—and beyond, to the offices reserved for those with seniority and supervisor positions.

When Kenzie was finished going over some interest rates with the customer, she bade the other woman a good day, slid off her headset and reached for the gold hoop earring she'd removed earlier. "I'm so glad you called," she told her sister. "I'm starving!"

"Buying you lunch seemed like the least I could do to help celebrate the new job. How'd your first week go?"

It was Thursday now, with the weekend—and her ill-advised "date" with JT—right around the corner. *Best not to think about that.* "Everyone here's great."

It wasn't Raindrop, where everyone knew her, but there was a certain relief in not being surrounded by colleagues who knew every detail of her life…such as what waitress Mick had spent the night with on his last visit to town. Her new coworkers seemed friendly, and her boss had three children of his own, which gave Kenzie hope that he'd understand when she had to leave early to pick up a sick kid or request a morning off for a school field trip.

Purse in hand, Kenzie rose. "So, what are we in the mood for?"

"Italian?" Ann asked hopefully. "We never eat it at home. Forrest says the acid in tomato sauce upsets his stomach, and Alfredo is too heavy."

"Sounds good to me," Kenzie said, wondering at the way her sister's mouth turned down when she said her husband's name. Ann could be opinionated, but she wasn't petty. If she was upset with Forrest about something, Kenzie doubted it was a lack of lasagna. "Everything okay?"

Ann blinked, her smile falling in place as automatically as if someone had flipped a switch. "Of course. What could possibly be wrong?"

In Ann's life? Good question. When Kenzie had been an impulsive teenager, she'd thought that her sister's approach of "thinking everything to death" was tedious and unimaginative. Time and circumstances had changed Kenzie's mind. If someone with Ann's discipline and organizational skills came into the bank for a loan, Kenzie would approve it instantly.

"What?" Ann asked, her smile replaced by a slightly more defensive expression. "You're looking at me funny. I told you, everything's okay."

"I believe you. I was just thinking that I'd like to be you when I grow up."

"Oh." Ann chuckled nervously, tucking a strand of hair behind her left ear. "Well, thank you."

They rode in Ann's car because it was outfitted with the baby's car seat, and Ann wound through several one-way streets, taking an indirect route to a small Italian café. She parallel parked with an ease Kenzie envied—*thank goodness we didn't bring the van*—and they climbed out onto the sidewalk. To the right of the front door was a patio enclosed with wrought-iron fencing and mostly shaded by a massive awning.

"You want to eat outside?" Kenzie asked. "Or will that be too hot for you and Abigail?"

"No, this is actually nice weather for August," Ann said. "You can almost tell fall is coming."

Fall. Kenzie thought ahead a few months, to the image of her Perfect House. She and the kids would be moved in by Halloween, trick-or-treating in their new neighborhood, officially starting a new life.

A dark-haired hostess with a wad of gum crammed in her cheek showed them to an outdoor table, and Kenzie watched her sister situate Abigail's carrier, raising the bonnet to offer further shade, and handing the baby a pre-prepared bottle. Looking back now, it was hard to believe Kenzie's own children had ever been this young. She'd been too preoccupied that first year with merely *surviving* to realize how little Mick contributed. It wasn't until much later that she'd started to come to her senses, and even then she'd been worried about whether she should have tried to make the marriage work for the children's sakes.

She was confident now that she'd made the right decision. Thinking of Drew's increasingly defiant expressions, she wondered how to convince her kids of that.

"So are the kids looking forward to school?" Ann asked once they'd ordered.

"Leslie is." School would be in session the week after next. "Drew's looking forward to finding out more about soccer leagues."

"Well, if they're looking to get out of the apartment in the meantime, y'all could come over this weekend," Ann offered. "We have that big community pool in the subdivision. Want to go swimming Saturday?"

Kenzie felt her cheeks warm and told herself it was the heat of the day. "Actually, the kids and I are going to an art museum on Saturday."

"Really? Which one? It's been a while since I've been to the High," Ann mused. "Maybe I—"

"We're going as the guests of someone else," Kenzie blurted, afraid that her sister had been about to volunteer her company. Since she and Ann had never been very close growing up, it seemed odd that suddenly her sister was so omnipresent—babysitting the kids on Monday, so that Kenzie knew they were in good hands on her first day, then buying lunch today, and now wanting to get together Saturday. Did she want to make up for lost years? Was she simply doing her best to help them settle into a new city? Or...was Ann somehow lonely?

In theory, Kenzie wouldn't mind having her sister join in on the museum to help defray some of the awkwardness—*sexual tension*—between her and JT, but it didn't seem right to add members to their party without first asking him. Besides, Kenzie could just imagine how her sister and the eccentric artist would hit it off.

"Guests of someone else? You're making friends fast," Ann said with a smile. "Is this someone from the bank?"

Kenzie fidgeted in her seat, probably looking as guilty as Drew did when he was attempting a fib. "No. From Peachy Acres."

"That Mrs. Sanchez you told me about? She sounds lovely."

"She is. But no, not her." Kenzie scanned the patio, hoping for some sign of the waitress approaching with lunch. Maybe food would distract her sister.

"So?" Ann asked.

"So what?"

"Who invited you to the museum? You're acting awfully strange."

"I've always been the weird sister, right?" Kenzie forced a laugh.

Ann drummed her fingernails on the table.

"There's a guy in the building who was...is...an

artist. He did some work for the museum, so he's giving us kind of a behind the scenes tour."

"Cool."

"Cool?" Hardly the reaction Kenzie had expected. "You're not going to grill me about who the guy is?"

"You just told me—he's a neighbor of yours and an artist." Ann studied her from beneath raised eyebrows. "Is there something else I need to know?"

When I see him, my heart beats faster. He's inspiring bubble-bath fantasies about acts my body forgot how to perform years ago. There's something about him that makes me want to share my feelings because I suspect he'd understand. "N-no. That's all there is to tell."

After her lunch with Ann, Kenzie managed to put her upcoming museum visit out of her head for the rest of the day. Friday passed quickly with high-volume business at the bank, and she was relieved to step into the lobby of Peachy Acres that evening. Mr. C. nodded to her on his way out, and she waited for the elevator, telling herself she should take the stairs for the exercise, but feeling too drained to motivate herself to do so. The doors parted with a ding and Sylvia Myer grinned at her over the top of her daughter's head.

"Afternoon, Kenzie."

"What number?" the little girl asked.

Sylvia shook her head. "I don't know why we ever spend money on toys. She'd be perfectly content to stay in the elevator all day."

They rode up to the third floor, and Kenzie could

hear the muted thud of music as she approached her apartment. She'd worked out a nice deal with Alicia from downstairs, who came and "hung out" with the kids for the bulk of Kenzie's workday. While Drew and Les would have chafed at the idea of a babysitter, they didn't mind playing board games with a pretty high-school sophomore and listening to top-40 tunes while Kenzie navigated rush-hour traffic.

The thought of traffic made her grimace. Once they moved farther out to their Perfect House, her commute would lengthen considerably.

Behind her, JT's door creaked open and she jumped about a foot, her breath catching in her throat.

"Sorry, did I startle you?" a good-looking blond man asked, his tone both apologetic and amused as he stepped out into the hall and closed the door.

Sean, she recalled. They'd met briefly before. A nice guy and unrepentant flirt, according to Mrs. Sanchez. His light eyes were full of humor and easygoing charm, the opposite of the shadows that seemed to haunt his friend's gaze.

"I guess my mind was just somewhere else," she said, feeling foolish. "I don't know why I reacted like that."

He nodded, but pursed his lips in a thoughtful way that made her wonder if he'd guessed she was unnerved by the prospect of seeing JT. "I hear you're going to the children's art museum tomorrow."

Curiosity raced through her. What exactly had JT

said about her and the twins? "Yeah, the kids are really looking forward to it."

Sean stepped closer, lowering his voice to a confidential tone. "I think the big guy is, too. Amazingly enough."

Although his words matched her initial surprise that JT hadn't graciously bowed out of the offer, she frowned. "Is it so amazing that an artist would enjoy a trip to an art museum?"

"Some days it's hard for him to enjoy much of anything."

Her pulse fluttered with a mixture of dread and excitement, as if she had inched closer to a secret she wasn't sure she wanted to discover. Would Sean fill in the blanks Mrs. Sanchez had left tantalizingly open? "He's been through a lot, hasn't he?"

He nodded. "Loss has a way of changing people. Be patient with him."

The implication of his words, combined with the intensity of his expression, rattled her. "Oh, but I— It's just a trip to the museum. For the kids. It's not like we're…"

"No?" Though Sean looked disappointed, he rallied quickly. "Sorry to have misread the situation."

"N-not at all," she stammered, more jittery than ever over tomorrow's date. *Get a grip. It hardly qualifies as a date when you're chaperoned by two nine-year-olds.*

Who was she kidding? Even if they were chaperoned

by the entire student body of the kids' new elementary school, going somewhere with JT was the closest thing she'd had to a social life in years.

Chapter 6

"You should wear shorts, Mom. It's too hot out for jeans." Leslie sat on the edge of Kenzie's bed, watching her brush her hair in the vanity mirror. She had a book in her hands, but ignored it in favor of dispensing fashion advice. "Plus, you still have nice legs."

Kenzie smirked over her shoulder. "Be careful how you say *still*."

"Or a skirt," Leslie said with a snap of her fingers. "I'll bet Mr. Trelauney would like you in a skirt."

Alarm bells clanged in Kenzie's head. "Honey, I'm not dressing to impress Mr. Trelauney. This isn't a… romantic outing. I'm focusing on you and Drew and my new job for the foreseeable future. I don't have any interest in dating anyone."

Leslie flopped down dramatically on the mattress. "I'm *never* going to have a dad."

"You have a dad."

"Not really."

At times like this, Kenzie could cheerfully strangle her ex-husband. "I know your father doesn't get to see you as much as any of us would like, but he loves you and your brother."

When Leslie wrinkled her nose, saying nothing, Kenzie moved to less dangerous territory and called out to her son. "Drew, we're leaving soon. Get your shoes on, please. And you'd better have paused that video game long enough to brush your hair."

He appeared in the doorway, scowling. "I can't find my other sneaker."

Before Kenzie could launch into an oft-repeated lecture about picking up after himself and staying organized, Leslie suggested, "Why not just wear your sandals? I saw them behind the couch."

"Thanks, Les." He turned to go.

"Tell Mom Mr. Trelauney would like her blue shirt," Leslie implored. "It brings out her eyes."

Looking back over his shoulder, Drew rolled his own eyes. "Mr. Trelauney's a guy. We don't notice that stuff."

"JT isn't a guy, he's a man. *Way* more mature than you. Plus, he's an artist, so of *course* he notices colors and composition."

Ann had taken the kids to a nearby library on Monday, and Leslie had been reading about art ever since. Motherly intuition told Kenzie they were on the cusp of Leslie's Next Big Phase.

The knock at their front door sent Drew scampering off for his sandals.

"I can answer it," Leslie told her mom, "if you want to finish getting ready."

Kenzie secured her hair in a simple twist and fastened the barrette clasp. "I am ready."

Still, she let Leslie hurry down the hall in front of her and open the door. Kenzie heard JT exchange greetings with the kids before she rounded the corner. Once she did, she froze in surprise.

The man smiling down at Leslie looked like a stranger, or at least an "after" JT, as if he'd participated in one of those makeover shows Leslie loved. JT had shaved since the last time Kenzie had seen him, and at first she thought he'd cut his hair, too. Upon closer inspection, she decided he'd simply tamed it into submission somehow. Gel, maybe? It wasn't slick or stiff. On the contrary, it looked entirely touchable. So much so that her fingertips tingled.

His clothes were notably different—wrinkle-free khaki slacks and a short-sleeved cranberry shirt with buttons down the front that were a shade or two brighter. It was conservative enough that he wouldn't have looked out of place in the bank, but different enough from his other clothes to make her realize that, for an artist, he didn't wear much color.

At that moment, he glanced up, his gaze colliding with hers. Her heartbeat stuttered, speeding up like an erratic recording before resuming its rhythm.

"Hi," she said, quickly breaking eye contact. "So…

everyone ready to go? Shoes on the right feet, no one needs to hit the bathroom first?"

"Mother!" Leslie's face was a mask of mortification.

With a teasing glint in his silvery eyes, JT made a show of checking his shoes. "I think we're good."

Once they reached the parking garage, Drew asked if they could go in JT's car.

"Whatever you drive has to be cooler than Mom's minivan," he told the tall man. "Which one's yours?"

"That one." JT pointed toward a blue station wagon. It was in desperate need of being washed and didn't look much newer than Kenzie's van.

"A wagon?" Funny, she would have imagined him as the owner of a motorcycle or something.

"Got a good deal from its previous owner. It gets surprisingly good mileage and provided plenty of space for…my artwork," he said flatly.

The tension in his tone might be due to his lack of inspiration lately, but she suspected it was more than that. Not sure what to say, she simply offered, "I'll drive, you can navigate." Behind the wheel, she'd have a specific activity to accomplish and would feel less tongue-tied. She hoped.

Inside the van, Kenzie just barely refrained from reminding everyone to buckle their seat belts. She sighed inwardly, knowing that the twins wouldn't appreciate being mothered in front of JT, and that the man himself would probably be amused. *I was interesting once,* she thought wryly. Surely she'd held conversations that didn't involve reminding people to tie their laces before they tripped, or to take smaller bites so they didn't choke.

Yes, and where did being interesting get you? chided a voice that sounded a little like her sister's. Kenzie wouldn't trade her kids for the world, but she hadn't set out to be a single mom. It was a lot to shoulder alone, and at times she felt a twinge of guilt that maybe she wasn't providing everything they needed emotionally. Everything they'd get in a two-parent family that included a *reliable* father.

"Kenzie?" JT's husky voice captured her attention, sending shivers along her spine. "You heard what I said about turning left, didn't you?"

"Oh." She'd pulled up to the exit of the parking garage, then stalled out in her own thoughts. "Right. I mean left. I'm turning left now and heading toward Harris."

Kenzie didn't know why she'd been worried about any awkward silences. Leslie didn't allow any.

"I've been studying art all week," the girl told JT enthusiastically. "I didn't realize there were so many types! Just in painting there's impressionism, pointillism, abstract—"

"He knows," Drew interrupted. "*He's* an artist."

Though Kenzie glimpsed the resulting glare in the rearview mirror, Leslie continued as though her brother hadn't spoken. "So what kind of painting do you do, JT?"

"Mostly I work with oil, but also hot wax. Have you ever heard of encaustic painting?"

"No. It sounds fascinating."

Drew snorted.

JT swiveled around, his tone sympathetic. "Art isn't your cup of tea?"

Understatement of the year, Kenzie thought. Her son would probably just as soon throw himself from the moving automobile into oncoming traffic as sit trapped in the van for another half hour while his sister breathlessly peppered JT with painting questions.

"I like sports," Drew said, a note of challenge in his tone. He wasn't as easily won over as his sister.

"Sports are cool," JT agreed. "To watch, anyway. I was too uncoordinated to succeed in playing them."

"Hmm." Kenzie hadn't meant to make the small, puzzled sound. But truthfully, with his build and unthinking, almost negligent, grace she was surprised JT didn't have a more athletic background.

Not that she planned on saying exactly that, but given the quizzical way he was regarding her, she should say something. "I was just thinking you can't be any less coordinated than *me.* After all, you do remember how we met?"

In her peripheral vision, she saw his lips twitch.

"I'm great at sports," Drew said with all the modesty of a nine-year-old boy. "I play soccer and baseball. Too bad you didn't paint something useful like Turner Field, or we could be spending the day—"

"Andrew Green!" Kenzie was appalled at her son's rudeness. "Apologize immediately. And then I suggest that you sit quietly for the rest of the ride and think about how to be more respectful of other people and their varying interests."

"Sorry," Drew mumbled.

Great. They'd barely made it five blocks, and JT probably already regretted his invitation. This did not bode well for the rest of their day.

The museum was doing steady weekend business, but didn't seem jam-packed. There were a dozen or so people lined up in the gleaming lobby to purchase tickets. JT bypassed the main booth, crossing the hardwood floor toward the white counter on their left. The sign hanging above the counter read Members and VIP Parties.

A young woman with a blond ponytail and navy blazer glanced up with a smile. "Welcome to the Wilkes Fine Arts Youth Museum."

"Jonathan! Is that you?" A redhead in her thirties hurried to the end of the counter, flipping up a hinged section to join them on the other side. She stopped just shy of hugging JT, squeezing his arm instead. "It's great to see you."

"You, too, Beth."

"Been too long," she reprimanded him good-naturedly. "You know we'll issue you passes for any time you want to use them. Dare I hope you've been hidden away because you're working on a new series?"

"Beth, I'd like you to meet Kenzie Green and her kids, Drew and Leslie."

The redhead paused, then turned to include them in her bright smile. "Nice to meet you!"

Drew grunted a perfunctory hello. Leslie excitedly explained that this was their first visit and that she'd already mapped out online the exhibits she was most interested in. Meanwhile, Kenzie considered the other woman's body language. It was obvious Beth and JT shared some sort of history and that she cared about him. Was she attracted to him?

What woman wouldn't *be?*

Dangerous thought. Kenzie herself couldn't afford to be attracted. While the broody, mysterious loner type might cut a romantic figure in books or movies, in real life they didn't make good partners. In real life—if Kenzie ever risked depending on someone else again— she'd need someone staid who would patiently help Drew with math homework and remember to take the trash to the curb on the appropriate pickup day.

Of their own volition, her eyes stole toward JT again. As he talked to Beth, he allowed himself one of his rare smiles, and Kenzie's breath caught.

"Would you guys like to get started and investigate on your own," Beth asked, "or do you want me to personally give you the grand tour?"

"Thanks, but I'm going to play tour guide today," JT said.

Kenzie wouldn't have read anything into the refusal, but there was something just a bit too quick about the way he declined. Beth's first reaction was naked disappointment.

But she masked that and raised a quizzical brow instead. "Have fun," she told them all, sending JT one more searching look before ducking back behind the counter.

"What do you want to see first?" he asked the kids

after handing them each a brochure with descriptions of the different areas and a rough map.

"Your mural," Leslie said loyally.

He chuckled, the sound rusty but endearing. "Suits me. Then I don't have to worry about following some particularly brilliant piece of art. You guys want to take the elevator up a floor, or the stairs?"

"Stairs are good exercise," Kenzie blurted, thinking back to when they'd shared the elevator down to the parking garage, and her heightened awareness of him. He was just such a big man, he dominated any space he occupied. When a man that size embraced a woman, she must feel incomparably secure in his arms.

The kids, not quite but almost running, took the steps faster than the adults.

Lagging behind with JT, Kenzie heard herself comment, "Beth seems lovely—former flame?" *What are you* doing? *It's none of your business! You're supposed to be saving yourself for math-and-trash guy.*

"Actually, no. Former friend of my wife's."

"W-wife?" The unexpected word hit her in the midsection like a physical blow. It was a wonder she didn't tumble down the cement stairs in a reenacted parody of their first meeting.

"Late wife," he said softly.

"Oh." Her heart constricted.

The natural inclination when hearing about a person's loss was to apologize, yet Kenzie bit her tongue; he'd stiffened…almost as if bracing himself against the automatic response. Besides, Kenzie was still so stymied by the news that JT was a widower that she wasn't sure she could string together an intelligible sentence. Dozens of unanchored words roiled around her brain, colliding into one another and spinning into new questions and speculations. Had she just discovered the reason JT rarely smiled?

After a moment, it became clear neither one of them was going to say anything else. She felt ridiculously insensitive, meeting the news of his wife's death with nothing more than "oh," yet JT seemed to exude silent relief that they weren't going to discuss it. Maybe it was too painful for him. *Maybe he still loves her.*

"Are you two coming or what?" Drew called from the top of the stairs.

"Sorry," Kenzie said. "I slowed down for a sec to catch my breath."

Drew grumbled in a low mutter to his sister. Kenzie thought she made out the word *old.*

"He's not the most patient child in the world," she said to JT. "Deep down he's a sweet boy, but he's been... I want to apologize for what he said to you in the van."

JT turned toward her, his smile sardonic. "Don't worry, he's not the first person who didn't think my art was 'useful.' At least he has the excuse of being a kid."

She sucked in a breath at the hurt in his eyes.

He shook his head. "I was trying for humorous, but it came out bitter, didn't it?"

Wounded, she would have said.

"Suffice it to say," he continued in a more nonchalant tone, "my par—my father wasn't keen to have an artist for a son. Saw it as a foolish hobby to indulge and a waste of my potential. All behind me now. I just didn't want you to think my feelings are so easily bruised that I'd hold it against a nine-year-old boy that he'd rather be at a baseball game."

Ironically, that same boy now seemed eager to get started. "What is taking so long?" he demanded, a pleading note in his tone.

"We're on our way," JT called back, not glancing in Kenzie's direction as he took the stairs two at a time.

She was glad for the moment to collect her thoughts. Whatever he might tell her—or himself—about having made his peace with his dad's disapproval, there was residual pain. Was JT so estranged from his parents that he hadn't been able to turn to them while coping with his wife's death? A sobering possibility. Much as she might wish in adult hindsight that her folks had raised her differently, with more structure, she'd never for a second questioned whether they loved her. She couldn't even fathom what heinous sin she'd have to commit to incur their disdain.

As a mother trying to do what was right by her own children, she experienced an immediate, albeit judgmental, flare of dislike for any father who alienated his son. Then again, was she being hypocritical? Did *she* respect JT's chosen career path, or did she also see it as wasted potential, a risky indulgence when there were monthly bills to pay? *Completely different circumstances.*

The benefit of not letting herself be romantically interested in a man like JT was avoiding those difficult

dilemmas. She could merely be a distant but supportive friend, unworried by how his choices would affect
her life or her kids'. It was best for all of them that he
remain off-limits.

If only she could do a better job remembering that
whenever a smile lit his eyes and his gaze warmed her
skin.

Chapter 7

"**W**ow! *You* did this?" Leslie asked over her shoulder.

JT almost smiled at her incredulity, which was simultaneously endearing and insulting. "Yep." He pointed at the initials slashed in deep purple at the bottom left corner.

The mural, a painting in bold colors of children playing at the Fountain of Rings in nearby Centennial Olympic Park, encompassed this entire section of wall. The kids in the picture were nearly as large as the two studying the work. Drew didn't share his sister's effusive enthusiasm, but he looked grudgingly impressed. At the very least, he didn't ask the kinds of questions JT might have expected: Why don't the kids have eyes or mouths? How come the sun is green? JT wouldn't describe himself as a Fauvist, but it was fair to say he'd been influenced by a Matisse exhibit his mother had taken him to see.

"This is really good." That hushed endorsement came from Kenzie.

Her praise affected him almost bodily, as if she'd reached out and stroked her hand along his bare skin. He couldn't help preening. Being an artist, neither could he resist asking what she liked about the work.

In response to being put on the spot, she glanced down, her tone turning shyly hesitant. "It's a nice sense of…motion? Something about the way you've drawn the children seems so realistically active." A wry smile touched the corner of her mouth. "And trust me, I know active children."

He quirked his lips in wry acknowledgment. Her two kids had already moved on to a nearby enclosure that featured "junk art" laid out as floor sculpture.

Kenzie studied the mural in front of her, then looked at JT. Obviously she had other thoughts on the painting, but seemed reluctant to share them.

"What?" he prompted. "Is there something about it you don't like?" His voice was neutral, almost academic, as though he were an art professor coaxing a reaction from a promising student, even if JT felt more like a nervous teen trying to impress a first date. Good grief—were his palms actually turning damp? He'd been reviewed by some of the foremost art critics in the country, for crying out loud!

"Oh, no," Kenzie assured him. "I was serious when I said it was good. It's just, those vivid colors…"

When she trailed off apologetically, he knew she didn't plan to finish her sentence, but he could guess. Had she expected something starker? God knows he'd become less vibrant in the past couple of years—not that some of his darker work wasn't beautiful in its own right, but where had the colors gone? He'd tried once, experimentally, to force them, and the resulting canvas had struck him as garish and obscene. He didn't remember the joy of green suns and purple clouds or why neon pink had seemed the perfect color for a German shepherd.

Kenzie excused herself to check that her kids weren't touching anything they shouldn't be, and JT lingered at the mural. It was as much a picture of who he used to be as it was of children playing.

Holly would have been disappointed in him. She'd been too full of life to want him to fade into a colorless existence. Her potential disapproval from beyond the grave carried more weight than his father's cold disdain ever had. *I'll try harder,* he promised his late wife. He also knew she wouldn't have wanted him to be lonely, that she would have wished him happiness. Catching himself staring after Kenzie's retreating backside, he wondered if it was also time to try dating.

Maybe. But not with a skittish divorcée who had her own emotional baggage and two kids with father issues.

JT had never visited an art venue with people who knew so little about art. As the day wore on, he found himself strangely charmed by the way Kenzie busied herself in the brochure and stammered whenever they encountered one of the many Do You Know…? stations located throughout the museum. Geared toward young guests, many of the trivia questions were intentionally easy, but it was clear she didn't have any of the answers. Even Leslie, who'd seemingly memorized half an art primer from the local library, had a full-fledged light-bulb moment, crying "Oh!" in the Impressionists' Hall when it dawned on her that Manet and Monet were not the same painter.

If Drew wasn't having the time of his life, he was at least participating in all the hands-on rooms that encouraged kids to put to work different principles of art. At the interactive display about sculpting, he went so far as to murmur "cool" before he caught himself. In contrast, Leslie was unabashedly getting a kick out of her day of culture and learning more about her newest interest. JT just wished Kenzie was having more fun.

Not that you did much to brighten her day.

What the hell was wrong with him? During their short acquaintance, he'd been thrilled she didn't feel sorry for him, so why had he blurted out two pieces of biographical information likely to evoke her pity? Though he'd never been particularly eloquent verbally, he couldn't believe he'd spoken so gracelessly about losing Holly. Yet when Kenzie had asked if Beth was a former flame, some part of him had wanted to make it immediately clear that she wasn't a romantic possibility…in the past or the present. Surely he hadn't been trying to reassure Kenzie that he was available?

He glanced to where she stood with Drew, discussing a piece of Colonial art and joking about life in pioneer days. Whenever her son had acted up today, forgetting his manners or talking too loudly, she was quick to correct him. Firm but fair. Once she'd addressed the problem, she let it go, resuming their conversations without holding a visible grudge. Whenever JT had disappointed his parents, the effects had been lasting. His mother had liked that he was more introspective than most boys his age. At the times he'd behaved in a more robust manner, she'd not only scolded him, but continued to send reproachful glances throughout the day, as if to remind him continuously that he'd let her down. And Jonathan, Sr.... Well, disappointing *him* was like inviting an arctic front, but without the snow to make it fun.

In JT's inexpert opinion, Kenzie had struck a nice balance with her parenting approach. He wondered if her kids knew how lucky they were. It was clear they missed their father and didn't see him often, but from what JT had pieced together, the man was selfishly temperamental. How did you explain to a pair of nine-year-olds that sometimes no father was better than a bad father?

As if feeling his gaze on her, Kenzie looked up suddenly, her eyes skittish.

"I, uh, was about to ask if you guys are getting hungry," he lied. "There's a café downstairs."

"Food!" Drew pumped a fist in the air, looking as

excited as if they'd just offered him season's tickets to the Braves.

Kenzie ruffled her son's hair, a move that left him squirming. "All right, a lunch break sounds fine by me. Les?"

"Hmm?" The girl didn't even look up from the plaque she was reading.

"Earth to Leslie," Kenzie drawled. "Why don't we go eat, then maybe hit another exhibit or two before heading out?"

"Already?" Leslie squeaked with dismay.

"Soon." Kenzie darted a glance toward JT. "It was very nice of Mr. Trelauney to come with us, but we don't want to hold him hostage for the entire day."

JT started to insist that he was enjoying himself in his own understated way, but he hesitated. Kenzie wasn't entirely comfortable with him. Instead of working to put her at ease, perhaps he should be glad of the subtle emotional barrier between them. They took the stairwell down to the restaurant, and JT was careful to stay in front this time, ostensibly showing them the way, rather than lag behind alongside Kenzie.

For lunch, he and the kids ordered sandwiches and Kenzie grabbed a salad. The small café was furnished with round tables, ideal for solitary diners or couples, and larger booths along the wall. He wound up on a bench next to Leslie and directly across from her mother.

"Thank you for today," Kenzie told him as she drizzled dressing on her salad.

"Absolutely!" Leslie chirped. "It's been so much fun, hasn't it, Drew? The exhibits are great. I love the quotes on the ceilings, too. Man, even the food is good here."

Drew grunted. "How would you know? You won't shut up long enough to eat anything."

"Andrew, be nice to your sister! And don't talk with your mouth full."

"Yes, ma'am," he muttered.

Taking a bite of her sandwich with exaggerated precision, Leslie gave her brother a *so there* look, then immediately started talking again once she'd swallowed. "You know what other food is good, JT? My mom's cooking."

Kenzie chuckled. "I'm surprised you even remember what my cooking tastes like, between the sandwiches we've been eating recently and the dishes Mrs. Sanchez has brought over."

Drew made a sound that might have been a moan of ecstasy at the mention of Mrs. Sanchez's food; JT could relate. He grinned in the boy's direction, and Drew's expression immediately turned stony.

"Don't be silly, Mom. Of course I remember your cooking. Like your lasagna! Can you make it sometime soon?" Leslie swiveled on the seat and batted her eyelashes at JT. "Maybe you could join us. We usually have leftovers, so I'm sure it—"

"Leslie!"

JT wondered if Kenzie knew just how horrified she sounded.

Leslie stubbornly persisted. "What? He lives just

across the hall, so it's not like he'd have to come out of his way. Drew, don't you think it would be a good idea for JT to join us for dinner sometime?"

At that, Drew's head jerked up from his sandwich. "No."

"Well, that's just rude," his sister said. "We owe him for today, and—"

"Not at all," JT tried to interject. "This was a favor with no strings attached."

"—*and* you talk about how you miss your friends back home and can't wait to make new friends once school starts. What about Mom? *She* should have friends, too. Male friends," the girl said with significant emphasis.

Kenzie's face had turned a red so vivid it reminded JT of his earlier work. "Now, Leslie—" she began.

But it was Drew who jumped to his feet, shouting at his sister, "I can't believe you! Don't you love Dad at all? We can't just replace him with some painter who lives across the hall. Mom doesn't need 'male friends.' She has us. And Aunt Ann! Her dating is a *stupid* idea…even for you!" Then he stormed off toward the diner's exit.

For a split second, Kenzie was too stunned by her son's tantrum to react, but the shock quickly evaporated, leaving two very different emotions in its wake. Mortification almost nauseating in its intensity, and worry for her son, which eclipsed her personal embarrassment.

She rose, mumbling a half-formed apology as she

turned to catch up with Drew. *It's getting worse.* His outbursts had steadily increased over the past year. She knew moving to Atlanta meant stressful change for the kids, but they were coping in very distinct ways. Leslie liked to lose herself in fantasy, whether through books or imagined romances between her mom and JT. Drew, on the other hand, simply seemed to be getting angrier. The twins had always had differences, but Kenzie couldn't believe the way he'd just screamed at his sister publicly.

"You owe Les an apology, you know," she said softly, reaching out to grab Drew's elbow before he could escape into the men's restroom. She led him toward a small bench between the water fountain and ATM machine. He didn't try to pull away, but he glared mutinously.

"Dating *is* a stupid idea," he reiterated. There was fire in his tone, but this was her baby—she didn't miss the way his lower lip trembled.

"For now, I agree. We have a lot on our plate, with my new job and school about to start. I'm not interested in finding a boyfriend. But worrying about that doesn't give you the right to be cruel to your sister."

His shoulders slumped. "Do you think after we move into the real house, you'll want a boyfriend?"

He looked so traumatized by the idea that she wanted to promise him that it would never happen. But that had been more Mick's style of parenting—saying whatever rash thing got him out of short-term trouble, with no thought toward long-range viability or consequences.

"I honestly don't know, Drew. What I can tell you is that we'll work out whatever happens as a family."

Apparently *family* had been the wrong word to use, for he grew wild-eyed. "We've been here over a week. Has Dad even… There was this movie on cable where the kid found out his father had been writing him letters that his mom didn't want him to have."

Oh, Drew. His tone was so beseeching, begging her to lie to him and be the bad guy so that he could hang on to illusions about his father. "You know that's not the case, don't you?"

Saying nothing, he nodded, his eyes welling with tears.

His abject misery was almost paralyzing. The right words of comfort and wisdom just wouldn't come. Did other parents have this problem? Did the articulate moms and dads she'd known in Raindrop secretly get tongue-tied and insecure in the privacy of their own homes? She tried to channel warm but no-nonsense Mrs. Sanchez, whom she couldn't imagine ever shrinking from being candid with her kids. Maybe if Kenzie simply faked it, inspiration would strike.

But when she opened her mouth, all that emerged was a sigh. So she reached out and pulled Drew into a hug, hoping the wordless gesture said everything her son needed to hear.

In a change of plans not even Leslie protested, they left the museum right after lunch.

By tacit agreement, no one tried to make conversation on the way home. Instead they relied on the radio and let Star 94 gloss over the awkward silence. Thank God, Kenzie had decided to drive today. She had a fool-proof excuse for staring straight ahead at the road and not even venturing a glance toward JT in the passenger seat.

What must the man think of her and her kids?

Kenzie eased the van into the parking space, and there was a small chorus of clicks and whooshes as her passengers unfastened their seat belts and let them snap back into place.

As he hopped out of the car, Drew asked over his shoulder, "Mom, is it okay with you if I take the stairs? Like you said, it's good exercise."

They both knew his request stemmed from embarrassment over what had happened earlier rather than dedication to physical fitness, but she saw no reason to humiliate him by making that point. "Sure. No running, though."

"Want me to go with you?" Leslie volunteered. It was an olive branch—she'd mostly ignored her brother since he'd yelled at her, and he smiled in relief and quick agreement.

They'd probably be arguing again before nightfall, but watching them walk away together, Kenzie was proud of them. Of course, this left her to share the elevator with JT.

"So," she began as the doors closed. "Eventful day, huh?"

The left corner of his lips twitched. "Don't take this the wrong way, but I'm exhausted."

"It would be hypocritical for me to take offense. I feel like exhaustion's been my natural state since they were born. But it's a good exhaustion," she added, not wanting to sound ungrateful for the two most important people in her life. "Fulfilling. Rewarding in a way that probably sounds ridiculous to someone with no children."

It was as if a dark cloud passed over his face, blotting out any sign of joy or teasing. His expression turned carefully blank. "Not at all. Paintings aren't kids, but many times I worked all night on a piece, found myself frustrated that I couldn't shape it the way I'd envisioned, later to accept that maybe it could be something even *more* than I'd imagined if I just had faith. So I'd slave away despite being tired, despite being exasperated, and when dawn broke and early sunlight spilled over what I accomplished, that's exactly what I felt— fulfilled. Rewarded."

Her breath hitched at the near poetry of his words. He spoke about his art with a passion that made her... Wincing, she reminded herself that Mick had spoken intently about his music, and that she'd once found his artistic dedication erotic, too.

"You were using the past tense," she noted. "Painting's not fulfilling anymore?"

"I wouldn't know."

The elevator lurched to a halt on the third floor, and as the doors slid open, Kenzie realized that someone sat in the hallway in front of her apartment. Not the twins, but her sister? A second look confirmed that it was indeed Ann and Abigail.

Along with several suitcases.

Chapter 8

"Ann! Is everything okay?" Hurrying toward her, Kenzie temporarily forgot JT's presence behind her, until her sister's wide eyes reminded her. "Um, Ann, this is Jonathan Trelauney, the neighbor I told you about. JT, my sister."

"Nice to meet you." He glanced toward baby Abigail in her car seat, then looked away with a tight smile. "I'll just go so that you ladies can— Goodbye. Nice meeting you."

With his long-legged stride, he was across the hall and inside his own apartment within seconds.

Ann pursed her lips. "Odd. Really, really cute, though."

Yeah, that was JT in a nutshell. "What are you doing here? I mean, you're always welcome, but…"

Careful not to disturb the carrier in which Abigail

was sleeping, Ann rose, stretching with a palm pressed to the small of her back. Sounding as casual as if she were asking Kenzie to pass cream for her coffee, she announced, "I've left Forrest."

And then she began crying, tears that had escalated to racking sobs by the time a startled Kenzie got the apartment unlocked. She ushered Ann inside, setting the baby on the coffee table in front of the new sofa. Kenzie was retrieving the luggage in the hall when the access door banged open and Drew and Leslie emerged.

Leslie drew up short. "What's all that?"

"Aunt Ann's bags. Your aunt may be staying with us for a couple of days," Kenzie guessed.

"Cool," Drew replied. "Think she'd make us some of that awesome roast beef while she's here?"

Kenzie rolled her eyes. "Baby Abigail is sleeping, so why don't the two of you tiptoe past and go watch something on the TV in my bedroom?"

Neither of them was terribly impressed with her television set, whose fuzzy resolution and limited color capabilities couldn't compete in today's Hi-Def world. They both nodded, though, and whispered brief hellos to Ann on their way through the front room. Kenzie was relieved to see her sister had managed to dam the tears. If the twins had paid better attention, they might have noticed that her eyes were swollen and her nose was red, but they were already engaged in a heated debate over what they should watch. Kenzie put the suitcases against the living room wall so that they were as out of the way as possible in the small room, then turned to her sister.

"Can I get you a cola? Wine?"

Ann's laugh was watery. "I'd take you up on that except I'm supposed to nurse Abby in the next half hour. I like a well-behaved baby, but I'm not trying to sedate her."

"Something else, then?"

"No, I'm fine."

"If you were fine," Kenzie pointed out gently, "I wouldn't find you sobbing in my hallway. By the way, didn't I give you the spare key?"

"Yes, but when I tried to reach you on the cell phone, it rolled over to voice mail. It didn't seem right to just let myself into the apartment without your permission."

The matter-of-fact statement stung. Even if they hadn't been close during adolescence, it disturbed Kenzie that her little sister was more comfortable lingering in the hall like a vagrant than assuming she'd be welcome.

"Ann, please, my place is yours." She sat beside her on the couch, searching her sister's gaze. "Truly."

"I'm so glad you said that. Because I was…kind of hoping I could stay tonight. Maybe a couple."

"For as long as you need," Kenzie promised. She didn't want to pounce with dozens of questions, but her curiosity was a welling tide. What on earth could have possibly happened to prompt Ann to walk out on Forrest? *Do not tell me he had an affair.* If staid Forrest was making illicit whoopee, all hope for the male species was lost.

Blinking rapidly, as if trying to fan away tears before

they had a chance to fall, Ann said, "I suppose you want to know what's going on?"

Yes! Preferably before her brain exploded from trying to puzzle through it. "Only if you want to tell me."

Ann tipped her head so that it rested atop the low-back sofa, addressing her response to the ceiling. "Do I look invisible to you? Am I invisible?"

"Of course not. Are you saying that Forrest's ignoring you?"

"Worse. If he just came home and didn't speak to me at all, I'd assume that he was preoccupied with something on campus. He knows I'm there. He comes right over to me every evening, gives me a perfunctory kiss right here—" she stabbed at her right cheek with her index finger "—and asks me what's for dinner. Usually without ever lifting his gaze from the day's mail as he sorts through envelopes. He doesn't ignore me in the strictest sense of the word, but he for damn sure doesn't *see* me."

Kenzie's mouth dropped open. She couldn't recall ever hearing her sister swear before. Though Kenzie could attest that if anything would urge you toward profanity, it was a failed marriage. This one didn't sound failed, however, merely in a rut. "It sucks that he's taking you for granted. Have you told him how you feel?"

Ann sat ramrod straight. "Ph.D. or no Ph.D., that—that *man* is an *idiot!* Last night I tried waiting for him at home in something a little more provocative than usual. Low-cut, with the perfume I thought he liked.

He didn't notice. So when he got home from his Saturday class this afternoon, I tried talking. And he had the *nerve* to tell me it was postpartum hormones and that I was overreacting. *Do* you *think I'm overreacting?*"

Since the question was voiced in a slightly hysterical way that suggested homicidal retribution should Kenzie say yes, she quickly shook her head. "You sure I can't get you anything?" *Water, tissues, a mild tranquilizer?*

"I just need to feed Abby, then get some rest. I'm drained. Would you be affronted if I slept through dinner?"

Kenzie snorted. "What, and miss my four-star peanut butter sandwich?"

Reflexively, she thought of her daughter's claims earlier in the day about Kenzie's fabled cooking skills, and Leslie's attempt to have JT over. When Kenzie's undisciplined mind envisioned a dinner with their neighbor, the image didn't include peanut butter or children. Instead, her imagination conjured a candlelit meal, during which he would pour them each a glass of wine and forget to eat because he was staring at her in the soft illumination.

Shaking her head, Kenzie tried to dislodge the crazy fantasy. While she was a reasonably attractive woman, she suspected she was past the age of being able to make men forsake sustenance. Besides, where were the twins in this daydream—at Ann's house? Unlikely, since Ann was here.

"Have you called Forrest?" Kenzie asked. "Just to let him know you're going to be staying with me, if nothing else?"

"Are you kidding? I left in tears and the big jerk didn't even bother calling my cell to make sure I was okay to drive. He can phone *me*…if he even notices the invisible girl is gone."

They should discuss this in more detail after Ann had had a chance to calm down. It was uncharacteristic for her to get so emotional, or to be critical of her steady husband. The fact that he'd been the kind of man who arrived home at exactly the same time every night and kissed her cheek in exactly the same spot had been what Ann loved about him. She'd been mature enough to admire predictability back when Kenzie had still thought relationships should be all about excitement and sparkle.

Well, I'm older and wiser now.

Pity, that. Because she suspected that JT, if it weren't for mourning his late wife, could provide enough sparkle to single-handedly simulate the Fourth of July.

Ann stayed for the duration of the weekend, claiming it was no hassle for her to sleep on the couch, even though it wasn't a sofa bed. Despite her sister's Saturday rant about invisibility, Kenzie had assumed that by Sunday afternoon, Forrest would have come to collect his wife and daughter, and that Ann would miss her much bigger mattress and 300-thread-count sheets. Yet, as the kids' first day of school neared, Ann and baby Abigail were still ensconced in Kenzie's teeny apartment.

"You know," Ann said as she helped dry the plates after Monday night's dinner, "this place is surprisingly homey. When we unloaded all your boxes here that first day, it didn't look like much."

Unpacking, hanging a few personal items, and the wafting scent of the enchilada casserole Mrs. Sanchez had brought when she heard Ann and baby were in residence did a lot to make the apartment cozy.

Kenzie glanced around, enjoying the rare approval from her sister. "Yeah, I did an okay job picking this, didn't I? Of course, luck had a lot to do with it." She'd been determined to find something affordable in the school district. Which reminded her... "Kids, you'd better be brushing your teeth! The first day of class might not be until Wednesday, but you need to get back in the habit of going to bed and getting up early."

Even from the hall, she could hear their groans. Once the twins were tucked in for the night, Ann asked if it would be all right to leave Abigail in her portable swing under Kenzie's supervision, and treat herself to a long bath.

"Take your time. There are bubbles on the shelf below the towels, if you want them." Kenzie turned on the electric swing. Soothed by its gentle metronomic sound, she stared into space and pondered her responsibilities as a sibling. Thinking aloud, she looked at the baby. "I'm her family. I'm supposed to interfere, right?"

Interfering hadn't been in either of her parents' nature, but Kenzie would bet everything she owned that Roberta Sanchez wouldn't hesitate to act if she felt it was in one of her relative's best interests. *I'm genuinely worried about Ann. I'm not doing this because I stubbed my toe on the portable crib while I was trying to leave for work this morning or because Abby cried—howled, really—from three in the morning to four.* Before she could talk herself out of it, she picked up the cordless phone from the coffee table and dialed.

It took several rings before Forrest answered the phone. "Hello?"

"This is Kenzie. Are you aware that your wife and daughter are staying with me?"

"Of course." He sounded vaguely baffled by the question.

"And are you planning to *do* anything about that?"

More bafflement. "Like what?"

Maybe Ann had been right and the man was an idiot. "Why haven't you called her?"

"Because I'm giving her space. That seemed like the patient thing to do. Ann is an eminently sensible woman. She's rarely overwrought. I wanted to give her time to sort through whatever issues she has. I'll be here for her when she's ready to come back."

Kenzie gritted her teeth. "Her 'issue' is that you don't pay enough attention to her! Now might be a good time to start."

"So you're saying she deliberately left in a manipulative bid for attention?" He sounded annoyed now.

Uh-oh. Why did Kenzie think she was the best person to assist with a marital spat when she was a divorcée who hadn't even kissed a guy since…since?

"Kenzie?"

"I'll let you get back to whatever you were doing."

"Before you go, can you ask Ann where my maroon

tie with the royal-blue stripes is? I wanted to wear it to tomorrow's faculty meeting and can't seem to find it."

"You'll just have to make do, Forrest." Kenzie disconnected. Should she tell Ann about the attempt to help? She stole a guilty glance at the baby, who was watching in wide-eyed curiosity as she swung from left to right. "If it comes up in conversation with your mama, I will definitely tell her the truth."

But Ann seemed happy to avoid the subject of her marriage. When she came out of the bath, she asked if Kenzie wanted to watch a movie. "A chick flick! We could microwave some popcorn and stay up late."

Kenzie winced apologetically. "Actually, I think Drew ate the last of the popcorn. And I'm kind of pooped." She'd been working hard each day to get up to speed on her new job, coming in earlier than she had to and staying just a bit later on afternoons when Alicia or Ann was with the kids. Kenzie knew from experience that once school started, there would be myriad disruptions to her schedule, and she wanted to make a solid impression on the new boss before then.

"Oh." Ann glanced down, her hands twisting in the pockets of her robe. "Sorry, I was being selfish."

"No!" Kenzie got to her feet. "No, the truth is, I've been thinking about us. Our childhood. Our relationship. Now that we're both in Georgia, I hope that we can grow closer. Do more sisterly stuff."

"I'd like that. I know I was…bratty when we were younger. I was jealous, I guess."

"Of me?" Kenzie asked, startled. "I figured you were just mature beyond your years, and it took me a while to catch up to you. Frankly, I've been struggling not to be jealous of *you*."

Ann's laugh sounded perilously close to a sob. "Why, because you've always had a secret yen to be the boring sister with the hollow accomplishments and inattentive husband?"

At least Ann still had a husband, while Kenzie's own marriage had disintegrated. "Ann, I know it's not exactly my business, but you and Forrest…"

"Yes?" She sat on the couch, her smile rueful. "Since I've invaded your home, I think you're entitled to an opinion."

But what was Kenzie's opinion? That it was better to be alone than with the wrong man? That good men who provided well for their families were in short supply and after investing so much time and effort in her marriage, not to mention the new baby, Ann owed it to herself to try to work things out before walking away from Forrest for good? That while Kenzie agreed Forrest could stand to be more affectionate, pregnancy and birth *did* jumble a woman's hormones, and being kissed on the same spot each day seemed like a dubious reason for jilting a faithful husband?

"You know what? Never mind. I'm the last person you should take advice from. I've only had one real relationship, and even my fifteen-year-old sister could tell *that* was going to be a disaster."

Ann flinched. "And I never let you forget it, did I? Man, I was a know-it-all."

Kenzie hid a smile. At times, Leslie reminded her of a young Ann. She loved both of them. "Okay, maybe you were obnoxious about it at times, but you weren't wrong."

"No, but I was scared. You flung yourself into your emotions. You experienced passion. I was always too afraid to do that. I carefully planned my relationship with Forrest, systematically seduced an older man. I mean, not necessarily in a sexual way. It was more of a domestic seduction. Now I'm just…tired."

"Having a newborn in the house will do that to you," Kenzie sympathized.

"It's not Abby's fault. She's a darling. But *I* picked out her pediatrician. *I* researched great preschools and already have her on a waiting list. I plan what we're going to eat every night and grocery shop accordingly. Hell, I practically lay out Forrest's clothes for him! I don't want to be in charge anymore. At the very least, I want to be a team, planning our life together. I want spontaneity, which I know isn't his forte. He doesn't have to sweep me off to Rome for the weekend, but maybe he could just call me around noon and say, 'Hey, instead of you cooking tonight, how 'bout I bring home a pizza?'"

Without meaning to, Kenzie laughed. "You don't ask much."

"I did," Ann corrected solemnly. "I asked for a perfect life. I demanded it, I created it. And now I'm not sure it's what I want. I wish, just once, that I'd done something wild and impetuous. That I'd been more like you. That my life was less khaki and more colorful."

Unbidden, the image of JT's mural rose in her mind, the bright swirls of color that created a high-energy picture of children having fun. It conveyed all the optimistic innocence of youth, when kids thought they were invincible and were content to draw neon-green moons and fluorescent-orange trees because they hadn't yet been told that they couldn't. Was that how JT had seen the world before his wife died?

"I guess none of us quite get the life we expected," Kenzie said softly. Thinking of her new job, the new school the kids were about to start and the Perfect House that awaited, she allowed herself hope, anyway. "Just because it wasn't what we imagined doesn't mean we can't find the beauty in it if we look."

Ann sniffed, considering. "I promise to keep my eyes open if you will."

"Deal."

"This is good." Sean blinked, moving away from the canvas to study it from another angle. "*Really* good."

JT chuckled tiredly. It was early evening on Wednesday and he'd barely slept more than two consecutive hours since Saturday. "Why does everyone always sound so damn surprised when they say that?"

Sean ignored the rhetorical question, still absorbed in the painting JT had created for the Owenbys. "You mixed in some darker colors than the original."

If the first abstract was a picture of the sea, this one was the sea on a cloudy day. The same waters, but more turbulent. "The palette's not too bleak, is it?"

"No. No, the new shades add depth, texture."

There was another subtle change JT doubted anyone but him would notice. In the first painting, there had been scattered impressions of marine animals, such as clouds that were shaped vaguely like laughing dolphins if you looked at the right angle. For this version, he'd added a sea horse. Holly had laughingly told him in her third trimester that sea horses were her new favorite animal, since the *males* gave birth.

I would've traded places with you if I could've. But that had never been his decision to make, hadn't even been a possibility. What he did with his life now? That was his choice. Since he hadn't been able to sleep since the trip to the museum—plagued both by inappropriate dreams of Kenzie and the eerily muffled, almost phantom sound of a baby crying through the walls— he'd painted instead. If he hadn't experienced the same feverish joy of creation he'd once known, his grim determination had at least yielded results.

And he could breathe again. Wondering whether or not he'd ever finish another painting had become a stone weight across his lungs. Now, oxygen was slowly seeping back.

Sean clapped him on the shoulder. "I'm proud of you, man."

"Thanks." They stood for moment, silently acknowledging their bond of friendship and what it meant to each of them. "You ever accept another commission without talking to me, I'll kick your ass."

"Nah, I make it a point to stay in shape. I doubt you could take me. When was the last time you slept or ate? Or—" Sean sniffed delicately "— showered? Tell you what, I'll check scores on the tube while you clean up. Let me buy you dinner to celebrate."

JT's first impulse was to politely decline and stay holed up in his apartment to rest. But at the last second he stopped himself. "Okay." He'd been in hiding long enough.

On Wednesday afternoon, Kenzie got permission to leave a smidge early—it had been the kids' first day of school and she wanted to hear all about it. More specifically, she wanted to hear that they'd liked their fellow students and had managed not to get into any trouble yet. As she pulled out of the bank's parking lot, her cell phone rang.

She noted that the call was coming from the apartment. "Hello?"

"Just me," Ann said cheerfully. "Kids got home safe."

"Thanks for letting me know." She'd walked them to the bus stop a few streets over that morning, threatening their lives if they didn't stay together on the way back in the afternoon. "I'm actually headed home now. Why don't we go out to dinner, and they can tell us all about their new classes?"

Ann laughed. "Sounds perfect to me…it was my night to cook."

Kenzie had to admit certain things had been easier with Ann pitching in to help, but she wondered how long she could offer her sister sanctuary without enabling her to hide from her problems.

By the time Kenzie made it through afternoon traffic and they had all three kids ready to go, it was nearly five-thirty. Waiting to lock the door, she was the last one out of her apartment—but the first to look up when the door across the hall opened. *JT.* Her heart skipped a beat in anticipation of seeing him. Somehow, despite their close living proximity, she'd avoided running into him since the weekend.

Disappointment so intense that it should have been comical hit when the man who emerged wasn't JT but his friend Sean.

"And who is this beautiful girl?" the man asked, smiling in Ann's direction.

"My sister," Kenzie replied. "My *married* sister, Ann." Apparently, twenty-eight was not too old for her protective big-sister instincts to kick in. Ann had recently admitted to wishing her life had included more passion; she might be vulnerable to the flirtatious attention of handsome strangers.

Sean glanced up with laughing eyes. "Actually, I meant the baby. Hi, Ann, I'm Sean, JT's friend and business partner. In fact, we were just headed out to dinner to celebrate his latest brilliant painting."

By now, JT had joined them in the hall. Dear heaven, he looked incredible. He wore a button-down black shirt with black jeans, and the monochromatic style was *really* working for him. His hair was damp and there was a gleam in his eyes that hadn't been there the last time they'd spoken. It gave him an irresistible edge of confidence.

Kenzie couldn't look away from him. "You've been painting? That's wonderful."

"Sean may be exaggerating the brilliance part," he said with a smile. "But it is pretty wonderful."

"We're going to dinner, too," Leslie said. "To celebrate the first day of school!"

"School isn't something to celebrate," Drew mumbled.

"Maybe we should all go togeth—"

"Leslie! I'm sure the men probably want to talk business and—"

"Not at all," Sean said smoothly. "I've been saying for months that what the big guy needs is more fun in his life. I know a great place where we can get decent food and play, too."

Drew looked intrigued despite himself. "What kind of playing?"

Kenzie tried again, feeling that she was rapidly losing control of the situation. If she'd ever had any in the first place. "Oh, but it's a school night. The kids shouldn't be out too late."

"Then we should get going," Ann said cheerfully. "It's not even six yet. We have plenty of time."

What are you doing? Kenzie demanded with her narrow-eyed glare.

Her sister fussed with the straps of Abby's car seat and pretended not to notice.

Despite the objections she'd tried to voice, fifteen minutes later Kenzie parked next to Sean's black car at a restaurant that boasted an indoor miniature-golf course, and hoped for the best.

Chapter 9

"Welcome to Course After Course!" A bubbly hostess smiled at them. "How many in your party?"

"Four adults, two kids and one baby requiring a high chair," Ann said.

We're just missing the partridge and the pear tree. How, Kenzie wondered, had she been railroaded into this? She glanced toward JT, noticing how the night-dark shirt made his silvery eyes even more dramatic in contrast. Oh, yeah. Now she remembered how she'd wound up here. She'd been too dazed to put up a sustained, coherent argument.

Also, everyone had ganged up on her. After the way Leslie had doted on JT the other day, Kenzie wasn't surprised by her daughter's behavior. She was more suspicious of Sean's motivation, though, and Ann's quick agreement. Surely her always responsible sister wasn't planning to do anything stupid?

Since they were a bit ahead of the dinner crowd and it was the middle of the week, they were seated quickly in a section of the restaurant designated Magical Dining. Waitresses wore witches' hats, and framed posters on the walls were from family-friendly movies ranging from *Bedknobs and Broomsticks* to *The Wizard of Oz* to more recent films. The spacious center of the building was devoted to the nine-hole golf course one had to pass to get a table; various dining rooms branched off like spokes from the main area. Drew forgot about his stomach long enough to scope out which holes looked the most challenging. Leslie was grinning as if she'd walked into one of her favorite books.

"So how'd you know about this place?" Kenzie asked.

"I'm an uncle." Sean helped Ann get the high chair situated. "I've become something of a regular here. I can highly recommend the wizard's filet."

Everyone took a chair, and somehow Kenzie found herself seated beside JT, which she'd hoped to avoid. Still, an undisciplined part of her—the old impulsive Kenzie—thrilled at his nearness and the subtly male scent of his soap. His eyes met hers, and she felt as if they were in their own little bubble since the kids were busily pointing out decorations to each other and Sean and Ann were both admiring a cooing Abigail.

"Tell me about this new painting," Kenzie invited.

"It's not really a *new* work. Sean found a couple that

had seen one of my bigger pieces and wanted to own a smaller re-creation."

"That still takes talent." She recalled his mural at the museum. "Which you definitely have."

He ducked his head in modest acknowledgment, the gesture endearingly boyish. "Thank you. I did manage to update the piece slightly. I'm happy with how it turned out."

"I can tell. You look…different. Good."

"You, on the other hand, always look good." He flashed a brief but charged smile of masculine appreciation.

Warmth blossomed inside her as if she'd just taken her first rich sip of hot cocoa and could feel the chocolate melting through her body. After a moment, she realized the table had grown quiet. No one else seemed to be conversing anymore. They were, she realized, watching *her* watch JT. Leslie seemed delighted enough to dance a jig, Drew was scowling and Ann actually winked at her.

Kenzie cleared her throat, glancing desperately toward Sean. "So, the wizard's filet is good then?"

Leaning back in her chair, feeling pleasantly stuffed, Kenzie smiled at Sean. "I have to hand it to you, you're great at picking out restaurants."

"I'm great at everything," he declared.

Over the past hour, Kenzie had grown accustomed to the man's joyfully outrageous nature. Sean was a flirt, but not in a sensual or discriminating way. He was the kind of man who could charm any woman between two and two hundred. He was fun to be around, yet so unlike JT that it was difficult to imagine how the men had become friends. Was it a case of opposite personalities bonding because their differences complemented each other, or had JT once been more like his business partner?

When Sean took the kids to get golf supplies and Ann excused herself to check Abby's diaper in the restroom, Kenzie found herself alone with JT and her curiosity. "Sean takes some getting used to," she observed with a smile.

"Let me know how long it takes. I still haven't managed it," he teased.

"You've known him a long time?"

He nodded, staring into the remains of his iced tea. "More than a lifetime, it feels like. He does catch me off guard sometimes. Accepting the commission for the Owenbys' painting, for instance. Personality-wise, we don't have much in common, but he looks out for me."

"Ann and I are kind of the reverse," she said. "As kids, we had little in common and were perfectly happy to go our separate ways. But I've enjoyed reconnecting with her now that we're older and have more life experience to help us relate. I don't have much practice doing it, but I want to look out for her. Sean wouldn't hit on a married woman, would he?"

JT laughed. "Is that why you think he went along with Leslie's idea to eat together? Actually, I think it's *you* he noticed."

"What?"

"The first time he ever saw you, he walked into my

apartment and called you 'hot.'" JT frowned. "I didn't much like that."

"Hot?" she echoed in disbelief. "Are you sure he wasn't talking about someone else?"

"Have you looked in the mirror lately? Those eyes alone. If I could paint..." He shifted in his chair. "I don't mean to make you uncomfortable."

She wasn't discomfited. On the contrary, she was becoming aroused. She swallowed, idly wondering if he ever painted nudes. Wondering if, after waddling through pregnancy with twins and now approaching thirty, she'd be entirely at ease letting a man see her body. She wasn't eighteen anymore, but the way JT was looking at her, he didn't appear to be cataloging the faint laugh lines at the corners of her eyes or the few-but-stubborn gray hairs that had recently appeared near her part.

"So, are you two ready to go for it?" a voice asked.

Kenzie whipped her head around to see Sean's smirk.

"Golf?" he reminded them, extending a pink-tipped club in her direction. "To the links!"

Ann declined play in favor of sitting on a bench while she gave Abigail the bottle she'd brought. "You five go ahead and have fun."

"It won't be mere fun," Sean said with mock gravity. "It will be a slaughter. I'm the Rory McIlroy of the miniature-golf circuit."

"Oh, yeah?" Drew challenged. "I'll bet I get a hole in one before you!"

Sean grinned. "We'll see about that, youngster. I was swinging a nine iron before you were born."

"That's because you're *old*," Drew said, his expression one of faux sympathy.

Laughing out loud, Sean made a smart-aleck retort that Kenzie didn't hear.

"He is good with kids," she remarked to JT as Leslie set her ball on the tee.

JT's face contorted for a second. "Yeah, he is."

"What?" she asked. It wasn't the first time she'd seen his expression darken at the mention of children, but now she found she couldn't leave well enough alone. Despite herself, she wanted to understand, and soothe the shadows from his eyes.

He took a deep breath. "Holly and I were expecting. That was my wife's name—Holly. We'd asked Sean to be the godfather."

Oh, God. Kenzie couldn't begin to comprehend the depth of his loss. As with the other day, it was on the tip of her tongue to say she was sorry, but the words were so painfully inadequate. Instead, unthinkingly, she reached out and squeezed his hand.

He glanced up, astonishment on his face, then down at their joined fingers. He returned her grip, his strong and warm. Awareness pulsed between them. If such simple, platonic contact could send sensation thrumming through her, what would it be like if he really *touched* her?

In recent memory, people had reached out to her as a mother, sister or daughter. The kids weren't so old that they were above cuddling when there was a storm raging outside, or one of them was sick. Ann hugged her, their mother stroked her hair whenever Kenzie managed to come home.

It had been forever since she'd been touched as a woman.

"I…" JT's voice was thick, a husky caress. "I think it's your turn."

Glancing at the putting green, Kenzie found the others were indeed waiting. "Right. My turn." She set down the sky-blue ball and hit it with more oomph than strictly necessary. It struck a woman at the third tee in the back of the calf.

Ouch. "Sorry!" Kenzie called, cringing.

Her children snickered, and Sean halfheartedly chided them while trying to stifle his own laugh. Even JT had sparks of amusement illuminating his eyes.

"I'm a little out of practice at this," she told him breathlessly.

He caught her chin between his fingers for a fraction of a moment before letting go. "That's okay. So am I."

Ann tactfully waited until the twins had gone to bed before broaching the subject of the evening's activities. "They certainly seemed to have fun tonight."

"Yeah. It was a good place to take them."

"And did *you* enjoy yourself?"

"Uh-huh. Are you all done in the bathroom? I was planning to hop in the shower."

Her sister leaned against the arm of the couch. "Would that be a cold shower?"

"I hope not. If the hot water heater's on the fritz, we

should let Mr. C. know," Kenzie babbled. "He's really quite handy. You hear horror stories about apartment supers in the city, but—"

"Mackenzie."

"Don't ask about JT."

"If you tell me, I won't have to ask."

Kenzie groaned, torn between the need to discuss him with someone and the fear that vocalizing her budding feelings would make them even more real. She was here only six more weeks, then she was moving to her Perfect House and he, hopefully, would continue rediscovering his former joy of painting. She did not need extra complications in her life, and it would be a lot easier to avoid temptation when she wasn't bumping into Tall, Dark and Complicated every time she opened her apartment door.

"He's attractive," she allowed, feeling as foolish as if she'd just proclaimed the Sahara "a bit sandy."

"Tell me something I don't know."

"He lost a wife and unborn baby."

Ann's breath hitched. "That's awful."

"Yeah." Kenzie stared into space. "The first few times I saw him, he never even smiled. Understandable, I'd say."

"He was smiling plenty tonight. Whenever he looked at you, for instance."

Kenzie tried to shrug off the observation. "I think he was just in a good mood. He's expressed frustration over not being able to paint. I guess he was creatively blocked. But now he's finished a piece he can be proud of. I noticed as soon as he stepped out of his apartment that he looked happy."

"He looked happy to see *you*."

"Ann, honestly, you might be overromanticizing the situation."

Her sister snorted. "Have you ever known me to romanticize anything? At all?"

"For all I know, he's still in love with his wife. Besides, he's all wrong for me."

"Which part of attractive, successful men who are good-natured about spending time with your kids turns you off?"

"You don't know him well enough to call him successful."

"Didn't you say he was specially invited to paint a mural for one of the city's museums?"

"And just because he was good-natured at dinner… Artistic types are notoriously moody. He was happy tonight, but what about the next time he gets stuck? The twins have already had one man in their lives whose emotional temperament was unreliable, who followed his muse at the expense of his family. I wasn't kidding when I talked about JT not smiling the first few times I saw him. I know he's capable of darker spells and, given his loss, I certainly empathize. But I won't put the kids through that again."

The teasing light had gone out of Ann's eyes. "The kids or you? I remember when you worshipped Mick, dreamed of all the places you'd see together and the family you'd build."

"Which was stupid. What did I think we were going to do, backpack two babies on tour?"

"You were eighteen and thought that anything was possible with love." Ann shrugged. "That's not a crime. I can't imagine how disillusioned you must have been to divorce him. That took courage, to do what was right for you and the kids."

In some ways, Ann was right. It did take a bitter kind of courage to admit you'd been so wrong about someone for so long.

"I just hope," she continued softly, "that you also have the guts to try again when the time comes."

Panic over how potent her feelings for JT were becoming made Kenzie defensive. "I don't think you can lecture me about courage. Why aren't you at home, bravely trying to work things out with your husband instead of being here, once again giving me advice on how I should live my life?"

Ann's face went slack.

"Oh. Oh, Ann, forget I said that. That was just plain bitchy."

"No argument there," she said with a feeble smile. "But there was some truth in it."

"A teeny, tiny kernel. I didn't mean to snap at you like that. I'm a horrible sister. I even called Forrest," she blurted in a fit of self-recrimination.

"What? When?"

"A couple of nights ago. I thought he needed a kick in the pants, figuratively speaking."

"His pants must be very well padded. Don't you

think if he cared about me at all he would have done, I don't know, *something?*"

This was a tricky area. "You know him better than I do. As you pointed out, even though he's older, you took the lead in the relationship. Maybe he wants to make things better but isn't sure exactly how. Maybe he thinks that, since you left, time and space are what you want and he's trying to give you that."

Ann said nothing.

"Please forget I made that comment," Kenzie pleaded. "You know you're welcome here as long as you like."

Ann nodded, but seemed subdued. By morning, however, she was smiling and joking with the kids about their putt-putt efforts the previous night. The school year was under way, and her family seemed comparatively happy. Kenzie went to work ensconced in a false sense of security. Then came Friday afternoon and the phone call at work she'd been subconsciously dreading.

"Kenzie Green speaking."

"Hi, this is Teena Arnold, the vice principal over at Carter. I'm calling about your son, Drew." The woman's tone was pleasant enough, but that didn't stop Kenzie from gripping the receiver tighter.

It's only the third day! What's he done? "Is there a problem, Ms. Arnold?"

"Not exactly, but we were wondering if it would be possible for you to come in this afternoon. Maybe you, myself, Drew and his teacher could have a little chat."

"About? I mean, of course I'll be there. I was just wondering…"

"Oh, I don't think it's a major worry, but Mrs. Frazer has some concerns about Drew's attitude, and some observations she'd like to share with you."

That sounded innocuous enough. Kenzie exhaled in relief that he hadn't started a fight by being overly competitive in P.E., hadn't stopped up all the toilets in the boys' bathroom, or done other destructive things she didn't even want to imagine.

Just some "observations." How bad could that be?

It was school policy that siblings not be in the same class, and Kenzie had met both the kids' teachers before the first day. When she walked into the vice principal's office Friday afternoon, she couldn't help again thinking that Mrs. Frazer, taller with stern, patrician features, was like Abbott to Mrs. Kane's Costello. Leslie's teacher was short, round, jolly, with a higher pitched voice that squeaked slightly when she spoke on a topic that excited her.

Drew was slouched in a chair, looking miserable, and Mrs. Frazer stood behind him. The vice principal, a silver-haired woman in pearls, leaned across her desk to shake Kenzie's hand.

"I'm so glad you were able to make time for us, Mrs. Green," the older woman said warmly.

"My kids are my priority." Kenzie tried to catch Drew's eye, wanting him to know she was on his side. "Honey, do you want to tell me what's going on?"

He shrugged. "Some stupid paper. I did the assignment. I didn't do anything wrong!"

Mrs. Frazer clucked her tongue. "Calling it a 'stupid' paper isn't productive dialogue, Andrew."

Kenzie resisted the urge to roll her eyes. Productive dialogue? Lofty expectations, indeed, especially since boys his age often considered armpit farts a valid form of communication. "What was the assignment, Drew?"

"Supposed to write about family," he mumbled.

She groaned inwardly. Was this about his dad? Both Mrs. Kane and Mrs. Frazer knew the kids came from a divorced home, but Kenzie hadn't expected it to be an issue so soon. After the twins had survived Father's Day with no word from their actual father, she'd hoped the next big hurdle wouldn't be until Christmas. Would it be wrong to buy gifts and say they were from Mick?

"Drew, you're not in any trouble," the vice principal interjected. "We just all care about you very much—"

He scoffed. "You don't even know me."

Kenzie squeezed his shoulder warningly, but the grandmotherly woman seemed unperturbed.

"We wanted to talk a little about your feelings and make your mother aware of them. Would you like to read her your essay?"

"Not really."

Mrs. Frazer had produced a pair of reading glasses and a piece of lined notebook paper. "If I may, Mrs. Green, here's a section of what your son wrote. 'My friend Jimmy back home has a cool family. He plays football every Saturday with his dad and brothers in the yard. I don't have brothers or a dad or a yard. I live in a small apartment with my mom, sister, crazy aunt and her stinky baby.'"

"Drew." Kenzie wanted to say a half-dozen things at once and landed on, "Aunt Ann is certainly not crazy."

"She cries as much as Abby, if she doesn't think anyone's looking."

"Women who've recently had babies can be a little emotional, honey."

"*I* didn't ask her to have a baby! Or to move in with us. We're too crowded already, and she and Uncle Forrest have a huge house. Can I go live with him? Just us guys."

She couldn't really see Forrest tossing around the pigskin with a little boy; the professor was more likely to consider checking the morning stocks together a bonding activity.

The vice principal leaned forward. "We certainly aren't advocating that he go live with anyone else, but it does seem as if he's surrounded by a lot of female influence. He's welcome to speak to our guidance counselor anytime he chooses—she's a wonderful listener and the kids all seem to respond to her—but Mrs. Frazer and I thought that perhaps he could benefit from a male presence in his life. A mentor of sorts. If his father's not available to help—"

"Not at this time," Kenzie said flatly.

"Then perhaps this Uncle Forrest?"

"Ah…that's a possibility." A complicated, awkward possibility, but worth discussing with Ann if it was in Drew's best interest.

"What about JT?" Drew said suddenly.

Kenzie's jaw dropped. "JT?"

"Yeah, he could be my mental."

"Oh, I don't think so, honey. I wasn't even sure you liked him. And he's so busy with his painting...."

"Yeah." Drew's chin thrust out. "Everyone's always so busy."

Her heart hurt.

The vice principal cleared her throat. "Well, we've certainly given you a lot to think about over the three-day holiday, haven't we, Mrs. Green? You and Drew talk, and let us know if we can be of any help."

"Thanks." Kenzie walked with Drew to the door and wished both of the other women a good Labor Day weekend.

Kenzie had arranged for Leslie to ride home solo on the bus and for Ann to meet her at the stop. That gave Kenzie and her son a few minutes to talk privately in the car. If he didn't want to, should she push? It turned out that worry was for nothing. He started firing questions at her even before he had his seat belt buckled.

"Is Aunt Ann living with us because Uncle Forrest doesn't love her anymore? Will Abigail grow up without a daddy, too? Is she going to move with us into the new house?"

"No, honey. You know how sometimes I have to separate you and Leslie when you're fighting?"

Despite his sullen attitude, he flashed a mischievous grin. "You mean when we're annoying you?"

"Ann and Forrest didn't want to fight, so they're kind of giving each other a time-out. I don't know how much longer she'll be staying with us, but she is not moving into the new house."

"Are you sure?"

Not entirely. "Why did you suggest JT as a mentor?" She would have been less surprised to hear him mention Sean. Though he didn't technically know the blond man well, they'd certainly hit it off. With JT, Drew was pricklier than a den full of hedgehogs.

"Dunno," the boy muttered. "He's a guy. He lives even closer than Uncle Forrest."

And JT had officially been on more outings with Drew than his biological father had all year. "Those are logical reasons," she agreed. "But I thought you didn't like him."

"I don't like art. At least, I didn't think so. Some of the stuff at that museum was kinda cool, I guess. Besides, Leslie's a suck-up. If you and JT start dating, I want to make sure he likes me, too. Or she'll get better presents at Christmas."

"Drew!" Kenzie gripped the steering wheel tightly, trying not to veer into oncoming traffic. *Back way the hell up, son.* "I already told you I didn't have any plans to date JT. I hardly think you need to start worrying about Christmas presents."

"Did you ever plan for you and Dad to, you know, end up living apart? Do you think he planned to be a better dad?"

How had her nine-year-old become so wise in the ways of the world? "I know it bothers your daddy that he isn't doing a better job. He's said so on more than one occasion."

"Then why doesn't he try harder?" Drew demanded.

"Sometimes it's hard for people to change, even when they really, really want to."

"If he ever gets a hit song on the radio, I'm not listening to it!"

"If you think that will make you feel better."

He stared out the window, not speaking again until she pulled into a parking space. "Mom, do you think JT would teach me how to paint?"

"I, uh… Honey, I really don't know. He's been having a hard time with painting lately, and we won't be here much longer," she reminded him. But Drew looked so unexpectedly crestfallen that she heard herself say, "I'll ask him. No promises, though!"

Life would be so much easier, she reflected, without promises. Fewer broken vows to spouses and disappointments to children. Even privately, promises could trip up a person. She'd sworn to be independent and responsible, avoiding men who might hurt her or have the power to wound her kids, yet she'd begun thinking of JT at random moments and as she fell asleep at night. Now her reticent son was beginning to carve out a place in his life and affections for the artist.

Please, please don't hurt us. Even if it were a promise she had the right to ask for, was it one he'd be able to keep?

Chapter 10

As soon as Kenzie walked into the apartment, she saw a huge floral arrangement dominating the coffee table. No point in asking who they were for, considering Ann's giddy expression.

"Can you believe he sent flowers?" she asked, beaming in Kenzie and Drew's direction. Then she sobered. "Everything go okay at the school?"

"Fine," Kenzie replied, cutting her eyes toward Drew and hoping to convey to her sister that they'd talk later. "Leslie make it home all right?"

Ann nodded. "She's in her room listening to her iPod and doing homework."

"What a nerd," Drew said. "We have three whole days before class."

"Yes, but your sister knows better than to procrastinate," Kenzie said pointedly.

"I guess I should go work."

She tousled his hair. "Good guess."

As he shuffled down the hall, she bent to inhale the fragrance of the purple and yellow bouquet. The last time a man had sent *her* flowers had been her boss in Raindrop when she'd discovered an accounting error in the bank's favor.

"So, was there a card?" she asked her sister.

"It said 'I miss you. Forrest.' If it hadn't had his name on it, I might have thought JT sent these for you."

Kenzie tried not to imagine how she'd feel if he made such a gesture. "'I miss you'? Simple, classic, to the point. I like it. Did you call to let him know you got them?"

"I left a message." Ann floated to the kitchen, where she lifted a pot lid and stirred something that smelled divine. "I told him thank-you. And that I miss him, too. And that Abby misses the way he sings to her when she's fussy."

"Forrest sings?" Kenzie couldn't quite picture that.

"Yeah, he has a surprisingly good voice. I try to soothe her with lullabies, but it's not the same." Ann worried her bottom lip with her teeth. "Do you think it's selfish of me, being here and separating her from her dad at a formative age?"

"I don't think you've scarred her for life, no, but I'm sure she'd be happy to go home. Drew asked me today if…"

"If what?"

"Well, if you were planning to move into the new house with us."

Ann gave a horrified bark of laughter, then clapped her hand over her mouth. "Oh, dear. Has my being here upset him?"

"He loves you. He really loves your cooking. He may not fully appreciate Abby yet, but that will come as they both get older. His teacher, however, is worried about estrogen overload. He's living with a sister, mom, aunt and tiny female cousin with a wardrobe of pink. They think he could benefit from some male influence. I wondered the same thing last spring, when he kept angling to get extra attention and playing time from his coaches."

Ann poured two glasses of ice water, handing one to Kenzie. "Are you thinking about calling Mick?"

Sipping the water, Kenzie considered the possible outcomes of such a call. "He's notoriously difficult to get ahold of. He doesn't stay in one place long, his cell phone gets turned off whenever he's low on funds, and he's slow to return messages. That said, if I *could* reach him and I told him about the vice principal's concerns, he'd ask if there was anything he could do and would immediately want to talk to Drew. He'd promise to come spend a weekend of special father-son time—he might even do it, if a gig didn't crop up in the meantime—but if he came and spent a wonderful weekend with Drew, it would hurt Les. And if he came and spent a wonderful weekend with both of them, full of resolutions to be a better dad and see them more, it would just leave more pieces for me to pick up when another six months pass before we hear from him again."

"That sounds like a no on calling him, then."

"He means well." Kenzie set her glass on the counter. "But intentions aren't enough. There needs to be action, follow-through." Speaking of well-intentioned promises… "I told Drew I'd ask JT for a favor this weekend. I expect to see him at the tenants Labor Day picnic. Think we could whip up some really great dessert I could use as a bribe?"

Ann struck a goofy femme fatale pose. "You sure you don't want to bargain with sexual favors, instead?"

"Rhiannon!" Kenzie paused, her mind departing on naughty flights of fancy. "We'll call that plan B."

As JT stared at his reflection in the bedroom mirror, he was struck simultaneously by two absurd bits of behavior—he was whistling a jaunty tune *and* he was considering changing clothes, inexplicably second-guessing whether his denim shorts and faded Shakespeare Tavern T-shirt were too informal for the annual rooftop picnic. The ringing phone interrupted his contemplation and he answered, half his mind still on wardrobe issues.

"Yo," Sean said in greeting. "Just wanted to let you know the Owenbys were thrilled. I knew they would be, but I thought you'd want to hear they loved the painting."

"Thanks," JT said absently, carrying the cordless phone toward the closet. Well, no wonder he'd gone with this shirt, he realized a second later. It was one of the few that had been clean and on a hanger. "Have you ever known me to be jaunty?"

"Not on purpose. There was that one Christmas party, though, with the eggnog incident."

"You've conveniently confused me with you."

"So I have. What's up? Feeling jaunty?"

JT had no idea what he was feeling. It was as if after months of living in the relative safety of dark numbness, he'd emerged into a kaleidoscope of bright emotion. Not an entirely pleasant sensation. As with a numb limb that had been "awakened," there were sharp needles of pain.

Along with returning responsibilities, he thought, glancing around as if seeing the dim room for the first time. He was an artist, for crying out loud, and there wasn't a damn thing hanging on the walls in here. When was the last time he'd made the bed? The pile of dirty clothes against the wall probably qualified for historic landmark status.

JT frowned. "I gotta go, man."

"Tell Kenzie I said hello."

"I didn't say anything about seeing her."

"You were behaving even more bizarrely than normal, so I intuited you must be nervous about spending time with a certain cute blonde. Plus, when we were at dinner, I overheard mention of the Labor Day picnic. Tell Mrs. Sanchez I said hi, too. Her cooking has ruined me for all other women."

"Why should I be nervous about seeing Kenzie? She's my neighbor. I see her all the time. She's…nice."

"I'll say."

"Don't think about her in that tone of voice." A wave of irrational possessiveness rose inside him.

"No lewd disrespect intended. I admire her wit and parenting skills and how adorably protective she is of her sister. But none of that precludes noticing just how—"

"I'm serious."

"All right." Sean paused. "So why *are* you nervous about seeing her?"

"Because I want to," he said finally. It had been a long time since he'd let himself look forward to something, since he'd truly wanted *anything*. Even though he'd complained about not being able to paint, that had been more frustration than the desire to create. On a basic level, he wanted Kenzie.

He wasn't sure if it would ever deepen into a more complicated emotion or if he was too damaged for that. For the time being, just wanting to be near her was something to savor. A rare gift he'd doubted he would experience again.

Now that he'd managed to answer Sean's question, though, JT was plagued with one of his own—did Kenzie want him?

In her mind, Kenzie always associated September and the start of each new school year with the changing seasons and the crisp bite of fall. In reality, however, today was approaching record-breaking highs and the baking heat stole her breath as she stepped onto the roof. Three minutes up here and she'd be sweating like a petty criminal during a tax audit.

A chorus of friendly hellos met her, and she smiled at Mrs. Sanchez and Mr. C. Alicia from downstairs approached and offered to carry the glass dish over to the food table. But Kenzie didn't see—

"Excuse me." JT's voice was an apologetic rumble and she felt more than saw him draw up short to avoid colliding with her.

She turned to look over her shoulder, drinking him in with her eyes. "No, it's my fault. I shouldn't be blocking the doorway." With him so close, taking a step away was the last thing she wanted to do, but she suspected he'd like to set down the heavy cooler he was toting.

"I don't cook," he said sheepishly. "Ice and sodas are my traditional contribution."

"Hey, don't knock the ice and soda. On a scorcher like today, they'll be a hit."

"Maybe next year we can do this in the parking garage instead. Think of all that shade. Then again, the view's nicer here."

Got that right, she thought, unable to resist watching as he walked past her toward the folding tables.

A moment later, he returned, carrying two different kinds of soft drink. "Take your pick," he offered.

"Thank you." She unscrewed the lid of one, toying with the plastic.

"Where's everyone else?" he asked.

"They'll be up soon. Leslie's helping get the baby ready, and Drew had to finish his video-game level before he saved his progress." All true, but Kenzie had ducked out ahead of her family on purpose, crossing her fingers for a chance to speak with JT alone. "I was hoping to run into you this afternoon."

"Oh?" His eyes were a hot liquid silver, and she almost blushed under their scrutiny.

She nodded, leaning against a section of decorative railing. "I need to talk to you about something. If you have a minute?"

"Fire at will."

The phrase might be more apt than he'd intended. He seemed a fairly private man, and she'd wondered if he ever felt under attack from his temporary but invasive neighbors. Leslie pushed for his company every time she saw him; Drew was barely civil. Now there were Ann and the baby, too. While JT had never complained, Kenzie suspected he could sometimes hear Abigail crying. Knowing he'd been expecting a child of his own, she better understood the way he quickly glanced away from the infant when he encountered her.

She swallowed. "My son, Drew? I realize you don't know us very well, but I'm sure you've noticed he's... working through some issues."

JT laid his arm across the rail, not touching her but close enough that she could feel the warmth from his skin. "Artists are supposed to be observant. I may not have known you long, but I think I'm starting to know you well. The twins are angry, with good reason, but they're amazing kids with lots of talent and strength. And you're a great mom who's doing a hell of a job with little help."

At twenty-eight, having someone praise her ability as a mother was about the headiest compliment she could imagine, far more potent than if he'd told her she had a lovely smile or shapely legs. "Thank you, but you give me too much credit. Ann's been helping, too."

"Seems to me that's a two-way street. Is she here to assist you, or are you giving her sanctuary through a tough time?"

"Both, I guess. Although her presence is part of why I need to talk to you."

His eyebrows winged skyward.

"Drew's teacher and vice principal called me in for a short conference yesterday. Apparently, one of the things he's unhappy about is being constantly surrounded by females."

JT grinned into his drink. "He'll grow out of that. In a few years, girls won't seem so bad."

"Even then, I suspect his mom, aunt and sister won't rate very high on his cool list. Meanwhile, the staff at his school feel he'd benefit from more, um, male influence in his life. A role model or teacher."

"I suppose that makes sense," JT said carefully, obviously starting to question how this applied to him.

"And then Drew surprised me on the way home from school with a request." She took a deep breath. "It was more a request for you, really. He wanted to know if you could show him a couple of things about painting."

"You want me to teach your son to paint?"

"I… It was Drew's idea, but it fits in nicely with the teacher's suggestion that he occasionally hang out with a guy." For the next five weeks, anyway. "They don't have to be formal, scheduled lessons. Unless that's what you want! I could even pay you whatever the comparable rate—" She stopped abruptly when she realized she had no idea what private art lessons with an acclaimed painter might cost. Wasn't she supposed to be saving up for all the miscellaneous expenses that came with a move?

"I don't want your money, Kenzie." With the metallic glint of panic in his eyes, he didn't look as if he wanted anything to do with her. Did he even realize he'd taken a step back?

"Never mind. This wasn't very well thought out," she admitted. "It's just that I promised Drew I'd ask, and now I have. So—"

"I'll do it."

"What?"

He scraped a hand over his jaw, gazing at something unseen beyond her. "Not to bash your ex, but I know what it's like to be hurt by your own dad. I can't make that better for Drew. I don't want to be a father or anyone's substitute father figure, but maybe I can be a friend. At the very least, I can let him come over to my apartment and throw some paint at a canvas on a semi-regular basis.

"Of course, if your son turns out to be some kind of prodigy, I want partial credit for having discovered him."

The joke he tacked on to lighten the moment barely penetrated her wonder that he'd agreed to help, when it clearly wouldn't have been his first choice. Fierce gratitude crashed through her. Rising on tiptoes, she swayed toward him. He didn't seem the huggy type, but perhaps he'd permit a quick peck of thanks on the cheek? He could easily evade her if he didn't want her this close.

It was hard to say which one of them redirected her intended gesture. Had she been deceiving herself in that split second when she'd told herself she was aiming for his cheek, or was it JT who'd had something else in mind when he bent his head down? Maybe it was both of them.

Regardless of how or why, JT's mouth, superficially cool from the icy soda, but burning hot beyond that, was pressed to hers.

Her lips parted in a sigh, and he explored them gently, running his tongue over the seam, sucking her bottom lip—a slight but intimate tug that made her tremble. She felt an answering pull deep inside her, and opened her mouth even farther. Cupping the back of her head in one large hand, he accepted the silent invitation. At the first velvety stroke of his tongue against hers, sensation shot through her. She clasped his shirt-front, making an involuntary sound that was only a few decibels shy of an honest-to-goodness moan. The man could seriously kiss.

Oh, dear. She was *kissing* JT! In full view of the other tenants, including the fifteen-year-old who some-times babysat for Kenzie's kids. Kids who could show up on this very roof at any second and catch their mom making out like Alicia's boy-crazy, teenage sister. It was that thought that overrode every other physical im-pulse she was experiencing and allowed her to pull free of his embrace.

"I j-just wanted to say thank-you," she stammered, feeling like an idiot.

Two small lines of confusion puckered his brow. "For the kiss?"

"No, before. That's what I was doing. Trying to thank you."

He looked startled for a moment, then threw his head back and laughed. "Remind me to do you lots of favors."

The suggestive pleasure in his tone kept her from feeling she was being mocked, and she smiled back. His uncharacteristic show of humor made her even more self-conscious, though, and she glanced around nervously to see if they had an audience. The Wilders from the first floor were sniping at each other as usual and seemed oblivious to everyone else. Alicia was standing at the food table, rolling her eyes at the way her older sister flirted with the building's resident college student. Mrs. Sanchez and her oldest daughter were furtively whispering to each other, and Kenzie experienced a frisson of unease, hoping that their hushed conversation was family gossip.

"Do you think anyone noticed?" she asked JT. "That was really irresponsible of me."

He brushed her hair away from her face. "It was just a kiss."

"Just?"

"Poor word choice. In all honesty, I'm not sure what words to use." He took a sip of his drink, glancing away before he spoke again. She appreciated the chance to regain her composure. "I plan to be up here for a while, if Drew wants to talk to me about coming over to paint."

"Thank you."

"You're welcome. Though I'm partial to the way you said it last time."

Unconsciously, she rubbed the pad of her thumb over her bottom lip. "So am I, but I didn't mean for it to be a spectator event." She'd all but sworn to her son that she wouldn't date JT. How betrayed would the kid feel if he'd seen her unguarded moment of lust? As habitually angry as he already was, she couldn't imagine what it would do to him if he felt he couldn't count on her.

"Next time," JT said softly, "we'll have to make sure it's just the two of us."

Her pulse raced. Did she want there to be a next time? Ludicrous question. Of course she wanted it. She ached with wanting. But did that mean kissing him again, letting him kiss her, was wise?

Noting her silence, he amended, "If there's a next time."

"Right."

If. A small, seemingly insignificant word for such a dizzying wealth of possibilities.

Chapter 11

Kenzie tossed and turned in bed, trying not to notice how large the mattress seemed tonight. There was way more space than one woman needed all by herself—even a woman as restless as her. She sat, irritably kicking at the sheets tangled among her calves. The apartment was unbearably hot. *I'll call Mr. C. in the morning, get him to double-check that the air conditioner's working properly.*

Her sigh echoed in the dark stillness of the room. Was she really deluded enough to convince herself that the problem was the AC and not that kiss she and JT had shared this afternoon? Maybe the reason she couldn't sleep was because she knew he was right across the hall. Was he painting during these late hours? Snoozing peacefully in his own bed? Or was he, like her, reliving the heady taste of their kiss, the contrast between the heat of their bodies pressed together and the slight, merciful breeze that had rippled over them for a moment?

She closed her eyes, remembering that moment, the sensations that had melted through her at the first touch of his mouth. *Bad idea.* Images like that were not going to soothe her into a more restful state.

Kicking her feet over the side of the bed, she thought of all the times she'd heard people recommend a glass of milk to fight insomnia. What about a giant bowl of ice cream? There should be plenty of milk in that, right?

Barefoot, she padded down the hallway, slowing when she heard a voice. At first she thought it might be Leslie talking in her sleep, but then realized it was Ann in the living room. She must be up with Abigail. Kenzie crept forward in a silent tiptoe, so as not to disturb the baby if Ann almost had her asleep.

"You know I do," her sister was saying softly, "but that's just the point…I don't *want* to come home so everything can be just like it was. If I'd been happy with everything as is, I wouldn't have left."

Kenzie froze. Her sister wasn't talking to the baby; she was on the phone with Forrest.

Suddenly there came the sound of a sultry, un-Ann-like chuckle. "Okay, that can stay the same. Wait— Kenzie's got another call, so… How should I know who's calling her at this hour? Of *course* I'm not inventing a reason to get out of our conversation, you lunatic." Despite her words, her voice was tender.

Someone was calling this late? Kenzie coughed delicately, alerting Ann to her presence as she rounded the corner.

"Hello?" Ann was pulling herself into a sitting position on the sofa, her eyes wide in the dim lamplight. "Yes, actually, here she is now."

"Who is it?" Kenzie asked, her mind irrationally leaping to JT. Not much of a leap, really, since her thoughts had been on him all evening. In addition to being a devastating kisser, he'd been remarkably friendly and patient with her son when Drew had finally shown up to scarf down three platefuls of food.

Ann cupped her hand over the cordless receiver. "It's Mick. Were you expecting his call?"

"Mick?" Shock paralyzed her as she reached for the phone. "The Mick I married?"

Ann nodded, making no attempt to hide her curiosity. "You think everything's all right?" she whispered.

"Only one way to find out." Kenzie took a deep breath. As she held the phone to her ear, she heard throbbing bass and background chatter. He was probably calling from a club somewhere. "Hello?"

"Mackenzie." He greeted her with gruff affection. "It's good to hear your voice."

Several sarcastic retorts came to mind about how he could hear it more often, but she bit her tongue as she carried the phone to her bedroom. Mick was who he was. Though she could harangue an apology out of him, that wouldn't make him less likely to lose track of time if he was jamming with the band, or more likely to pay his cellular service bill.

"I got your message that you were moving to Atlanta."

"That was weeks ago," she pointed out gently. "Thank goodness I wasn't trying to get ahold of you because of an emergency."

He gave a self-deprecating chuckle. "Hell, what right-thinking person would call *me* in an emergency? We both know I stink in a crisis. The kids are lucky to have you as a mother, Mac. You're better at everything than I am. Except maybe an inverted guitar chord."

"It's true the kids won't inherit any musical ability from me."

There was a pause, followed by rustling and the fading of ambient noise. He'd either gone outside or walked somewhere more private. When he spoke again, it was easy to hear the waver of emotion in his voice. "How are they?"

"If you'd called a couple of hours ago, you could have asked them that yourself." With a sigh, she got back in bed. "They miss you."

"I miss them, too. Which is part of the reason I've quit."

"Quit what?"

"Performing. I've left the band."

She couldn't have been more astounded if he said he was giving up *breathing*. "You're kidding."

"You know I don't kid about music."

That was true. "Are you looking for another band? Or attempting a solo career?"

"No, I'm serious. I've quit. You reach an age when you can't keep lying to yourself. If it was gonna happen for me… 'Course, the industry's in my blood now. I've met dozens of musicians in the past few years, many of them really talented. Maybe I can help."

"I don't understand."

"I'm going to represent other musicians! I've made connections," he said proudly. "Just because I wasn't able to make them work for me the way I'd hoped doesn't mean those connections won't come through for the right band, the right singer with that 'it' factor."

"Um…" She wanted to be supportive, but she'd always seen him as more adept at making music than having business sense. Even if he were successful in this new venture, would he be happy watching someone else reap the accolades he'd dreamed of for more than a decade?

"In fact, I'm out tonight with new clients! I'm going to focus on their set and help them figure out how to improve it before next Tuesday. They've got a gig in Nashville that could be their big break!"

God. She prayed for patience as she battled back the unwanted déjà vu. If she had a dollar for every "gig" that was supposed to have built a career, she could single-handedly buy one of the houses in Ann's neighborhood.

"I've saved the best news for last!" Mick told her excitedly.

Her body tensed in nervous anticipation of what other bombshells were in store.

"Atlanta's developing quite the recording scene. If all goes well, I'll be in the city on a semi-regular basis. The kids and I can reconnect."

"That would be… Mick, you're free to come see them anytime. You don't have to wait for a professional reason to come to the city." It would have been great if he'd make plans surrounding, for instance, the kids' birthday. Or the upcoming winter holidays. Thanksgiving would be here before she knew it, Christmas close on its heels.

"Don't worry, it'll be soon! But I should get back inside before the boys get started. The opening number is really important for winning over the audience, setting the right mood. Hey, don't tell the kids yet about my coming to see them? It would be a cool surprise."

She wasn't sure. Drew in particular might need some time to sort out how he felt about seeing his dad, but she agreed not to tell them just yet. After all, Mick's definition of "soon" wasn't necessarily the same one the rest of the English-speaking world used. The less she told the twins now, the less disappointed they might be when his plans unraveled later.

When JT awoke midmorning on Tuesday, he realized he needed more supplies—and not, for a change, because he'd let paint dry out or because he'd thrown a stylus against his studio wall. No, he was actually using the pigments and beeswax that had sat untouched for so long. Until recently, he'd considered the tubes and jars silently mocking, belligerent in their disuse. Now they seemed sad, neglected. JT felt repentant and eager to make up for lost time.

He hurried through brushing his teeth and threw on pants and a shirt that may or may not have technically matched. The sooner he got to the store and back, the sooner he could get to work.

He was still shoving his left foot into a sneaker as he opened the door to his apartment. Preoccupied as he was with half-formed plans for a treated piece of wood, it took him a moment to realize he was staring at the back of some guy. Not necessarily a notable event, except that the guy was standing in front of Kenzie's door, making no move to knock. He wore a pair of glasses, which he pushed up on his nose twice in less than a minute, muttering to himself the entire time. In his lightweight blazer and slacks, he looked like a well-dressed but slightly deranged encyclopedia salesman.

"Can I help you?" JT's voice came out more menacing than he'd intended, but he felt somewhat protective of Kenzie and her children.

The man jumped about a foot, then turned to face JT. He was older, by around a decade, JT guessed, and pale—a nervous potential suitor? After all, he didn't appear to have any encyclopedias, vacuums to demonstrate or literature inviting her to consider spiritual salvation. Then again, why court a woman in the middle of the workday? If he knew Kenzie, surely he realized she was at the bank now.

"I'm Dr. Forrest Smith," the man replied. He lifted his chin, a flinty gleam of determination showing behind the lenses of his wire-rim glasses. "And I'm here for my wife!"

"Oh." The guy was here for Ann, not Kenzie. Suddenly, JT liked him much better. "Well, good for you."

"Yes." Dr. Smith's shoulders slumped slightly. "She was. Maybe too good for me."

A mild and abstract kind of alarm pulsed through JT at the other man's confiding tone. Visions of that wood panel and his unrealized hopes for it fluttered through his subconscious. Still, neither the art store nor the wood were going anywhere, so he shoved his hands in his pockets and waited.

"Have you met Ann?" Dr. Smith asked.

"A couple of times. I don't know her well."

The other man was nodding absently, talking almost more to himself than JT. "She's younger than I am. I was surprised when she showed interest in me, but I got used to it. Used to her. She keeps everything so organized...."

If JT had just awakened half an hour sooner this morning, perhaps he would already be at the store, sorting through the—

"Are you good with women?" Dr. Smith asked suddenly.

"Hmm? Oh, no. Not really." What this guy needed was Sean, a natural-born charmer who never thought it was weird when total strangers asked him for opinions. JT wasn't charming, he was...isolated, awkward.

Although, holding Kenzie on the rooftop hadn't felt awkward. It had been instinctive and effortless, finding her mouth with his, kissing her as if he already knew her shape and taste and just how she liked to be caressed. Holding her against him, he sure as hell hadn't felt isolated.

Ann's husband was muttering again. "Damn, I

should have brought flowers. I'm here to ask her to come home. Do you think I should have brought flowers with me? It would have been more romantic."

Truthfully, JT had no idea. He didn't know if Ann craved romance or if she even intended to go home, though Kenzie seemed to think her sister's separation was temporary. Since this nervous-looking husband had asked for advice, JT spoke from his gut.

"I had a wife and child once. I'd give anything to spend another day with them. If you love your wife, tell her now. Stop dithering out in the hall, don't waste time going for flowers. Just. Tell. Her."

The man considered this, shoving his glasses up on the bridge of his nose in a move that was clearly more habit than necessity—they'd barely moved since the last time he'd pushed them into place. "Right. Right, why am I wasting time?" Without waiting for an answer, he pivoted and rapped sharply on the door.

JT hoped Ann and the baby weren't out running errands, or the results of her husband's resolve would be rather anticlimactic. JT breathed an inward sigh of relief when the door swung open. He was already turning to go when he heard a quizzical "Forrest?" from behind him. As he stepped inside the elevator, he glimpsed the embrace at the end of the hallway. From the way Ann was kissing her husband, he suspected she would indeed be going home soon.

JT averted his eyes quickly to give the couple more privacy, even though they were oblivious to his existence. Recalling Kenzie's nervousness about an audience the other day, he couldn't help wondering...

what would have happened if they'd been alone when he kissed her? His blood heated at the thought, at the memory of her mouth.

What he'd told Forrest seemed like a split truth. JT would always hate the tragedy of Holly's death, that she'd sacrificed her life trying to give birth to the baby that hadn't made it, either. There had been plenty of days when he would have sold his own soul to spend five more minutes with her. Yet she hadn't haunted his dreams in the same way for months. While it would have felt disloyal to say it—even to himself—he knew he'd slowly been getting over her. This was more than simple healing, though. He was actively waking up with another woman's face and laugh and kiss on his mind. Kenzie had become the woman he wanted to spend time with.

She'd be gone soon, and part of him took comfort in that, a finite end rather than a shocking jolt.

After the wrenching double loss he'd suffered, he doubted he would ever again be capable of long-term emotional commitments...or that the wary single mother would even welcome one. Kenzie's moving would help them part ways naturally, without a lot of drama, and he welcomed the easy out. Still, he hoped to see her as much as possible before that happened.

JT knew it was Kenzie by the sound of her knock—light and quick as if she were both eager and shy. Or possibly, despite the open windows, he was strung out on paint fumes and turpentine.

"Just a sec," he called, cleaning his brush with a rag as he walked to the door.

As he'd expected, Kenzie, along with her son, who'd obviously changed out of his school clothes, waited on the other side. Drew wore denim cutoffs with ragged hems at the knee, a black T-shirt and a huge grin.

JT arched an eyebrow at him. "You look excited to get started."

"Yeah, I'm psyched. Leslie is torqued. Kept whining about how *she's* the one who—"

"Andrew." Kenzie squeezed his shoulder. "A little sensitivity, please. Remember your manners, or JT can punt you back to our apartment."

Frankly, JT was surprised the kid would rather be over here messing with art supplies instead of back home with his video games. Was it just the novelty of getting to do something that didn't include his sister? JT knew the boy's teachers thought he needed time around an adult male, but JT had a hard time seeing himself as a role model. Still, he was happy to help. Partly because he recalled the confused misery of his own adolescence…and, selfishly, because of the way Kenzie's eyes lit with gratitude. A look like that made a guy feel as if he could leap tall buildings in a single bound.

"Don't be too late," she added, and JT wasn't sure if the instruction was for him or Drew. "You promise you've finished your homework?"

"Yes, ma'am." If Drew didn't technically roll his eyes, it was implied in his tone.

"All right. But you still need to eat din—" She broke

off, her gaze jerking up to meet JT's. "You should join us! I mean, if you want to. As a thank-you."

He couldn't help thinking of how she'd thanked him on a previous occasion. By the rosy flush climbing her cheeks, he guessed she was remembering the same thing. His eyes held hers, and if it hadn't been for Drew standing between them, JT would have leaned in to kiss her again. Her lips parted, and he forced himself to look away.

JT cleared his throat. "What time's dinner?"

"How about an hour?" she offered.

"Sure." When JT was in the creative zone, he could lose whole hours at a time, but he suspected that Drew would get bored long before then. An hour sounded reasonable for an actual art lesson, not that he was planning anything too formal.

He ushered Drew inside and began to give him a brief overview of paints. "As I told your sister, I do a lot of work with oils, but we probably won't start with that for you today. Acrylics are a fast-drying option, and watercolors don't involve much cleanup."

"Good," Drew said. "I don't like to clean."

"Artists have to take care of their equipment, though. There's a lot of discipline and hard work and routine involved. It's not just standing in front of an easel waiting for inspiration to strike and then breaking for a latte."

"Latte?" Drew wrinkled his nose. "That's a kind of coffee, right? Why would I want one of those?"

"Never mind. Let's round up some supplies and go up to the roof."

"You don't work in your apartment?"

"Sometimes I do, but a change of perspective can be good, not to mention the fresh air and natural light."

Drew trailed him to his studio, hanging back in the doorway as JT gathered some basic tools. "Thank you for letting me come over. I think Mom was nervous about asking you. She likes you, you know."

JT straightened, having no idea what the appropriate response was. Every time he looked at Kenzie, his temperature soared ten degrees, but he could hardly tell Drew that. "I like her, too." In fact, he liked the whole family a lot more than he would have thought possible in such a short time.

A disquieting acknowledgment. How much more emotionally invested would he become before it was time to bid them goodbye?

"Mom?" Leslie was supposed to be setting the table, but was instead leaning against the kitchen counter, getting under Kenzie's feet as she tried to finish preparing dinner. "Are you okay? You look...kind of like I feel when I throw up."

Lovely. "I'm just busy, trying to get dinner ready." Although, if she *were* feeling the tiniest bit apprehensive about cooking for JT, it might be because a certain daughter had once tried to make her sound like Julia Child and Betty Crocker all rolled into one.

Kenzie was never going to be an award-winning chef, but she ought to be able to produce a decent-tasting, well-balanced meal. She had biscuits in the oven, chicken breasts in a pan with basil and white wine, and green beans boiling. *What am I forgetting?* Salad! She'd meant to put together a salad.

"Can you grab me carrots and a cucumber from the fridge? I'll chop, you wash lettuce leaves."

Leslie obliged. "You know," she said as she took the lettuce to the sink, "I would understand if you were feeling nauseous. My new friend Angel feels that way when she sees the boy she likes."

Aside from a twinge of motherly panic that girls Les's age were already noticing the opposite sex, Kenzie was relieved to hear Leslie casually mentioning friends—the kind that didn't exist solely in fiction. At least one of the twins was settling into the new school. "Maybe you could invite Angel over sometime."

"Cool. I bet she'll like the view from the roof. I like going up there to read and think," Leslie said. "I'll miss it when we move."

When they moved… Kenzie should take the kids for a drive by their future house this weekend. She could hardly recall what the place looked like. Oh, she had vague impressions, but the details were getting fuzzy. She needed the reminder that *that* was home, not Peachy Acres. Despite its cozy community feel and the neighbors she was getting to know, the complex was just a way station. Still, the apartment felt comfortably roomy with Ann and Abigail gone. Her sister had called Kenzie at the bank to say she and Forrest were going to work on resolving their problems—and that *he* was planning to cook an early dinner for *her*.

When the front door opened, Kenzie's heart thudded in anticipation. While she liked everyone she'd met in the building, there was no question that one neighbor in particular had become special to her.

Drew rushed in first, talking a mile a minute. "You want to see what I did? I used paper today, but JT said I could use canvas next time. I thought he was supposed to tell me what to draw or arrange a bowl of fruit or something, but he just gave me some colors and told me to go for it. He's a really lousy teacher."

Yet Drew was grinning from ear to ear and JT, entering the room behind him, wore a similar smile.

JT held his palms up in front of his body. "Hey, I never claimed to be a good instructor, kid. It's not my fault if you chose unwisely."

Leslie was peering at the paper in her brother's hand. "So, what is it?"

"I don't know yet. But remember some of those pictures we saw at the museum?" Drew adopted a pompous tone. "*Untitled in Yellow, Big Fat Splotch on Wood Circle.* JT said I can think about what the painting means to me, but that not all art has a… What was that word again?"

"*Literal?* Literal meaning?"

"Yeah! I'm gonna go wash my hands. When do we eat? I'm hungry."

"There's a surprise," Leslie muttered, obviously still put out that no one had invited *her* to come paint. Kenzie made a mental note to plan a fun mother-daughter activity the next time Drew went across the hall. Maybe if she and Les were giving each other pedicures and enjoying some boy-free quality time, her daughter would be less resentful.

"Something smells good in here," JT said. "Anything I can do to help?"

Kenzie smiled up at him. "No, that's—"

"You could set the table," Leslie said. "I was going to earlier, but then I came in here to calm Mom down."

"Calm her down?" He repeated the words to Leslie, but angled his questioning look at Kenzie.

Kenzie sliced a few more pieces of carrot, thinking with fond nostalgia of the days before the twins could speak. "Leslie, why don't *you* go set out the dishes, instead of trying to foist your chores off on our guest?"

"Okay." Lowering her voice to nowhere near a whisper as she passed, Leslie instructed her mother, "If you do feel nervous, you're supposed to take deep breaths. They're, like, soothing or something."

With a sardonic glance over her shoulder at the skillet, Kenzie reflected that perhaps the white wine would have been put to better use in a glass rather than in the chicken recipe.

JT came to stand next to her, leaning against the counter and clearly enjoying himself. "Anything I can do to help with your jittery nerves?"

Yes, go stand in the next room. But then she wouldn't be able to bask in his nearness, enjoy the unique smell of *him* that was noticeable beneath the astringent perfume of paint and whatever soap he used to scrub with after.

"My nerves are fine, thanks. My daughter, as you may have noticed, has an overactive imagination." Given the things Leslie had no compunction saying right in front of Kenzie, she shuddered to think what an unsupervised Drew might have said in the past hour. "So, how did it go?"

"Seemed okay. We sat on the roof, working on separate pieces. Every once in a while he'd ask my opinion or share something random from school. At first, he was tense whenever he thought he'd messed up. I explained that no stroke is wasted—sometimes the work goes in a different direction than you'd planned, but the very unexpectedness can be inspiring. It's always a learning experience, an exploration of sorts."

"I could listen to you talk about art all day. You have a way of making it sound interesting and personal."

"I could talk to you all day," he rejoined. "You make me feel more interesting than I am. What are you doing Friday night?"

"Uh, Friday?" she echoed, caught utterly off guard. "This Friday?"

"Yeah." He grinned, but a shadow of uncertainty passed in his gaze like the outline of a shark swimming just below the surface of the water. "Sean and I have been asked to a private gallery showing, with the invitation to bring guests, of course. I thought maybe you'd like to come with me and we could…talk about art some more."

Or kiss some more, thought the impulsive, undisciplined Kenzie. "*Yes*. Oh. No. I mean, it's kind of you to ask—"

"But you'd like to think about it?"

"Well, there are the kids to consider." Donning protective mitts, she sidestepped him to retrieve the biscuits from the oven. "I don't know if I can find a sitter in the next few days. Alicia comes by some afternoons, but she mentioned she's looking forward to the high school's first away game this weekend. Maybe Ann."

"She's gone, isn't she?" JT's tone was surprisingly satisfied. "Did she go back to her husband?"

"Apparently he came by today and swept her off her feet. Or at least convinced her that he saw her as more than a glorified administrative assistant. They should be fine."

"Good. It's nice to see people get happy endings," he said softly, almost to himself.

As they all sat at the table, Kenzie kept replaying his words in her head.

Was it naive for people like her and JT, a divorcée and a widower, to believe in happy endings? That took a kind of pure-hearted faith she was afraid she'd outgrown. Still… She watched JT pass Drew the green beans and laugh at Leslie's imitation of Mrs. Kane. Vowing to call Ann first thing in the morning to ask about babysitting, Kenzie finally wrenched her gaze away from JT's handsome face.

Maybe she lacked the childlike optimism to believe in happy endings, but she couldn't help being seduced by the possibility of new beginnings.

Chapter 12

The surprise on Sean's face would have been comical if JT wasn't feeling so abashed. He was part owner of the gallery, yet how long had it been since he'd set foot here?

"Well, this is a red-letter event," his friend said, recovering. He took in JT's white shirt and jeans—the only pair he owned without obvious paint smears. "You even look halfway civilized. Wait, do I *know* you? For a second, I mistook you for someone else."

"Practicing for that career as a comedian in case the gallery closes?"

"Think I should put in a call to Punchline first, or the Funny Farm?"

Looking around, JT ignored the hypothetical question about Atlanta's comedy clubs. As far as he could tell, the two of them were the only people here. "*Is* the gallery in danger of closing?" He remembered how excited he, Sean and Holly had been when they first opened. JT shouldn't have neglected everything. He felt like a man coming out of a coma.

"No." Sean blinked. "I didn't mean to give you that impression. It's true that we made more of a profit when you were…"

"Painting?" His identity as an artist was supposed to have lent the gallery cachet.

"More active in the art community, I was going to say. We still get customers. You just came at a slow time."

"Well, I come with good news." JT shoved his hands in his pockets, wanting to share his joy but not wanting to make more of it than it was. After all, a few colorful blotches did not a career reinvention make. "I, uh, started a painting."

Sean's eyes widened, but he kept his tone casual. "Yeah?"

"Yeah. I mean, it's not entirely right. I may scrap it and take another stab, but…it felt good."

His friend let out an excited whoop. "This is fantastic! We'll celebrate this weekend. You want me to call Whitney and see if she has a friend free on Friday? We could double."

"About that…" He hesitated. "I invited Kenzie to the showing."

Sean's jaw dropped. "Wow. I knew you liked her, but I didn't think you were ready to take the next step. I'm proud of you, man."

JT squirmed. "It's not that big a deal. I like her company, so I asked her to join us."

"Not that big a deal? Isn't she the reason you're painting again? The reason you're out and about in clothes that don't look like they came out of a rag bin?"

"No." *Maybe.* "So I did some laundry. It was time."

"Way past." Sean rounded the short, curved counter to clap his friend on the shoulder. "Whatever spurred you, I'm glad to have you back, buddy. Tell Kenzie I look forward to seeing her Friday night."

"She hasn't actually said yes yet. She needed to look for a sitter."

"Ah, right. Brave of you, getting involved with a mom. I love my nieces and nephews, but still…"

JT rolled his eyes. "'Involved'? It's one night in a group setting. You have a more overactive imagination than Leslie."

"Le—?" Sean stopped short. "Did you just compare me to Kenzie's kid?"

The words had just popped out, but JT was still adjusting to having the Greens in his building, much less cropping up in his everyday conversation. "You should be flattered. Kenzie has great kids."

Sean started laughing then, barely managing to stop long enough to gasp, "Oh, yeah, you're not *involved* at all."

JT gave him a one-finger salute and decided his time was better spent back at the apartment working on his painting, than dealing with the mockery of his so-called friend.

At home, he turned on his music—a local rock band

he liked—and changed into a T-shirt and jeans that were more paint than denim. Then he dived into work, losing all track of time until he was distracted by a knock at the door. Jarred out of his creative flow, he swore under his breath, then realized guiltily that his music was probably too loud. He hit Stop and answered the door. Instead of finding Mr. C. with a noise complaint, he found Kenzie, looking beautiful and shy.

"H-hi." Her smile was tentative. "Am I interrupting?"

"Not at all." He followed her gaze to the small splatters that had accumulated on his hands and clothes in the past few hours. "Okay, you caught me. I was definitely working—I'd hate for you to think I look like this all the time—but it's no bother. What can I do for you?"

She lowered her eyes. "You've already done so much. Even when he was getting ready for school this morning, Drew was talking my ear off about ideas he has for possible artwork. And trust me, Drew is *not* a morning person."

Was she? JT wondered. He couldn't stop himself from imagining how Kenzie woke up in the morning. Refreshed from sleep, did she rise efficient and ready to tackle the day? Or was she softer, dreamier? That was a Kenzie he'd like to see.

There was also the possibility that she woke up as cranky as a bear, but he suspected she could make even that adorable.

"JT?"

"Mmm?"

"Your mind's still on your painting," she guessed apologetically. "I won't keep you. I just wanted to let you know that I talked to Ann today. She said she'll pick the kids up from school on Friday, and they can spend the night with her."

She blushed as soon as she'd finished the sentence, and JT raised an eyebrow.

"In case it's a late night," she added hurriedly. "We don't have to worry about getting back at any p-particular time."

"Right. That makes sense." But didn't explain the blush. He grinned inwardly. "Tell your sister I owe her one."

She nodded. "Will do. I, ah, guess I'll see you Friday."

"It's a date." Belatedly, he recalled saying those words to her once before and getting blasted with an automatic disclaimer.

This time, however, she didn't disagree. Instead, she sank her teeth into the full lower lip he suddenly couldn't stop staring at. Though she looked a bit skittish, her eyes sparked with the blue fire of excitement, too. As if she wouldn't mind his kissing her again.

Before he did exactly that, she gave herself a slight shake and smiled at him. "It's a date."

The woman with the loose curls and black dress appeared so different from the one who went to work at the bank every day that Kenzie almost panicked when she heard the knock at the door. *I should change! JT can't see me like this.* He was perceptive enough to take one look and know she was a fraud, a harried single mom impersonating someone glamorous.

Too bad Leslie wasn't home tonight to allay her fashion fears. Kenzie alternated between elation at not having to worry about any unwanted witnesses for a good-night kiss and sheer terror. While she'd never consciously used her children as a shield against romantic entanglements, they'd certainly created a buffer.

Tonight, bufferless and wearing such a comparatively short skirt, she felt naked. Which did nothing to help her regain her composure as she opened the door.

She forced a smile. "H— Mick!"

Her ex-husband's wide brown eyes were filled with only slightly less surprise than she was feeling. "Mackenzie. Wow, look at you. *Nice.*" His gaze swept down her form in frank appreciation.

There was a time in her life when getting that look from him would have weakened her knees, but when she recalled her reaction now, it was so distant that it felt like seeing someone else's memories rather than experiencing her own.

His grin was crooked as he teased, "Didn't have to get all dressed up on my account."

"How could I have when I had no idea you were coming?" Her date was scheduled to arrive in a few minutes, and here stood her ex-husband. She was hard-pressed to imagine a more awkward social situation.

"I told you I wanted it to be a surprise!" He looked so damn pleased with himself that she wanted to scream.

Even if he'd been trying to do something sweet, did he ever think about the three of them? Understand that they had lives of their own and weren't just sitting around waiting for him to have an opening in his schedule?

"You gave me the address in case I wanted to send the kids anything, so I looked you up on the internet," he continued. "Where are they, by the way? I've got presents for them both."

She started to shove her hands through her hair until she remembered how much trouble she'd gone to with the curling iron, then gritted her teeth instead. "It's nice that you came to see them, and I'm sure they'll be thrilled to know gifts are involved, but they aren't here. They're with my sister and won't be back until tomorrow."

He grimaced. "They're with Annie? Well, they aren't going to have any fun with that sourpuss. Why don't I—"

"Ann's not a sourpuss. She was just always mature for her age." *Which is more than I can say for some of us.*

"I still think the kids would have more fun with their dad tonight. Come on, Mac, I'm not going to be in town long, and—"

"Of course you're not!" She threw her hands in the air. "Mick, they're not toddlers anymore. They aren't content to giggle while you tickle them for twenty minutes, then wave slobbery fists goodbye when you leave. Again. They're old enough to ask questions, to want explanations—from *me,* thank you very much— about why you can't keep the most basic promises, why you can't be relied on to send freaking birthday cards. They're twins—you only have to remember one date."

His posture had turned defensive, his jaw clenched. "I'm here now, aren't I? I'm trying. I told you I was working to change, and all you can do is bust my chops about the past?"

She sagged in the doorway, wanting to kick off her high heels and spend the rest of the night hiding in her room within the folds of a comfy robe. "I get that you're trying. I applaud you for it. But I will not rearrange this family's plans to make life more convenient for you. I tried to tell you when we got divorced—it can't always be about you, not when you're a parent."

His gaze, scathing this time, raked over her again. "Fairly self-righteous coming from a woman who got rid of her kids for the night and looks ready to—"

"If you finish that sentence, I will slap you."

He reddened.

As well he should. Even when they'd been married, he'd flirted with band groupies and women at nightclubs. Before the kids had been born Kenzie had always been there to keep a proprietary eye on him, indulging him as he winked at females who would hopefully go on to buy his music. But swollen to three times her normal size in the eighth month of pregnancy, and later at home with crying infants, she'd had the occasional stab of insecurity about his faithfulness. It was a question she'd never brought herself to ask as their marriage ended—what would be the point when she was already bitter over so many other issues? She liked to think he'd never strayed, but after the divorce, he sure as hell hadn't been celibate, and had no right to require it of her.

Not that she'd already decided to sleep with JT!

No, it was just the principle of… Suddenly she was too distracted by hazy but provocative images to complete her thought. She fanned her face with her hand.

"I apologize," Mick said formally. "I was being an ass. Whoever he is, he's lucky to have you. You were always my biggest fan, and I screwed it up. I'm sorry I hurt you."

"Don't worry about me. Worry about your children. It's not too late, Mick. Don't screw things up with them."

"I—" He broke off, both of them turning as JT came out of his own apartment, looking incredible in black slacks and a lightweight black turtleneck.

Very sophisticated, very sexy. A giggle welled up in her throat as she considered her own all-black ensemble. Together, they would look like a pair of over-dressed cat burglars.

JT had drawn up short, noticing Mick, but flashed Kenzie a warm smile. "Sorry, I lost track of time painting. Any man who keeps a woman like you waiting should be shot."

"Thank you. But let's forgo the firearms. Buy me a drink, we'll call it even."

Next to JT, Mick suddenly looked older, even though the two men couldn't be far apart in age. Still, there was something haggard in her ex-husband's face—too little sleep, too many late-night sessions fuelled by alcohol and nicotine. He stuck a hand out in her date's direction. "Mick Green."

JT's expression was inscrutable as he shook his hand. "Jonathan Trelauney."

Glancing back at her, Mick managed a smile that looked at least half-sincere. "You two have fun tonight. I'll...call you tomorrow morning about seeing the kids."

"That would be good." Feeling strangely melancholy, she watched him stride down the hall and disappear into the elevator.

He was making a renewed effort, which as a mom she appreciated, and nothing had changed between them in years—she was more than free to date—so why did she feel sad? *Pity.* She felt sorry for the man who'd lost his family in pursuit of a dream, only to eventually lose even that.

"Hey." JT reached out, lightly cupping the side of her face. "You all right?"

She nodded wordlessly.

"We could alter our plans if you want, maybe stay in. Although that would be a *huge* sacrifice on my part. As you may have noticed, I'm quite the crowd-loving extrovert."

In spite of her mood, she giggled. "That's the very first thing I noticed about you."

He leaned closer. "Would you like to know the first thing I noticed about *you*, Kenzie?"

"I'm not sure."

"Proportion is important to an artist, ratio and dimensions and the different ways to manipulate them.

And you seemed out of proportion, with so much life and spirit in such a relatively small frame. Although the frame is quite nice." He trailed his gaze over her face, collarbone, the straps of her dress and the hint of cleavage below, then back to meet her eyes. "You steal my breath, the way you try to be stern but then smile. You have a great smile."

"So do you." She reached out to trace his lips with her finger. "I wish I saw it more."

Capturing her hand, he pressed a featherlight kiss to her palm. "I can guarantee I've smiled more since I met you than in the entire past year."

A flattering comment, but she wasn't sure she wanted the responsibility for making him smile. Seeing Mick tonight had reminded her of her former role as a cheerleader. Supporting his artistic dream and cajoling him out of moody doubts when a song wasn't coming together or a purported talent scout didn't show had required nearly as much effort and energy as raising twin babies. Barely an adult herself, she hadn't had it in her to nurture all three of them without losing her own sanity. She was more stable now, the children less mindlessly demanding, but she didn't want to carry the burden of someone else's happiness.

At least, not on a long-term basis.

Right now, JT's complimentary gaze and deadpan jokes were making her happy, and she hoped to return the favor. She had one whole night free to selfishly spend on herself, and she planned to devote the evening to their mutual pleasure.

"CAN I GET YOU ANOTHER glass of wine, Kenzie?" JT offered, one hand resting comfortably at the small of her back.

Before she could answer, Sean grumbled good-naturedly, "Better let me get it. At least that'll give me something to do besides stand here like a third wheel."

Earlier, Sean had told Kenzie how thrilled he'd been to learn she was joining them. Unfortunately, his own date had canceled because of a cold. Before this evening, Kenzie couldn't remember ever being so pleasantly spoiled. She was accompanied by not one but two handsome men who possessed tons of knowledge about art as well as senses of humor. They'd kept her thoroughly entertained as they squired her through the small upscale gallery, studying photographs and sculptures. In fact, they were so solicitous and charming she feared the attention was going to her head. She felt unnaturally light, nearly giddy.

"I think I should pass on a second wine," she said. She'd noted that JT had stuck solely to soft drinks all evening. "But thank you."

"Well, I'm going to get myself some refreshment," Sean said, the twinkle in his gaze belying his gloomy tone. "At least *pretend* to notice my absence."

JT grinned at Kenzie. "Did you hear something?"

She elbowed him gently. "You're going to wound his ego. He's very delicate."

Sean snorted. "I don't have to stand here and take this abuse. I can go get plenty of abuse on the other side of the room."

As his friend walked away, JT chuckled with wry

admiration. "He'll probably end up with some pretty woman at the bar buying him a drink to make up for the way his friends are ignoring him."

"So his date tonight wasn't a girlfriend?"

"No. Sean's a great guy, but he doesn't have a lot of interest in long-term romantic relationships."

"I can understand that," Kenzie said without thinking.

JT cocked his head. "My experience is limited, but usually women cluck their tongues and say that settling down would be healthier for him."

"Maybe it would. But that's not everyone's experience, is it?"

"No," he replied softly.

They both turned back to the framed black-and-white photograph in front of them, but there was only so long they could pretend to be studying its unique focus on the background, instead of the deliberately blurred subject in the center of the shot.

"Did it upset you to see your ex tonight?" JT asked. "You've been a really good sport about being here."

"A rare night on the town with two guys who keep me laughing? Yeah, that's a hardship." She squeezed his hand. "I wasn't upset. His unannounced presence just threw me at first. He thought it would be fun for the kids if he surprised them."

"And you don't agree?"

"I wish he'd think about more than 'fun.' He's been the glamorous parent, the one off in a band who shows up for a few hours without sticking around for middle-of-the-night flu or teacher conferences. I'm the one worrying about homework and orthodontist visits and bills—all the daily grind that isn't sexy."

"Don't sell yourself short." JT's expression took on an almost predatory gleam that was both disconcerting and thrilling. "Even in day-to-day routine, you're plenty sexy."

She lowered her eyes. "Flatterer."

He shook his head. "I watched you put away dishes in your kitchen, the way your clothes slid and clung to the curves of your body. I openly ogled as you popped a bite of warm, buttery biscuit between your lips."

For a man who made a living evoking emotion visually, he was pretty skilled verbally, too. He had the ability to wring powerful reactions from her without even touching her. Which was kind of a shame—she really, really wanted him to touch her. The desire had grown throughout the night into a sweet, sharp craving she saw no reason to deny.

Her throat felt so dry it was hard to get words out. "So, um, how much longer do you think we should stay?"

"Why, you tired?" There was a silky, teasing note in his voice.

"Ready to go someplace more intimate," she corrected.

She looked around in search of Sean. They'd arrived in separate cars, but it only seemed polite to bid him farewell. Raising his hand above the rest of the crowd, JT waved for Sean's attention and made their goodbye by pointing toward the exit as he ushered Kenzie through the room. Ten minutes later, they were on the road. Although he was driving at a nice, safe speed—below the limit, by Atlanta's standards—Kenzie felt as if she were hurtling toward something overwhelming and inevitable.

And she couldn't wait to get there.

Chapter 13

In an endearing gentlemanly fashion, JT quickly got out of the car and rushed around to open her door. The September night was still warm enough to be muggy. To Kenzie, it felt as if even the air was throbbing and heavy with expectation. He took her hand, and, dazed, she let him lead her inside the building.

The elevator doors slid apart to admit them. For a change, Sylvia Myer wasn't present with her button-pushing daughter. *Must be after the little girl's bedtime.* Tonight, Kenzie and JT were all alone. A wave of wanting swamped her, and she watched him hungrily.

As soon as the elevator jolted into motion, he reached for her. His arms, bands of gentle steel, encircled her in a fierce embrace. Ducking to her height, he claimed her mouth, absorbing her breathy gasp. Had she ever wanted a man so intensely?

The elevator halted. *Thank goodness.* Somewhere in the course of the evening—perhaps when he'd first made her laugh after Mick's departure, or when he'd held open the gallery door, or when he'd told her how sexy she was—she'd subconsciously reached the decision to make love with him. But she needed to get him into one of their apartments before she had time to lose her nerve.

As they neared the end of the hallway, JT asked, "Should I walk you home, or do you want to come over for a little while?"

"I'd like to see your place." She'd never made it past the threshold.

He'd barely ushered her inside before he pressed her against the wall, kissing her with even more fervor than in the elevator. He nipped at her bottom lip, saying between kisses, "I'm…a lousy…host." Pulling back slightly, he trailed a hand over the side of her neck, toward the modest swell of cleavage revealed by her dress. "I should offer you a drink or something."

She tilted her head back, arching toward his touch. "I'll take the 'or something.'"

When he kissed her again, she could feel the smile on his lips. They took their time, necking like a couple of teenagers. There was no doubt in Kenzie's mind that he wanted her as desperately as she wanted him, but they had the whole night ahead of them. The sensual side of her appreciated the tantalizing foreplay; the part of her that was nervous about having sex for the first time in years was grateful for the slow seduction.

Finally they drew apart and JT chuckled wryly. "I

really am a bad host. The least I could do was find a more comfortable spot. We could move to the couch?"

Or the bed. Was that too forward? "Actually, could you show me around? I'd love to see where you work."

"All right."

His floor plan was a lot different than hers. Where the space in her apartment was carved up for a maximum number of rooms and vanity nooks, his was considerably more open. The living room was larger, flowing into the kitchen, with very little separation except the breakfast bar divider. There was a single bathroom and two bedrooms, one of which he'd converted into a studio. His apartment looked recently cleaned, not as messy as she would have expected from a bachelor.

The studio was fascinating. There were several easels set up, small electric tools she didn't recognize sitting atop a square table, shelving units full of paint and other supplies placed against the walls. Some sort of respiratory mask hung right beneath the light switch. Everything clearly had a place…except for the art itself, which was scattered everywhere. A large piece of wood lay on a window seat, half its surface covered in colors and waxy texture, and on the floor below were wadded-up pieces of sketching paper. Old canvases were stacked in a corner, and one had slid off the pile. The surface of a desk had disappeared entirely under an inch-thick layer of drawings. There was a palpable energy in the room; she could easily picture his artistic mania, JT sketching and muttering to himself as he tried to produce just the right image.

Kenzie glanced around, taking it all in. "How long have you been— Oh!" Her gaze fell on a picture that lay crookedly across a chair.

He quickly moved between her and the object she was studying. "How long have I been painting, you were going to ask?"

"Was that picture of *me?*"

He shot her a helpless look, obviously embarrassed that she'd spotted it.

"Can I see it?"

"It's not very good. My work is more abstract by nature. It's difficult for me to accurately capture a real person."

A grin tugged at her lips—he sounded like her kids when they were stalling. "Please?"

"Here. Don't say I didn't warn you."

She took a step closer to reach for the paper, and their fingers brushed. The fleeting contact gave her a warm *zing,* but it was nothing compared to the dizzying sensation that went through her when she looked at the picture.

"Good heavens," she breathed. "Is this… This is how you see me?"

Earlier that evening, she'd looked at her own reflection and felt a jolt of fractured identity, knowing the woman she saw was Kenzie Green, yet in many ways not recognizing her. Seeing JT's drawing was similar, only a hundred times more powerful. She didn't think her mouth was really that sensual. And she was amazed at how expressive the eyes were even without color. Despite his modest claim about not capturing people well, he'd done a phenomenal job.

He'd focused mainly on her face, her hair a smudgy free-form impression of loose waves on the edges of the picture. Thank God he hadn't drawn her body. She didn't think she could take the effect of seeing that.

She glanced up with amazement, meeting his nervous gaze. "This is beautiful."

"I was depicting a subject who's beautiful."

It was on the tip of her tongue to protest that she wasn't that beautiful, not really, but he was there, kissing her, before she could.

She'd expected a studio to smell more like the paints she'd had occasion to use over the years, mostly poster paint or spray paint, but it was difficult to describe the sweet scent permeating the room. Earthy and ripe. Between the aroma, the colors and textures and most of all the man who held her cradled against him, standing in JT's studio was the most pleasurable assault on her senses she'd ever encountered. As he kissed her, he traced lazy patterns up and down both her shoulders, stopping at the top to fiddle with the straps of her dress.

His voice was nearly hoarse. "Maybe I could show you the rest of the apartment now?"

The only part left was his bedroom. "Yes."

When they reached his room, instead of flicking the light switch, he crossed the dim interior and turned on a lamp—a delicate-looking stained-glass piece.

"Pretty," she said. The riot of illuminated colors reminded her of the mural he'd done for the museum.

"Thank you." He studied the fixture. "I just recently pulled it out of storage to give the room more life."

She took a guess. "Was it your wife's?"

"She gave it to me for Valentine's Day one year." He glanced up with a rueful smile. "This is inappropriate, isn't it, standing here with my gorgeous date and talking about Holly?"

"You loved her. That makes you the man you are...a man I'm extremely attracted to. Acknowledging the woman you shared your life with doesn't bother me."

"Thank you. Let me show you the other thing I rescued from storage." He pointed to the left, at a segmented painting that was clearly one work but took place over three different panels.

"Yours?" Unlike the children's mural, there was no clear image in this, but it was a rich mass of reds and violets in broad, lush strokes. Though not graphic, it was indefinably erotic.

"Mmm. One of my earlier pieces. It was featured in a magazine once, and I had offers to buy. At the time, I was so proud of it and so afraid that I might not produce anything else quite as good that I refused to let go."

"It's fantastic." She crossed the room for a better look, hearing his footsteps, smelling his cologne, as he approached. At the first touch of his lips against her bare shoulder, she shivered with anticipation. He pressed a kiss to the nape of her neck, then traced the shell of her ear with his mouth. She moved restlessly against him, ultimately turning in his arms so that she had better access.

She meshed her fingers in his hair. "You make me so… I haven't felt like this in a long time."

After that, neither of them spoke. The only sounds were of their mingled breathing, whispers of fabric as clothes brushed against each other or were removed, and muffled jazz from the apartment below. JT was adept enough at keeping her in a sensual haze that Kenzie didn't get nervous when her dress pooled at her ankles. Besides, she was preoccupied with removing his shirt. It wasn't the first time she'd seen his quite impressive naked chest, but before, she hadn't been free to touch him. Now she trailed her fingers over the flat muscular planes and the modest dusting of dark hair. Warm male flesh. She'd seen beautiful sculptures of the human form before, but no matter how masterfully rendered, cold marble would always be vastly inferior to the original subject.

Not until JT reached behind her to find the clasp of her bra did real apprehension ripple through her.

He must have sensed her infinitesimal withdrawal because he stopped immediately. "Am I rushing you? We don't have—"

"No, everything you're doing is perfect." The thought of him seeing her body wasn't nearly as daunting as the prospect of his no longer touching her.

Her breasts were aching. Taking control of the moment and banishing her own timidity, she unfastened the bra and shrugged, letting the lacy black material fall. His expression turned to one of near reverence, a supremely gratifying reaction from a big, strapping man like JT.

He ran his thumb along the swell of one breast, curving to the sensitive underside in a lazy circle, tracing smaller and smaller spheres until he finally brushed the peak with the pad of his thumb. Her eyes closed involuntarily, and her legs trembled with the effort to remain standing. He cupped both her breasts, then dropped his hands to her satin-covered backside, pulling her closer for another soul-searing kiss.

Desire quaked inside her, leaving her weak and breathless. She clung to him. "JT." Was that her voice? The husky rasp sounded like a commercial for an adult phone line.

He kissed her throat again, his fingers continuing their exquisite ministrations across her breasts. "I'm right here, sweetheart." Taking her hand, he tugged her gently toward the bed.

Kenzie sank into the mattress, savoring his weight atop her, squirming at the feel of him so close to where she most wanted him. He moved away to shuck the pants he'd been wearing, and her mouth went dry at the sight of him in formfitting boxer briefs. *Oh, my.* She was a very lucky girl. If her body wasn't throbbing with such excruciating pleasure, she might even be a little nervous at the thought of this man inside her.

He didn't allow her much time to think, however. Bending his head over her, a dark contrast to her pale breasts, he drew a nipple into the damp heat of his mouth. Even though she enjoyed every touch, she could have sobbed in relief when he finally retrieved a condom from the nightstand drawer. She tilted her hips, helping to guide him, and gasped at the sensation. For a moment, neither of them moved, and she met his eyes, the visual connection somehow as intimate as being physically joined.

Then he began to thrust in long, slow strokes, and Kenzie's breath became uneven as she responded with answering movements. He braced himself with one hand, keeping the other entwined with hers on the quilt next to her head. She squeezed his fingers, nearly writhing as delicious spasms built deep within her and radiated through her limbs, from the top of her head to the tips of toes curled in satisfaction. At the end, she cried out in wordless ecstasy, and JT crushed her against him, murmuring against her hair.

Kenzie's heart was racing so hard she expected it to fly free of her chest. For a brilliantly colored, suspended moment in time, her entire body had felt that way—free of all worries and soaring.

She licked her lips. "That…that was…" So much for being articulate. But who could blame her for not being one hundred percent coherent after the most powerful climax of her life?

"Agreed." They lay there in a sweaty, contented tangle for a few more minutes before he attempted to speak again. "Stay tonight?"

She nodded. Right now, there was no place in the world she'd rather be.

"Mmm." Eyes closed, Kenzie moaned in bliss. "Lord, this is good."

"Careful." JT, shirtless and grinning, shot her a completely ineffective look of reprimand. "I'm going to think you get more pleasure out of the enchiladas than the sex. Horrible for my self-esteem."

She giggled. "No disrespect to Mrs. Sanchez's cooking, but the sex was definitely the high point of the evening."

He regarded her with a skeptically raised eyebrow. "Are you just saying that to get another bite?"

"Maybe." She tucked the sheet more firmly around her and reached for the fork in his hand. After making love earlier, they'd cuddled in sleepy contentment until Kenzie admitted she was starving. She'd forgotten just how energetic sex could be, and it seemed to have revved up her appetite. Of course, there was also the fact that she'd been so nervous earlier in the day about her date with JT that she'd barely eaten.

So he'd microwaved a plate of leftovers and brought it back to bed with a couple of chilled bottles of water.

I'm lounging in bed, being fed by a half-naked man who has the body of a Greek god. Did life get any better?

He swallowed his own bite of food and smiled. "And to think I was aloof to Mrs. Sanchez the first few times she came by."

"Aloof? A people person like you?"

He reached around to swat her on the fanny. "You're not allowed to hang out with Sean anymore. I see his sarcasm is wearing off on you."

She laughed. "But I like Sean. I had so much fun tonight." Truthfully, when JT was relaxed, he was every bit as humorous as his friend. It was a thrill to see him playful and happy. "Were you…"

"Was I what?" he prompted.

But her mouth had been running faster than her thoughts and she winced now at what she'd been about to ask. "I was just...thinking...about what you might have been like in the past."

He studied her for a minute. "You mean when Holly was alive?"

Kenzie nodded, hoping she wasn't casting a pall over the moment. "When you met her. You were probably less, as you put it, aloof then." If he'd flashed that devastating smile often, his late wife had probably fallen in love within moments. If Kenzie wasn't careful...

"Actually, I was always fairly guarded. I didn't come from a very demonstrative family, and the emotions my parents *did* demonstrate didn't leave me eager to open up to anyone. I didn't think I had much emotion to offer, except through my paintings."

The first few times she'd met him, Kenzie might have agreed. Now she knew better. He was a man who cared—and hurt—deeply.

"I know I wasn't the world's best boyfriend or husband, but she put up with me." He ran a finger along Kenzie's jaw. "She would have liked you."

"Thank you." Kenzie was touched, knowing she'd been paid a very special compliment.

Their gazes locked, and Kenzie felt longing swirl through her. Not just physical longing—although that was there, too—but the longing to erase any pain he'd ever suffered, the longing to show him how much he had to offer, and prove to herself that despite her post-divorce cynicism, she, too, had a lot to give another person.

Like what? Love? It wasn't a question she wanted to face right now. So instead, she stole the last bite of enchilada, eliciting a mock growl of protest from JT.

"There are going to be consequences for that, woman."

With a shriek, she came off the bed. "Should I make a run for it?"

"You could." He grinned. "But I plan to catch you."

She'd never looked forward to facing consequences so much in her life. Yet as the two of them laughed and wrestled, a tiny part of her heart warned that, sooner or later, there would be emotional consequences, too.

Chapter 14

Huddled in a borrowed sweatshirt that fell past midthigh, Kenzie stood at the large window in JT's living room. Streaks of burnt-orange and scarlet had appeared on the horizon and were slowly streaking across the early dawn sky in a beautiful blossom of color, but she couldn't help resenting the sunrise. Her magical night with JT was at an end.

The wafting aroma of coffee preceded his footsteps. A moment later, he joined her. She gratefully accepted the mug he offered.

He lifted his chin toward the window. "Gorgeous, isn't it?"

"I guess."

"You *guess?*" He laughed, kissing the side of her neck. "You're definitely tough enough to be an art critic."

She ran her fingers over his stubbled jaw. "I'll need to leave soon."

No matter how much she wanted to spend the next few hours lounging in JT's bed, she needed to get in touch with Ann first thing this morning and arrange to pick up the twins before Mick called. While Kenzie had refused to change everyone's plans last night to accommodate his surprise arrival, she didn't want to deprive her kids of spending whatever time possible with him before he left again.

JT rested his head on top of hers. "Let me make you breakfast first? You're probably famished."

"True," she said with a grin. She should be exhausted, too, but up until she'd seen those first rays of sun, she'd felt invigorated, buzzing with excitement and life. She hadn't had a night with so little sleep since the twins were babies.

After the late-night enchiladas, she and JT had showered. Eventually they'd made love again, a slow, sweet union that left Kenzie glad there'd been no men in her life for years, that she'd waited for this one very special man. JT was a night person used to being up during the wee hours, but he'd insisted she try to sleep. Instead they'd wound up talking for hours. In the intimate darkness, he'd told her candidly about selling the house he'd shared with his wife, and coming to Peachy Acres, where he'd begun to heal. Kenzie told him about her own upcoming move and the Perfect Home. Yet even as he said the house she was buying sounded wonderful, she'd been assailed by unexpected misgivings.

Living here had spoiled her in some ways. She'd

had more help and more time with the kids. Once she moved, there'd be an increased commute, plus weekend hours that would be eaten up by lawn and garden maintenance. There would be no companionable meals with Mrs. Sanchez. And what would Kenzie do when a gasket blew or a fuse shorted? In Raindrop, if a repair job outstripped her own skills, she'd known who to trust for affordable assistance. Here, she'd relied on Mr. C. whenever there was a problem. Even though she'd only been here a short time, she'd miss the people.

Especially this one, she thought, staring into JT's eyes.

"Hey." He touched her cheek. "You okay?"

No. Suddenly, she wasn't. "Can I get a rain check on that meal together? I appreciate the generous offer. I just…"

"Need to go." He stepped away.

"JT, thank you for last night. It was extraordinary." Choking back the lump of emotion in her throat, she held up her still-full mug. "And thanks for the coffee, too."

"Feel free to take that with you," he said.

"I'll, uh, just return the cup later," she promised. After he'd seen and touched most of her exposed body, would it be awkward to run into him? To pass him in the hall or bring Drew by for painting lessons? *Not that I'll be here much longer to run into him.* Which was for the best. Even knowing they weren't right for each other in the long range, Kenzie's heart might get different ideas if she remained in JT's proximity for an extended period.

"Sure." He gave her a sad, understanding smile, making no move to touch her. "You know where to find me."

The tension in Kenzie's apartment was so crushing that she expected light fixtures to start shattering at random. *Mick, if you don't call, I will hunt you down and beat you to death with your own guitar.* Or, at the very least, give him a really strongly worded piece of her mind.

Despite being tired, she'd dutifully crossed town to pick up the kids at Ann's that morning. On the way home, she'd shared with them the good news that their dad was nearby and wanted to spend some time with them. Lunchtime had passed hours ago, and still no word from her ex.

After pushing away an uneaten sandwich and declaring himself not hungry, Drew had gone to his room, punctuating his retreat with a slammed door. It was the kind of behavior Kenzie would normally reprimand. Today, she had neither the heart to chide him nor the energy. Leslie, predictably, had curled up on the couch and sought escape in a book. Kenzie couldn't help noticing her daughter hadn't turned a page in a long time.

Kenzie sat down and scooped her daughter's feet into her lap. It seemed only yesterday Kenzie had been playing "This Little Piggy" with tiny baby feet. Now Leslie painted her toes neon colors and wore shoes only a few sizes smaller than her mom. "You want to talk about it?"

"My book? Sure. It's a mystery," Leslie began. "There's this girl named Turtle who—"

"I meant about your dad," Kenzie clarified, even though she was pretty sure her daughter already knew that. "You must be disappointed."

Leslie affected a nonchalant shrug. "Not really."

"This is partly my fault," Kenzie said, second-guessing her selfish impulse to spend last night with JT. "Your dad came by last night, but you were already at Aunt Ann's. I should've—"

"We had fun there," Leslie interrupted. "We made cookies and I got to help give Abby a bath. It's way easier at their house than it was here because there's more space. And Uncle Forrest showed us a computer game that uses math. It's kind of hard, but Drew figured it out better than I did."

Kenzie's heart squeezed with gratitude, even as her eyes filled with tears. *She* was supposed to be comforting her daughter, yet, mature beyond her nine years, Leslie had reversed their roles. "Thank you, honey."

"You're a good parent," Leslie said fiercely. She hugged her mom, but a moment later pulled away, looking sheepish. "I mean, at least you didn't give us goofy names like Turtle or anything."

Kenzie ruffled the girl's hair. "Well, I *was* thinking of Salamander for you, but changed my mind at the last minute."

Chuckling, Leslie returned to her book. *One down. Now, to deal with the other....*

Armed with napkins and a handful of Drew's favorite cookies, Kenzie knocked on his door. "Can I come in?"

"'Kay."

It was worse than she'd anticipated. He wasn't even angrily crashing toy cars into each other or blowing something up via handheld video game. He was merely lying on his bed, scowling at the ceiling.

"I brought you some chocolate chip cookies," she said coaxingly.

"You never let us eat dessert if we don't eat nutritious food first."

"Well, today I'm making an exception."

"Because of Dad," he said flatly.

"Because you're my son and I love you and I thought you could use a little cheering up." When he didn't reach for the cookies she was offering, she placed them on the nightstand and sat next to him. "Your dad really wanted to see you last night."

"Sure he did."

"Did you understand when I was explaining about his changing jobs? He's trying a different path that will hopefully allow more time for you and Leslie. Maybe he got busy with one of his clients today and plans to call us later."

Drew glared. "So these clients are more important than us?"

"Of course not!" Kenzie stifled further thoughts of homicide and tried to get her foot out of her mouth. "It's just that—"

Mercifully, she was interrupted by the ringing phone. She jumped off the bed. "I'll bet that's him now!"

"Yippee," her son intoned.

By the time Kenzie returned to the living room,

Leslie had already answered. Her daughter glanced up with wide eyes. "It's Dad!" She said it with the same wonder as if she'd just discovered Santa Claus setting out presents Christmas morning.

"That's wonderful, honey." Kenzie held out her hand. "Do you mind if I speak to him for a minute?"

Leslie nodded. "Mom wants to talk to you…. Okay, see you soon!" She hopped off the sofa, passing the phone over before running down the hall to share the news with Drew.

"Mick." Kenzie bit down all greetings along the lines of *what the hell took you so long* and kept her tone even. "I'm glad you got a chance to call. I have to confess, I thought we would hear from you earlier in the day."

"Well, I wanted to make sure I wasn't disrupting anyone's plans," he said caustically.

Be the bigger person, Kenzie. "Everyone's here now, no set plans to speak of. Do you maybe want to bring over those presents you mentioned, join us for dinner?"

"Actually, I thought I might take my kids out for supper, if you don't object. Dinner and a movie with their old man?"

"Depending on the movie you had in mind, that sounds great." She paused, softening. "I really *do* want you to have quality time with the kids. Last night was unfortunate timing."

"I appreciate that, Mackenzie. Why don't you ask the kids what films they're interested in seeing, and I'll be there in, say, half an hour?"

It took fifty-five minutes, but considering Atlanta traffic, he could be forgiven the brief delay. Rather,

Kenzie could forgive it. Leslie, who'd read three chapters while waiting for her dad, didn't seem to notice. Drew, on the other hand, practically met his father at the door with a stopwatch.

Mick froze at the sight of his son. "Look at you! Lord, you've grown. Look a lot like I did at your age."

"I'm nothing like you."

Startled, Mick glanced toward Kenzie. Drew had always worshipped his father. Kenzie had tried once last spring to explain to Mick their son's growing anger, his misery that his father missed his sporting events.

"Tell him his soccer picture's in my wallet," Mick had said. "In spirit, I'm at all his games."

Nine-year-old boys could give a collective rat's ass about "spirit."

Leslie began chatting about a current movie that was based on a book her teacher had just started reading to them. "We should see that one! It's a cool story. Drew, I think you'd like it."

He hitched a shoulder. "Don't care what we see."

Mick looked baffled but didn't comment on the boy's attitude. Kenzie tried to figure out a way to pull her son aside tactfully. She understood his anger, but she'd rather he enjoy his father's company today than regret the lost opportunity later. In the end, though, she couldn't think of anything to say that wouldn't put him in an even more belligerent mood. Perhaps this was simply something father and son would have to work out for themselves.

Normally she welcomed periods of kid-free quiet; once they were gone, the silence seemed oppressive.

Following her daughter's lead, Kenzie picked up a novel she'd started weeks ago, but after rereading the same paragraph three times because she kept losing her place, she conceded defeat. Then she flipped through the television channels, but Saturday-afternoon programming wasn't exactly riveting. Restless and craving comfort, she eyed the plate of chocolate chip cookies on the kitchen counter.

Don't even think about it, they'll go straight to your hips. Maybe what she should do was use the free time to exercise. In her defense, she had burned plenty of calories last night.

Heat flooded her face as she recalled the vivid details, details that conjured longing. It had been mere hours since she'd left JT, and already she missed him. Her gaze darted across the kitchen again, this time landing on the mug she'd hand washed. The mug she'd promised to return.

She grabbed the cup and exited her apartment before she could stop herself, not even pausing to put on shoes. Barefoot, she padded across the hall and knocked once on his door.

He opened it a moment later, his immediate surprise giving way to a pleased smile. "Kenzie."

"I, uh, wanted to give this back." She held up the mug, feeling foolish.

He eyed her with affectionate cynicism. "That the only reason you're here?"

"Well, I..."

"Because it's one of a set of six, and I live alone. I do dishes enough that I don't foresee a shortage."

"Hey, I'm doing the polite thing. Besides, I live with kids. If I don't return it ASAP, you run the risk that it could get taken out by a baseball thrown indoors."

He glanced past her at the closed door of her own apartment. "Where are the kids now?"

"With their father." She slumped, unable to contain her earlier worry. If today's outing was a disaster, would Mick be even more reluctant to get involved in the children's lives? She didn't want Drew blaming himself for that down the road.

JT searched her gaze. "Why don't you come on in?"

"I can't stay." She wasn't sure why she put up the token resistance. After all, she easily could stay for the next three or four hours. It beat being at loose ends in an empty apartment, she thought as she followed him.

In the kitchen, he pulled her into his arms. "You looked like you could use a hug."

She cuddled closer, grateful for his perceptiveness. "I wonder if I'm doing a good job. There aren't enough concrete right and wrongs. Most days I just hope I'm faking it enough to fool everyone."

"I can't claim to be an expert, but from this observer's point of view, you're doing a wonderful job. The fact that you're doubting yourself because you want to do what's best for them just shows what a caring mother you are."

That earned him a kiss. How could it not, when he held her and said what she most needed to hear? But as he kissed her back, her feelings of gratitude quickly flamed into something more carnal.

When he fumbled for the buttons on her blouse, she said, "This isn't why I came over."

He rubbed a thumb over the tight peak of one breast. "Do you want to stop?"

She shuddered. "Hell, no."

"I am so glad you said that."

He scooped her up into his arms, making her feel tiny and deliciously feminine, and carried her back to his room. Last night, he'd stroked and kissed most of her, but that had been under the cover of darkness. Lying naked before him in the stark light of day was a new vulnerability, a new intimacy she hadn't intended, bringing them even closer. The first two times they'd made love, they'd been learning each other's bodies and desires. JT was a quick learner. He touched her now as if he were an expert on her every erogenous zone, knowing just how far she could tolerate his erotic teasing.

When he slid inside her, all her muscles clenched, trying to bring him even closer, hold him even tighter. As the pressure built, she moved more frantically, the ripples of pleasure becoming a crashing tsunami. She heard herself call out his name. He echoed her cry with an incoherent shout as he thrust home.

For long peaceful moments, neither of them moved—Kenzie wasn't sure she could if she wanted to. But then he shifted, rolling off her, though his gaze was still locked with hers.

"Kenzie. I…" He glanced down, then straightened suddenly, going pale. "Damn."

Her warm fuzzy feelings of afterglow cooled considerably. "What? JT, what is it?"

He stood. "The condom broke."

Chapter 15

People mentioned awkward mornings-after. Kenzie had never heard the protocol for a hellishly awkward "later...that same afternoon."

She and JT had both cleaned up and dressed, yet part of her felt painfully exposed. He looked so angry. She realized the emotion was directed at the defective prophylactic, but that didn't quite stop her from feeling hurt.

"I'm sure it will be okay," she said from the middle of his living room. "I, ah, have pretty regular cycles, and it's not the right time."

He stood at the same window where they'd cuddled that morning, seeming an entirely different man than the one who'd brought her coffee. "I don't ever want to get a woman pregnant. I'm not sure I could live through that again. I know—rationally, I know—that thousands of women have healthy babies every day. But Holly didn't. I killed her."

"JT, no." Kenzie was horrified by the naked blame in his tone. While fatal labor complications had become mercifully rare, they occasionally happened. "What happened to her was a tragedy, but no one's fault."

"That's what the doctors said, too." Still not looking at her, he shivered. "I can't go through any of that again. Not just the labor or the pregnancy but all of it. Falling in l—" His voice broke.

Human compassion would have been enough to motivate Kenzie toward him even if she barely knew him. Now that she was familiar with him in the most personal of ways, seeing the pain on his face was like a knife in the stomach. She wanted so badly to embrace him and somehow absorb his suffering. Yet he moved away just as she reached him, his expression one of subtle panic.

"I can't. Don't you see that, Kenzie? I've been letting myself grow attached to you because I thought it was safe. You'll be gone soon. It won't be like when Holly was ripped away. I *know* you're leaving. And it's really not the same thing, because she was my wife and I loved her. You were just going to be… I don't know what. I'm a jackass. I persuaded myself that I wasn't falling for you, but it's not true. I can't let that happen again." He took a shaky breath. "Losing her may not have killed me, but there were plenty of days when I wished it had."

"You plan to never love again?" It struck Kenzie as unbearably sad, even though she'd clung to the same safety net he had—her leaving in a few weeks would help them part ways naturally, giving him little chance to complicate her and the kids' life.

"I was lucky enough to have those years with Holly." His face softened as he added, "And lucky enough to have this weekend with you. That's far more than some men ever get."

She opened her mouth to protest his denying himself a chance to be happy, but what could she possibly say? While she'd like to think fate would never be cruel enough to take someone away from JT again, there were no guarantees. He had so much to offer a woman, but she understood his self-protective instinct. More than she cared to.

"If you don't mind, until we move, I'll still let Drew come over and paint with you. But it's probably best if I don't…see you. Alone, I mean."

"Probably," he echoed in morose agreement.

"Goodbye, JT."

He didn't answer. When she let herself out of the apartment, he was still standing fixed in place, his posture one of dejected solitude. She told herself that he'd recover once she moved away, find a happy medium of painting and spending time with friends without getting too involved with any one person. But she knew his expression of naked loneliness would haunt her for many nights to come.

Especially when she was lying awake and missing him, battling her own lonely heart.

"So." Ann handed her sister a plate of burgers fresh off the grill. They were taking them inside to stick on buns for the kids while Forrest started the next round.

Meanwhile, Drew and Leslie chased each other through the lush backyard. "I waited all week to hear from you in the vain hope that babysitting the kids would earn me some deets."

"'Deets'?" Kenzie laughed. "You've been hanging around too much with my daughter."

"Details, woman! Spill the details about JT."

The plate wobbled in Kenzie's hands, and only Ann's reflexes kept the burgers from becoming lawn ornaments.

"Sorry." Kenzie bit her lip, scolding herself for her overreaction. So Ann had mentioned JT—big deal; Drew had been talking about him all week. Even though the boy had mastered the right terminology, he persisted in teasing JT about being his mental rather than his mentor. JT had given Drew an actual canvas to paint on, and the results now hung in the boy's room.

Even Leslie had been impressed with her brother's efforts. "Who knew he had talents beyond soccer and creating clutter?" she'd asked, still a touch bitter that no one was helping to develop *her* artistic abilities.

Ann didn't say anything until they were inside, safely out of anyone else's earshot. "Are you okay? I noticed you sounded tense on the phone this week, but I thought that was the weirdness of Mick being in town."

"No, for the kids' sake, I'm glad Mick was here." Although she hoped it wasn't a case of too little, too late. He had indeed taken them to dinner and a movie, but Drew complained that the man had spent half the meal on his cell phone with newly recruited clients. "He's supposed to come back the week we close on the new house, hang out with the kids while I take care of things."

Ann scowled. "You ask me, you end up taking care of way too much. I'd love to see you with a guy who could take care of you for a change."

"Honestly, I'm not looking for that." Kenzie opened the refrigerator, grabbing the mustard and ketchup while Ann sliced tomatoes. "I'm okay taking care of myself. Less chance for disappointment."

"You sound cynical."

"No, just practical. See? I'm learning in my old age."

"But what about the yummy artist? Where does he fit in with practicality?"

"He doesn't." Kenzie sighed wistfully. "We both came to that conclusion last Saturday. I'm about to move out of the apartment complex, you know."

"Yeah, but you won't be living that far apart. If you really wanted to date—"

"That's just it—we don't."

"I saw the way you two looked at each other! You like him. And he's surprisingly good with the kids. Did I mention yummy? Is it that you don't want the same things?"

Actually, they did want the same thing: security. Kenzie needed stability for herself and her kids, and JT was desperately trying to safeguard himself against possible hurts.

"Ann, he's just now returning to his life and career after getting over his wife. He doesn't plan to ever really get involved with anyone else, but if he does... well, he's going to need someone with a lot of patience, a lot of extra time and TLC. Meanwhile, I have two kids, one of whom is increasingly angry and confused and in need of a lot of extra attention himself. JT's great. I wish him well, but trust me, there's no future for the two of us."

Ann thought this over, staring intently at the cutting board. "What about a present?"

"I don't follow."

"What if, instead of obsessing about the possible future or dwelling on the hurts of your past, you two just concentrated on the present? Being happy today. You both deserve that much."

"Live for today?" Kenzie shot her sister a gently teasing grin. "What kind of radical thinking is that? What happened to carefully planning ahead? That's what got you where you are now."

"Yes and no. Forrest and I spent a lot of time preparing, planning, strategizing ways for him to get ahead at the college, when the best time to have a baby might be. Sure, most of our organizing has paid off, but somewhere along the way we forgot to enjoy the here and now. Forgot to enjoy each other." Her cheeks flushed a rosy pink. "We're working hard to make the time to do that."

"And no one's happier about that than me—"

"Especially since you got your apartment back." Ann smirked.

"No comment."

Just then, a rap at the sliding glass door drew their attention. Kenzie's son stood on the other side. When he saw that he had his mom's eye, he slapped a hand to his forehead and pantomimed being dizzy and weak from hunger, eventually "passing out" on Ann's porch.

Ann laughed. "Think he's trying to tell us something?"

"Let's get the burgers that are ready outside before rioting begins." She lifted two paper plates and headed for the door.

"Kenzie?" Her sister's voice stalled her. "We don't have to keep talking about it, especially not with the kids around, but will you think about what I said?"

"Sure." It was an easy promise to make. After all, she'd thought about JT and the way he made her feel every day since she'd walked out of his apartment.

A better question than would she think about him was how did she go about forgetting him?

At the heavy footfalls behind her, Kenzie's heart sank. She kept her eyes on the lit elevator button, hoping for the best. Even though she'd heard the door open at the far end of the hall, that didn't necessarily mean JT was approaching. Maybe it was Sean or another acquaintance.... But by the time the man stopped behind her, she was already reacting to the subtle scent of his cologne and the familiar warmth of his body.

"Hey," he said softly.

Curse her laziness; she'd been doing a great job of avoiding her neighbor, and if she'd only taken the stairs instead of waiting around for the elevator, she could have spared herself this encounter.

"Hi." She gave him a feeble smile over her shoulder. Even that one brief glance shredded her willpower.

He looked fantastic. More than anything, she wanted to reach out and touch him. Hold him and ask how he was doing, kiss him and let him know how much his continued tutoring meant to her son.

She felt so on edge that she almost jumped at the sound of the *ding.* They filed into the elevator together, and she couldn't help thinking of the night they'd returned from their gallery date, when JT had grabbed her the second the doors closed and they'd spent the duration of the brief trip locked in each other's arms.

Her breath quickened.

"You okay?" JT frowned. "I didn't think you were claustrophobic."

"I'm fine. Just…a lot on my mind. Getting ready for the move and all." With the closing next Tuesday, she had taken this afternoon off work for the final walk-through of the house. It was a routine check to verify that everything she and the sellers had agreed on after the inspection had been addressed, and that no undisclosed last-minute damage had occurred to the property.

JT nodded. "Drew mentioned that you guys have started packing. Or, more specifically, that you've started assembling boxes and have been on his case about packing."

She lifted an eyebrow. "I—*whoa,* what was that?"

The elevator had jerked to a halt with some kind of screeching metal-on-metal sound.

"Good question." After a second, he added, "I think we might be stuck."

"What? No!" She heard the panicky note in her own

voice. "I—I have a scheduled walk-through I have to get to." More to the point, being trapped in a small space with JT was—*heavenly*—her idea of hell.

"Hang on." He hit an intercom button labeled Emergency. "Hello? Anybody out there? This is Jonathan Trelauney. We're stuck in the elevator."

A moment passed, then there was the crackle of static. "JT?" Mr. C.'s voice had never sounded so good. "Don't you worry, I'll check out the problem and see if we can get you going again in a jiffy."

If he could manage it in the next five minutes, Kenzie thought wildly, she'd send him an enormous gift basket as a goodbye.

"Great, Kenzie and I would appreciate it."

"She in there, too?" Mr. C. asked. "When do your kids get home from school, hon? I can have Mrs. Sanchez meet them in the lobby and take them to her apartment if you're still in there."

It made Kenzie smile to have someone else worry about her children. "Thanks, Mr. C.," she called past JT's shoulder, "but Alicia's staying with them this afternoon anyway, because I have an errand to run. Besides, they won't be here for another hour. We'll be out by then, right?"

That was answered with silence. Then an upbeat, "I'll do my best."

Gulp. She couldn't handle being in this elevator with JT for sixty minutes—not without losing her mind, entertaining some seriously adult fantasies or both. She sat against the back wall of the elevator.

JT leaned against the short wall to her left. "If this

were a movie, we'd probably bounce up and down to get the elevator moving again."

She was so not bouncing up and down in front of JT.

"Or we'd try the trapdoor on the elevator ceiling," he continued. "That's always a popular escape route in cinema."

She smiled. "I didn't realize you were such a film buff."

"Only recently. I had some friends in college who did indie movies that I supported, but I haven't paid attention to what was in theaters in years. Earlier this summer I went through a period of insomnia and started catching a lot of stuff on cable. Old black-and-white movies, new blockbusters, action flicks…marathons of makeover shows," he admitted sheepishly.

A guffaw escaped her. "Really? You and Leslie could watch them together. That's her favorite television." It had been a stupid thing to say, of course. As of next week, Leslie and Drew wouldn't see JT anymore. *And neither will I.*

She wasn't moving to the far side of the moon, but, in this case, it might as well be. If she and JT were different people committed to trying to make a relationship work, it would be worth the traffic and distance, fitting him between the kids and getting settled in their new home and community. But the last time she'd been alone with this man, he'd point-blank told her that he was looking forward to her being gone, that he just wasn't ready to share his heart.

She fell silent, but it wasn't a relaxed silence. Half the time she could feel his gaze on her; the other half, he was trying too hard not to look at her. But aside from each other, there wasn't much else to occupy their interest. Neither of their cells worked inside the elevator. She read and reread the inspection notice and safety code information. Finally she realized she did have something to say—it was just painfully embarrassing to figure out how.

"JT? I thought, in case it was something you were worried about, that you should know I…" *Spit it out. The man's seen you naked, for crying out loud.* Strangely, that thought didn't soothe her. "Last week, well, I'm definitely not pregnant."

He blinked at her, as if first trying to figure out what she was talking about, then nodding vigorously. "Oh. Good. Thanks for, um, letting me know."

"You betcha." This felt like the most absurd conversation she'd ever had. And she'd spent entire days with chatty twins. "Would it be obnoxious of us to check back with Mr. C. and find out what's taking so long?"

"I just hope he doesn't mention our predicament to Mrs. Sanchez," JT grumbled. "She'd try to talk him into some crazed notion of not rescuing us, so we could have more time together. She brought over dinner last Friday and chewed my ear off about letting you leave."

"'Letting me'?" As an independent woman, Kenzie didn't know if she should be appalled or amused.

"I know, I know. She harbors some old-fashioned idea about how I'm supposed to stop you from following your own path by declaring my—" He broke off suddenly, clearing his throat. "She's a meddling busybody."

"But you love her anyway."

He looked Kenzie in the eye. "Against my better judgment, yeah, I do."

A lump of emotion swelled up in her throat, making it momentarily impossible for her to speak. Which was probably just as well. Now that she and JT were safely platonic again, why admit anything she might regret later? *Then again,* an internal imp demanded, *you move next week, so what do you have to lose by speaking up now?*

"I do have my own path to follow," she told him. "But I'll always be glad about the side detour to Peachy Acres. I...I've come to care about you a lot. I'll miss you. All three of us will miss you."

He bent forward to grab her hand and squeeze it. She held on as tightly as she could.

Then Mr. C.'s voice boomed through the intercom. "Okay, folks, the bad news is we can't get the elevator started again right now. So we're going to pry open the doors and pull you out. You've stopped just below the second floor. We'll help you out and let you take the stairs down."

Kenzie stood, staring at the doors that would soon open. When they did, she and JT would each go their own way.

JT rose, too, reaching for the back pocket of his jeans. He pulled out a worn leather wallet. The business card he handed her was a plain white rectangle, but each line of information, JONATHAN TRELAUNEY, ARTIST along with his phone number and email address, were printed in a different font and color.

"You are one of the most capable people I've ever met," he said. "For months, I've been trying to figure out how to best take care of myself, and you're single-handedly taking care of a family of three, along with miscellaneous relatives who have problems of their own and some crazy guy who lives across the hall."

She laughed at that. "I'm not sure my sister qualifies as 'miscellaneous' or that I've done anything for you. Quite the reverse, actually."

"We'll just agree to disagree about that. As capable as you are, I doubt you need others often, but if you ever need anything…"

"Thank you." Touched, she closed her fingers over the card.

Outside, she could hear Mr. C. and someone else working to pull back the doors. Lightning fast, she stretched up one last time and pressed a final kiss to JT's lips. Then she sprang back. Moments later, Mr. C. and the building's college student managed to get the doors far enough open that Kenzie thought she'd just be able to squeeze through.

"You go on ahead," JT said chivalrously. "You have that house inspection. I won't be able to make it through something that narrow, but I'm in no hurry."

He went down on one knee in front of the opening, letting her use the other leg for a boost. Mr. C. and the younger man reached down and helped pull her through. Once free of the elevator, she thanked all three of them and hurried to the stairwell.

She couldn't help thinking of how she'd first met JT here. As he'd helped her pick up her slightly muddied belongings and decapitated panda bear, his expression unsmiling and his sheer size imposing, she never could have imagined the warm, caring man who would become an accidental but important part of her and the children's lives. At the bottom stair, she glanced back up, but she wasn't sure why. After all, there was nothing to see here and she had someplace to be.

Her Perfect House and pragmatically planned future awaited.

Chapter 16

"Mom? Earth to Mom?" Drew snapped his fingers, looking across the kitchen table at Leslie. "What's that word you used the other day? Something about cat comas?"

After a second's thought, Leslie was able to translate. "Catatonic."

"Yeah. I think she's that," he said. "Maybe Alicia should have stayed to look after us tonight. Mom may have been turned into a pod person."

Kenzie set her fork down on her plate and gazed at her son. Between discussing stories with his sister and JT's artistic influence, Drew's imagination seemed to be taking on a life of its own lately. "I am not a pod person. I was thinking about the house."

"Is it as gorgeous as you remember?" Leslie asked dreamily.

"Um…" Was it? She'd had a weird vibe during her walk-through this afternoon. The front yard looked majestic, but she'd suddenly panicked over not only the monthly check she'd have to write for the modest acreage, but the upkeep required. In the gleaming, spacious kitchen with its modern flat-top stove, she'd had the sense that the room seemed…a little sterile and without personality. She glanced up from her kitchen table now, enjoying the comfy warmth of the place. They weren't living in a mansion, but they were living well within their means. *You're just having last-minute cold feet. Perfectly normal.*

But what if next week the cold feet became buyer's remorse, and it was too late to do anything about it?

"Oh, who wants to hear about the house?" Drew said impatiently. "We'll be there soon and can look at it as much as we want. *I* wanted to tell Mom about what happened at school today."

Pride filled Kenzie. Over the past two weeks, Drew had become more and more engaged. He had a small group of friends he mentioned regularly, and he'd fallen into the habit of sharing weird facts he'd learned in social studies or science. "What happened?"

"First, I got a B on that test yesterday, and it was *really* hard, too. But also, Mrs. Frazer talked about how we're going to have fine-arts week in November, and I told her I knew a local artist who's famous and everything. I don't think she believed me at first, but she's heard of JT. She was impressed! I told her JT would come talk to our class, and now I'm, like, her favorite kid. She asked me to bring in one of the paintings I've done to discuss during art week."

Kenzie's mind went blank. On the one hand, it was thrilling for a mother to have her son so enthusiastic about school, and she didn't want to dampen what he was feeling right now. On the other, he couldn't just go around volunteering adults—especially not *that* adult— for class events. She'd expected the move to provide a clean break between JT and her family. It was surprising to realize it might be more complicated than that.

"Mom?" he pressed. "Did you hear what I said?"

"Absolutely, and great job getting that B! But, sweetheart, we don't know if JT will be available to come to your classroom."

"I'll ask him tonight," Drew said matter-of-factly. "I'm supposed to go over there after dinner. I'm sure he won't mind."

"Maybe not, but… You know we won't be seeing much of JT after we move, right?"

"I've been thinking about that. Couldn't I still come and paint with him after school? You could just drive over and get me, then take me home."

"That will take forever," Leslie complained. "I don't want to be stuck at the house waiting for you guys to come home at night."

"Drew, you told me he was working on a new abstract series. That will probably take up more of his time. And Leslie's right, it won't be convenient to slog through evening rush hour once we live in the opposite direction. Atlanta traffic is totally different from Raindrop's."

"It doesn't have to be every day," he wheedled. "Just sometimes. Can we at least ask JT about it? He likes having me around."

"I'll tell you what, let's drop that for now, but you can go ahead and ask him about November. Please don't be disappointed or angry if he says no."

"I won't, but I'm sure he'll say yes! JT's the type of guy you can count on." Drew carried his empty plate to the sink. "I'm going over to decide what to do for art week. Knowing Mrs. Frazer, she'll want a painting that manages a 'dialogue' or something. I think she's a little nuts."

Kenzie could empathize. Her world wasn't making as much sense these days, either.

As had become their habit, JT and Drew went up to the roof to work. Even if the kid wasn't moving away, they wouldn't be able to continue their lessons in the evenings, not now that daylight saving had kicked in and the sky darkened much earlier with the approaching winter.

This would probably be the last time Drew came over. It was funny how JT had started this as a way to help the boy—or, more accurately, the boy's blue-eyed mother—yet he felt as if he'd really gained something indefinable and special. Maybe he'd talk to Sean about trying to set up some part-time teaching gigs, or even once-a-month free classes for kids at their gallery.

Drew had been nervous when he first arrived tonight, but once he'd asked about his elementary school's upcoming art week and was reassured JT didn't mind attending, he'd calmed down and turned his attention to his painting.

It was JT who was now nervously obsessing over the November appearance and couldn't focus on his work. Was the school's art week something that parents attended, too? Would he see Kenzie there? Both she and Drew had mentioned Mick's attempts to be in Atlanta more, so maybe *he'd* show up, as well. For the kid's sake, JT hoped so.

He hadn't been able to get Kenzie out of his mind since their interlude in the elevator earlier—or her confession of how much she'd come to care about him. It was the kind of thing he knew he wasn't brave enough to say, because those admissions led to deeper feelings, the exact opposite of the safe distance he craved. Yet even knowing that separation was safer, he'd had to fight the urge to ask Drew about Kenzie's week or how she was doing. *Or whether she's mentioned me lately.*

Pathetic. No self-respecting man would use a nine-year-old as an unwitting spy.

Glancing toward Drew, JT chuckled to himself. Nor should a self-respecting man let a nine-year-old outshine him with a better work ethic. With that thought, he turned to his palette and got down to the business of painting.

When Drew came over to say it was time for him to go, JT was so engrossed in the burgeoning creation that it took him a minute to realize the boy was speaking to him.

"That's cool," Drew said. "Does it have a title?"

"Not yet." JT stepped aside so that his protégé could take a better look.

"I think it looks like people." He studied the different colored blobs on the canvas. "These smaller ones could be kids, the bigger ones the adults. Like a family. Maybe that's what you should call it—'Picture of a Family.'"

JT raised his eyebrows; there were a lot of blobs. "That's a pretty big family."

"Like Mrs. Sanchez's. She has a lot of relatives. I think she's the red blob." Drew pointed toward a blurred sphere near the upper corner of the canvas. "I'm gonna miss her when we move."

"You'll make new friends. After all, you and Leslie didn't want to move from Raindrop, either, and you made new friends here."

"I guess." The boy looked unconvinced, but nodded anyway. "Do you want to go downstairs so I can clean my brushes, or should I just leave the stuff up here?"

"I'll clean up for both of us," JT promised. "You run along so we don't get in trouble with your mom."

Drew looked unperturbed by this possibility. "I don't think she'd ever be mad at you. She likes you too much."

JT laughed. "Your logic's flawed, son. After all, she *loves* you—does that stop her from getting mad?"

At that, Drew scooted promptly toward the door, calling a quick good-night over his shoulder.

After the boy was gone, JT continued painting until the evening grew chilly and his fingers uncomfortable. Then he took everything back to his apartment and kept on painting, ignoring the passing hours. Finally he stopped to look at what had taken shape on the canvas. A family, Drew had said. JT had grown up feeling disconnected from his own, then had violently lost the one he and Holly had formed. It was something that, deep down, he could admit he desperately wanted...but was afraid to reach for.

He looked again at the picture, a miasma of colors dominated by a rough rectangle. On top of and surrounding the rectangle were blobs of different sizes and shapes. His mouth twitched as he found himself thinking of the red splotch as Roberta—red was a good shade for her passionate temperament and spicy dishes. Maybe the white, skinny oval toward the bottom could represent grizzled Mr. C. And the bright yellow in the middle of the canvas, the unintentional sun the other shapes revolved around? Definitely Kenzie. He'd winced when she moved in, afraid she would disrupt his existence. God, he was glad she had. She'd brought with her such a brightness that...

I have a family.

The thought came out of nowhere as he glanced back to the canvas. Sean was like a brother to him, Roberta Sanchez an opinionated but favorite aunt. The people in this building had slowly taken up space in his hollow heart, none more so than the beautiful woman across the hall and her two children. What she'd said earlier today was true—he did love Mrs. Sanchez. And he would be devastated should anything bad ever happen to Sean, yet that didn't stop JT from treasuring the man's friendship or going into business with him.

Wasn't it just as possible to lose one of those people as someone he loved romantically?

It's not the same. A dull phantom pain ached in his chest. If Sean got hit on the head with an asteroid tomorrow, it would suck, but it would be different than the I've-just-been-torn-in-half mindless sorrow of losing Holly. Just as the risks of romantic love were greater, though, weren't the rewards, as well?

Did he want to be a colorless, solitary blob on his own dark canvas, or did he want to be part of a family, a returning member of the world that he painted but too seldom participated in? He didn't even have to think about the answer.

Instinct and raw emotion, the kind he'd been trying so hard not to feel, propelled him out of his apartment and straight to Kenzie's door.

Even though it hadn't jostled her from sleep—she was too restless for that—a knock on the door at one in the morning was startling. Was there some kind of emergency in the building? Was her ex in town, looking for a place to crash after an event at a nightclub? The very last person she expected to find was wild-eyed JT, his hair standing on end, brightly colored smudges on his sleeveless white undershirt and jeans.

"JT? What's wrong?" She stepped out into the hall, pulling the door partially closed behind her so they didn't wake the kids.

"No, it's what's *right*." His expression was one of

almost manic joy. She was still trying to decipher it when he grabbed her and kissed her passionately.

Momentary shock turned to a flame of bright arousal, her body much faster to respond than her confused mind. Heat pulsed within her, and she opened her mouth, seeking closer contact. But the insistent part of her asking *what the hell?* finally made itself heard long enough for her to pull away.

"JT, I don't understand. What—"

"I love you. Mrs. Sanchez was right. I should declare my love and try to keep you from leaving Peachy Acres. Or at least from leaving me. Don't leave me, Kenzie. I need you. You've changed my life. I still don't know if I could handle having a woman being pregnant with my baby, but my time with Drew… I always wondered if I would be a good dad and now, I think, yes. Even though my chance was taken away from me, even though my own role model wasn't— I could be a father. And I can paint again! Come see what I've just finished. Maybe I could explain it better that way than in words, but—"

"Stop!" Her head was reeling. She felt dizzy and was frantic to get off this unexpected roller coaster. She couldn't keep up with the information he was throwing at her. "I need a minute."

"I love you." He repeated it almost more to himself than to her, and her heart leaped with joy at the statement.

He loves me. Her toes curled inside her fuzzy pink socks. No. She tamped down her budding euphoria. At least one of them had to stay grounded in reality—a role with which she was too familiar.

"JT, this is insane."

He offered her a lopsided smile. "Artists usually are crazy."

Tell me something I don't know. Though he was joking, he wasn't helping his own case. "Look, you know how much I care about you, but I'm not a teenager anymore. I can't allow myself to be blindly swept off my feet. I have two kids to think of."

"I know, and they're wonderful kids. Like I was just telling you—"

"It's one in the morning! You're jubilant because you've just finished what I'm sure is a brilliant painting. You're coasting on artist endorphins or adrenaline or whatever, but that's no reason for deciding you want to be a father figure. Especially not to two children who already have one wacky dad in their lives."

JT stiffened. Her rejection was starting to sink in. "I'm not 'wacky.' It's not fair for you to automatically paint me with the same brush as Mick, if you'll pardon the expression."

Part of her wanted to agree with him, assure him that she thought he'd be a much better and selfless father. The rest of her was fleeing in blind panic and wasn't willing to stop to entertain the possibilities.

"I've already been one man's muse," she heard herself say, not liking the note of hysteria that was creeping into her tone. "You're crediting me with you being able to paint again. I don't _want_ that responsibility. What happens if you get stuck, or a critic hates your latest piece? Are you going to blame me for that, maybe without even meaning to? Are you going to growl that the kids are a distraction, that none of us understand…? It's one in the morning, JT."

"I'm aware of the time." He sounded angry, but there was sheepish acknowledgment in his gaze that perhaps he'd acted too impetuously. "Could I come back tomorrow, at a more civilized hour, so that we could discuss this?"

She gripped the doorknob behind her, retreating. "I don't think that's a good idea. You yourself told me not long ago that you didn't want to fall in love."

"That's when I was arrogant enough to think I could control it, but you—"

"No, I didn't do anything. Not intentionally. We were both honest about not wanting anything long-term. I…I can't."

Rocking back on his heels, he assessed her. "You're as scared as I was. I thought you were more courageous."

"I never claimed to be."

"It's all right." His voice had gentled. "We can work through our fears together. We can—"

"There is no we!" She opened her door and turned to escape. "Goodbye, JT."

She didn't slam the door in his face, but it somehow felt like she did. Inside, she leaned against the frame, letting the tears come. *I'm doing the right thing.* He was clearly not in a rational mood, and she was making the adult choice for both of them. Just as she'd done repeatedly in her marriage. She was not going down that road again.

No matter how tempted she'd been to tell him she loved him, too.

She was gaining a house but losing a dress size, Kenzie thought in the ladies' lounge of the lawyer's office. Lack of appetite the past few days meant that the once sharp business suit she'd chosen to wear to the house closing was hanging limply on her frame. It wasn't a good look. Still, she was about to walk into that oval conference room and sign away her life savings, so new wardrobe additions were out of the question.

After applying more lipstick, she slid the tube in her purse and checked to make sure she'd remembered all the necessary items for today—checkbook, driver's license, social-security card. She had just finished her inventory and stepped into the lushly carpeted corridor when her cell phone buzzed. Probably Ann calling to wish her luck. Or Mick rescheduling again. He'd been due to arrive last night, but had to postpone. At least he'd bothered to let her know, something he hadn't always done in the past.

"Hello?"

"Mrs. Green? This is Ms. Taylor, the school nurse. We need you to come pick up Andrew. I'm afraid he's just thrown up. There is a nasty stomach bug going around."

Oh, the poor baby. "Is he all right? Do you think I should get him to the pediatrician?"

"He's resting comfortably, no fever. I wouldn't be

too alarmed, ma'am, but he definitely can't stay here with the other students."

"Of course not." She peered through the glass at the real estate agents and attorneys already seated at the mahogany table. "I'm not in an area of town where I can reach him anytime soon. And I'm supposed to be... Can I have someone else pick him up?"

"You'll have to call us personally with the name of the individual and they'll need to show photo ID in the office."

"I'll get right back to you." She disconnected, holding up an index finger at her frowning Realtor. Damn. If Mick had been able to make it, that would be a quick solution. Ann lived too far away; by the time she got Abigail all ready and into her car seat... Mrs. Sanchez was a likely possibility, if she were home this afternoon, but Kenzie didn't have the woman's number with her and would need to call information.

Or.

Peeking into her purse, she fished out the business card JT had handed her. If you ever need anything, he'd said. But what kind of woman coldly refused a man's love, then phoned him for a favor? *A mom whose pride isn't as important as her kid.*

She punched in his number, holding her breath until he answered, and cut him off in mid-hello. "It's Kenzie. I need to ask—"

"Aren't you supposed to be closing on a new house?"

"Exactly. But Drew's school just called. He threw up. Even if I walk out on the closing—"

"I can get him. Just give me directions."

Five minutes later, she'd authorized the plan for the school and was able to go into the conference room. But her mind wouldn't focus on all the contract clauses the attorney was trying to explain. *I can get him.* That had been JT's immediate reaction to her needing help. There'd been no hesitation, no snarky response.

He'd caught her so off guard the other night, when he'd rushed over to share his 1:00 a.m. epiphany, that she'd been startled and disoriented. If she hadn't been panicking, would she ever have compared him to her first husband? She cringed, recalling that she'd implied he was wacky. JT had disrupted his own comfortable solitude to be there for her and her kids. Even a nine-year-old could see that. What was it Drew had said, confident his newfound hero would want to help with art week? *JT's the type of guy you can count on.*

He sure as hell was.

"Mrs. Green?" The lawyer smiled at her, but sounded vaguely impatient. "Are you with us?"

"No. I mean, I am, but I shouldn't be. I'm sorry, a few moments ago I received a call about my son, and I...I need to be somewhere else." She stood as her agent turned to the sellers and tried to do damage control, mentioning a family emergency and rescheduling. Kenzie could barely hear the words over the buzzing in her head of thousands of lightbulbs coming on at once.

She loved JT.

She loved his artistic side, loved his big heart, evidenced by how much he'd adored his first wife and by how he'd let Kenzie and her kids into his life. And she loved how steady he was. He was *not* Mick. Maybe her first husband was going to follow through on his attempts to become a better father, maybe that would be a short-lived fiasco. Either way, she and the kids would be all right, and she had no business punishing JT for another man's failures.

The length of the red lights seemed to grow in direct contrast to her need to reach home. *Home.* That truly was what she considered Peachy Acres these days, although she imagined she could feel that way about any place where her children were and where JT was nearby.

When she reached the apartment building, she parked the car and raced to the stairwell. She wasn't taking her chances with the elevator. By the time she banged on JT's door, she was breathless.

He frowned down at her. "Kenzie? I thought you were—"

She grabbed him by the front of his shirt and simultaneously launched herself upward in a kiss that said all the things it would take too long to vocalize. For a shining second, she understood what he'd said about thinking in colors. Starbursts of light and joy exploded behind her eyes, her longing for this man obliterating anything as mundane as words. To her delight and relief, JT did not hesitate or push her away. He cradled her to him, meeting her kiss with fervent, openmouthed abandon.

"Mom!"

Oh, dear heaven. How had she forgotten about Drew? She angled her head away from JT—not willing to let go of him, though—and saw her curious son sprawled on JT's couch beneath a quilt.

"Um…hey, honey, feeling better?" She was officially the worst mother in the world, but her son wasn't glaring.

"Well, I've managed not to yarf in JT's apartment," he said.

She could feel JT's silent laughter beneath her fingers. "That's much appreciated," he said.

Drew narrowed his eyes. "I know what you said before, Mom, but does this mean you two will be dating, after all?"

She bit her lip. "How would you feel about that, kiddo?"

Her son's face took on an exhilarated expression and he pumped his fist in the air. "Cool! Leslie is gonna be so mad that I found out first."

Kenzie took JT's hand and led him a few feet away, toward the kitchen, where she could speak quietly and not with an audience. "I am sorry about the other night."

"Don't be," he told her with a tender smile. "Some of what you said was true. It was unthinking of me to bang on your door at one in the morning. On a school night, no less. What was I expecting you to do, sweep me inside and let me make love to you with impressionable children down the hall? I was a bit out of line."

"And I was a lot out of line. I let my past build up fears about the future."

He ran a hand over her hair. "I know a little something about that. To tell you the truth, those fears are still there, but they're not as strong as what I feel for you."

Moved beyond speaking, she kissed him again, incredibly grateful that they had each found this second chance at love and happiness. All that was missing was an orchestral swell of beautiful music to make this a movie-perfect moment.

"Hey! When you guys are finished sucking face, could someone get me some ginger ale?"

Kenzie felt JT's smile against her lips and thought, *Close enough.*

Epilogue

It was a gorgeous June wedding, with Sean serving as best man and Ann, pregnant *again,* glowing in her matron-of-honor dress. Since weather delays had made it impossible for Kenzie's parents—doing humanitarian work in South America—to attend, Mr. C. had agreed to give her away. The whole of Peachy Acres turned out for the small but lovely rooftop ceremony, and Mrs. Sanchez made the wedding cake. If anyone thought it was odd for Kenzie's first husband to be among the guests, they kept it to themselves. For her part, Kenzie was thrilled that he'd honored his promise to be here and to keep the kids while she and JT went to the beach for a weekend honeymoon.

As she walked down the "aisle," she couldn't help thinking of JT's first marriage. *I promise to love him as much as you did,* she vowed to the unseen Holly, who she liked to think was here in spirit and approved.

After their honeymoon, they'd be moving to a nearby suburb. It was older than the neighborhood Kenzie had almost ended up in, but the house had character and the perfect small building in the backyard to serve as a studio for her new husband, whose recent abstract series *Family Portraits* was garnering critical acclaim. Leslie and Drew did not share in their mom's demurring that she couldn't take responsibility for his talent.

"We take full credit for inspiring him," they bragged to their friends.

As Mrs. Sanchez cut slices of cake for the happy couple, she reminded them, "I expect to see you both at the Labor Day picnic!"

"We wouldn't miss it," Kenzie promised.

The older woman raised her eyebrows. "Maybe by then, your sister won't be the only one pregnant, eh?"

"I don't know. I'm pretty happy with the two I've got." Returning to diapers and sleepless nights after a decade? Probably not. But if she and JT made that decision, she knew she had an equal partner in parenting.

For his part, JT had told her when he proposed that the possibility of her carrying his baby still terrified him, but that he was trying to let go of the fear. "After all, I received one of the biggest blessings of my life when I stopped being scared and let myself love you."

Now that love was evident on his face for all to see. "Dance with me, Mrs. Trelauney?"

"Happily." She snuggled into his arms as someone

turned up the music. In her peripheral vision, she saw Drew waltz by with the much taller Alicia, and grinned.

"That's the smile I like to see," JT murmured.

"Good." She lowered her voice to a wicked whisper. "Because once we reach our hotel, I plan to spend a lot of time wearing that smile and not much else."

"Nude, hmm?" Her husband matched her teasing tone. "Maybe now would be a good time to talk to you about a new series of paintings I'm thinking of...."

* * * * *

*If you enjoyed this story from Tanya Michaels,
discover a sneak-peek from her exciting new tale
TAMED BY A TEXAN, available in April 2012
from Harlequin® American Romance!*

"Incoming," Ty said under his breath to Stephen, as a woman in a formfitting green dress stalked toward them, her long black hair bouncing against her shoulder blades.

Stephen took a quick look, then shook his head. "Tell me you didn't date her and break her heart."

"You!" The woman had reached them. Her narrowed eyes were sharper than the best set of knives he'd ever owned. "You have a lot of nerve."

Ty gave her a disarming smile. "It's true, ma'am. I've always had more nerve than brains. Have we met? Ty Beckett."

"Oh, I know who you are, Mr. Beckett. You're the competition and you've come to spy."

"Spy? Ah. You must be Grace Torres," he deduced. "Look, it isn't as if I came in here to steal your recipes. Although, kudos on this salsa verde. It would definitely be worth stealing." He waited a beat to see if the compliment improved her opinion of him. *Nope.* "I was just stopping by on my way to the reception because I was intrigued. You were a mystery. I've heard of all the other finalists."

When Stephen coughed, choking on his chip, Ty realized his phrasing might not have been the best way to break the ice, insinuating she was a nobody in the culinary world. To cover his uncharacteristic gaffe, he introduced her to Stephen. "This is Stephen Zigler, my friend and business manager. It was his idea to come in," Ty fibbed cheerfully.

Stephen reached across him to shake her hand. "The manager designation is true. The friend part is debatable."

When Grace laughed, her entire face lit with warmth. She'd already been lovely, but as her lips curled into a smile and her eyes lit… *Damn*. Ty was jealous of his friend, annoyed that Stephen, the married soon-to-be-father, had been the one to coax this from her.

"You I like," Grace said, ignoring Ty's presence completely. "I'll see you at the reception."

Then Grace turned and left without another word to Ty. Stephen hooted with laughter. "There goes the winner of this cooking competition," he pronounced between chortles.

"What? Now, that's just mean," Ty complained. "You're only saying it to wound me. A great salsa verde is no basis for determining whether she can win the whole kit and caboodle."

"Oh, I wasn't basing it on that." Stephen's grin was full of admiration. "She's possibly the only woman on the planet completely immune to the Ty Beckett charm. In my book, that makes her a superhero with mystical powers. Dude, you're toast."

Will Ty and Grace be able to stand the heat?
Both in and out of the kitchen?

Find out in
TAMED BY A TEXAN

Available April 2012, from Harlequin® American Romance®
wherever books are sold!

Harlequin®

American ★ Romance®

Save $1.00 on the purchase of
TAMED BY A TEXAN
by Tanya Michaels

Available in April 2012,
or any Harlequin® American Romance® book!

Available wherever books are sold, including most bookstores, supermarkets, drugstores and discount stores.

Save $1.00
on the purchase of
TAMED BY A TEXAN
by Tanya Michaels
or any Harlequin® American Romance® book!

Coupon valid until June 22, 2012. Redeemable at participating retail outlets in the U.S. and Canada only. Limit one coupon per customer.

52610295

5 65373 00076 2   (8100)0 11786

NYTCOUP0312

REQUEST YOUR FREE BOOKS!

2 FREE NOVELS
FROM THE ROMANCE COLLECTION
PLUS 2 FREE GIFTS!

YES! Please send me 2 FREE novels from the Romance Collection and my 2 FREE gifts (gifts are worth about $10). After receiving them, if I don't wish to receive any more books, I can return the shipping statement marked "cancel." If I don't cancel, I will receive 4 brand-new novels every month and be billed just $5.99 per book in the U.S. or $6.49 per book in Canada. That's a saving of at least 25% off the cover price. It's quite a bargain! Shipping and handling is just 50¢ per book in the U.S. and 75¢ per book in Canada.* I understand that accepting the 2 free books and gifts places me under no obligation to buy anything. I can always return a shipment and cancel at any time. Even if I never buy another book, the two free books and gifts are mine to keep forever.

194/394 MDN FELQ

Name		
	(PLEASE PRINT)	

Address		Apt. #

City	State/Prov.	Zip/Postal Code

Signature (if under 18, a parent or guardian must sign)

Mail to the **Reader Service:**
IN U.S.A.: P.O. Box 1867, Buffalo, NY 14240-1867
IN CANADA: P.O. Box 609, Fort Erie, Ontario L2A 5X3

Not valid for current subscribers to the Romance Collection
or the Romance/Suspense Collection.

Want to try two free books from another line?
Call 1-800-873-8635 or visit www.ReaderService.com.

* Terms and prices subject to change without notice. Prices do not include applicable taxes. Sales tax applicable in N.Y. Canadian residents will be charged applicable taxes. Offer not valid in Quebec. This offer is limited to one order per household. All orders subject to credit approval. Credit or debit balances in a customer's account(s) may be offset by any other outstanding balance owed by or to the customer. Please allow 4 to 6 weeks for delivery. Offer available while quantities last.

Your Privacy—The Reader Service is committed to protecting your privacy. Our Privacy Policy is available online at www.ReaderService.com or upon request from the Reader Service.

We make a portion of our mailing list available to reputable third parties that offer products we believe may interest you. If you prefer that we not exchange your name with third parties, or if you wish to clarify or modify your communication preferences, please visit us at www.ReaderService.com/consumerschoice or write to us at Reader Service Preference Service, P.O. Box 9062, Buffalo, NY 14269. Include your complete name and address.

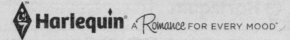

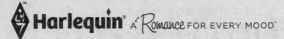

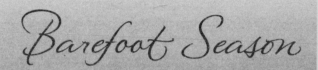

NEW YORK TIMES BESTSELLING AUTHOR

SUSAN MALLERY

returns with a poignant new story about finding love
and freeing oneself from the past....

Barefoot Season

Available March 27, 2012 wherever books are sold!

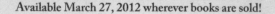

www.Harlequin.com

MSM1338